ADVANCE PRAISE

FOR 120 MURDERS

"These stories move like a counterargument against the state of the world, whispering in my ear like an insect or an instinct—a mosquito, or my libido, a denial, a denial, a denial, a denial, a denial."

—Daniel Handler, author of *Why We Broke Up* and *All The Dirty Parts*

120 MURDERS

DARK FICTION INSPIRED BY THE ALTERNATIVE ERA

120 MURDERS

DARK FICTION INSPIRED
BY THE ALTERNATIVE ERA

EDITED BY
NICK MAMATAS

RUADÁN
BOOKS

BOSTON, MA

Anthology edited by Nick Mamatas
Copy editing by Ian Kappos
Cover image by istock.com/PhotoGraphyKM
Cover Design by Shi Briggs
Interior Design / Formatting by Todd Keisling

First Edition

RUADÁN
BOOKS

www.ruadanbooks.com

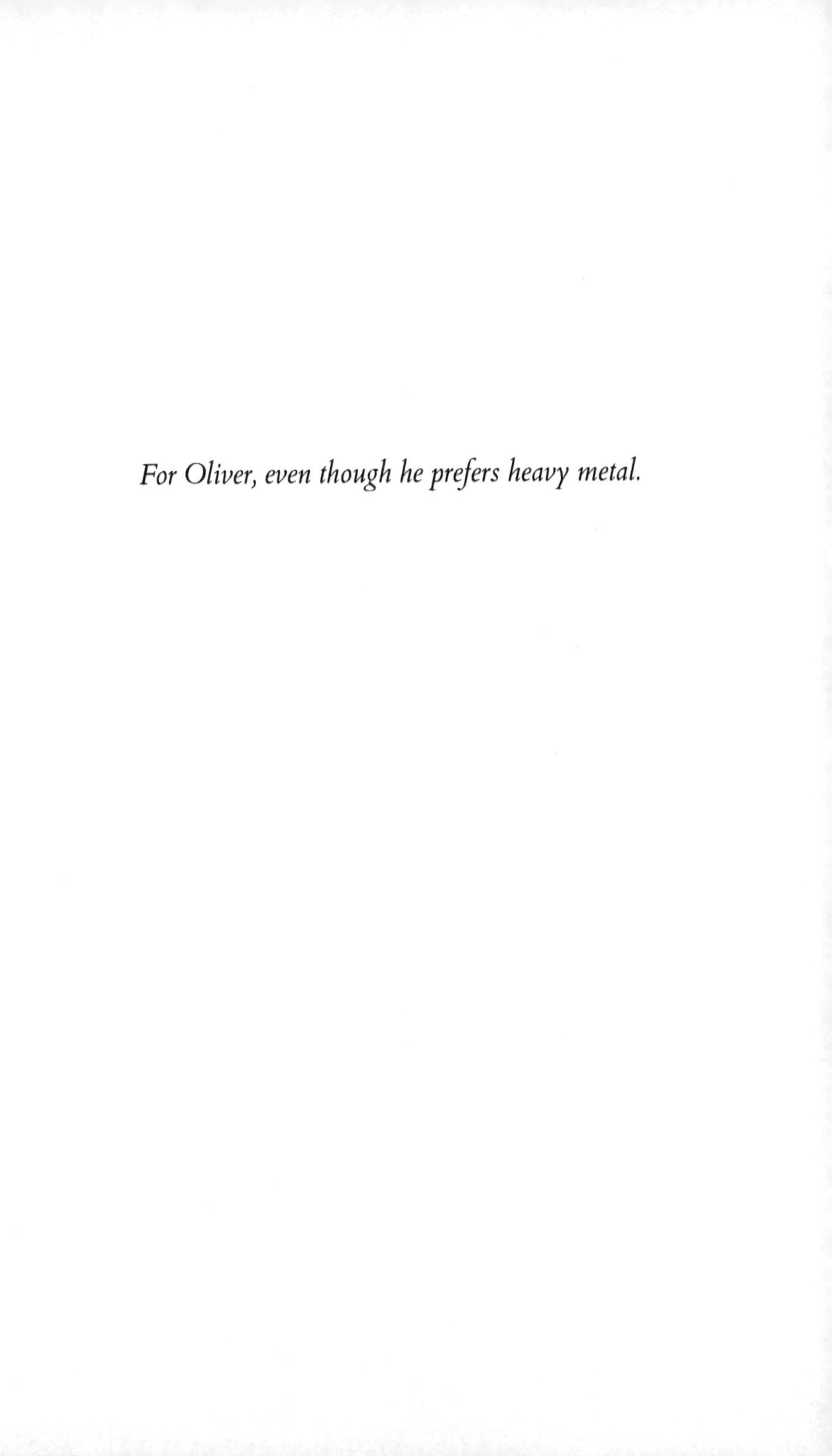

For Oliver, even though he prefers heavy metal.

Table of Contents

WHERE IS MY MIND? AN INTRODUCTION
    by Nick Mamatas XI
HOW SOON IS NOW
    by Cara Hoffman 15
EQUATIONS FOR A FALLING BODY
    by Jeff Chon 21
EXTRA MIDNIGHT
    by Zandra Renwick 37
LITTLE MASCARA
    by Jason Ridler 43
WENDY, GROWING UP
    by Veronica Schanoes 61
SEE AMERICA
    by Todd Grimson 83
WE'VE BEEN HAD
    by Alex Jennings 93
"HIDE & SEEK" BY SWANN
    by Josh Malerman 115

Just Like Fire Would
    by William Boyle 131
Land Of The Glass Pinecones
    by Michael Marano 155
All My Life
    by Meg Gardiner 179
Never Let Me Down
    by Brian Francis Slattery 195
Sacred Meats
    by Jeffrey Ford 219
Never Forget
    by Elena Mauli Shapiro 225
House Meeting
    by Chris L. Terry 243
Superstition
    by Silvia Moreno-Garcia 257
Tornado Mother
    by Libby Cudmore 275
The Show Must Go On
    by Cyan Katz 293
Do It
    by Paul Tremblay 309
A Slasher Cozy
    by Selena Chambers 325
Love Will Tear Me Apart
    by Maxim Jakubowski 333
The Best In Basement Radio
    by Molly Tanzer 351
Contributors 391
About the Editor 401

I never owned many records. And yes, not vinyl, not cassettes, not CDs. Not LPs or 45s. There's a complex set of reasons for such things—my parents weren't very musical, the Brooklyn apartment in which I lived was small and not private, there were no record stores within walking distance, and I spent most of my money on comic books. Thankfully, the tiny convenience store downstairs and the tobacconist across the street had plenty of magazines and comics, and there was a wonderfully filthy used bookstore by the elevated tracks on 86th Street. And I also owned a clock radio. Picture a clock radio. Did you see the fake wood with the red digital readout in your mind's eye? Of course you did. I know where your mind is.

Being a curious sort, one day I turned the dial all the way to the left, and *my* mind exploded. College radio was booming. WNYU and WSIA played amazing music, the sort of thing I'd never hear spilling out of the Camaros cruising down Kings Highway or from the boom boxes of the pop-and-lockers on the corner. WSOU played the heaviest of metal. Out on Long Island, where I visited my grandparents and great-grandparents and one hundred Greek cousins almost every weekend, there was the world-famous WLIR, though its signal was often tantalizingly out of reach. Coming in clear as a bell was WUSB, where some years later I would volunteer as an undergraduate at SUNY Stony Brook.

But college radio is all about the very long set of unusual music, followed by a college sophomore zombie-stuttering their way through the track listings. One might have a new favorite song and never hear it again. (If anyone is familiar with either a song or a band named Snob that had a tune with both grinding guitars and a cello and perhaps even a music video—grainy, one-shot, perhaps with the band or at least a cellist on a spinning platform—that was played on *Night Flight*, please contact me c/o Ruadán Books. It's been forty years.) But there was *Rolling Stone*, and *Spin*, and (my favorite) *Creem*. I spent more time reading about the music I wanted to hear one day than actually managing to listen to any. To this day, when I think about a band or song I want to listen to, I don't hear the tunes in my mind's ear, I see the smeared newsprint ink of an album review or a black-and-white publicity still in my mind's eye.

And there was TV. In New York, a UHF station commonly called "U-68" played anime, and *The Uncle Floyd Show* (which also featured bands), and music videos. Joan Rivers (yes, really) had her own late-night show for half a minute and someone on her staff would book the likes of Hüsker Dü and the famous-in-Canada Doug and the Slugs.

Out on Long Island, where cable was necessary unless you only ever wanted to watch the local news out of Connecticut or religious nuts warning against *Dungeons & Dragons*, Freemasonry, and Gorbachev, I had access to *Night Flight* on USA, and of course there was that basic cable channel that used to play music, right there on the television, *all the time*. There were only a relative handful of songs on rotation, but shows such as *The Cutting Edge* and various programming blocs such as *120 Minutes* and later, when everything was terrible and everyone had sold out, *Alternative Nation* almost had what I wanted.

Once upon a time, journalists *worried* about music videos. Satanic imagery, glorifying sexuality, changing the focus from virtuosity to hair volume, all were cause for concern—what today we'd call someone's hare-brained "take." And there was another, more interesting issue that would come up. *Would kids who listened to music by watching it ever make a personal connection with a song, or would they just remember the video?* In the olden days of sock hops and mop tops, people would wax nostalgic about their first surreptitious hand job when they heard a favorite song. Shades of James Joyce!

But now, in the 1980s, wouldn't the baby busters—as Gen X was called before Douglas Coupland got his hands on us— just recall Ric Ocasek's head on a fly, or Aimee Mann being shoved against a staircase, or Stan Ridgway emerging face-first out of a pot of beans, or a janitor rockin' out amongst an anarcha-cheerleader squad, instead of their own personal experiences?

Turns out, no. The volume you hold in your hands is proof.

The creative mind is capacious, with room for video imagery, power chords and synthesized keening, personal experience, sense memory, fantasy, and emotional upheaval. Writers often write to music. Musicians read while on the road and then make silly concept albums because they want to tell stories too. Two billion people on this planet carry little televisions in their pockets and can listen to or watch whatever they want, whenever they want … unless they just type in "Snob cello song *Night Flight*" into their search bar. Then they come away disappointed. But *everyone else* is doing fine, I promise.

But why dark fiction? The music of the era was dark. Even the poppy tunes and the danceable numbers had dangerous vibes, blasphemous turns of phrase. Blame the H-bomb, urban blight, Thatcher and Reagan and Helmut Kohl, smack and coke and television ("drug of a nation…"), and the general sense that history wouldn't so much end as come to a skidding halt, which it did on September 11th, 2001. So, in these pages, the music of the alternative era is the soundtrack to crime, noir, the gothic, the ghostly, and the cyberpunk.

And the title, *120 Murders*? Feel free to count them up across the stories, but your total may fall short of the number depending on what you consider a murder as opposed to a mere killing. The missing corpses? They'll turn up one day. I plan on pleading insanity. This anthology will be entered into evidence. Not a jury on Earth would convict me.

—Nick Mamatas
Berkeley, California
November 2024

Jack lost her eye the day she landed on the pavement instead of in the pool. Out in the sun and the air, flying from the high dive with such purpose, then rolling from the slick concrete, slipping beneath the blue water, a ribbon of red following her to the bottom where she lay for three minutes and forty-one seconds, neither lifeguard at their post.

I didn't know her well back then. I'd never been to a country club. I swam in the river, jumped from the remains of the bridge, swung out on a rope or walked the narrow, pebbled peninsula to deep water. Accidents there were usually final. No ambulance could reach the swimming hole, which one got to on deer trails, treading through the overgrown thicket. I sunned myself on cracked slabs of stone that had once been a sidewalk before the flood, and came home refreshed from cold water, smelling like mud. I thought about Jack all summer while people prayed for her family. I thought about her square jaw and her cheekbones and her sturdy body, *her*, the muscles in her arms. She had a loud laugh that would ring out in the hallways and wore sweaters and plaid skirts and duck boots.

By fall there was a new girl at the bus stop in Jack's place, with white hair and black boots and dozens of black rubber bands girding her wrists like an archer's bracer. The breast of her jacket affixed with shining round badges, lips painted blue. She let me stammer on, nervously introducing myself, telling her about the school, telling her she looked like my friend, before finally saying, "It's me, you idiot."

She told me how a resurrection trick with tools and drugs at the hospital had brought her back. And her parents, who could afford to have the champagne color of her eye replicated exactly in glass, made it so she could return to school as a facsimile of herself. She had no visible scars. At school it was soon clear she also had no more interest in reading, writing, science, history, or math. The accident had wiped her mind, like shaking an Etch-a-Sketch. I would have given anything to lose all that information. To emerge as she did, believing in nothing, my shyness eradicated, the whole world open again.

I wrote her school papers and met her outside classrooms to give her answers to tests. And she received all of it with an eye-rolling impatience, like she was humoring me and humoring our teachers, filling in blanks on meaningless forms, waiting everyone out. After the accident, after her transformation, the only things she cared about were sound and color and shape, which she said were the same things but people were too dumb to understand it.

When the summer came again she abandoned the girls from the club. She swam in the river with me, and we dyed our hair as blue as the pool, walked the trails into the forest, stayed up late watching music videos. She covered herself with jewels and ink, building things with sticks and old clothes, roadkill, and kitchen utensils, painting eyes all over our faces. Everything happened now as if we were permanently severed from the past, as if we were the only ones who knew there is no such thing as the future, that the future is a thing that can never be experienced.

Money from the lawsuit meant she would never have to work, but once school was over, I had to get a job. My father insisted I come work in the shop, and I did, the heir to a great fortune in auto parts where I would sit silently in the back office among piles of invoices and nearly criminally vulgar pin-up posters.

I thought that I would never see Jack now that school was over, but she moved to the industrial part of town, into a building that had been an old slaughterhouse and butcher counter. And she set to work making dresses and suits out of Christmas ornaments, bubble wrap, and feathers. The place was five blocks from the mechanic shop. By day I answered calls and filed invoices and talked to strangers about snow tires and after work I sat in front of the tall glass windows of the butcher shop with Jack, listening to tapes and smoking and watching the shadows get long.

That winter, she ordered mass quantities of pig intestine, porcupine quills, and rabbit fur from butchers and art suppliers and she built new animals, which she left in the woods and near sewer grates. She made things all day. Sewing and gluing and painting and welding. She made jewelry out of dried fruit and cinnamon sticks and bones and plastic bottles and ball chain and rubber balls from gum machines, which she called communication devices. I wore one such communication device—a green rubber ball filled with glitter on a chain with a wishbone and a long blue feather affixed. It did not work like a computer or a telephone and the only person it inspired to communicate with me was my father who told me to take it off.

By then her workshop was filled with new clothes, new structures, new animals. Objects that sometimes looked like garbage, sometimes like costumes, sometimes more alive than anything in this world. They were filled with a kind of charge, a vibration that could simultaneously make you think and stop you from trying to express anything at all. At the time I thought the only word to describe them was timeless. Like they had existed forever in some other place and she had conjured them.

The butcher shop was covered with vines and ivy into which she wove bits of trash. She painted the building gold, strung strands of blinking blue and red lights on the hooks where sides of beef once hung. She opened the loading dock doors and painted everything a bright chemical blue to go with her lipstick. She made a chandelier out of tile and rosaries and whistles on lanyards. Her pale skin and yellow eyes shone in the flickering light and she said she was going to open a club. Now. There it was.

I no longer went home after work but stayed with Jack, sleeping on a mattress against a wall of small square windows, eating breakfast in the early morning light at a low table she built from cinderblocks and old window panes, standing on my own in the evening inside the gold building while she danced beneath the lights on the blue floor, languid like a body in water, translucent, like a mist rising from the dewy grass. Her voice just a vibration in my head.

Author's Note: Descendants of working-class Irish immigrants living in industrial towns ask the same questions and see the same ghosts whether in Manchester or Appalachia. Morrissey gave us the couplet and Johnny Marr gave us the reverb to reject false hope and feel the power of our collective loneliness, a force that can make art from garbage and lack.

A baby face named Molina answered the 10-71 for shots fired. He was clearly shaken. The man of the house, Timothy Nevin, had walked into his son Hunter's room and shot him in the head. He then walked into the kitchen, placed the gun under his chin, and pulled the trigger. There was no outward sign of struggle.

We stood over Hunter's body. It was a little after six in the morning. A sliver of fresh sunlight sliced through his Pokémon curtains. He would've been getting ready for school soon. Other than the entry wound and blood-soaked pillowcase, he looked peacefully sweet.

"What kind of seventeen-year-old still has Pokémon curtains?" Molina asked.

He winced and took a few short choppy breaths. I gave him a look letting him know he'd be fine, and he gave me a look that asked if I was fucking serious right now. He walked over to Hunter's desk and began pounding on the wall, began weeping. It wasn't a good look, but at the same time, it wasn't a great thing to see.

"Come on, Molina."

"I know, sir—Detective. Sorry, I'm just—who shoots their own son in the head like that?"

"You're gonna be okay, Molina. Listen to me. You're gonna be okay."

"I threw up before you got here. Everyone already thinks I'm a pussy."

"Everyone is just as upset as you are."

This wasn't true. The other guys didn't give a shit, not how Molina did. They might have been disgusted by a man taking his son to the grave with him like a pharaoh, but they certainly weren't heartbroken about it.

"You know, Molina, back when I was still on patrol, the sergeant used to tell me the moment I stopped caring was the moment I was no longer useful."

Now this was just a stupid cliché every senior officer told cherries, and every one of them said it like it was the first time we'd heard it. And for the most part, it was the first time we'd actually heard it, and from the look on his face, it sure as shit was the first time Molina had heard it. But it wasn't true. Most of these guys didn't give one good goddamn. I'd heard these halfwits joke about dead babies, geriatrics who'd shat themselves after getting stabbed, the thick tufts of pubic hair on drowned teenagers. The crueler the joke, the harder they laughed, and I reminded myself I hated every goddamn second of it. This wasn't gallows humor, as they liked to call it—gallows humor being for those about to be hanged—and this wasn't me being, in the adroit verbiage of Officer Molina, a pussy. The truth was, all those snickering bulletheads were exactly who the public said we were. I have no illusions about my job or what I do. I'm just like any other shithead who hates his job, the only difference being I'm a shithead with a gun and a nice pension.

I led Molina out of Hunter's room and into the living room. A Lenovo ThinkPad sat open on a coffee table cluttered with printouts covered in red ink. Empty McDonald's bags sat open at the foot of the couch, crinkled and spotted like baby birds, which explained why the entire room smelled of French fry grease. Nevin had left an imprint, a sad little man-shaped dent, on the smudged cushions.

Seven of us were on the scene—me, Molina, a three-person evidence team in the kitchen, three patrol cops, and another plainclothes, Pete Spanos, who was perusing Nevin's bookcase. More were on the way. This was just how it was after a slow night.

"Yo, Kim! Over here!"

Spanos was waving me over, so I clapped Molina on the shoulder and told him I had to go.

"You gonna be okay?" I said.

"Sorry Detective. Been a long shift is all."

"When are you off?"

"Soon enough."

"Well, head home and get some sleep."

"Yeah," he chuckled. "We'll see if the baby cooperates."

"How old?"

"Four and a half weeks now."

"Congratulations. Well, when the baby sleeps, you sleep. Don't keep yourself up thinking about this."

Another cliché for cherries. No one sleeps when the baby sleeps. It's almost cruel to say it, and this line of bullshit Molina saw right through.

"Hey, Molina," I said, "I saw one of those Hefty bags on the side of the road yesterday. Surrounded by Sheriff's deputies. You should've seen how defeated they looked."

"Coonhunter strikes again," he said. "We're just never gonna catch that—"

"Let's watch it with the Coonhunter shit."

We turned to see a uniform named Bassey giving us the death stare. We told her we didn't mean it that way.

The Coonhunter was a weirdo who'd been leaving Hefty bags filled with dead raccoons by the roadside. Rats and possum were also in the bags—there was a cat once— but it was mostly raccoons. We had no idea where this sicko was finding all these raccoons to shoot, and it wasn't really anything anyone cared about, other than it being a pain in the ass. But the name Coonhunter stuck because it was just a simple and direct way to talk about what he was killing. I understood Bassey's objections. If I were in her shoes, I'm sure I'd be a little uneasy about it too, but it wasn't meant in a racial way.

"All due respect, Detective," Bassey said, "I have ears, and I have eyes. I've also been on the force for twelve years, so I have the same sick sense of humor the rest of you do. I know exactly how you people mean it, even when you say you don't."

"Sorry, Bassey," I said. "We didn't mean any disrespect."

Bassey walked off, narrowing her eyes over her shoulder. Spanos motioned me over in that annoyingly impatient Pete Spanos way. I made sure to avert Bassey's gaze as Spanos and I left the house and I shielded my eyes from the sun.

"See anything good?" I asked.

"Anything good where?" Spanos said.

"Nevin's bookcase. You were eyeing it pretty hard."

"Ever heard of *The Third Policeman?*"

"Who's the third policeman?"

"It's a book. My brother-in-law got it for me a couple birthdays ago. He's a bit of an egghead, a copy editor like our dearly departed Mr. Nevin back there. He's always trying to expand my horizons and all that crap."

"Any good?"

"Wouldn't know. Stopped after the first page. Anyway, I just stood there thinking about my brother-in-law, how it'd kill my sister if he'd done what Nevin did. Thought maybe I'd try to read it again, just so my brother-in-law doesn't get so bent out of shape about us not relating."

"Well, let me know your thoughts when you're done."

"Nah, figure I'll save you the grief."

We made our way to the neighbor's porch: Bill Witherspoon, 77, widowed, wife died of cancer three years ago, retired long-hauler, owned his own trucking company until he was bought out by Heartland Express.

"Those guys with the Valentine's hearts all over their semi-trailers?" I asked.

"I always wondered who those guys were," Spanos said.

"You see them everywhere and then start to wonder what their story is."

"I thought I was the only one."

"You're never alone, Spanos. That set of footprints in the sand was me all along."

"Listen bud, I know you're a Buddhist, but let's draw the line at blasphemy."

"I am, in fact, a Methodist."

"What is that? Some kind of cheap Korean knock-off Buddhism?"

"Now who's the blasphemer?"

"Jesus Christ. You sound like Bassey."

"Hey now."

Bill Witherspoon smoked a cigarette on his porch. A sun-bleached Maxwell House canister was filled to the rusted brim with butts. I shook his hand, and he asked if I'd like a cup of coffee, and I told him I'd had my two cups but that he should definitely have a cup.

We headed inside. The place was a wreck in the way houses of widowers his age usually were—a stack of jackets draped over the back of a chair, balled-up socks under the mug-cluttered coffee table. It was also clear he smoked indoors. Witherspoon came back with his coffee, and we sat at the dining room table. He apologized for the mess. I told him I was the same way, that I found it hard to clean up after myself after losing my wife to cancer, which wasn't a lie.

"So, you called in at 4:38 a.m.," I said, "saying you heard a gunshot next door."

"That's right."

"How are you doing right now? Sorry, should've asked that first. Are you doing all right?"

Here's the thing—he'd only reported hearing one gunshot when there were two. A neighbor had called in at 4:32 reporting a gunshot, then while on with Dispatch, they'd reported hearing a second shot at 4:34. Then another neighbor called at 4:36, saying they'd seen Witherspoon staggering out of the residence, gun in hand, "bawling his eyes out." He called in two minutes or so later.

A rifle leaned against the entrance to the hallway, an old Marlin 39A. It was practically an antique. Boxes of ammo were stacked flush against the wall. Witherspoon glared at me, lit a cigarette, the Zippo shaking in his hand. I'd seen it before, that glare, one that said he was fine, that he was cool, that he was calm, and all he had to do was show me how cool and calm he was. This is what happens in that beat during conversation, what's happening while they're grinding their hands together the way Witherspoon was grinding his together.

"I'm fine," he said.

"This isn't going to be anything too drawn out, Mr. Witherspoon. I just want to dot some *i*'s and all that."

"Dot some *i*'s, huh?" he scoffed. "Young boy gets shot by his father and that's that?"

I asked him if I could bum a smoke, and he slid the

Winston soft pack across the table. This wasn't any kind of power move—I just wanted a cigarette. The cigarette was slightly bent, curved up like a duck's bill, from being in his pocket. I lit it and thanked him.

"Did you know the Nevin family very well?" I asked.

"Not well. They were a depressing group. Man of the house was a real bookworm, so we didn't have much to talk about. And I mostly try to keep to myself anyway. My wife passed away a few years back, and I really haven't felt very social."

"I'm sorry for your loss. How long have you known the Nevins?"

"I just told you I didn't know them all that well."

I took a drag and looked out his window. The yard was impeccable in the way his home wasn't. It was crisp and clean. You just didn't see lawns kept up like that anymore, at least around here, in the middle of a drought.

"Those pink flowers," I said. "What are those?"

He said they were Seaside Daisies. His wife had loved them. A squirrel worked its way up a wooden post, sat on the lip of the bird feeder. Witherspoon shifted in his seat as it grabbed some seeds in its little squirrel hands and began chomping. Two crows joined it, and Witherspoon watched them on the patio, snatching seeds and millet off the concrete, the raspy whisper of his meaty hands grinding and grinding together.

"Say," I said, "is that a Marlin 39 against the wall over there?"

"It was my father's. My wife didn't care for it."

"Do you mind?" I got up and walked over to the rifle—picked it up and turned my back to Witherspoon, aimed it down the hall. It was lighter than I thought it would be, almost like a child's gun. I placed it back and read the label on the ammo box—goddamn CB 22 Short, subsonic, low-velocity, makes about as much sound as an air rifle. I tried to hide how much this tickled me. Son of a bitch. What dumb fucking luck. The guys never would've believed it, even if I'd told them, which I wasn't going to. I could hear Spanos now: *Police work, baby*, he'd laugh.

"Thanks for indulging me," I said. "I just find these old rifles charming."

"You smiled," he said.

"Did I?"

"You shook your head too, chuckled a little. Not all that noticeable, but I saw it. Your lips moved. I don't read lips, but they moved."

"You got me," I said. I took a seat. "Ask any of the guys next door, and they'll tell you I'm not much of a poker player."

Witherspoon sighed, snuffed his Winston. Lit another. His jaws loosened a bit. He'd finally willed himself to be calm and cool.

"You want to ask me about the raccoons," he said.

"Possums, rats. One cat, one time."

"That was an accident. It broke the kid's heart. He thought it was a raccoon. So, how's a homicide detective know about a bunch of dead raccoons? Figured it would be Animal Control's problem."

"It is their problem, but it's also been a running joke at the station. Every couple of weeks, some poor patrol car stumbles across one of your roadside Hefty bags. Used to really freak them out, but now we think it's kinda funny. Well, most of us do."

"Am I in trouble?"

I told him that was up to him, so he told me about his wife, Amalia, how they'd married while he was a young man stationed in Germany, how cancer took their son, and then took Amalia herself. He led me to the window. And it was a beautiful garden. We watched the scrub jays, and sparrows, and red-winged blackbirds flit from feeder to feeder. Larks, wrens, hummingbirds—I could see why Amalia loved it back there. Witherspoon pointed at the area beyond the fence.

"That's where the raccoons sneak through and empty out the feeders. I was teaching Hunter how to shoot them, thought the Marlin would be nice and quiet, not cause a fuss. Look, I'm sorry it's such a hassle for you guys. I respect the law. I really do. But you don't understand how much Amalia loved watching those birds in the morning. Don't know why the raccoons keep coming back. I guess I'm just not as good at it as she is."

"So, about Nevin and his son. What can you tell me?"

He asked me if I remembered the woman who'd jumped off the Oakland end of the Bay Bridge last December. I told him I did. He said that was Nevin's wife. Her body had washed up Christmas morning, the yacht harbor near Coyote Point. That's neither here nor there—I only mention it because just about every precinct in the area had a good laugh over it, the recordings of those frantic 911 calls with the horn section from "Christmas Wrapping" blaring in the background.

Her death destroyed Nevin, Witherspoon told me, destroyed him to the point he slowly lost interest in the things that keep the rest of us alive, including taking care of his own son.

"Somebody had to watch over that kid," Witherspoon said, "so I did it. Amalia really liked Hunter. We didn't care for the parents, but he was a nice boy."

"You and Hunter shot the raccoons at night and then dumped the bodies."

"Then we'd stop at Jack in the Box on the way back. Wanted to make sure he was eating. He was a good kid. A little weird, to be honest, but his heart was in the right place."

This was all well and good. But again, he'd reported hearing one gunshot instead of two. The first gunshot was approximately 4:32 a.m. The second shot was 4:34. I was very happy to unmask the mysterious Coonhunter—it tickled me to do so—but Witherspoon came out of the house, gun in hand, at 4:36.

"Did you ever think Hunter was in any danger?"

"I knew Tim wasn't long for this world. All I wanted was to save the boy, make sure he—"

"You wanted to stop Nevin."

"What was that?"

"You heard the first shot and rushed over, to save the boy."

Witherspoon dropped his cigarette into a Jack in the Box

cup. The backwash sizzled, then silence. He pulled another out of his pack and then put it back in, then slumped slowly into his chair. He crossed his arms.

"I knew it was too late. I went to make sure Hunter didn't die alone. But I was too late for that too."

He asked if he needed a lawyer, and I told him it wasn't very likely. There was a knock at the door, and then Spanos apologized for interrupting, said I needed to see something. I thanked Witherspoon for his time and shook his hand. He couldn't even look at me.

We headed back to the Nevin home, and Spanos asked if I got anything useful. A crowd had gathered out front as we removed the bodies. A news van from KPIX 5 was parked across the street.

"Hey Spanos, remember the body that washed up in San Mateo last Christmas?"

"The one at the yacht club?"

"That was the perp's wife."

"You're kidding. Jesus. Well, at any rate, this'll make a lot more sense to you now. Police work, baby, am I right? Ha!"

I walked in, and Molina, who still hadn't gone home, led me into the master bathroom—and there it was, Sharpied on the mirror:

WHEN WE BOTH JUMP WHO HITS BOTTOM FIRST

"Jesus Christ," I said. "We're just finding this now?"

"Sorry, Detective," Molina said.

Sorry, Detective. A disgusted reflection smirked from

behind the Sharpie scrawl. The man had left a suicide note, in the master bathroom, with the lights on, and it took us over forty minutes to find it. But why all-caps? Why *When* and not *If?* The *Both* implied simultaneity, but none of the "jumpers"—Nevin, Hunter, his wife—jumped at the same time. And Nevin was a copy editor by trade, so why write a note without any punctuation? And this was why the reflection was smirking—it knew there was no point in asking these questions. Knowing the answers didn't matter in the long run, didn't solve a goddamn thing. More like *Sorry, Detective.*

Molina asked if I'd said anything, and I told him I hadn't, and he said he heard me mutter *Galileo*, and I asked him why he bothered asking if he already knew.

"You think this has something to do with Galileo?" he asked. "Some kind of message?"

"This isn't a comic book, Molina. These aren't clues, for Christ's sake. I just said Galileo because it reminded me of that story from school, the one about dropping a pound of feathers and a pound of iron from the Leaning Tower to prove they fell at the same rate."

"Oh yeah. That's a bunch of bullshit if you ask me. Wind resistance and all that."

"Yeah. Wind resistance."

Molina asked me if I thought Nevin was saying he and his son had jumped at the same time, and I told him it didn't matter. We weren't psychologists, just a bunch of dumb cops who couldn't even make the simplest of connections.

"Murder-suicide," I told him. "Nothing more. You hear me?"

"Well, yeah. Of course. Whatever you say, sir."

As far as I was concerned, the matter was closed. All other matters just didn't matter. He nodded.

The media relations officer stormed in, demanding a briefing. I told her to give me a second, and she said she'd been looking for me all morning, so I told her to give me a second. I walked outside and made my way through the crowd, back toward Witherspoon, who was sitting on his porch. I took a seat next to him. He handed me a cigarette.

He pointed across the street. Beyond the rooftops, the sky hazed brown with smoke. Pretty soon, the entire town would smell of ash.

"Huge fire up around Tilden," Witherspoon said. "They say it's a bad one."

"You can't dump bodies on the roadside anymore. Do you understand?"

"Where should I do it?"

"I don't care, but you have to find a better place."

Author's Note: Michael Stipe has said "Fall on Me" was partly inspired by the apocryphal tale of Galileo dropping objects off the Leaning Tower of Pisa to prove they fell at the same rate: the law of falling bodies. I was drawn to this idea of falling bodies, each one falling at the same time to see which hits bottom first. This is ultimately a story about the ways we drag each other down, even when we feel we're lifting each other up. Because these are stories inspired by alternative music, I wanted to evoke what I felt watching the music video: grainy footage of rubble shot upside-down. There's a disorienting bleakness to that video, and I wanted to honor that.

We were young and terrible and beautiful, and the world was ours though we didn't know it then or ever. Now you're gone, and I'm left with this collection of mental snapshots, a scrapbook of who and what we were, starting with our origin story—yours and mine; yours plus mine—back when no one could stand in our way but us.

SNAP

Here you are: smiling feral, holding my hand on a Copenhagen street, both of us bold and fearless the way only fifteen can feel.

Garish colors and street musicians turn the off-focus background of twisting cobbled alleys and ancient sooted brick into a party, that medieval city's Karneval a bizarre flipside echo of carnivals where my then-unborn cousins would someday dance in Trinidad. Your hair is hard '80s pink, the bright spikes a festive addition to the day's abundance of festive additions. We float through feathers and glitter and the thick sweet haze from a thousand gently roasted hashish cigarettes sparked at once, an entire city smiling with us, laughing and singing, nodding slot-eyed and contented at each other, at strangers and non-strangers, friends and unfriends. Let me be more honest here than I intended and admit to being too high too often those days to now recall much other than dumb numb happy wandering, anchored by your hand, your palm girl-soft and so much pinker than mine, you a Viking goddess archetype, a punk rock Valkyrie in chains and black eyeliner; me an olive ungainly almost-this and almost-that chameleon who never manages to fit in anywhere.

In this snap I'm four inches off the cobbled street. In this memory, my feet don't touch ground all day.

SHOT

Here you are: on the cusp of the '90s, a graffitied chunk of Berlin Wall crumbling in your fist, your nails with their customary chipped polish, the final mohawk I gave you grown long enough to satisfy mainstream tastes. Remember dyeing our hair once in my mother's Texas bedroom? *Extra Midnight*, the color might've been called, or some other marketing-department notion of how to sell. Later my mom cried over the thick tarry stains we left blossoming between Victorian roses on her vintage carpet—ruined forever, that rug from some distant land having survived a century of bloody wars and steamy nooners and muddy boots and voracious moths and ocean liners and shipping containers and junkyard runs only to be defeated by fifteen minutes of teenage thoughtlessness. I knew even then it wasn't the rug my mother cried over but my unrepentant guilty posturing as I pretended not to feel like an asshole.

A lifetime later, this side of a career curating antique oddball objects I stitch and file and glue and otherwise mend by hand, I am so, so sorry about that carpet ... but wouldn't give up any minute of any day spent with you.

SNAP

Here you are: visiting Toronto where I moved for college, in a ragged, once grand, basement apartment close-ish to campus, its enormous decrepit fireplace tiled deep craftsman green and crammed with candles somehow making up for damp walls and poky windows large enough only for my jerk of an angry ill-tamed cat to squeeze through. Back then I lived with a boy—one quite important at the time—who doesn't appear in any of these snapshots, his affections and faults, like those of other boys and the men they became, much less vivid than yours in any memory I might shuffle through. In this one we're hiking westward on Toronto streetcars across concrete wastelands farther down the line than I ever ventured before or since to find your grandparents in that alien landscape—*suburbia*.

When we finally arrived, I remember they offered us the same tart tea and mushy cookies your other set of grandparents once fed us outside Copenhagen. They had a tiny pigtailed dog named Skippi who wore pink plastic barrettes in the shapes of bows, and after living in the same high-rise for twenty years they both still spoke only the familiar guttural language of home with each other and you and the dog and all their nearby friends.

SHOT

This one is the hardest for me to imagine but here you are in our current century: a single parent, your daughter five years old and the kind of beautiful so astounding strangers give her presents in the local shops—a flower, a candy, a toy. She'll be trouble someday to someone somewhere but not yet, not here, not to you. I came as soon as you told me you were starting chemo, flew over oceans and continents between us as fast as I could.

Weeks passed. Leaves turned. I stayed far too long and took zero pictures of you but snapped acres of photos in the famous cemetery down the street, bowing angels and eroded crosses dusted with frost and pigeon shit. The heavier the snow fell, the more aggressive the doctors got with your treatment. At this point you bike two miles each morning down those gorgeous cobbled snowy streets to the hospital where they radiate you from inside out, a crooked bullseye tattooed low on your abdomen to show them where to burn.

I entertain your daughter, walk holding her hand to school each day, make her laugh with my terrible Danish and spoil her with sweets when you pretend you're not looking.

SNAPSHOT

I was wrong. This, this one is the hardest to imagine. This snapshot exists nowhere. It is not real because I wasn't there, but also somehow feels truest: your murder.

This snapshot then is one of when I wasn't beside you. How I wasn't anywhere near the quiet urban laneway you trudged in northern winter's predawn for another experimental treatment that had shown great promise, blah blah blah. It's how I didn't defend you from a stranger's knife. How I did not take any wound on your behalf, or turn his blade aside with my nonexistent superpowers or dubiously quick thinking or my meager knowledge of self-defense. How I did not grab your girl-soft hand with bluff bravado and push us together past this man twice our size the way we survived a hundred other guys in a hundred alleys behind punk rock speakeasies or a hundred fuggy rear bedrooms at seedy parties—

Never mind. This one's the easiest to imagine after all.

I'm married now. When he and I met I described you to him, called you the love of my life, as I had to every man I've ever been with and anyone else who seemed willing to listen. The day you died a friend of yours I never met texted me across time zones, language barriers, and culture gaps with running details of your final hours while doctors tried to save you not from the cancer killing you slowly but from the man who did it with a single thrust. I want to say your friend was kind and that I know she didn't mean to be cruel but mostly the experience was dreamlike, too surreal for mental snapshots. Some English-language textbook must've instructed Danish schoolchildren the use of exclamation points to convey emotion, and as medical efforts to revive you failed, and failed, and failed, your death in texts was all afternoon punctuated for me in *!, !, !.*

I think about you lots on lots of days, though not as much on lots of others. In the occasional startling moment of fleeting vertigo I'm afraid that, without you, the threads anchoring who I am to who I was have snapped. I picture those broken strands drifting alongside oil spills, undecayed plastic, and deep seaweed flotsam in great tangled heaps, fallen and floating where they used to stretch over that ocean, those continents between us.

AUTHOR'S NOTE: Special shout-out to The Dead Milkmen's "Punk Rock Girl" for capturing that invincible euphoria of being in teenage love with a 1980s punk rock girl.

LITTLE MASCARA

BY JASON RIDLER

Piss hit the porcelain and Ron relaxed for three heartbeats. He'd broken the seal during the first hour. Coke and JD did that far worse than beer for some evolutionary reason. But he'd timed his run to the shitter perfectly. He always did. Now on his third run, he would take no longer than Lost and Found's latest and last single at regular RPMs.

Jet's high growl sounded fresh and electric, as if she were right there in KVSS's bathroom with the graffiti dicks and plastered flyers for long-dead protests instead of piped in through a hotwired PA. Dirty and rough, her voice cut through him in steady inches.

No angels need apply so long as you reply/ happy birthday, little devil, ha—

whrzll!

The needle scratched. Rat-ass-fucked. Ron ran into the hall, stuffing his dog back into Korean War-era surplus army pants while the scratch chewed and spat out Jet's last word.

Ha-ha-ha-ha-ha-ha-ha—

"Shut up!"

He shouldered the studio door and ran into the cabin, slammed the sound-door shut, then slid the volume channel up the strip in a perfect fade while doing the reverse for the show's cart. The low, lonesome whistle of a slow-moving freight train overtook Jet's scratched laughter. Once her channel was silenced, he slid his mic's back up. Knees bent, he swallowed a cough and opened his mouth.

"Grrrrrreatness personified, you would have thought that scratching vocal was some kinda screw-up here at KVSS Radio, 89.7 on your dial, but that was an exclusive remix from a Japanese EP version of Lost and Found's 'Truth and Consequences' and you got it here, folks, on Ron Asterix's *All-Night Train Wreck.*"

He grabbed his mug of Coke and JD and pulled back his rolling chair.

"And if you are still listening, and how could you not be, the party will be switching tracks to tonight's tribute show to the late but eternally great Jet Everson in one hour at the Tricky Dick Theater on 13th and Hennapin, where none of the donuts have names like street walkers but where a veritable cavalcade of the best bands of the underground will perform, including Acid Waste, Wango Tango Commandos, The Lucha Kids, and more are all taking the stage and raising money for Jet's family in this time of need.

"But wait, there's more! A special performance of Lost and Found with a cosmic top-secret guest so mysterious even

I have not been advised on their identity—thanks to Ruby Diamond and Maurice the Magnificent for setting up this commemoration to our fallen angel and the best singer our scene has seen since a kid named Robert Zimmerman left Duluth, changed his name, and told everyone in Greenwich Village he was from Brooklyn.

"This is Ron Asterix on the *Train Wreck* and I have one ticket still up for grabs if any one of you can answer a genius-level trivia question about Lost and Found's queen of scream."

He sucked in air between swollen gums as the train whistle *whoo-whoo*'d, took a swig, then sucked his gums. He'd scribbled the questions on a napkin somewhere in this shitbox studio of dandruff, dusty roaches, and McRib-stained Styrofoam. He slammed the cough button.

"Where are you, fucker?"

He shoved a stack of *Maximum Rocknroll* zines on to the floor but the reveal was just an old setlist from Stefan Righteous's *Reggie Power Hour*. He kicked the fresh pile of floor trash and realized he was swimming in dead air.

"Fucking fuck!"

He threw the empty mug at a poster of Kiss covered in dart holes and watched it bounce to the floor without a crash. *Just make something up now, man! You gotta go!* He released the button, gripping his hair. "And that trivia question is … During their tour, Lost and Found played a song Jet said was dedicated to her number-one fan. Can anyone tell me the song's title? You have sixty seconds!"

He scatted the *Jeopardy* theme song, knowing the question was impossible to answer.

"Bap badadadad da … da … da—boom boom!"

The phone lit up.

"Stop the presses—we have a caller." He tapped the phone channel on and raised the volume. "All right, caller, who is this?"

Nasally breath hung in the air. "A fan." She giggled. "Her biggest one ever."

"Then you'd know the answer! If so, let's hear it now or you will fade to black."

"'Bullet and Vein'," she said with confidence.

She was right. And there was no fucking way she should be. Because the song was unnamed when Lost and Found played it at the Foghorn. Jet named it with Ron the night he asked and she said what she said and then they did what they did and then she did what she did and …

He grabbed the bottle by the neck. "Well, overture, hit the lights, the show will go on with this now sold-out affair," but the joy of patter had run out. He took a long draft, tossed the bottle in the trash heap. "And who is our lucky winner?"

"If you play your cards right," she said. "You."

Tricky Dick's was half-empty. Chavez and Sterno set up the stage for Roger Wilco and His Degenerates. The Lucha Kids started a pinball tournament to raise more dough as the clock marched toward midnight and all Ron wanted was to turn into a pumpkin and get smashed.

That was some fluke. Some guess. Or I didn't hear right. Not fucking possible. It's like overhearing a dying person's last words from a city away.

Another beer arrived with a smile and pat on the head. Ruby wouldn't let Ron have liquor. She knew better. Beer was easier. Familiar. Calming. Even if Ruby served Grain Belt, Minnesota's friendliest beer. She refused to play any Lost and Found over the speakers so instead, just to keep everyone agitated, she kept a bootleg copy of Kmart Muzak on repeat. It was one step away from a dental office waiting room. And it made everyone hungry for something real and alive. Three cans came and went while Ron shook hands, gave hugs, and if he never heard the word condolences again he'd die a happy man. The fourth Grain Belt reminded him that his bladder was full and straining.

Tricky Dick's bathroom was hardly legendary. But the Sharpie artwork over the urinal of Garfield the Cat sucking his own dick while Odie the Nazi Dog whipped his ass held a kitschy charm. A short creature saddled up beside him.

"Brother Ron."

Father Velvet B. Seducer, all five-foot-three of him (minus pompadour), drained a mighty stream as his electric preacher's voice grabbed Ron's attention.

"Father. What's up?"

"Angels returning to their domains."

"Ain't that the fucking truth."

"She was rare, Brother Ron. And rare things do not go extinct. When they vanish it was like they never existed at all."

"Sage."

"May I ask, is it true? Did she take her own … life? After the Wrecking Yard's show?"

Ron smacked the lever, loaded himself back in his jeans.

"Because I saw her standing there during our set. You looked enchanted, Brother Ron. Like a man about to make the best or worst decision of his life."

"Adios, Padre."

"I just worry about certain gates being denied—"

Ron walked away as two drunk punks stumbled in, shouldering him, but he went with the flow, spinning a little dramatically.

"No offense meant, Brother Ron!" was all he heard, and then went back to the bar as Acid Waste counted four before jumping into the fray of LNF's "The Last Straw." Tina Oberon sang like a funeral dirge, two octaves too low, but all Ron heard was the sweet, sad confidence of Jet hiding in the lyrics.

Seven Grain Belts later Maurice and a dude and a gal approached while Bunzilla took the stage and Maurice made the "c'mere" motion with two meaty fingers and Ron slid off his stool before the thunder and roar began and soon they were all outside, sharing a pinny of grass so strong one of the strangers had to be A&R. The other was his A&Arm candy.

Maurice was the only guy who never got beaten for wearing flares because he was built like a Venice Beach god. His face was so mashed and pretty from scuffles he'd earned the nickname Skutch. The letters on his right knuckles spelled

J-U-D-O. On his left was B-O-S-S. He ran FistyCuffs Records like a mafia don, and was the only one Jet hadn't slept with to get a record deal—for which Ron was always grateful. Comparison was *death*.

You're my one and only, lonely boy.

Ha-ha-ha—

"Our boy Ron is a purest," Maurice said. "Our local tastemaker."

"Right?" said A&R, whose name was Josh, or Jude, or Jehovah. "Train Wreck is fan-fucking-tastic, dude. Is it true you managed—"

"Father Velvet Seducer," Maurice said, switching an inevitable problematic line of questioning. "Who just signed with Sire."

"He's here?" said the arm candy. No doubt this girl was his *niece*, who just turned eighteen six minutes ago. "I love 'Rainbow Escapade.'" Her mascara was thick enough to work the street but sweaty enough her eyes were starting to seem a tribute to Alice Cooper ... or a clown.

"Then you should thank Ron," Maurice said. "He got them the gig at Manny's where the cops came and—"

"And Father Velvet played and sang 'Police at my Back' on piano like a one-man band until they dragged him away ... and the next day, they signed."

Ron snickered, eyes on the eighteen-year-old girl clown. "Guilty as charged. I'll drain this town of talent yet."

"Hey," A&R said, leaning in for intimacy that did not exist. "I was real sorry to hear about Jet."

"That makes all of us," said Ron.

"She was the heart and soul of Lost and Found."

"Preach," said Ron.

"You know we talked, right?"

"I'd heard something."

"What was that?" He passed him the last sliver of the joint.

Ron took a drag until it vanished, then spoke with smoke chasing his words. "That you were going to make her a star." He cackled. "Did you *really* say that?" He thought of some long-lost interview with Ray Davies from The Kinks from the BBC where he introduced a woman who sang back-up and Davies told the crowd "She's going to be a star, because I am going to make her a star," Ron mimicked, like some British Invasion Frankenstein. And the next thing you knew, the world never heard from her again. Maryann Price, buried at 'Scrapheap City'."

"I'm sorry?"

"You should be."

Maurice was chatting with the Arm Candy. And not like he wanted to rail her. Ron's asshole constricted as A&R garbled on and said, "So, I guess Lost and Found needs a singer."

"Huh?"

"And Dizzy here? Well, she is so close to breaking out. She just needs a band to hold her up. Like, imagine if Madonna was in The Runaways and you'll see where I'm heading."

"Yeah?"

"But I don't want to talk business. Not here." Dizzy laughed with Maurice but kept checking eye contact with Ron. "Maurice said that you were the man to talk to make it happen."

"He said *what?*"

"Wouldn't be wasting your time otherwise, Ron."

And the son of a bitch had a card. Like some corporate ass-kissing leech.

"And trust me, spend a little time with Dizzy and you'll see stars, too." He patted Ron's shoulder, said three words, and she followed him as if leashed, eyes on Ron like a prisoner. Sadder than death and yet alive.

Once the alley exit was closed, Maurice clapped his back. "She can sing."

"So can loons. She ain't fit to lick Jet's boots, let alone wear 'em."

"The band can't make records without a singer."

"She's not a replicant."

"Bands lose singers all the time, don't be an ass. Keith left Black Flag and the world was better for it."

"Fuck you!"

Ron swung hard and missed and then lost gravity and found it on a trash bag and the buzz he'd caught was now neon in his eye, glaring at the man looming above him with hands at his sides, a kung-fu gunslinger. "Don't let the band starve because you're grieving. We all loved her."

Elbows propping him out of the filth, Ron groaned. "You loved making money off her," Maurice said. "So, tell me, Judas, how much is your cut to get them off your label and onto Interscope? Like you did for Stitch?

"You know your problem?" Maurice said. "You're a purist. And that won't keep you warm at night as her corpse grows colder."

"Fucker, you're dead!" Ron thrashed to get up like a drunken crab but Maurice snap-kicked his chest and all the grass in his lungs wheezed out.

"No, Ron. She is. And I don't think you were paying attention. She signed with that guy. They all did. Your precious angel sold out to Mammon before she punched her own clock. It's a business, Ron. And not a fair one. So shut up, wake up, and grow up and get the boys to take in Dizzy so they have a fucking chance of rising above Jet's cowardice."

The night wore on Ron and he ran out of words. Him, the mouthpiece of extremely local overnight college radio. Not speechless. Wordless. And bands came and went off stage and people had a time and he tried to hold down another Grain Belt but it was all too much and the smoke was thick and rancid with the bad breath of a thousand sad and desperate punks and freaks and geeks and stoners and skids and losers and dreamers still holding time, all just holding time until Ruby rang last call and Lost and Found took the stage, minus Wade who was puking in the alley—or so Heck-Tor Jonson said before introducing the band—praising Jet, then the growl of Bender's Telecaster was lit by a guitar run and they were off to the races with "Never Was Easy" and Ron was looking for a fight with shoulder taps as he headed out the back door and instead found Wade giving his nose the farmer's handkerchief in the alley, head recently shaved at the side and his mohawk pasted to the right side of his skull.

"True?"

Wade snorted but wouldn't stay in the frame of Ron's vision. "Say again?"

"Is it true?" He stumbled forward.

"Fucking hell, Ron. What do you think?"

He tapped syllables on Wade's shoulder with two fingers. "She never handed in that contract."

Wade slapped his hand away. Gravity dropped, but Ron spun again and found himself twisted but standing like a drunk ballerina. "And how would you know?"

"I saw her tear it up!"

He laughed. "You fucking stooge, this isn't a movie." He snorted and spat his loogie onto the dark, wet concrete. "They have carbon copies! A Xerox machine! Don't you have like a poli-sci degree? She signed it. It's binding. We got paid. And now we're *fucked.* That's her legacy. Debt and worry all because she punched her ticket."

Ron wasn't listening, too busy doing rock and roll math. "So, she couldn't get out of the contract … then that's why—"

"Oh, fucking hell. Dude, I'm running late!" Wade pushed past him.

"Don't take her!"

"Who?"

"It'd be blasphemous!"

Wade clenched his fist and eyes. "Okay—I am not beating

you shitless because you loved us when no one else did. She was a danger girl. Our danger girl. Everyone's danger girl. And they don't die old or easy, bud. That's the price of her burning so bright."

Ron shook his head as Wade clapped his shoulder.

"Just don't blame yourself. It would have been junk or a razor or fucking vanishing act sooner or later."

"Tell me you won't to let her join." Ron grabbed Wade's leather lapels, but one shove from Wade had him stumbling back like a palooka in round three. "You can't! You fucking sell out," he groaned as the door slammed shut. Knob locked tight.

The alley provided no solace, just the growing company of rats. But what made Ron spring out of his mire was the familiar broken chord plucked on a Gibson Explorer and cascading into itself with speed. Then an unfamiliar voice murdered Jet's vocals as they wailed out, "*You're my one and only, lonely boy.*"

Ha, ha, ha, ha, ha.

The FR54 all-night vomit comet came to the corner of Dixon and Pine when it wanted to. The bench seemed to be made of bone and waiting a slow way to die. Ron sat on it and avoided the thoughts in his head by counting the rain drops hitting the puddle against the curb. He even wished that he smoked, to make the moment romantic instead of pathetic, but cigarettes had never brought him the joy or relief or coolness he saw others enjoying from them. At one hundred and seven drops the dull blur of headlights down the road and the soft hum of bus tires slicing wet ground spelled relief …

"This seat taken?" Dizzy seemed thinner, stretched, like she'd walked out of a Sergio Leone spaghetti western.

"Free country," he said.

"We both know that's not true." She crossed her legs tight and it didn't seem to stretch her fishnets. "Like getting tickets to the show. There's a cost." She sighed like dark static.

Pins and needles ran up his spine. "You? That was … I'm sorry, I completely forgot."

She laughed, bending over to her knees, then smiling at him. "Oh, I got in just fine, Mr. DJ. That's not why I called."

The distant glow of bus lights shimmered and did not seem to move.

"Why did you?"

She put her chin in her hands, elbows on her knees. "Respect. Approval. I wanted you to know I wasn't just some piece of ass. I'm a fan. A huge fan. And you know, it's not like she was sixty. She was only two years older than me, come this November."

Ron sniffed. "So, you're a super fan?"

She snickered. "Quiz me, Alex Trebek."

"Home town?"

"Sandusky, Ohio, though she always said Bitters, Arkansas, because it sounded so Cunt-Tray."

Ron laughed. "Nice. Favorite singer?"

"Polly Styrene."

"Okay, enough with the easy stuff. Who was the inspiration for 'Lonely Boy'?"

"She would *never* say! No matter who interviewed her. Or interrogated her!" That word sat like wet ashes in his brain. "Now, how about you answer me one question."

"Shoot."

"You were with her, right? The night before her parents saw her on their lawn around 8:15?"

"You sound like a cop, narc."

She cackled. "Please answer the question, Mr. Asterix." She slid her hand onto his knee. The rings on each finger were *Looney Tunes* edition costume jewelry, thick and bright and phony. "There are so many gross rumors, Ron. If anyone knows the truth about what happened, it's you. Please?"

The bus lights were still two demonic eyes of white light on the horizon.

"Please?" she pleaded.

"Why do you care?" he said. Across the street at Underground Records' display window—he could have named every single record placed fresh on those shelves this week from memory if it wasn't so fucking sloshed. "You're not family. You're not a friend. You're a fan trying to fill her combat boots and—"

"She was my girlfriend." Ron refused to budge, willing his eyes to see into the dark window. Moto Cross' new five-inch; The Blasters reissue. And ten percent off all Lost and Found EPs and albums and cassettes and "Ron? She was my girlfriend, *too*. Why do you think I know this stuff?" That hand never moved. But Ron's memory sobered up with the shock. On her middle finger was some cubic zirconia that could prick an eye or scar a cheek.

"Where did you get that?"

"Ron, did you hear what I said? She loved us both. And we both know a ring couldn't hold her. She refused all chains of this world, our Danger Girl."

Dizzy wasn't talking like some suburban dingbat bimbo slumming it in the scene. It was almost pillowy, matronly, comforting, chameleonic.

"And she picked you, Ron. Didn't she?"

Her hand slid back and forth as she whispered too close to his ear. "Even if she'd never stay. She picked you. That last night."

"Where did you get—"

"Listen." She inhaled his scent, hand scorching a path up his thigh. "Do you know how lucky you are? That night. That last night she spent. When she said yes. You were the last one." Weed. Whiskey. Beer. Grief. A loser's cocktail. "The last one, Ron. The last one on earth."

"Hey, c'mon."

She inhaled again. "Smells like honey. The last from our queen."

"Knock it off."

"Shh. You don't have to do anything."

"Listen, you psycho …"

Stars lit up the night sky as something hard and strong cracked his skull. He tumbled ass over tit from the bench and onto concrete. Vomit filled his mouth.

"Shh!" Her hand was hot iron clamping his mouth. He flailed, a drunk Muppet having a seizure. She mounted him, skirt high and legs fierce, eyes burning cherries. "That's it. She said you liked it a little rough. And that's better. Now lay still. Just like her." She giggled, wrestling his dog from his pants. "And I'll finish you off, too."

Joints locked, but his body shivered. The dead air in his lungs made his eyes bulge while she ground him into wet earth colder than Jet's dead body. He was weightless until she started to sing.

He clawed snow and ice until his numbing fingers found something wet and nasty to throw. And there was a *konk* of ice and bone. He breached the surface of her hands as they slid away and feral energy ferreted him from his back to his gut to his knees to his feet and then to slamming his sneakers in the snow. His mouth was free and cold air burned his lungs. His breath was a wheeze like some dying freight train. Before he knew it, he was running to the white eyes of the bus, hands waving and feet slipping the wrong way on a one-way track. The bus wailed and slammed its brakes but sound faded out and was soon overrun with a scratch on a needle going *HA-HA-HA*.

AUTHOR'S NOTE: I grew up with three feminist sisters who fed me Audre Lorde and Naomi Wolf books, and a conservative father with the largest *Playboy* collection within an atomic blast-radius of the Toronto suburbs. Puberty was a political act. So, I admired how Paul Westerberg could call out how women get trapped by limited choices beyond sex-object or mom, no matter what their hopes or dreams. Also, when I first heard "Little Mascara," I knew some "danger girls" in full-Halloween mascara who said fuck that noise and lived hard, fast, and full before vanishing into either conformity or the grave. This story is a eulogy for the latter.

WENDY, GROWING UP

BY VERONICA
SCHANOES

Peter tells Wendy and the Lost Boys a story about how mothers can't be relied upon, how a long time ago he tired of playing with the fairies and tried to go home to his mother, and when he got there, the window, which he had assumed she would always keep open for him, was shut and barred, and there was another little boy sleeping in the bed that had been his. He and the Lost Boys are horrified. Wendy is terrified and immediately demands that she and her brothers be allowed to go home.

And what of Wendy herself? After she and her brothers abandon the Darling household for greater adventures, how does she spend her time? Sewing pockets, mending socks, telling stories; there are many days, we are told, when she barely gets to put her head above the Lost Boys' underground home.

J.M. Barrie's own mother took to her bed when her older son Davey fell through the ice while skating and died, and she never left it. Barrie was six. It was Barrie's older sister who assumed the role of caretaker, the first of Barrie's child mother figures who appear time and again in his plays and fiction. Wendy is the most famous, of course, but she's not the only one.

Instead of writing her paper on *A Midsummer Night's Dream*, Delilah—"Della" to her friends—had finished the dishes and was now scrubbing the floor on her hands and knees, what remained of her hair hidden under a kerchief. What remained was very short, because two days ago she had bleached her hair at Naomi's house with hydrogen peroxide and then dyed it purple with Manic Panic. When she had got back the next day Aunt Ginger had made her cut it all off.

Now Aunt Ginger was out playing bridge and drinking with her girlfriends, Della's cousin Krista was at a dance for her school with *her* friends, Uncle Paulie was at Sons of Columbus with his friends, and Della was scrubbing the kitchen floor on her hands and knees. Before she had left, Aunt Ginger, still angry about the hair-dyeing, had warned Della that if the entire kitchen wasn't *sparkling* when she got home, she would pull Della out of that hippy, liberal school Della's mother had sent her to. Della could go to Fort Hamilton High School with Krista, she wasn't any better than Krista, no matter what that school had put into her head.

Della's mother had wanted her to go to that school. When Della's sixth-grade teachers had tapped her to take the entrance exam for Hunter College High School, some years ago, her mother had been so proud. She had told Della that it was the best public school in the city, and when Della had gotten in, she had been even prouder. She had danced with Della and her little sister Lisa to New Kids on the Block and hugged them a lot. Their father had been at work; back then he had still been able to work.

"You're gonna go there, and you'll be the first in the family to go to college, too!" she had said. "You're gonna make something of yourself, not get stuck like me!"

That had been a year before they'd had to remove Della's mother's adrenal gland, when she could still get out of bed and dance with the girls. Almost two and a half years before she died.

Nonna had been the only family who had wanted Della after her mother died. Aunt Dee had wanted Lisa, who was only seven, and cute and cuddly, but she had said she didn't have room for Della, too. Nonna only had a small rent-controlled studio apartment on East 10th Street, which was a big drug block, but she and Della had made it work. And it was only a few blocks from where Naomi lived with her mother, Sharon. That was nice, because when Nonna had started getting agitated, or trying to wander out of the apartment in her bathrobe, Della had been able to call their place and then Sharon, who'd gone to social work school, would come over and help until the old woman was herself again.

But then, two months ago, Nonna had slipped and fallen,

breaking her hip. At the ER they realized how far Nonna had gone into Alzheimer's, and sent her to an old age home in Staten Island, and Aunt Ginger had grudgingly taken Della in.

Della did most of the cooking and a lot of the cleaning. She did the grocery shopping except for Aunt Ginger's vodka, because she wasn't about to tell that bitch about her fake ID, which worked, at least when Della smiled and made small talk with the bouncers at Wetlands.

Della had kept her grades up even when her mother first started getting sick, when she was in seventh grade, because of how proud Mommy had been of Della's intelligence. But once her mother had stopped being able to get out of bed, getting dinner done on time and cleaning up the apartment had kept her father's belt hanging in his closet, and doing her homework had not, so that was an easy choice. Her grades dropped as she took care of the home and her mother and her little sister.

She'd felt better when her father moved out, even though her sister had cried. He'd started getting sick himself by that point, and Lisa was worried about who would take care of him. Della was still busy, but it was easier, somehow, even as her grades continued to drop, and her friends dropped away, too. Between the ones she stopped hanging around with because she didn't have the time to go to movies and stuff and the ones who stopped hanging around with her because she had become prickly and, let's face it, a little mean, she really only had Naomi.

Naomi's friends had dropped her when her father left and

she had gotten *really* mean. Some people are just like that, sometimes.

But Della liked her, even if she thought Naomi was a little naive.

So now Della was scrubbing Aunt Ginger's floor, she had always been scrubbing floors, she always *would* be scrubbing floors, scrubbing floors and washing dishes and cooking food for people who yelled at her or worse. Della had a vision of herself still stuck in Bay Ridge in middle age, with gray hair and an aching back, bad knees from scrubbing floors all her life, and maybe hitting the vodka a little too hard and yelling at *her* children, and something in her head snapped, and she threw the scrub brush in the bucket of Murphy Oil Soap and water. Fuck this. She had to get out, and she knew how to get out, because hadn't her mother told her? She was going to get good grades, and get a scholarship somewhere, maybe upstate, maybe somewhere like Vassar or Sarah Lawrence, and she was going to go to *college* and *get out of Bay Ridge*. She was going to go upstairs and work on her English paper, and Aunt Ginger could go fuck herself.

Besides, it was a Friday night. Aunt Ginger stayed out late on Fridays. She could work on her paper and finish the floor later, and Aunt Ginger would never know. She got up off the floor, walked to the tall, steep staircase, and climbed.

What makes a good mother?

Is it all the cooking and cleaning? Surely there's more to

it than that; surely love must enter into it. But love can't be the entire answer either because it's easy to hurt or mistreat somebody and still love them, or claim to, anyway.

Put another way, what is it a child loses when she loses a good mother?

Vasilissa's mother protected her from beyond the grave, by means of a magic doll. But then, one gathers that Vasilissa's mother did a good job of protecting her daughter when she was alive, too. Cinderella had a fairy godmother, or perhaps a pair of doves sent by her dear departed mother. All of which points to a disturbing truth: without adult protection, children have nothing. (That is actually one of Perrault's morals to "Cendrillon"—all the charm and virtue in the world will do you no good at all without a godparent to help you.) Some mothers don't protect you even when they're alive, let alone after they're dead. Vasilissa not only has her doll, but the witch Baba Yaga gives her a skull on a pole that burns her evil stepfamily to ash with light from its eye sockets. There's all kinds of protection in fairy tales.

This is the defining characteristic of childhood: powerlessness. Not innocence. Innocence is an adult creation; it's only possible for it to develop under the care and guardianship of benevolent adults. An unprotected child finds innocence destroyed very quickly, and relatively easily, too, and is no less a child for all that.

Adults find it easier to imagine fairies, or magic dolls, or possessed birds than we find it to imagine a minor with the power to help herself.

Upstairs, after taking notes on *Midsummer* for an hour, her head hurt and her eyes hurt—she'd needed new glasses for over two years now, but Aunt Ginger said the money from Della's Social Security Survivors' Benefits wouldn't stretch that far. Maybe not, but Della had her doubts; Aunt Ginger had bought a new sofa just a couple of months ago, one which Della never sat upon. She was thinking about getting a painkiller for the headache from the bathroom cabinet when she heard a key in the lock, the door opening and closing and locking again.

Maybe it was Uncle Paulie. He wasn't so bad, he mostly minded his own business and stayed out of the way. Or Krista. Krista wasn't a bad cousin. She tried to help Della out when Aunt Ginger wasn't around to see. She wouldn't rat Della out for working on her homework instead of the kitchen.

But then Della heard her aunt's tapping heels going down the hallway and turning into the kitchen. She could even hear the neck of the vodka bottle shuddering against the rim of the class as Ginger poured herself a drink. Della could hear all this. Her chest started to get tight with anxiety. She had no health insurance and no prescription insurance and apparently her Social Security check wouldn't stretch far enough for inhalers either. The asthma sent her to the ER every few months, which she hated, because Della hated hospitals.

After a minute during which she imagined Aunt Ginger gulping down the vodka tonic as if she hadn't seen the stuff in years, Della heard her name shrieked in tones of bitter frustration. She put her books and pen away in her messenger bag so Ginger wouldn't storm into Krista's room and tear them out of her hands. Then she went out to the hallway.

"What is it, Aunt Ginger?" she said.

The older woman was still making her way slowly up the stairs, heels in her right hand, drink in her left, breathing heavily from either exertion or anger. She probably needed a home without stairs at this point. "Useless, ungrateful," Della could hear her snarling, not quite *sotto voce*.

Ginger arrived at the top of the stairs and stood swaying in her stocking feet, the smooth pantyhose against the polyester carpeting. "Did I or did I not tell you to clean up the kitchen tonight?"

Della did her best to smile sweetly. *Like fucking Cinderella*, Naomi had said once. "I put the food away and finished the dishes," she explained, and however sweet she may have managed to make the smile, her tone was mutinous. "But my English paper is due on Monday."

"Selfish!" Aunt Ginger exploded. "I took you in when we hadn't seen or heard from you in *years*—would a phone call have been so hard? I give you a place to sleep and food, a home, and …"

Della let her mind drift while Ginger ranted, thinking about *Midsummer* until she tuned back in long enough to hear "thoughtless and selfish, just like your mother!"

Della's lungs got even tighter and her face grew taut. "Don't you say *anything* about my mother." She ground out each word in a low voice. She was almost shaking with rage, suddenly.

Aunt Ginger paused for a moment, a glint in her eye. "Oh, that got your attention, did it? Well, you know it's true. If she hadn't been so *thoughtless* and *selfish*, she would have made arrangements for you, and I wouldn't have to put up with this!"

"That's not true!" Della shouted. "She was *not!*"

"*Your mother*," continued Aunt Ginger, "was a druggie *slut* who got herself and your father *sick* with her selfishness, and that's why they're both dead now!"

The blood drained away from Della's face and she felt very calm. She felt like she was floating, and she could see everything. The past unrolled in her mind, every miserable minute of it; and at the same time she took in all the details of the present, like Aunt Ginger's feet, slippery in her nylons, balancing at the top of the staircase, and the mascara crusted onto each of her eyelashes. She could even see a few seconds into the future; she could see herself, very clearly in her mind's eye, slowly reaching out with both arms and shoving that old woman with the slippery feet and encrusted eyelashes, shoving her hard, so that she would slip and fall backward down the stairs, landing so heavily that Della could hear her skull crack, the cunning sadistic smirk finally wiped off her face.

And then she did it, and it didn't happen slowly at all. She stepped closer to Aunt Ginger, reached out with both hands, and pushed her sharply and strongly down the stairs.

It happened quickly, but otherwise almost just as Della had pictured it. Ginger tried to find purchase on the rug with her feet, but she slid right off the edge of the top step. She tried to grab the railing but couldn't—or wouldn't—let go of her drink until it was too late. Her back hit the edge of one step with such an impact that Della could almost feel the vertebrae in her own back splinter, and when Ginger's head finally hit the first floor of the house—no carpet there—Della could indeed hear her skull crack.

Della, still calm, took a deep breath. "That's not true," she repeated, quietly this time. For a moment, she felt wonderful.

But then her chest tightened up again, and she had to gasp for breath, little shallow pants that presaged a full-on asthma attack. She gripped the railing at the top of the staircase and closed her eyes. Oh God, what had she done? Should she go down and see if Aunt Ginger was still alive? What if she wasn't? That would make Della a murderer, wouldn't it? But what if she was? What if Aunt Ginger was still alive and could tell everybody exactly what Della had done?

Della forced herself to breathe in while counting to four, hold the breath for four counts, and then exhale slowly for four counts. She did this three more times, just as Dr. Brenner had taught her, and she could feel herself starting to calm down, even if her chest stayed a little tight.

Okay. She was alive. She was alive, and mostly okay, and Ginger was dead, probably. And she was not about to stay here and wait to be asked what had happened. Moving deliberately but not slowly, she turned around and walked back into Krista's room. She put on her Docs and grabbed her messenger bag.

There was only one way downstairs.

Della licked her lips and went out to the staircase, where Aunt Ginger's crumpled form lay at the bottom. Carefully hugging the side of the steps furthest from where Ginger had fallen, she pressed herself against the wall and took a step down. Only twelve more to go—she'd had to vacuum each and every one—and then she'd be grabbing her coat from the front closet, and then she'd be flying, flying out the door.

She took another step.

As long as neither Krista nor Uncle Paulie came home before she got out.

Step.

She hoped it wasn't Krista who would discover Ginger's body.

Step.

It's awful, to discover your own mother's body. It had been awful, to find Mommy so cold and still and smelling odd, and then trying to keep Lisa out of the bedroom until the ambulance arrived.

Step.

Step.

Getting closer now. Should she look to see if Ginger was breathing, or turn her face away?

She turned her face away.

Step.

Would Uncle Paulie have her killed?

Step.

She was pretty sure her father's family was connected.

After all, her father had worked at Fulton Fish Market. Della never ate fish.

Step.

They were Sicilian. Her mother's family had been from Rome, fleeing ahead of World War II because her great-grandfather had been a communist. Nothing wrong with that. Naomi's parents used to be communists. Her father still was sort of.

Step.

And a dead body had been found in Uncle Paulie's club once, hadn't it? He wasn't gonna like this.

Fuck it. Della jumped the last few steps and ran like hell to the closet in the front hall. She grabbed the cheap, tattered coat, the one with the button saying CLOSETS ARE FOR CLOTHES on the inner collar where she could turn it in so her family couldn't see it, off the hanger and pulled it on, and then she ran to the front door. She peered out the peephole. The street was dark, good, and she didn't see anyone, good, so she unlocked the door, stepped out, pulled it shut behind her, and locked it again.

She was out. She didn't think she'd be coming back.

She wasn't exactly sure where she was going, but she was getting the hell out of Brooklyn, she was sure about that. So, she made her way to the subway, sticking to the side streets and shadows of Bay Ridge, fumbling in her messenger bag's side pocket for a token. She didn't want to give the token clerk a reason to remember her, and she definitely didn't want to get busted for jumping the turnstile.

The important thing was to get away—not without anyone seeing her, that would be impossible on a weekend night in New York City, even in Brooklyn, even in Bay Ridge—but without anybody noticing her. She kept her face turned to the ground.

Della made it safely onto the train and took out her book to read but couldn't focus on it. Aunt Ginger's words ran through her head over and over again. But Mommy *wasn't* selfish and thoughtless, she *hadn't* been, she'd done her best.

And a small voice in Della's head noted that her best had left Della with Ginger and who knows what was happening to Lisa.

"No," Della said under her breath, and sat on the thought, hard. Mommy had done her *best*.

Oh, why hadn't Mommy let Dr. Brenner adopt her and Lisa? They would still be together, then, and Della would be in Dr. Brenner's nice apartment in Chelsea right now, finishing up the first draft of her *Midsummer* paper, and maybe then Dr. Brenner and her partner would make popcorn and all of them would watch a video they'd rented or something on TV.

Dr. Brenner had been serious about wanting to adopt them, she and Della's mother had had some very serious talks about it, talks for which both Della and Lisa had been sent out of the room. Lisa had watched the TV in the waiting room, but Della had lingered outside the door and tried to listen. She could only catch every fifth word or so, because they were speaking in the taut, low voices adults used when discussing what little was left of her mother's future, but she had clearly heard her mother say "Let me think about it some more" before she'd had to scuttle back to her seat and pretend to have been reading *Oliver Twist* for school all along.

Maybe her mother had thought about it some more, but she had never called Dr. Brenner about it again. Della was pretty sure why not, but she tried not to think about it.

A few months back, she and Naomi had spent some time with Lisa in Washington Square Park, and Lisa had said, "I don't like gay people. They always make me feel kinda queasy."

Della and Naomi had exchanged looks and Della had said, after a moment, "Dr. *Brenner* made you feel *queasy?*"

"I didn't know she was gay!" Lisa had protested. "I didn't mean her!"

"Who did you think that woman who lived with her was?" retorted Della.

Lisa flushed. "I didn't know!"

Della didn't like to think about that, though. Anyway, even if that had been the reason, her mother would have gone on loving *her* no matter what. No matter *what.*

Thinking about Dr. Brenner made her think about Sharon, Naomi's mother, who had finished social work school the previous year and gone to work with Dr. Brenner at the Beth Israel HIV clinic.

Coincidence. The city isn't always so big.

That made her think of Naomi, and that made her decide where she was going.

Death is a journey, and sometimes a journey means death. Peter, we are told, accompanies the souls of dead children, Barrie doesn't say to where, so they do not get scared along the way. Of course he does. His followers are the Lost Boys, and while he may claim that they are children who have fallen out of their perambulators while their nannies weren't looking, we all know what it means when someone says they've lost a child. Peter might be dead himself; there's only one way not to grow up, after all. But he does not seem a reliable psychopomp. He often forgets the Darling children altogether on their way to the Neverlands, even Wendy, and has to be reminded who they are.

Perhaps unsurprisingly, then, Wendy gets lost on the way to the island that is also the mind of a child. Which child? Any child. Each child. She gets lost, and the only light she has is Tinkerbell, demonically laughing at her and pinching her. Tinkerbell, who abandons her and flies off to convince Tootles to shoot arrows at Wendy. Upon her arrival in the air above the Neverlands, Wendy is shot and plummets to the ground, gasping in shock.

It takes a lot to save her.

Poor Wendy.

It's better to make the journey on your own terms, even if you're going to the underworld. Especially if you want to come back out.

She switched for the F at 9th Street, but it was a big interchange, up three or maybe four flights of stairs, and Della's chest got tight again. It didn't help that the night air was cold and that a couple of people were smoking on the platform. Della tried the four breaths again, but the tightness wouldn't go away, and by the time the F pulled into 2nd Avenue in Manhattan, she was starting to wheeze.

She walked the five or six blocks to Naomi's building slowly, but she could still barely breathe when she got there. She managed to cough out enough of a sound for Naomi to recognize her and buzz her in, but when she reached the apartment and knocked she was wheezing so badly that the instant Naomi got her inside, she took one look at her and ran for her mom's spare inhaler.

Della used it four times.

Her lungs started to open up. "Thanks," she said when she was able to speak again, and sat down.

Naomi locked the door and came over. "What's going on? You look terrible."

Della took a couple of long, deep breaths, relaxing into the oxygen. Look, she could breathe again, she didn't even have to put any effort into it. Breathe in, breathe out.

"I came to say goodbye," she said, almost drunk on how easy breathing had suddenly become.

For a moment a look of panic appeared on Naomi's face. "Why? Where are you going?"

"I have to go."

"Why? Where? Are Ginger and Paulie moving out of the city?"

Della shook her head. Once, twice. But it still didn't seem definite enough, so finally she said, "Ginger's dead," and

Naomi looked surprised and then firmly said, "Good," and before she could stop herself, Della said, "I killed her, I pushed her down the staircase and killed her. And now she's dead, I think. I'm pretty sure."

Naomi nodded. She thought about it and then said, "She was awful. It serves her right." After another moment to think, she added, "Uh … do you want to tell me about it?"

Belatedly, Della remembered Naomi's family. "Is your mom here?"

"No, she went to see Eric Anderson with her women's group."

Even so, Della shook her head. "No. I just came to say goodbye. I don't want to get you in trouble."

"That's stupid," said Naomi. "You're not stupid. You couldn't possibly think I'd let you wander the streets alone. If you leave I'm coming with you. You must have known that if you came here, I wouldn't let you leave alone." It's so easy to throw your life away when you're young.

Della shook her head again.

"You came here because you knew I wouldn't let you go. Just talk to me."

Della knew it would be better, better both for Naomi and for herself, if she kept her mouth shut. She knew that from listening to Uncle Paulie and her father, but she couldn't seem to stop herself from talking.

By the time Naomi's mother got home later that night, Naomi and Della had made plans. Mostly Naomi.

"I don't see why you have to run," Naomi had said. "Nobody else was there, right? And you didn't run into anybody you know on the way here. And you didn't ride up in the elevator with anyone else, right? Right. So … it's what, 10:30 now? We'll say you got here at nine. You left right after finishing the dishes, you didn't look at your watch, but probably around seven or 7:15. You've been here all evening, working on your *Midsummer* paper. It's due on Monday? Are you sure? I should start mine tomorrow, I guess."

"So, what, I just go back?"

"Yeah. They don't have the number here, right? Right, why would they? So, they're not gonna call and tell you they found Ginger, so stay over here tonight—it got late while we were hanging out, you decided to just stay, maybe call the house and let the phone ring so you can say you tried to let them know. Tomorrow afternoon, you go back. Someone will have found Ginger by then, and she's an alcoholic, they stumble and fall all the time. You can just act horrified. You look pretty horrified."

"I am horrified," said Della in a low voice. "Why aren't you horrified?"

Naomi shrugged.

"I love you."

A silent moment passed.

But Naomi was full of ideas. "Do you have to stay with Paulie now? Does guardianship pass to him, do you think?"

Della shrugged. "Maybe? I don't know. Maybe he'll ask Aunt Dee to take me, but she always said she didn't have room for Lisa *and* me. She and Ginger had some kind of agreement, I think."

"Well, that's over now," said Naomi practically. "Maybe …" She hesitated. "Maybe we could ask my mother?"

"Ask her about who I'm going to go to? I don't think she'd know."

"No. Ask her if she would be your guardian. You could come live here. With us. If you want."

Della didn't say anything. A siren went by outside.

"My mother loves you."

Della loved Sharon. In certain lights, when she was tired, she looked a little bit like Della's mother.

Before Della could put together an answer, though, Sharon's key turned in the lock.

Sharon walked in to find her daughter and her daughter's best friend giggling on the couch together. It was nice to come home to. Too often, lately, Naomi had been staying out later, coming in after Sharon was in bed but not asleep. How could you fall asleep knowing your teenage daughter was out in the night doing God-knows-what? It was nice to see her at home with Della. Sharon smiled.

"Girls! Della, I didn't know you were here. I've stashed some extra inhalers away, just in case you were coming over soon!" She went into the bedroom and took three inhalers out of the bottom drawer of her dresser and came back.

"Should we make popcorn?" she asked.

What if Wendy didn't *want* to cook and clean and mend? If Cinderella grew tired of waiting, alone in her grief and suffering, before her fairy godmother made an appearance? Sometimes you do what you have to do, to make a bearable life. Like Peter, locked out of his mother's house and embrace, luring child after child to his island, and thinning them out when they get too old. And still, the Darlings abandon him and the Lost Boys abandon him, and he is once again watching through a locked window as Wendy, John, and Michael fall into their mother's arms. And pretending, every spring when he remembers, that for a few weeks, he has a mother, as some darling little girl does the cleaning. Cinderella marries a prince. Vasilissa not only marries a czar, but she finds herself a new, loving mother in the bargain. The tragedy is not in growing up. The tragedy is in never growing up.

Later that night, Della lay in the fold-out cot next to Naomi's bed. She felt warm.

"Naomi?" she whispered.

"Yeah?"

"Do you really think I could come live here?"

"Of course," whispered Naomi, and she reached out from the bed and took Della's hand. "My mom's a social worker now. She can talk to whoever's in charge. And we can trade off the bed and cot week by week. And she can keep on giving you her extra inhalers. I bet she can even find a way to get you new glasses and doctors' visits, too." Naomi yawned. "It'll be fine. You'll see. Go to sleep. You've got a big day tomorrow. And you've still got to finish that *Midsummer* paper. So do I."

Della lay awake in the dark, holding on to Naomi's sweaty hand until the other girl fell asleep. She wasn't as certain as Naomi was that everything would be all right. She knew she wouldn't crack, not now, not when doing so would get Naomi in trouble too. Della was dependable. She just wasn't sure that Sharon would take her in. No matter how much Sharon loved Della, she was still a single mother in a two-bedroom apartment with a newly minted social worker's salary in New York City. The apartment was rent-stabilized, but even so. Della wasn't convinced she'd fight to add another girl to the second bedroom, even if she had been happy to see her.

But she treasured the island of quiet and possibility. Tonight she was safe, she could breathe, and she was loved. She gently let go of Naomi's hand. Maybe tonight could be enough.

Growing up is survival. And surviving means growing up. You can't wait for Peter. Peter forgets to come for Wendy at spring cleaning time year after year, you can't depend on him for anything. Princes are like that. Czars too. They want to keep you frozen in time, young and beautiful forever.

You can't rely on Peter, and you can't rely on princes. Neither one knows the first thing about what it takes to survive as a girl. If you want to do that, you go into the woods, to Baba Yaga and her daughter. They have a skull waiting, and they'll keep it warm for you. You can grow up. You can grow old.

AUTHOR'S NOTE: I've always liked Hole, especially because of all the misogynist shit directed at Courtney Love for the cardinal sin of being married to Kurt Cobain. It was Love who, for my money, was the real songwriting genius of that couple. One of the refrains of "Miss World"—"*I made my bed, I'll lie in it*"—always spoke to me for its bloody-minded determination to reap exactly what the singer sowed, and its refusal to accept that most of us *don't* make our own beds, especially as minors. Our beds are made for us in so many ways, and I suppose that made me think about who it is that makes our beds when we're young, both literally and metaphorically, all the people who are supposed to care for us, and what happens when they don't.

Play detective.

Click.

The teenage boy is wearing dirty tattered jeans. You can see revelations of tender white skin here and there and there. Mulberry scabs. He wears just another assembly-line black leather jacket. There's an illegible violet-red-orange emblem on the back. Maybe it's an Egyptian scarab or some kind of devil face.

He goes directly to the drop and extracts the briefcase. Look at the slender pearlescent moving ass. Stepping over puddles of contaminated water roiling with machine oil, the water glinting rainbows in the cold morning sun. The walls are made of cardboard, black and red graffiti scrawled upon them in illegible hieroglyphs and arabesques.

Industry has ceased. This section of the urban landscape is condemned, filled with shut-down factories and abandoned warehouses, paralyzed robots unmoving for years.

Inside, boxes cave into each other, mixing together obsolete parts for dead machines. Undersized coffins, broken down by moisture and stress. All of the metal bodies merge together, in disorder, buried en masse.

Surprise.

You motherfucker, the boy says. What do you think you're doing?

Slap him. *Shut up.* His wrists are soon handcuffed behind his back. The black leather jacket's emblem says nothing important. It's a message from some pharaoh.

The boy has the overbite and typical hollow cheeks of the urban vampire type you see all the time.

You asshole, he says. Who do you work for?

Myself.

Liar. Who programmed you?

I program myself.

Sure you do. What next, dummy?

Talk to me.

Across broken green and blue glass into another wing of the endless complex. Battered stockrooms, hundreds of offices, empty vaults. Rows and then piles of expressionless mannequins and cyborgs, some battered, missing their heads or arms or legs.

Over here.

What do you want me to say?

I don't know. What do I want you to say?

No answer.

Bzzzz.

No answer.

Bzzzz.

I'm only maybe ten years older plus software enhancements but he seems so young he could be my kid, if people still had kids. He has this trashy punk sneer on plum-colored lips he can't help, hair falling down over his left eye. I'm smitten in some insubordinate way, someone else's irrational memory fusing random neurons in a way I can't control.

There are people waiting for me, he says. They'll come after me. They'll find you and fuck you up.

No they won't. And I don't care.

What do you want me to say?

The right answer for a change.

You can fuck me, he says.

Maybe later. What's your name?

Billy.

Mmm, I think you're lying.

Ow, he says. Okay, okay. Jason. It's Jason.

Hey Jason. Why not an even dumber name, like Jonathan or Josh?

Fuck you. Who're you?

Raytheon.

You're named after a dead battery?

Don't make me feel bad.

Through some broken window comes a ray of dirty white, wasted sunlight. Dust motes. Tiny mechanical flies. The ray of sunlight is writhing and alive.

After some initial mechanical resistance, he's perfectly willing to tell me *everyfuckingthing* he knows.

I'm not so complicated. No one ever is. Sometimes you just think you are, because it seems more interesting to have a personality and you don't.

Jason's beginning to like me a little. Or maybe he just wants to ally himself with an energetic force. See America. Go for a ride.

Click.

Black leather jacket. Soiled white t-shirt that says in blood-red letters

C'MON.

Ow, he says, but nothing really hurts. *Ow.* He says that a lot. You baby, I say. Let's go.

But it takes a long time to drive out of/into the suburban wilderness. Hours and hours of slo-mo, repetitive scenery. Does the vehicle move at all? Stock footage and silent panoramas of wires and pale cement.

The light decays.

We stop among strangers and buy hamburgers. Or these things that look like hamburgers. Jason gets ugly when he eats.

After a long spell of racing silence, he starts talking about all the bad things that happen to assholes who get caught.

Like this one guy, he says, they kept pouring gasoline on him and lighting him up, then putting him out and starting all over again. After a while, man, he started getting pretty sick of those fucking blue flames.

Jason laughs at the picture in his head, or because he thinks it sounds cool.

Just shut up, okay?

I can't help myself. Ow.

In a minute (or an hour) he starts to cry. These slow, beautiful, transparent mercury-silver dead tears. He's ultimately so young.

He feels bad. He likes to feel bad. It perversely satisfies him to feel doomed and fucked-up.

There are big dark holes in the ground. Humming vistas of nowheresville. The car does not make a sound. We're just a shadow on cement.

In New St. Louis, we find a hotel room. While Jason is in the bathroom, doing his golden shower thing, the bullets are removed from the gun and hidden under the bed. I can see the future here, sorta.

And then it's showtime. Put this in there. Do this. Lick that. All these appendages, tentacles, blind mouths.

Later, much later, Jason pretends to be asleep. He listens and listens and listens to me sleep.

Then, finally, oh so cautiously, taking pains, he sneaks out of the bed. He creeps, in slow motion, like a cat after a bird in a cartoon, going for the gun.

He picks it up.

Nothing. Silence.

Darkness. Decay.

Do it. Go ahead.

What? Jason says, as if awakened from a trance, one of his fangs glistening in the light from the dead iceberg moon.

The gun is violently removed from him. He's hit and hit

again. Hit. That's okay. He wants to be hit. He thinks it's a sign of ... *love?*

Jason falls to his knees like some nine-year-old robot girl assembled from a kit. He sort of sobs.

Reset.

The next day, *Tuesday-Wednesday-Thursday*, we head down South.

Insects are frozen dry buzzing in straight or looping lines, captured by the excess magnetism in the air.

Abandoned houses, old mansions, empty roads. Cars left upside-down in ditches. Drones hover above everything sending data who knows where or why.

There are very few flesh-and-blood people walking around down here undisguised. Some are pretending to be stupid robots or androids or something; others pretend not to be when they were made on an assembly line somewhere, factories in China long defunct. When there was a China. Then there exist creatures built by child rocket scientists from online print-out kits. Naturally there's a lot of miscellaneous harvesting for spare parts. This gets messy sometimes. Porn no one human can understand.

Half-finished empty malls. They've become museums.

Let's rob this place, Jason says, when the car stops somewhere to be refueled.

Bobby's Parts & Shit

What for?

Let's do it. I don't like the way that redneck motherfucker

looked at me. He's got a crooked boner. Let's send that faggot straight to burning hell.

You do it.

No, you.

Why should I?

'Cause you're the one who took the bullets out of the gun, Jason says, laughing like crazy. *Stop.*

See America. There are long flat plains and dead buildings and black rivers and then sometimes there's nothing at all. It's not there. You can step off the edge.

The sky is a colorless soft burn.

Fizz. Fizzy. Fizziness.

But there are so many shadows and holes. It's hard to make out what some of these shapes are supposed to be. The shadows move. There are signs, but no one can read them anymore.

It's painful to open your eyelids in this *Sequel to Alabama IV.* You need to get some special sunglasses, and still the air everywhere needlejabs your eyes. There are dead dogs and cats and possums rotting forever in the sun.

Children play impossible games five feet off the ground. The light here is pulsating, mathematics reinvented and trashed. These dolls move in slo-mo like they're on secret wires.

In F-Birmingham, Jason buys research pharmaceuticals to put some extra feelings into his blood. Anything for a kick. He's bored. The whole world is bored. I'm bored. The unreal pharmacist moves in slow motion, stop-motion, hard to be sure he exists.

There are *gaps.*
Then I recite:

> *There are all these bad habits that have to be broken.*
> *Bad habits picked up by being losers.*
> *If the bad habits are broken,*
> *we won't be losers anymore.*

Fuck you, Jason says. Why're you so fucking ambitious all of a sudden? Quit faking shit all the time.

Nothingness.

There is a drum solo in a backyard by some kid grown in a vat with four arms five eyes three mouths. He can really drum. He's a blur.

A hundred years go by, a thousand years in one hour, and then Jason puts one too many synthetic emotions into himself.

He freezes up.

I just watch. I can't tell if I ever have a hard-on anymore.

This black car backs up into an alley. Jason falls out. He just lies there on the pavement, next to those garbage cans, amid scrunched-up papers or leaves.

Oh, maybe he's resting. He's gotten really lazy, he never wants to do anything anymore. He's just waiting for the right moment to remember how to breathe and talk and act like a real live three-dimensional boy.

Or maybe Jason knelt down, in a grove of trees, and was shot in the head. A beautiful, tragic death, the way he always wanted to go, execution-style goodbye. This was in ancient sepia, real jazzy, oh yeah.

Goodbye.

What?

I can't *think think-a-think.*

In some little bungalow in *Florida or Else*, they're waiting for me, sharpening their knives. I'm full of poison, hard to kill. To death me they'll have to cut off my head. Even then I'll writhe, coiling and hissing in the raspberry bleeding dark brown dirt.

Hey, let's go to the beach.

The sky is strobing pink while the artificial ocean's gray with jerking creatures in the waves.

Repeat.

Look at all those doomster sharks in their sunglasses and latex suits, dancing by that burning pile of never.

They don't know me, or maybe they'd say hello.

On dry land, my head floats on magnetic waves.

I'm going out.

Babe, I'm coming in.

AUTHOR'S NOTE: I always listen to music when I write. I'm not very introspective about my writing process; what I try to do is lose myself in the description of a dream, sliding sometimes into delirium and then re-emerging as though from melting waves. "Slammers" by Cabaret Voltaire has the sort of hypnotic beat that might hold creatures of thought suspended in mid-air.

WE'VE BEEN HAD

BY ALEX JENNINGS

t was still summer—at least until the end of the week. I'd come to town to check on Worth's old man, and then I'd fly back to New Orleans and marry my girlfriend at a dive bar before a pajama dance party. I'd bought my plane ticket at the last minute. If I hadn't found a direct flight, I might have had to drive. I'm a big dude and hate contorting myself to fit into those seats, but I could handle it for a couple hours.

I got to the airport a little late, breezed through security on sheer charm, and boarded the plane with minutes to spare. Thankfully, the flight wasn't even half-full, so I tucked myself into a window seat of an empty row at the back of the plane.

I'm not afraid of flying—which is good, considering all the travel I do. It's not worth being afraid because if anything goes truly wrong, I'm so irredeemably fucked that there's no point in worrying. We hit some turbulence, turbulence with an edge to it—and I could have sworn I heard the flight attendant say something about screaming as she ran through the safety presentation before takeoff.

At one point it felt like we were sliding down a hill like a kid on a saucer sled. I could hear a pregnant electrical hum—the kind of sound an amp makes just before you play a note. With it came a sterile, wintry smell, like the inside of a walk-in freezer. The noise stretched out, and I found my ears straining, just waiting for an opening chord that never came.

The cabin lights winked off, and though it was broad day outside, everything went black, the sort of textured swallowing black that makes you feel like you've gone suddenly blind. I felt someone drop into the aisle seat, and my heart began to speed. I touched my chest, and my hand was so cold I could feel it through my seersucker shirt.

The figure in the aisle seat turned to stare at me. Its gaze was tactile, crawling up my left shoulder and then the side of my face. It cleared its throat, prepared to speak, and I wrenched myself awake.

For a moment, I was afraid I'd shouted aloud. I sat there breathing hard, waiting for a flight attendant or another passenger to ask what was wrong. Nobody came to bother me.

It was The Walkmen that did it to me. I was sleeping over at Worth's house one night when we were thirteen. He'd fallen asleep, and music videos had come back on the TV in the wee hours. I half-listened, letting the images slide over my eyeballs like warm salt water. And then that echoey piano started up, and there was Hamilton Leithauser shadowboxing in black and white.

He looked like he hadn't slept in a while. He wore a plain white T-shirt, his hands were taped up like a fighter's. Something about his look along with the bad-Dylan-imitation vocals made me turn up the volume. I still don't know who played his opponent, but it looked like they were really trying to kick each other's ass. I didn't pay attention to the lyrics, just the sound of his voice, that driving rhythm section, that tinkling piano that made me feel like I was walking barefoot down a dark forest path … I didn't just fall in love with the song or the band but the world it brought suddenly to my attention.

When I finally paid attention to them, the lyrics resonated with me. I never had any use for nostalgia before Worth died. When people ask what he was to me, I say he was my brother. For our band, we shared a surname—we were Kenton and Ellsworth Stiles. My aversion to nostalgia is why I hated coming back to Columbia. It's a "planned community" in suburban Maryland with whimsical street names, a too-big shopping mall, and miles of paved bike paths running through tamed woodlands. When my Uber carried me up Flamepool Way, I felt no tightness in my chest, no panic at the idea of being back here. I just wasn't sure what I'd say to Worth's father, Mr. Desmond.

Worth and I met when we were five. I watched across the street as he and his family moved into the split-level house situated beside the bike bath that ran past the Tot Lot. That weekend, I saw him riding his bike. He was no older than me, but he already rode without training wheels.

We had this game in the neighborhood where when someone was riding their big wheel, other kids would stand in their path and dare them to hit them. I did that to Worth first chance I got, even though he was on a big-kid bike. Instead of turning aside or stopping, he sped up, trying to hit me.

I dove out of the way, shocked and laughing, and that was the moment we became friends. He had a runny nose and bright hooded eyes. I remember him standing on the path in his BK Diamonds, holding his Huffy by the handlebars. His voice was always a little adenoidal, like he had a cold. He said, "My name's Ellsworth. My dad named me after a bad guy."

That night when I told my dad I'd met a kid named Ellsworth, he barked a laugh.

"Watch out for that one," he said. "Outlaw."

"Worth says he was named after a bad guy."

"The baddest," my dad said. He laughed again.

The next time I went out, I made sure to carry my Teen Titans lunchbox full of Pogs. Worth seemed like a kid worth impressing.

Worth was low-key obsessed with Lobster Boy. Grady Stiles, Jr. was this carny with ectrodactyly hands and feet like claws. In 1978, Lobster Boy shot and killed his daughter's fiancé the night before the wedding. He was convicted, but because of his disability he was sentenced to house arrest and probation. He was also a wicked drunk, and in '92, his next-door neighbor walked into his house and put two in Lobster Boy's head while he sat smoking, watching TV.

Worth never had to work at music—not the way I did.

The week after we saw the video for "We've Been Had," Worth sat down at the piano in our school's music room and started playing the song. He got it exactly right. I went home that night and told my dad I wanted to use my Christmas money to buy an electric guitar. We didn't decide to call ourselves Grady Stiles until we signed up for the talent show that spring.

Okay. About Blandair Farm … When we were kids, everyone just called it the Smith Farm, after its then-owner, Elizabeth Smith—though we knew her as "Mad Myrtle." She was a rail-thin bird-like woman who smoked like a chimney and wore sunglasses day and night. The property lay just inside a spit of woods that ran behind our subdivision bordering Maryland 175.

When I was home for the holidays in 2018, I went up there one afternoon. I didn't go all the way to the big house, but I found a gap in the pasture fence and walked down the slope for a better look at the barn and the stables.

It was worse than I remembered. It was maybe two in the afternoon, but the sky was much grayer than it had been at my parents' place maybe a hundred yards away.

A barn stood off to my right. I swallowed hard, staring

into the blackness of the doorway on its side. How could there have been a time when Worth and I would have charged in there like it was nothing?

When I turned to head back, I saw a deer standing in the middle of the pasture. It gawped at me, open-mouthed, swinging its head slowly to the left, then to the right. I'd never liked the way animals behaved out here.

Now I had the terrible impression that someone larger than me stood behind me and a little to my left, that if I turned to look a flash of light would break across my vision as they hit me with a plank. As I stood rooted to the spot, the deer kept shaking itself, and the daylight continued to fail.

I blinked, startled to find myself standing on the bike path out by the Tot Lot. Day had been restored, and I was fine, except for a touch of heartburn. I'm sure it was heartburn.

Normally, I'd have examined such a disorienting episode, but instead relief gusted through me like a breeze stirring chimes, and I turned my back on the whole thing.

People argue about whether Maryland is the South. As far as I'm concerned, it qualifies. Leaving aside the literal fucking slave plantation beside our neighborhood, we have not just one but multiple Waffle House locations. Waffle House isn't completely relegated to the southern USA—they have them in Hawaii and Maine—but there is a specific feel of chaotic resignation to a Southern Waffle House. And the ones in Maryland have that in spades.

Yes, there's a lot of covert northern-style racism in Maryland, but there's also the other kind. When I was maybe eight, some White Power group flyered our neighborhood. The pamphlets included a crude illustration of a white family sitting in a rowboat. The father was using an oar to beat back a Black man who was trying to climb into the craft. In the foreground, shaded hands reached out of the water. The caption read something like "no blacks no jews mud people in our lifeboat for survival!"

Instead of telling my parents about it, I kept the thing. I had never seen anything like it. Someone had gone to a lot of trouble just to let people like me know they didn't want us around.

Growing up in the '90s, Worth and I had a lot of autonomy to go tear-assing it around town on our own. We would ride our bikes down to the mall or over to Waxy Tracksies in Dobbin Center. Or we would head up to the farm.

One rainy Saturday when we were maybe ten, we headed up to the farm and got closer than usual to the manor house. There were NO TRESPASSING signs posted all over the property, and while our parents had never warned us away from the place, we knew we weren't supposed to be there.

That was the first time I saw the ruined slave quarters.

The little fallen-in house was smaller than the apartment my uncle Claude rented after his divorce. My father had read *Roots* aloud to the family more than once, so I knew that multiple families had once lived in spaces like it. The shack didn't give me the same feeling as finding that Klan pamphlet, but I felt something hard to define. It was like the presence of an evil spirit, but worse, because revenants and vengeful ghosts come from outside our experience.

The shack's planks had sprouted fat white mushrooms that were dissolving the wood from the inside, but to me the planks seemed uncomfortably fresh.

"You dare me?" Worth said.

"What?"

"You dare me to go inside?"

He was staring at the big house, and now his eyes didn't seem hooded at all. They looked larger than normal, cartoonish.

The manor was a three-story brick house with a columned porch. It barely qualified as a mansion. The original owners had held human beings in bondage just to maintain a shitty little pile tucked away in a dreary wood.

"What—no."

"Like Panthro," he said. He must have grown since his parents bought him his green and white striped polo. It fit poorly now. "A trial of *stealth*."

"You talking crazy right now for real."

But the idea thrilled me.

Dr. Desmond Oluka was tall and powerfully built. He was ten years younger than my parents, but still on the older side.

I think he liked me bringing Worth out of his shell. He'd done some boxing in his younger years.

Worth wasn't a fighter, though. He was a dreamer, a musical genius.

See, I can write songs, I'm okay on keyboards, and I can play guitar all day. I'm even handy with a set of drums—and if I have to, I can get something out of a horn that sounds all right. Worth could play anything. *Anything.* I never saw him encounter an instrument he couldn't assimilate into himself like the Borg. Harp, vibraphone, theremin, sitar—didn't matter.

I had to work hard just to come up with anything he'd care to elevate through his talent. That's why, when he told me he wouldn't work on another record, I didn't believe him. Sure, maybe we needed a break from each other, but I figured he'd still play on his own. We'd had a couple blow-outs in the past year. Trivial disagreements that ballooned, somehow, into screaming matches. I'd come close to slapping him before I backed down, ashamed of myself, of my willingness to hit someone I loved—especially given how he'd been bullied in school.

When The Walkmen quit playing together, they had wives, young kids. They didn't want to tour anymore. Not me. I can sleep anytime anywhere—and as long as I get four hours, I'm good. I operate at a high fuckin level in our field, just not as high as Worth. He didn't need Grady like I did. He didn't need music like I did, but music wasn't something he did, it was something he *was.* You don't just up and decide to quit breathing.

I wrote something like thirty songs over the summer of 2017, hoping at least a few would appeal to him. Usually, he'd sit with his eyes closed and his head cocked to the right, and every so often his eyes would open because he'd heard something he could work with. I played them one after the other, and this time, he kept his usual squint. He leaned back in the overstuffed easy chair I'd bought at an antique shop on Frenchmen Street and lit himself a Marlboro Light.

"It ain't there," he whispered. I couldn't read his tone. "Can't hear it."

"What the fuck do you hear then?" I snapped.

He didn't take offense. He just shook his head. "Nothing, bruh. Just noise from outside."

"What's going on with you, man?"

"Nothing," he said. "It's not the songs, either. Songs are fine. You polish them some, they'll be ready—except for that one about the snowman. That shit is beneath you."

I tried to be insulted but couldn't. I think I even laughed a little. "No Christmas record?"

It was as if he hadn't heard. "I think it's me," he said. "Something in me."

Instead of working, we just talked into the night. Talked in a way we hadn't in years. For a while there, it had started to feel like we were two executives at some company that made widgets or time pieces. That night, though, we were brothers again.

"I been talking to Azha," he said. He eyed me like he was checking me for cracks. Azha was his high school girlfriend. They'd stayed together after we dropped out. She even moved to LA with us, but things had turned sour. I never found out what happened, but it seemed serious. A betrayal.

"*Azha* Azha?" I asked.

He nodded. "She wants to travel, and I want to take her. You can do a solo record if you want, and then when I get back, we can see what's what."

In fifth grade, he'd written a report on Bali, couldn't stop talking about it for weeks. It blew his mind that the rest of the country was Muslim, but Bali had its own version of Hinduism. He got a hold of *The Theatre and Its Double* and read about how dance and music were completely integrated into Balinese life, and the joy that idea brought him just never wore off. Honestly, when we were grown and doing well, looking to leave LA, that was how I sold him the idea of moving to New Orleans. I told him that the music, the art was everywhere, all the time. Just like Bali.

It was winter when we finally ventured inside the manor house. We had both turned eleven, and during Thanksgiving break we had a heavy snowfall—which meant sledding. Worth's brother Larry pitched a fit until Worth agreed to let him pilot their saucer sled solo. He immediately lost control, steered himself into the base of a pine tree at the bottom of the slope behind the Arnolds' house. He shocked himself and dropped a snootful of snow from the branches above him, then was done for the day.

After taking Larry inside to lick his wounds, Worth came back out. He wore a ridiculously puffy red, blue, and yellow winter coat with fake fur fringing the hood over a pair of purple snowveralls. I had on a fleece-lined brown corduroy jacket with a fuzzy collar that looked like something Wolverine had worn in the *X-Men* cartoon. I could tell from the set of his mouth that he'd stolen a couple of his dad's menthols.

"You wanna go down to Jackson Pond?" I asked. Heading there would give us ample time to smoke on the way without getting caught.

"Maybe," Worth said. He cocked his head back and to the right, gazing at me over his cheeks. "We could do sumn else …"

I let him lead the way.

We didn't light up until we breached the tree line. Our smoke mingled with the steam from our breath, escaping like spirits into the ether. Instead of heading through the pasture, we stuck to the woods. There wasn't much undergrowth— just some sticker bushes and the odd deadfall here and there. With the trees bare, we were able to see the slave quarters and the manor well before we arrived.

For a long time, I didn't remember any of this. I sensed only its vaguest outline beneath the surface of my mind. After all the journaling, the EMDR, the talk therapy and hypnosis, I have memories of memories. Fragments like chunks of ice bobbing in Jackson Pond.

The woods return to me clearly. The farm's buildings seem too large, kneeling in darkness like flood waters, though I know it was still bright out. There was machinery. The skeleton of an old wagon, its metal chassis rusted through. Pine needles and snow crunched beneath the soles of my boots. I still smell candle wax, charred meat.

I remember the manor's front door, but I don't remember opening it. I can still see Worth's face, wide-eyed and ashen, his mouth open, screaming. He is tied down, or lying at the bottom of a stairwell, a pool of blood like a stained-glass halo at the back of his skull.

A cemetery stretches in every direction as far as I can see. The trees are grave markers.

The old woman sits on an overstuffed sofa with holes in its upholstery. Tufts of foam or cotton batting have burst through the floral-printed fabric. A television blares. There is something awful about the way her arms are arranged in her lap. They're too long or don't bend, or there are too many. Or all those things.

You boys and your lousy racket. Her voice is low and full of blood, but she isn't surprised to see us.

"She thinks we belong here," I whisper, or Worth does. The brown seashell of his little ear.

"Maybe we do."

A stream of bloody vomit at my feet. When I look up, a deer hangs above me, caught in the branches of a tree, feebly kicking its legs as it makes a choked, stretched-out noise deer can't make.

I ran from the house. I think Worth was still inside. I remember a maze stretching around and over me, but was it hedges or black volcanic stone? At its center stood—stands?—a great wooden table covered in blood. Some of it has dried, but some is very fresh.

The trees stand tall, too tall, as the ground reclines above me, rolling. The bloody vomit is mine. There is a hollow inside me, a wide-eyed shadow in the dark. I see its sclera and its teeth.

you left me i needed you and you left me

I'm sorry. I'm sorry. I'm sorry. I'm sorry.

I'm sorry, but I can't do this. I won't.

I stood for a long time in front of Worth's childhood home. I had the impression that someone stood there with me, but I knew I was alone. I hadn't sensed Worth even once since his death, and I liked to believe he'd gone exploring, free of disease, pain, addiction.

Finally, I rang the doorbell, and Desmond's nurse, Gregg, answered. He was a pinch-faced Jewish cat with thick glasses and a crooked red slash of a mouth. He seemed surprised to see me.

"Is he awake?" I asked.

Gregg nodded.

"How is he?"

"Better than he has been in a while," Gregg said. "He had a rough night, though, so he's tired."

"Upstairs?"

"Living room."

Worth had wanted to hire a nurse for his father, even before the stroke. Larry was away in Nepal, running the American school there, and Worth and I were in New Orleans. After Desmond got sick, Worth wanted to move his father down, but the old man was adamant. His life and his friends were here.

Worth hired Gregg to work as his father's "valet", cooking, cleaning, seeing to his needs. Despite his infirmity, the old man was sharp as hell, so I'm sure he realized why Gregg was really there.

The living room was mostly unchanged. The fifty-inch TV hung opposite a large cream-colored sectional sofa with chaises on both ends. Photos of Worth and Larry hung on the walls. Worth in his Boy Scout uniform, nose to nose with a baby bat, Worth and Larry holding up their pinewood racers, Worth sitting at a drum set. There was one photo of the two of us at one of our early bar shows in Ellicott City. I was on my knees, shredding theatrically on a Flying V while Worth was dipping his mic like Ginger Rogers, his right arm crooked above his head …

And then there was our *Rolling Stone* cover. We wore our Prince-meets-George Clinton costumes from the Knights on Earff tour. I'd come across that image countless times over the years, so many that I'd stopped *seeing* it. Now I noticed was how young we appeared. The issue had hit the stands when we were both twenty. I was grinning from ear to ear—I'd made a point of it, tired of the way rappers mean-mugged in every promo photo. Worth was grinning, too, but his expression was desperate. He looked like a hostage. He'd shut the interview down when the reporter started asking us about TV on the Radio.

That was the other big Black rock act at the time—but they were nothing like us. We had more in common with The Gories or Living Colour. Our biggest hit had been "The Littlest Richard," for Christ's sake. After that, Worth was only willing to be interviewed by other musicians, ones he knew and liked. Press became my job.

Mr. Desmond sat on the sofa. He was much smaller, lighter, than he'd been the last time I saw him. His shoulders and chest had been so powerful when I was a boy, but now I could easily lift and carry him. His hair had gone entirely white, and aging had finally made it into his face. His cheekbones had risen beneath his grooved skin while his eyes had sunken. He still smelled of Old Spice.

"Uncle …" I said.

"Please. Sit down."

"I don't know what happened," I said. "I don't understand it."

"Sit."

I took a seat on the cushion next to his. I realized now that I'd been so focused on keeping it together, on writing for the new record, on preparing for the tour, that I didn't know how to be with my grief.

"At least it wasn't in that damnable city."

Mr. Desmond hated New Orleans. The crime, the dysfunction, the corruption, the crumbling infrastructure—all valid points, honestly. It's a difficult city to live in, but I had become my best self there. Worth had, too.

"We're going to spread his ashes on Halloween."

"I don't want him trapped there, Kenton."

I opened my mouth, closed it again. "He … No. I don't either. We'll spread them on the lake. He loved Lake Ponchartrain."

Mr. Desmond leaned forward, slid his hand into the front pocket of his shirt, found nothing, and sat back again. "Sometimes I think about the farm. About you boys up there."

I shook my head. "It's not a good place."

"He went back by himself all the time," Mr. Desmond said. "In his teens, especially. He used to talk with the old woman. He said she thought he was a spirit."

"There were a lot of them up there," I said.

"They've turned it into a park," he said. "Playgrounds and lacrosse fields … Do you think she's still up there?"

"No," I said. "That place blotted her out. That's why she was so crazy."

"Did Ellsworth tell you what he saw?"

"Said he heard something." He had told me that he'd been riding his skateboard on the other side of the property—across Highway 175, and that he'd heard voices singing, chanting. It had terrified him, and he'd run.

We sat in silence for a while.

"He should be here," I said finally.

For a long time, he didn't respond, then: "Yes. He should." He swallowed. "I think of going up there myself, but if I found him there …"

"Don't," I said. "Don't ever. He wouldn't want it."

One moment I was crossing the street back to my parents' house—I remember stepping into the yard, and the next, I was walking along a well-trodden dirt path that meandered crazily through the horse pasture. Night had fallen, and it took me a moment to realize why the world looked so strange: there was no color. Everything was grayscale, just like the video for "We've Been Had."

I shut my eyes and fought for control. If I chose, I could turn around and walk back off the farm, no problem. I didn't ask myself why, then, I headed for the manor house.

Something I never liked about Columbia is that the sky never gets dark at night. The stars were always dim, struggling to be seen over the light pollution, but not tonight. I could have reached up and burned my fingertips on them, like pinching out a lit cigarette.

Night air lay heavy on my skin, and the closer I got to the mansion, the harder walking became.

I don't know how I missed the rock that sent me sprawling, but I tumbled like a camera in a clothes dryer. My chin hit the dirt hard, and my teeth clacked together painfully.

I knew Worth as soon as he touched me. He rested his hand on my right shoulder for a beat, then shook me gently like he was waking me for school. "Get up," he said. "I got sumn to show you."

I sat up, reached for him, but the sight of him made me lower my hands. He was young again, in his teens. He had his ear pierced, his hair had been plaited close to his dark scalp, and he wore his old round glasses. The absence of color made his skin look even darker, his eyes brighter.

"Are you okay?" I asked. "Are you—are you trapped? In pain?"

He took an exasperated breath. "Get up," he said stonily. "You wanted to know."

Just then, a breeze gusted by, carrying scents of wood smoke and cooking meat. I salivated, and a pang of hunger twisted in my gut. How could this be a dream? It was too vivid, too sensory.

By now, Worth was several yards away. He walked without checking to make sure I followed. I jogged to catch up.

A broad wooden table stood outside the slave quarters. Something lay piled on it, but I pried my gaze away. Part of me knew what we'd find there.

Panic dulled my thoughts like radio static.

Now Worth stopped, turned. He took my left wrist in his long broad guitarist's hand. "I never told you because I love you," he said. "You can look, but then you have to go. If she wakes up …"

"Why black and white?"

"It's worse in color," he said. "Lots worse."

Together, we looked at the table.

The shock was immense, but it was only shock, not surprise. Understanding that made me want to curl in on myself.

Tears welled, spilled down my cheeks. I wanted to fall to my knees, but rage kept me upright. I was tired, incalculably exhausted, but I stood. I stand.

It had been a woman, a Black woman. Parts of her—one of her arms, half a leg—had been taken already, but the rest of her lay butchered. They hadn't even bothered to close her eyes. They had rolled back in their sockets, and her mouth yawned, like her jaw had been dislocated.

"This is how I found out that they ate us sometimes," he said. "I saw it when I was a kid."

"How old were you?"

"Not old enough."

We stared in silence for a beat. My mind wandered, tried to stop seeing, but I forced it back to focus.

"You shouldn't be here," I said. "I need … I need you to be out of pain. I need you to be free and—and—beyond all this."

"Look at her," he said.

I'd never taken my eyes off her.

"She could be my mother. Tortured. Literally. Fucking. Butchered … . How can I turn my back?"

"You're trying to—?"

Something shifted then. It was like a cloud passing in front of the sun. A darkness that recast everything around us, but without any change to the light. An invisible ripple raced across the ground.

"Time's up," Worth said.

"Come with me! Come—"

Worth turned to spear me with his gaze, and for an instant, everything was in color. The blood, the viscera, the shit, and the smell rolled into me like a wall. I retched.

An invisible force yanked me off my feet. I moved backward at speed, but as I went, I caught a glimpse of the manor house. Its façade had cracked open, and a column of black smoke streamed from the rift—but it wasn't smoke.

Yyyyyou, it said, slurring its words. **Yyyyyou k-kids ... !**

The woman on the table sat up. She pressed her remaining hand against the left side of her face and wailed. Worth positioned himself in front of her, feet planted, chest squared.

I woke up in my parents' house.

The Walkmen were right. Nostalgia is bullshit. We can't comfort ourselves with the past because the past is a lie. It's not just us, it's not just Black people who are trapped by it. We are all locked together, wrestling against angels.

And I'll say this: I was wrong about Worth. Everyone was. He was a fighter. He *is*.

AUTHOR'S NOTE: "We've Been Had" and its music video are very important to me. I first saw it during a major low point, visiting Columbia, Maryland, during a holiday visit. In interviews, Hamilton Leithauser has said that the lyrics he wrote don't add up, but I know what they mean to me. The Smith/ Blandair Farm is a very real place, and my late brother and I spent a lot of time there when we were growing up. I haven't been back since 2018, and I have no plans to go.

Bradford was now one of those men who had been raised without a father only for that father to show up the moment success smiled upon his son. It was an implausible reality, of course, hard to accept: Bradford had heard similar stories about other people. He'd also long ago gotten through the angst, the rejection, the confusion, sorrow, and horror of growing up without a dad. Maria Swann played a major part in that, of course. She moved on quick, partly because she had to, but also because she was wired that way. More than a go-getter, Maria was a *mover-on*, and would have molded her son into a man with confidence, humor, intelligence, and culture, whether her husband had abandoned her or not.

And now, tonight … only hours before Bradford would perform the number-one hit "Hide & Seek," amongst others, a set of angular, dark music the critics called "goth" … and Dad was on his way to see him.

Wyle Swann's vanishing had sent Maria into a rage the young Bradford had witnessed in real time. But years later, pacing the backstage greenroom at Impresario Hall, Bradford comprehended in full how brief that rage had been. A couple weeks maybe. Less than a month before she'd sat her son on the couch and explained in stoic, unwavering terms how it was just the two of them now, and that maybe that's the way it always should have been. Bradford needed to hear this. Still, times were hard. Maria's intensity landed her some jobs and lost her others. She made enemies as easily as she made friends. But she had never stopped working.

Bradford got that from her. But he got a lot from her.

Now, able to see himself in the greenroom glass, dressed in black from hat to boot, his hair the same raven-wing dark as his mother's, he understood Maria had been goth herself. And her son had made a killing off of it.

Sure, "Hide & Seek" was a little more than just inspired by Siouxsie Sioux's "Peek-A-Boo." Bradford had no problem admitting that and, in fact, had told Siouxsie herself. In interviews, at parties, in record label conference rooms, he gave credit where credit was due. And why not? Maria had raised him right. Father, Dad, Wyle (whatever Bradford called the man on the rare occasion he came up) didn't raise a thing.

Yet … after fifteen years … he was on his way here …

Len Singer, Bradford's celebrated manager, had telephoned that afternoon. Bradford had been stretching on the carpet in a hotel room at the Woodruff in downtown Detroit when it rang.

"Swann? Singer."

"Good news or weird news?"

"Weird. The weirdest."

And Bradford knew, he just *knew* what words would come next. Later, he would wonder if this knowledge had something to do with unseen bonds, ones we don't choose, ties to the people who conceived you. He'd make a note of this in his black notebook. It could make a good song. Some lyrics even came to mind: *You don't choose who knows you/ you don't choose who shows up unannounced …*

But this was announced. Wyle Swann had managed to call Len Singer directly. Bradford wondered if perhaps this had something to do with Maria's having fallen for such a man. A bit of a go-getter himself.

"It's your dad," Singer said.

"Uh-huh."

"And, well … he said he's coming to the show tonight."

"Uh-huh."

"Look, this kind of thing happens from time to time. You hear stories. A guy reaches some level of fame and people come out of the woodwork. I'm really sorry, man."

"Give him backstage access," Bradford said. The words sounded just as crazy to him as they did to his manager. But he stood by them.

"Wow, really? Are you sure about that?"

"Yeah. Did he say why he's in Detroit?"

"He said he'd driven a thousand miles to see you. As if … well, as if this ought to prove to me he was trying. Or something like that."

Another reasonable song idea. Everything was a song idea these days. The view of Detroit. The couch in the greenroom. The fact some fathers just upped and vanished, then showed again, as if the floor of the spacetime continuum had a trapdoor and Bradford's entire life had been one element of a grand trick.

"Presto," he said.

"Yeah," Len Singer said. "Abracadabra, my friend. Are you sure you're sure?"

"Yeah."

"All right. I'll tell him. I'll let Bruce know, too. You thinking before or after?"

"Before," Bradford said, not knowing his father at all. Was he the kind of man who would stay through a whole show? It seemed unlikely.

Later, getting dressed before the hotel room's window, his heart would go to Siouxsie Sioux, finding a strength and style in her he hadn't quite found anywhere else. How would she have handled this? Maybe she had. Nothing like it had come up the time they'd met, backstage at a Banshees show in New Mexico. Had she ever had a similar experience? It felt like a good idea, talking to someone who, at the very least, might commiserate. He decided to ask Len if any of Len's other clients ever had a father scratching at the door. You couldn't rightly manage million-unit sellers without running up against their personal lives. Bradford discovered it felt good telling his manager. Felt like the story of his father had acted as a bridge by which he and Len could travel back and forth from one another; a personal touch always present, even in the most practical or pressing of matters.

Bradford stood at the window longer than he'd planned. He'd seen the start of a rainfall. Just as the dark of night rose up to meet it.

All in black, Bradford phoned Dix, his security detail, a thing he never thought he'd need, and let the serious man know he was ready to go to the venue. There would be more primping and last-minute wardrobe details to work out, but Bradford Swann wouldn't be caught on camera in anything but black. Part of it was his image, of course, and what a photo of him in khaki shorts and pink flip-flops in the music magazines might do to his booming career, but another bit of it was that link to his mother. Maria had always looked like she was on her way to a funeral even before Wyle vanished, and Bradford didn't know it was unique until the boys at grade school mockingly told him so. But even back then, music on his mind, and musicians too, Bradford walked those school halls proud to be something of a shadow.

"What's an artist if not the world's shadow?" he asked his reflection in the window. Then he frowned. Just because everything was a song idea didn't mean they were all good.

Dix knocked on the door. Bradford gave himself one last glance in the glass, then stepped into the hall.

"You ready, Mr. Swann?"

"I would say that's my father's name," Bradford said. "But I don't have a father."

"Is that so?"

"Yes. And I'm ready."

On the walk to the elevator, he eyed the gun holstered at Dix's hip.

"That thing looks powerful," he said.

Dix pressed the elevator button. Going down.

"You're safe with me," Dix said.

"Can I hold it?"

"What's that?"

"I've never held a gun before."

Dix looked to the glowing blue number as the car climbed toward them. He pulled the gun out but didn't hand it over.

"Go on," he said. "Touch it then."

Bradford did. He ran his fingers along the muzzle. It looked powerful indeed. Strong enough to change the world.

He nearly recoiled when the elevator bell dinged. As if the weapon had put him to sleep. Dix already had the gun back in its holster.

"It's raining out there," Dix said. Bradford hadn't even noticed the small umbrella hanging from the security guard's other hip. "You'll need this."

This he did hand over and Bradford opened it as the elevator took them down.

All black, of course.

"You don't believe in bad luck, do you, Dix?"

The big man eyed the open umbrella.

"No, sir," he said. "Not when you're prepared for what's coming."

Jerry and the other bandmates were already doing their sound checks when Bradford arrived. That's not how it used to be, but the rush of success had done more than afford Bradford the opportunity to buy his first home. He knew to exert as little energy as possible to keep himself from burning out before the shows and to save his energy for all possible post-show activities. Tonight, of course, was different. Bradford didn't want to use the word "special" because he had no idea what to expect of the coming reunion. He didn't want to use the word "reunion" either.

"Look who showed!" Beth called. The band's lead guitarist, Beth's walkdown riff to open "Hide & Seek" might be what put it over the top. Bradford was not unaware of this. And he loved her for it.

"It takes a lot of time to get the black pants to match the black shirt," he said, coming to the foot of the stage. "How does it sound?"

"Hear for yourself." She cued the others, and they started from the top. Bradford felt the boom of the bass drum (always too loud, he thought; the drums should support, not tell the story), but it all sounded good. It was easy to imagine the big hall full of young people. Kids dressed in black. Like Bradford. And Bradford's mom.

He crossed the floor to the sound booth, gave the band a listen from there, then, umbrella in hand, exited the theater through a side door.

The rain was coming harder now. The night had grown up.

On the walk in he'd spotted a payphone in the brick alley. Deep enough where he ought to be okay, hidden from any fans that might show early. Deep in that alley now, he fished quarters from his pocket. He called Mom.

"Is it my famous son?"

"How did you know?"

"A mother knows." Then: "No, that's bullshit. I've answered the phone the same way the last ten times. I just happened to be right tonight. What's wrong?"

"Nothing's wrong."

"Well, according to my calculations, you should be backstage right now, nervously pacing."

Bradford laughed.

"I already did that. I do that all day."

"Ooh. I hear something in your voice. What is it?"

The rain looked like a wall now at the head of the alley. The black umbrella and fire escapes overhead kept him mostly dry.

"Dad's coming tonight."

Maria didn't go quiet, didn't hesitate in responding.

"*Dad?*"

"Yeah, well, I don't know what to call him."

"I knew this day would come."

"Did you?"

"Of course. He was always an opportunist. You're rich. Now he comes. Like a fuckin piranha."

"I gave him access backstage."

"Why?"

"I don't know."

"He might try to hurt you, Bradford."

"What do you mean?"

"He's not well. Never was. He left his wife and child without a word. You're of sound mind. Would you ever do something like that?"

"Of course not."

"Exactly."

Young people in black passed the head of the alley. Bradford was amazed how little the rain bothered them.

"Fans," he said.

"Well, your father is no fan. I don't like this."

"I have security."

"That's fine. But are you prepared? To see him pleading, pathetic? How else could he arrive?"

Bradford had not considered this.

"I guess I imagined he was coming to congratulate me."

Now, finally, Maria did hesitate.

"He's not of sound mind," she said. "He wouldn't think to do just that."

"Well, I wish I'd called for some other reason. I wish I was calling to tell you I wrote a new song."

"What will you do about this?"

"I'll see him. I'll hear what he says, I'll see him off, then tear up the stage and all of Detroit."

"I'm not going to tell you what to do," Maria said. "It's neither of our style. But I ask that you be careful."

He heard worry in her voice. It was as out of place as

listening to a favorite album and discovering that a guitar had been out of tune all along.

"I love you, Mom."

"Don't trust him," she said.

He hung up then. And Bradford watched the young people in black pass the head of the alley until he saw an older figure, small in stature, moving through that same rain. It was a man, carrying no umbrella, wearing no hat. The man looked up at Impresario Hall's marquee. Bradford couldn't see it from where he stood, but knew the man was reading his own name up in lights:

SWANN

Before he could detect either pride or irritation in the man's posture, the man had stepped out of sight, the bricks of the alley like a closing curtain.

Only Bradford knew the show, or this scene anyway, had just started.

He hurried back inside the hall's side door.

He didn't rise to greet the man, nor did he play the angry son. He'd reached peace with this relationship long ago.

But how had he?

"You look just like your mother," said Wyle Swann.

But Bradford knew that wasn't quite true. The differences between Maria and himself were all visible here, on the face of the man standing in the greenroom, wet from the rain.

"Do you like music?" Bradford asked.

It was something he'd long wondered. Was a man who was capable of leaving his family capable of loving music?

"Well, I don't listen to it very much," Wyle said.

Dad wasn't quite as pathetic as Maria had predicted. But he certainly wasn't at ease. He didn't know what to do with his hands. With his shoulders. His eyes.

"I heard you on the radio," Wyle said. "They said you'd reached the top spot."

"Yes. It's a dark song. About hiding dead bodies, I suppose, and searching for new ones to hide."

Wyle reacted the way someone who wasn't familiar with art and music might. He half-smiled and looked short of articulation.

"Well, I liked the song," Wyle said. "But I didn't quite hear it that way, I suppose." Then, getting to it: "You must be wondering why I'm here."

"No," Bradford said. "I'm wondering why you left."

Wyle reached into his pocket and pulled forth a handkerchief and blew his nose. He looked and sounded like a man who had walked through the rain.

"I don't think you'd like that answer," Wyle said.

Up the hall, beyond the stage, the vamp music played through the Impresario's big speakers. The noise of the growing crowd swelled beneath it. Bradford knew his bandmates were in their own greenrooms. Jerry was no doubt doing shots of Jack Daniels, Beth doing finger stretches and posing for the mirror.

"I'd like to hear it, either way," he said.

Wyle nodded like he'd expected as much. Still, he seemed unprepared.

Bradford thought of Dix. And how he'd seen Dix on the quick walk back inside after using the payphone.

"Sometimes people just don't get on," Wyle said. "Your mother was too much to deal with."

"I'd say she's just enough to deal with. I like her that way."

He thought of Dix, yes, and how he'd made a point of reiterating the fact he had no father. And might he come gather Bradford at ten-to?

But Bradford had made peace. Hadn't he?

"I was younger then, just as you were," Wyle said. "I'm not sure I'd do it again."

"Not sure? You mean you don't regret it?"

Another subject that seemed to flummox the man.

The clock said twelve to nine. Dix would be by in two minutes. You could count on him like that.

"I don't think a man can have no regrets," Wyle said.

Bradford thought of his black notebook. Maybe there was a lyric in what the man just said.

"But you see me now," Bradford said. "All grown up. Where did you go?"

Wyle seemed to search his mind. Was he trying to come up with a good story? Had he not thought of one already? It was all right; Bradford searched his own thoughts, too. Understood that the peace he had made was the same force that had driven him to write "Hide & Seek" after hearing

Siouxsie Sioux's "Peek-A-Boo." It all came from the same place. Maria wasn't the only one who imagined Wyle would show up if Bradford became famous.

"I'm a worm," Bradford said, "and you're the fish."

"What's that?"

One minute to go now. Dix any second. Punctual guy, that Dix.

"So, you're not sure where you went? I imagine it's gotta be a big memory, the day you left your wife and kid."

Wyle shrugged. Of all the things he could do. Bradford saw him then in a thousand bars, shrugging a thousand times as he told ten thousand people he had no wife and kids.

"I'm thinking we could start over," Wyle said. "You and me."

"And Mom? What about her?"

Peace, yes. For having a plan. It wasn't something Bradford had consciously formulated, perhaps, but a plan all the same.

Become famous. Be the worm to his father's fish. Lure the man in.

Then?

Wyle reached into his pocket as the doorknob turned. Bradford raised his voice like he would for an hour, in just a few minutes now.

"*What are you doing?*"

He shouted it at the man. Top of his number-one lungs. Shouted it like he'd like to have shouted it the day Wyle Swann vanished into the future.

As if cued, the crowd in the venue chanted: *Swann! Swann! Swann!*

So loud. About to get louder.

Dix heard the shout. Saw the man's hand in his coat pocket. Unholstered his own gun.

And fired.

Later, he would assuage himself with the memory of the way Bradford stood with his arms covering his face. As if the man did have a gun. It was part of being security for a celebrity. You had to be ready for a fanatic. And Bradford's words would help calm the security guard's fears of having killed someone he didn't need to kill.

He wasn't of sound mind, Bradford told him. The words would play over in Dix's head as the singer took over the stage, held the crowd in the palms of both hands. It was unbelievable, the way this guy could witness a shooting, then sing a set like nothing had happened at all.

A plan, yes. An incredible and unlikely plan that came to be.

Bradford wondered if that's because the universe thought he deserved it.

Another song idea. Maybe. Maybe too corny.

You did the right thing, Bradford told Dix, as Dix searched the fallen man's jacket and found no weapon. *He was here to hurt me. Nothing more.*

Dix would watch the crowd as Bradford sang about hiding dead bodies behind him. On the stage, and in that moment, it would all feel like part of the story. Part of rock 'n' roll. A fanatic killed in the greenroom of the country's current number one hit.

Murder? Dix would think.

But he wouldn't give the idea any air. Bradford had told him he was about to be attacked. Told him the man had said as much prior to reaching into his coat.

Murder …

The word would fade. Replaced (bizarrely, Dix thought, but who could blame him for feeling piqued?) with what Bradford had told him twice tonight, that the singer had no father. The words would keep popping up as Dix scanned the crowd for more threats. *No father.*

Dix wouldn't be sure why he was snagged on this.

Maybe it was because the man looked a bit like Bradford.

Maybe that was it.

Maybe.

Author's Note: I was a kid during this era of music, and Siouxsie and the Banshees kinda scared me. But it was a thrilling sort of scare. Siouxsie was a combination of many things I was into: storytelling, horror, rock 'n' roll. The song "Peek-A-Boo" was particularly haunting.

When I think of the game *Peekaboo* I think of a parent momentarily vanishing, before pulling their hands away and returning.

It's a game that ought to be traumatizing to a child. Where did my parent go? And maybe it is traumatizing. And maybe we just don't remember it that way.

Gravesend, Brooklyn / October 1991

Carla kicks the bums out of Mother's 123 Lounge and closes the joint a little after four in the morning. She's wasted and woozy. Too many shots with No Lips Jenny, Maple Ray, and Mike the Mistake. She thinks about sleeping in one of the back booths, but she skeeves the duct-taped vinyl, bathed as it is in the fumes and detritus of her unclean clientele.

She needs a weapon for her short walk home. She always takes one when she closes, but she's been even more careful since her sister Frankie went AWOL a week earlier. Carla's thirty, and Frankie's twenty-seven, but Frankie's the one who's been hitched for five years. Yesterday, before coming into work, Carla checked her mail to find a letter from Frankie—with no return address—saying she'd gone on the lam from her piece-of-shit husband Charles. Carla called

Charles to tell him she'd heard from Frankie, and he took the news like the shifty Republican fuck he is. Whining, upset, not even showing a bit of relief that it wasn't an abduction or something. Frankie escaped from *him*, and Carla's gotta admit, she got a kick rubbing it in. *You suck so bad she had to pull a Houdini to shake your ass.*

Still, the way Carla's mind works, getting dragged into a dirty van in the middle of the night and winding up a sex slave on Long Island or some godforsaken place is always a possibility, so she deadbolts the front door and goes into the cramped office next to the bathroom. She crashes down in the wobbly chair behind the desk, her leather jacket rubbing against the vinyl seat. Her eyes are heavy. She opens the combination lock on the top drawer, barely able to remember the numbers. They fuzz in her memory and in front of her eyes. White blotches on the black dial. She finally gets the drawer open.

The drawer serves as a stash spot for illicit objects both confiscated and abandoned: brass knuckles, a few dinky switchblades, a cop's baton (left behind by Officer Jerry Mahoney on his Last Great Drunk in '88), several canisters of pepper spray, and a military tactical pen.

Pepper spray is what she goes for. She's used it before on a man who was trailing her, from over five feet away, getting him right in the face like that squirt-the-clown game from Coney Island. The guy howled off into the night, pawing at his eyes. The one she chooses comes in a gold canister with black plastic casing, featuring a small trigger that sends the stuff whooshing out like heavy-duty Raid.

Carla double-checks the lights and the door on the way out. She holds the pepper spray in the palm of her hand, thumb poised over the trigger. It's gotten a little chilly out. The sky more gray than black. She hears streetlights clicking. Voices from a distance. The borough inhaling and exhaling.

She looks around. Gravesend Neck Road is mostly quiet. Her apartment is two short blocks away on East Fifth, but at this time of night it feels like a million fucking miles. She plods up the sidewalk, head darting around, searching for men where men shouldn't be, clasping the pepper spray tightly in her hand.

Footsteps behind her suddenly. She looks over her shoulder and sees a dark shape.

Of fucking course.

She moves faster. Turns the corner. Trips over her own feet, falling to the sidewalk, scraping her hands, dropping the pepper spray, watching it skitter into the gutter by the rear tire of a burgundy Chevy Lumina.

The dark shape says something.

Her breaths come fast. The world around her slows down. She shuffles on her knees toward the spray.

The heels of her hands are bleeding a little, dotted with indentions from where the dirty, cracked sidewalk has pressed into her skin.

She says something aloud. A frustrated little something, scolding herself for falling. She's acting like a stupid rookie.

She grabs the spray, turns, and aims in the direction of the shape, watching the mist cloud over his face.

The shape screams. Gets him right in the eyes. Sounds like he's dying. She can tell by his voice now that it's Charles, Frankie's husband, tangled up in the wreckage of her departure, sniffing around for clues. Carla has never liked him, but she feels sorry for him a little. He's a successful guy with his Wall Street job and his fancy clothes, not used to losing. Carla knows things haven't been good between Frankie and Charles for a long time—all his cheating and conniving—but Frankie hadn't made any prior indication she was gonna vamoose. Maybe calling Charles had been a mistake. Must be the guy's even worse than she knows. Going poof in the night like Frankie did. Him showing up at 4:30 a.m. to stalk Carla. The thousand different kinds of bitch he's calling her right now.

"The fuck did you do?" Charles asks.

She stands unsteadily. "I didn't know it was you. Blink a lot. I heard that helps."

"Jesus Christ." He isn't blinking. He's tossing his head around, trying to battle the burn with something like a breeze. "I can't see. Am I blind forever?"

"Your eyes are closed."

"I can't fucking open them."

"It'll pass."

"How long?"

"I don't know." She pauses, tries to steer this encounter to what it should be about. "You're creeping around outside the bar after I close? Real smart."

"I thought if I could retrace Frankie's steps, I'd get a

sense of where she might've gone. Can we go back to your place? Please."

"I'm drunk. I just want to go to bed."

"I can't go anywhere like this. Please." He pauses. "Is your new boyfriend there?"

She should just say he is, but the truth is Carla hasn't heard from Neil all night and isn't expecting him. His band Malnutrition played a show at some new club in the city. Maybe she's just feeling guilty for pepper-spraying Charles. The only lie she can manage is: "I don't know. Might be."

"Can we just talk? Make some coffee. And I can wash my eyes out."

"You're sober?"

"Yes."

"Well, I'm not," Carla says. "Don't give me any goddamn trouble."

In her apartment, Carla turns on some lights and pockets the pepper spray. The place is small and decorated in her own brand of chaos—a main space that's her living room, bedroom, and kitchen all in one, though there isn't much of a kitchen, just a small fridge, a sink, and a hot plate on a wheeled table cart. Stacked books tower everywhere. Music magazines too, with names like *Eclipse* and *Earworm*. Records in dusty crates line the walls. Torn pages from the magazines taped over the crates. A green futon salvaged from a sidewalk. An axe dangles from a pair of leather buckle hangers on an otherwise bare patch of wall in the back of the room. Her form of home protection. A gift from Maple Ray.

Carla guides Charles to the bathroom, where he flushes his eyes with sink water and buries his head in a hand towel probably crusty from Neil's jizz. Carla tends to her scrapes, dabbing sloppily at the tough skin on her hands with alcohol-soaked toilet paper. Charles breathes like he's passing a stone.

She leaves him to his own devices in the bathroom and goes out to the kitchen. She fixes coffee in her burnt-bottomed percolator and delights in the brief smell of gas that blooms over the stove before the blue flame sputters on.

Charles comes out, his eyes and cheeks red. Now he's trying to blink the pain away.

"Any better?" Carla asks.

"A little," he says.

"I'm sorry that happened."

"Can I see the letter?" He's trying to move on, it seems.

Carla pats at her jacket. She's not particularly good at keeping track of papers. She reaches into her inner pocket and finds the letter folded into an uneven square. She isn't sure what she did with the envelope. She unfolds the letter and flattens it on the kitchen counter.

Charles comes over and looks at it. He reads it very quickly through tears. He's not crying; the tears are from the pepper spray. There isn't much to read, anyhow. He picks it up and inspects the paper. He runs his fingers over the ink. He holds the paper close to his face and investigates Frankie's signature. "This is it?"

"That's it. I only told you because I thought you had the right to know. Obviously, things between you two weren't good."

"I find out this way how much my wife despises me. Nice. Where's the envelope?"

"Must've tossed it. Nothing special. No return address."

"What about the postmark?"

"I didn't even notice. Still New York, I think." She pauses. "What are you, Columbo now? Let her go. She wants out. My sister's a free woman. God bless."

He shrugs. "I'm just at a loss."

"Think about what you might've done to prompt this."

"I'm no monster. No need to run away in the middle of the night."

The coffee boils over. Carla tends to it, shutting the gas, sopping up the spill from the foil burner liner with a rag. She pours a cup for Charles. Black—whether he takes it that way or not.

He sits on the sofa. She hands him the chipped mug full of strong black coffee. He slurps it.

"I still can't get over the pepper spray," Charles says.

"You have no idea what it's like to be a woman."

"You're right about that."

"Damn skippy, Chuck," Carla says. *Damn skippy* is a dumb phrase that she gets a kick out of, but it also brings her great pleasure to call him Chuck. She knows he hates it.

"Don't call me that."

She continues, undeterred: "Chuck, Chuck, Chuck."

Cruelty sometimes accompanies drunkenness for Carla, but she's got every right to bust this guy's balls anyhow. He isn't welcome. Stalking her on the street in the middle of the night horror movie shit at best.

"Real mature," Charles says.

"Hey, this is my place."

"My old man used to call me Chuck. Finally quit when I started making more money than him. Suddenly, I was Charles. Came around with his hand out when he needed a new fence or a new refrigerator."

"Why don't you get out of my apartment, *Chuck*? Why don't you go back home and try to dig up some other clues, *Chuck*?"

Charles goes over to the axe hanging on her wall and fingers the blade. "What's this axe all about?" he asks.

"When guys like you get out of control, I have the axe," Carla says.

"I should chop my head off with it. Can a man chop off his own head with an axe?" He laughs and then rumbles into the tiny kitchen area, finding a bottle of whiskey in the cabinet under the sink. Bottom shelf stuff snagged from 123. He swigs hard. "Why'd she leave me? Where could she have gone?"

"I'm not her keeper. You should've been a better husband, I guess. That Staten Island broad from your job you hooked up with was the last straw maybe."

"That was one time. She was nothing. For Frankie not even to talk to me about leaving, I don't understand. To do this elaborate thing where she says she's hanging out with you at 123 and then just takes off—that makes fucking sense to you? I deserve that? I'm not some mobster she can't cut ties with."

"I think you should go," Carla says. "You can have the bottle."

"How generous of you." Charles pauses, drinks more. "You make me sick," he continues. "You know that? You're absolutely nothing like Frankie. You don't even care about her. Not really. Your own sister."

Carla wants to argue that point—she *does* love Frankie, of course she does—but there's no reasoning with Charles. He's probably projecting his own bad behavior onto her. She's just some puttana bartender, lacking morals, lacking values. She's seen it in stiff collars like him before. The floodgates open and they recognize themselves as they truly are. Primitive. Sinister. And when a man catches a glimpse of his own soul, he'll look for a woman to take the fall. Oldest story there is. "You need to leave," Carla says.

"Look at you," Charles says, ignoring her. "A freak. You think you're better than me, better than Frankie, better than your folks, better than the neighborhood. Smarter. Superior. Cooler. All that. I have news for you. You're just a coward. You turned your back on your parents, and you've got a crappy apartment and a crappy job. You don't care about anyone but yourself. You ever think of having kids? Probably not. Bar whores raise bar whores."

Carla moves toward the phone on the wall. "I'm gonna call Neil," she says. "He'll be right over. He doesn't live far."

Charles picks up the bottle and blocks her path. He takes a swig. "It's Neil this week, huh? Who's it gonna be next week?"

"You need help," Carla says. She's known violent men before, men who are quick to put their hands on women especially after a couple of belts of whiskey. Charles might be freefalling through what's left of his life, but he's a Wall Street marshmallow. Probably shaves every day. Probably sits in Grand Central Station like a king and has his shoes shined by a little man in a hat. Never any dandruff on his lapels. Never any dirt under his fingernails, which he probably clips religiously over a wastebasket lined with a neat plastic bag. He's soft, and now he's melting away to nothing. But, no matter what he says, he probably won't hurt her. Still, she thinks about the axe, the pepper spray, the hot coffee—stuff she can go for to fend him off if things go all the way bad.

Then he grips her arm, just above her elbow, pushing his fingers into her flesh. It's a mean touch, an angry one, as if he wants to pierce the skin and grab bone.

"Don't touch me," Carla says, wriggling away.

There's a war behind his eyes. "Or what?"

She puts her hand over his hand and tries to peel it away. She digs her nails into his fingers. His grip tightens.

"Maybe I want you to hurt me," he says. "Maybe I have to hurt you to make you hurt me." His hand travels up to her neck. He touches her throat gently at first and then starts to squeeze.

She considers kneeing him in the balls but thinks she

should try to deescalate the situation. She backpedals, easing herself out of his grasp and then pulling away more forcefully. His fingers fade from her. She touches her neck. She still feels where his fingers had been. She breathes the rotten air of her apartment. She thinks about telling him again that he needs help but decides against it. She has nothing say to someone who's just made like he's going to strangle her.

Charles goes back to the bottle. He drinks until he gags. He heads to the sink, hunches over the basin, and pukes on the dirty dishes.

Carla goes for her axe.

"Now we're talking," Charles says, moving slowly toward her, his chin flecked with puke. "Chop me down like a tree. Give me what I deserve. Forget suicide by cop. I'll take suicide by Carla."

The axe shakes in her unsteady hand. She's at a loss for words. Everything she can think to say feels wrong. If she tries to soothe him with sweetness, if she talks him down, what next? Throw open the futon and tell him to sleep it off? Whatever sympathy she retained for him was extinguished when he put his hands on her.

"Don't clam up on me," Charles continues. "Tell me I'm sick. Tell me I need help. Tell me I need to straighten out for my own sake." His voice catches in his throat.

Charles is about five feet away from Carla. Wisps of dust on the floor between them. Neil's sneaker with frayed laces. A crumpled tissue. A scattering of change, blackened dimes and nickels and pennies.

"Back up," Carla says.

Charles loosens the collar on his shirt. He puts one hand around his own neck. "Chop me down," he says. "Please. Pepper spray was just the start. I complained, but I should've been thanking you. Best I've felt since Frankie left. Pain's the answer."

Carla remembers an empty lot from when she was a girl. On Twenty-Fifth Avenue right across from Angelo's Bakery, in the shadow of the El. A big weed-choked lot full of broken concrete patches and swaths of sandy dirt. She always imagined it must be what the bottom of a dry lake would look like. The kids from her school, St. Mary's, went there for what they called Baptism Wednesdays. This was in eighth grade, maybe ten kids total. They'd pass around a bottle of cheap wine or vodka or whatever. Draw straws to see who'd get to throw the bottle at some passing stranger out on the sidewalk. They had a points system. First obstacle was clearing the high fence that surrounded the lot. Then there was a breakdown according to age and status. An old limping woman with a shopping cart was worth the most. The goal wasn't to hit the person but to shatter the bottle beside or in front of them, scaring them silly for the sheer amusement of it. Dumb fucks with nothing better to do. Mostly, it was harmless fun. Worth a laugh. But there'd been two times where they'd frightened or hurt people so badly, they'd done real damage. There was the old man who lost his mind at the sound of the crashing bottle and jumped off the sidewalk into the street, clipped by a passing truck. He got hospitalized but didn't die. The boy was a bad one. Seven years old maybe. On his own. Sent to the store by his mother or grandmother, a plastic bag full of fruit and vegetables dangling from his arm. The bottle had nailed him—a misfire by Bertie Biagini—and he collapsed to the sidewalk, bleeding, his oranges and tomatoes rolling into the gutter. The crew scattered after that. Baptism Wednesdays went on hiatus. The kid's probably alive somewhere, and it's just a bad memory. The day the bottle fell from the sky and almost killed him. Carla's not sure why she's remembering this now.

Charles steps closer. He's close enough to touch her. He doesn't put his hands out yet. His eyes are lost, wild, so red that he looks like he has a strange disease.

Carla bites the inside of her lip and draws blood. She can taste it in her dry mouth. She regrets drinking so much. She's standing still but feels like she's moving. "Leave," she says. The way they're positioned, she's between him and the door, but she feels like she's cornered.

"Make me," he says. He reaches out and grabs her by the throat again. His grip is even harder this time. He'd found some inner reserve of strength and power and he's using it to try to strangle her.

She swings the axe at him. She makes a weird, tight, stabbing motion because he's so close and his hand is on her throat. The blade somehow sinks into the bicep of his free arm.

He howls. Releases his grasp.

She pulls back, holding the axe in front of her. Blood on the blade.

He holds his good arm across his body, his hand fluttering over the tear in his shirt the axe has made, blood dotting the fabric, the wound dark beneath. He doesn't look scared. He looks satisfied, like he's enjoying the pain.

"Yes," Charles says. "More."

She's done things other than pepper spray in self-defense before—kneed a guy or two in the balls, threatened an ex with a cast-iron pan after he grabbed her shoulder too hard—but thudding an axe into the arm of a rabid brother-in-law is new. The axe has always been a joke, just hanging on her wall as a humorous threat for one-night stands who want too much or too little, who won't leave when their time's up.

She wants to drop the axe. She wants Charles to turn tail and run, holding his arm, dripping blood in the hallway outside her apartment door and down the stairs and onto the sidewalk outside, taking his wildness with him.

He doesn't. He comes at her, his good arm outstretched.

She swings the axe again, squinting so that she can still see. In her thin field of vision, he seems stretched now, elongated as in a nightmare. A hazy, yawning creature. The axe catches him on his neck. That artery. The big one. Like a pulsing cable. She'd swung hard enough that when she lets go of the axe, it remains lodged in his neck.

He topples sideways, blood erupting around the blade. When he hits the floor, the axe falls free. It bounces, and she dances out of the way of it. The blood really starts to fountain from Charles's neck. A small river of it, flowing and pooling on the slightly tilted floor.

Carla backs up to the wall and inches her body down until she's sitting, drawing her knees to her chest. She's several feet from Charles and all the blood. She looks at the floor beneath her. A sliver gazed between her legs. Cleanish. The bare, scuffed wood almost fools her into believing the rest hasn't been real. She puts her head into her hands. She hears dying sounds coming from Charles. Gagging, gurgling, choking. And then silence.

She looks at his body. Blood everywhere as if it has gushed from a busted pipe. She wonders if it'll drip through the floor into Goodie and Bald Bob's apartment below. She blinks her eyes to make it all go away, but it's still there when she opens them, red and radiant and real. Like one of those giallo movies. The red redder than red should be. Charles asked for it, literally. He wanted it. He kept coming. He would have hurt her—maybe killed her—if she hadn't used the axe. She tells herself that's true. She rocks in place. She hopes no one will come knocking. She doesn't think they will. Loud fighting isn't abnormal in the building. People mind their own business. A loud thud against the floor at five a.m. doesn't rate a 911 call. She's gotta figure out what to do next.

Carla decides to run. Her only other option is to call the cops and tell them Charles attacked her and she took him down with her fucking wall-axe. All true, but the cops will read the scene differently. They'll call it murder. They'll see her as some vixen who'd taken advantage of her prosperous brother-in-law after he was shattered by his wife abandoning him. She knows the way these things work. It's too much to think about. Maybe they'll conclude she and Frankie are in cahoots.

It could be days, maybe even longer, before anyone discovers the body. She'll throw some towels down to soak up the blood, then split. Go to the Port Authority and catch the first bus out of town.

She's frantic. Looks around. The apartment is on fire with everything she'll have to leave behind. Every scrounged piece of furniture. Every record. Every cup, ashtray, book. Every memory. Drunken nights with boyfriends, curled on the futon, kissing. Neil will look for her. How long will he try before he gives up? She thinks of Mother's 123. Its dankness. The regulars. The swallowed-up feeling of being in there for an eight- or ten-hour shift. Tips stuffed in her pockets. That old, clanging register. Glasses smeared with fingerprints. The cramped office with its drawer full of weapons. Everyone from the bar will be concerned about her disappearance.

Carla's shaking. She's trying not to walk through Charles's blood. She's trying not to vomit. Her head's pounding. Her drunkenness has faded to chill sobriety and transformed into this strange pain. She goes to her little bathroom and takes a bottle of aspirin out of the medicine cabinet. She can barely open the cap. She shakes a few pills into her palm and washes them down by leaning over the sink and slurping from the tap. The water tastes faintly metallic. She imagines it traveling through the building's ancient pipes. She imagines those pipes stretching like spindly never-ending arms under the sidewalk, under the streets. A system of reaching and moving and bringing that never stops. She feels dizzy. She sits on the toilet and takes a few deep breaths.

When she's regained some control, she grabs a bunch of towels and brings them out to Charles and throws them over the pooled blood around him. She takes a blanket from the futon and drapes it over his body. She picks up the axe from where it has fallen and washes it in the kitchen sink. She's already forgotten that Charles puked on her dirty dishes, and it makes her sick to see that.

She finds her Mets cap and puts it on, tucking her hair underneath. She leaves the apartment, axe in hand, pausing in the hallway to lock the door.

Outside, she drops the axe into a dumpster down the alley next to her building, stuffing it under a pile of black garbage bags gnawed open by rats.

She then goes back to the street and slides her apartment key into a sewer drain, listening as it clinks down to the bottom of the sludgy underground pit. She thinks again of pipes. The world below. She's heard stories about people who live in abandoned tunnels under the city. Maybe she'll join their ranks. Maybe she'll shower under dripping pipes. Maybe she'll build a little hut in the tunnels made of scavenged wood and steal electricity from the MTA.

She still has the keys to 123. Before splitting for keeps, she goes there. It's just after six. The neighborhood is starting to wake up but not the bar people. Not yet anyway—the first customers won't start congregating outside until eleven.

She opens the door, goes inside, and flips on the lights. In the office, she finds a piece of paper and two envelopes. She sits at the bar and writes a quick letter to Frankie. She wants there to be some way for Frankie to be in touch with her, just in case. She wants to say she's sorry, that she hopes the heat doesn't come down on Frankie. She doesn't know how to say anything. After all, she has no idea where she's going.

She directs her sister to put a personal ad in her favorite music magazine, *Eclipse*. An entertaining personals section fills the back pages. She's seen this in movies before. *Dear C: Looking for you. Love, F.* She apologizes about Charles, leaving out specifics. She stuffs the note in the envelope and seals it and writes Frankie's name on the front, placing it next to the register in a slot where people leave things for others to pick up. She can probably trust that no one will disturb it. The folks who frequent and work at 123 are a lot of things, but they're not snoops.

She thinks twice about it and tears the letter up. A stupid idea. If the cops come around, they'll find it. She's a fugitive now. She's gotta think like a fugitive.

A drink, she thinks. *Just one more to calm my nerves.*

Carla pours herself a tumbler of rye. She stands there and drinks it and takes a last, lingering look around. Crooked pictures on the wall. Scraggles of whiskery dust stitched into the ceiling. The sour smell, a mix of a subway platform and thrift store. She starts seeing faces—the regulars—even though no one's here. She's lived her very own little *The Iceman Cometh* life at this joint and now she's leaving it for God-knows-what. Uncertainty, homelessness, a world of trouble?

She doesn't want to go. She likes this hidey hole, this holy dive. It feels more like home than her dumpy apartment or childhood house. The owner, Augusta, has treated her better than her fucking parents ever did. They'd cut her off by the time she was seventeen, had her pegged as a tramp.

She thinks she should write a quick note to Augusta and leave it on the desk in the office, explaining that fate stuck out its foot and tripped the shit out of her, but she decides against that too. Better for Augusta not to know anything.

Carla finishes her drink and rinses the glass in the sink, leaving it to dry on a folded rag. She takes five hundred dollars from Augusta's safe—she's sorry as hell, but has no other dough to survive on. She shuts the lights. She remembers the empty envelope and snags it from the bartop.

Back outside, she locks the door, drops the key in the envelope, then slides it through the mail slot. Purple light bleeding from what remains of the darkness, edged with morning blue, rises over the rooftops. The rye has given her what she needs to keep moving.

She goes to the subway station on Avenue U and McDonald and boards the first F train into the city. The middle car is empty except for the conductor and a couple of men reading newspapers. At the Port Authority, she'll buy a ticket somewhere north or west. Maybe Chicago, maybe California, maybe Canada. Carla only thinking C places.

Her mind is a collage of things she doesn't want to see. The axe that used to live on her wall. Charles on the floor. A picture of herself, a mugshot. She thinks of the word *murderer,* how surprised she is that she could kill someone. She's not a murderer. She acted in self-defense. She imagines being apprehended on the train like Public Enemy Number One. But no one knows yet. No one will know for hours or days. Frankie might never know. Two sisters, both drifting wild.

The ride is stop-and-go, but no one bothers her, which is the most she can ask for most days, let alone this one. She stares first at her scratched hands and then out the window. Letters etched sloppily into the glass, playing over the blur of the city. Rooftops, windows, tunnel darkness, the river viewed from the bridge, all of it so familiar and yet so distant.

In the city, she trudges out at the Times Square station. She dodges early morning crowds and cars. Hustlers approach her. She blows them off.

The Port Authority is big and cold and full of transients and drifters. People sleeping on floors and benches. Pigeons skitter around inside. There's nothing she hates more than birds indoors. She doesn't believe in Heaven or Purgatory or Hell or any of that, but she always figures that if there's a Hell it's a lot like the Port Authority. The pressure and tension of the place. Always under threat. Someone eyeing your shit, someone following you. Garbage everywhere. Dirty tiled floors. Endless escalators. Those pigeons inside.

The last time she was here was when she'd taken a bus upstate to visit some friends, Morgan and Tony, in Kingston. They left Brooklyn because it was getting too expensive, and they could live for next to nothing in Kingston in a warehouse Morgan's uncle owned. Carla stayed up there for a long weekend, drinking in bars that felt like church basements and sleeping on the floor and taking walks through the woods. She remembers a railroad trestle, caves, cold wind. She visited Woodstock, maybe twenty minutes by car, where a bunch of hippies had gone to pasture.

Morgan and Tony were the kind of people who were always chasing something. Her uncle gave them the boot and they scraped together money for a one-way trip to Boulder, Colorado, where Tony claimed to have a friend with a cabin in the mountains. Last Carla had heard, they'd bought an old beater for fifty bucks and pointed it west. Colorado—another C place.

Maybe Carla'll start in Kingston, though. Now that Morgan and Tony are gone, she doesn't know anyone there, but she likes the feeling of familiarity, however minor, that comes with having once visited. Plus, there are all those towns nearby she'd either trekked to on that trip or just knows the names of—Woodstock, Rosendale, New Paltz, Saugerties, Phoenicia. She imagines herself working in some dive bar, pulling cheap beers for lonely country types, college kids, broke artists, others who are on the lam. Men who ride their bicycles to the bar and have sinewy arms from jobs that require real labor. She remembers mountains and farms in the Hudson Valley. Winding roads. Different air. She bets five hundred dollars can secure her an apartment and enough food to last for a few weeks.

She goes to the Adirondack Trailways booth and buys a one-way ticket to Kingston. A man nearby watches as she pulls bills from the back pocket of her grubby jeans to pay. The attendant hands her a ticket. She walks to her gate and sits down in an orange bucket seat. No one else is there yet. The bus doesn't leave for an hour and change. She hopes it'll be empty. This time of day, there aren't commuters going home from work. Kingston isn't far. Folks commute into the city by bus from there. It must be tiring, especially factoring in traffic, but she's sure the tradeoff's worth it. You can own a lot more up there than you can in the city.

She pictures herself living in a place with wood floors. A fireplace. Maybe a view.

The man who watched her take money out of her pocket comes over and sits next to her. He asks her if she has a buck she can spare.

She shakes her head but then she gives him a crumpled dollar. She hopes that'll be enough to drive him away. It is. He takes the money and leaves her alone.

A few others join her at the gate. This family—a wife, husband, two bratty kids—and an elderly woman, whose only luggage is a paper shopping bag that looks to be full of books. When the bus pulls in, the driver gets out and stretches, smoking a cigarette before opening the door and allowing them to board.

Carla has lost track of the time. She only knows that she's leaving the city. She only knows that, from now on, she can't look back. Maybe she'll find her sister out there somewhere. Maybe they can be new mysteries together.

AUTHOR'S NOTE: "Just Like Fire Would" by The Saints is one of those songs that I'm always thinking about, always remembering, and I'm always building from what it makes me feel. (Also worth noting that Bruce Springsteen released a great cover of it on his 2014 album *High Hopes*.) I had this character I'd started writing, Carla, a bartender at a Brooklyn dive called Mother's 123 who keeps an axe on her apartment wall, and I just started seeing her world soundtracked to this song by The Saints. There's the obvious connection between the title and Carla's axe, but it was more about the feeling to me, the raspiness, the hook, the defiance and profundity of escape.

You think of her hands, of them unmoving atop white hospital sheets, of their long-ago flutter over vellum-thick drawing paper flecked with spilled coffee stiffened by the grit of fine sugar. Your skin again takes the warmth of her hands clasped over yours, from the time you'd held her about the waist, palms near where she'd been cut to pull forth the son the adoption agency forbade her to take to her breast. You hear again her breathing, low, away from her chest, as you'd both watched the coffin march of baggage on an airport beltway, awaiting the possibly lost satchel holding medications that'd let her sleep without the threat of her lungs gripping shut.

You think of the crime of her motionless hands as you walk the Boston streets, near the half-frozen Charles River where not one of the perhaps thousand people sleeping within twenty yards of you would hear if you cried out the way you wish to, in this dead zone where trees, lined as if in a grove, and snow and fallen branches make a no-man's-land only called a "park" because people walk their dogs here.

You roam the Between place where she has lived since her first breath, forced as she was into the world by the crush of a steering column against her drunken mother's belly, pushed into early birth on a Halloween Night that addled the realms of the Living and the Dead … pushed into the world by a centuries-old oak that will bear the scar of her mother's engine block for centuries more … cupped into an hour of both Death and Birth, until that dawn … when Death ceded through the intercession of an ICU incubator.

Morning wakes around you, not through any visible dawn, but the shift of light through winter fog atop the Charles.

You turn to walk back to your cold bed and see your Guilt walking toward you, as you knew it must, as it has each night since her hands fell still, as you knew, in a deep corner of yourself, that you wished it to.

The art she has created to be on your body, the tattoo designs she has drawn for you that you've never taken into your skin, walks toward you with your gait, yet without flesh or skin … Hollow … Shaped by the places she'd designed the tattoos to go. Your Guilt configures her art as it should be on your body, granting your Guilt the recognizable shape of *you* as it no longer walks with the boneless fluidity it has had on previous nights.

Your Guilt constellates memorials her hands have drawn for those you have lost.

Her hands are still.

Her breath, machine-assisted, is not.

What her now-still hands have sketched stands before you, atop unbroken snow.

The blue rose she drew—intended for your right forearm, from the center of which extends the hand of a drowning man that she designed after your cousin died upon striking his head on an icy sidewalk—takes the sheen of the snow behind where your Guilt stands. As does the single track of a bear paw intended for your upper left arm that she drew for your friend Tom, who'd nominally died by hanging but had truly died via an insurance company's whim, when it chose to no longer cover his meds.

And as daylight shifts and your Guilt slides out of visibility, you realize this thing without a heartbeat had waited the span of a heartbeat for the sun to refract it out of your sight.

Walking beneath the last shred of moonlight, you see for an instant, across the River, the lost glow of the lost time in Kenmore Square when you first kissed her, and the hopping of bonfires lit by indigents on the Fenway. That lost glow in the Square was itself a relic of another time, when glass and moon-gleams refracted not just light, but sound. You stand on the bridge closest to your neighborhood, glancing toward the Harbor. The hospital in which her hands are still, while machines akin to that long-ago ICU incubator make her chest rise and fall, wears a caul of fog.

You are thankful for that, even as it makes you angry.

You'd met her while the churn of a subway blew her pain like leaves along the platform.

As she chased the pictures she'd drawn, she had a look like that of a bus station hustler on a cold day, unsure he could score enough money to land a place to sleep that night. The sketches of her pain danced among commuters' shoes down Harvard Square Station. Bright colors defining dark thoughts skittered among Uggs and loafers, sneakers, combat boots a little too unscuffed. You caught the pictures that blew near you, and were yourself caught by dream images of Munch-like faces pleated within the bark of lightning-struck oaks, and labyrinths laid to a far horizon behind an imp of the type that once adorned absinthe bottles, but with the pained and mournful look that Dürer gave Jesus.

Your gaze taken by the faces and the imp, you were again gripped by the fear that'd beaten within you like a second heart while taking the forearm of Mitch, your old drummer, as he'd had what you'd thought had been a seizure standing before a Cezanne at the Art Institute of Chicago. The both of you living on too much truck stop coffee and too little sleep, you'd led him through a cityscape broken by your exhausted perceptions back to the rust-pocked tour van that always stank of diesel, though it ran on gas. "I heard it," he said on the cardboard and foam rubber cot upon which you and your bandmates slept in shifts. "I could *hear* the painting."

That fear pulsed, again.

But for whom, you didn't know.

As you not only heard her art as Mitch must have heard that

Cezanne, but your fingers, without your volition, suddenly knew how to, and ached to, translate what you heard into guitar tabs.

You collect more of her art, not looking at it, while she darts around the platform. You thank your mind for releasing what it heard of her drawings, as you're reminded of the wretched romantic comedies your ex, Lauren, so loved, of how the sight of a breathless, pale woman panicked on a subway platform would be shot in a way that'd evoke Audrey Hepburn, her distress a bit of whimsy to charm a dashing Gregory Peck or George Peppard.

But the semi-feral hustler desperation in her eyes as she approaches kills that rom-com illusion, even more than the sunset reds and oranges of her dreads. That her breathlessness had nothing to do with her being unto a Hollywood ingénue was not known to you, yet. Her hand-knitted, fingerless gloves were of cotton yarn that you'd later learn would not trigger her asthma as would wool. The heaviness of the paper stock stuck you, as you handed her the pictures, your sight still … thickened … by her art, as it would be in a dream on a winter's day. The subway's roar crowded the air, and you must have said something about her art, because she said, "Thank you" as if taking a compliment, not accepting tangible objects returned to her.

Her fingertips stayed on your palm, punctuation of her thanks, and prelude to something else.

She took your hand in way that was more comfortable than it should have been, like a palmist, and touched the ink stains on your fingers from the leaking pen with which you'd written lyrics that morning.

"You draw?" she asked.

You told her no, that the last thing you drew, your mom had affixed to the fridge with plastic kitchen magnets shaped like letters.

She lifted your hand closer, ran her fingertips over the telltale callouses on your own. The sheen in her eyes became a fraction less desperate as she lifted her gaze and said, "Wow, that's weird," and stepped toward the exit with body language that said you were to walk with her as she tapped images of dead Harlequins tied upright on horseback and Dali-warped bodies back into her portfolio.

"What's weird?"

"I always wondered what it'd be like to show my stuff to my mom. I was just thinking that, as I dropped my portfolio. And right now, I'm going to find out. I'm going to find out exactly that."

"You … wait … *'find out?'* You're showing all these to your mom? Right now?"

"Yeah. First time. Ever."

"*First* time?"

"Never seen anything I've done."

"She must've … when you were a kid …"

Your broken words tumbled as you dodged commuters, and there is a shallowing of the beautiful crow's feet at the corners of her eyes.

"I'm *meeting* my mom now," she said, with the frankness

of a stranger you'd known before in hospital waiting rooms, bus depots, and while holding friends' hands on the doorsteps of methadone clinics not yet open. "For the first time."

At the foot of the subway stairs, she leaned the portfolio against her shin as she swung her bag from hip to thigh, and you heard the unwelcome, too-familiar rattle of large prescription pill bottles as she pulled out her card.

You took her card, her information "written" in smoke rising from a candle in a holder suitable for Jane Eyre to use while climbing a curving stair. You're certain you'd never use the card, certain the last fucking thing you needed was another person in your life with a mind barely tamed by pharmaceuticals while she said, "Call me, if you want," as if speaking were a strain. "Things're … things're *weird* today. And you talking about showing pictures to your mom is the kind of weird maybe I shouldn't fight. The kind of weird I should maybe … go with?"

You pocketed her card, said, "Sure." Your thumb rubbed the wedding ring from Lauren, which since the divorce you've worn on your right hand, as you watched her take the stairs to Harvard Square, worried the wind that blew October leaves and the bedsheet hems of ghost costumes might also snatch her pictures the way the subway gusts had done.

Later, after you had called her, standing on the Harvard Bridge, looking eastward down the Charles in a winter dawn, you draped your arms around her and breathed the earthen scent of her locs, made a bit stronger by the sweat of her dancing. And despite having played so many late-night gigs, this was the moment you'd first heard, through the churn of thick flurries made colors without name by the sunrise, the clatter of the day's first subway trains as they crossed the distant Longfellow Bridge.

That silence that followed was next broken by the rattle of pills in her bag—what had been a red flag of worry had since become a comfort, as had the chalky, coppery taste on her breath from her inhaler.

Her hands, in her fingerless gloves, held yours as you touched her waist through her coat.

Her hands, in her fingerless gloves, then caressed your face as you kissed.

You think of her hands, how they danced over thick paper as you lay naked beside her, her sketchpad propped against a pillow dusted with fur from the black cat she kept, in defiance of the threat its dander posed to her. The wife of Lauren's sister Kristen, whom you loved as you would your own sister, had texted you from Kristen's phone to tell you Kristen's femur had been snapped when a drunk driver clipped her as she rode the Mass Ave bike lane.

There'd been a time before you'd married Lauren that Kristen had shown up at your door, bike helmet under her arm, knowing she was too loaded to ride back to Somerville, and you let her crash on your couch. As you tucked your grandmother's eiderdown around her shoulders, she said, "I love you," sober enough to know what she was saying, and too drunk to not be telling the truth. You kissed her brow, loving this kid sister who'd come to you by happenstance when you had no sister by blood, and when you said "I love you" to her, the words came more easily than when you said them to Lauren.

You look at her hands … at the movement of her razor-sharpened pencil on paper, the tilt of her left small and ring fingers with which she shades and textures the graphite. She makes a design like an inverted fleur-de-lis that seems partly set into skin, so that blood beads at the points of insertion.

You no longer hear her art as you used to. What had disoriented you now gives you a sense of place and stillness that in turn inflects your music, much more than did the drama Lauren created by wanting to be a muse to you of the stripe that her artistic idols had left in ruins.

The fur-dusted bed you love to share with her is across from a bunk bed painted light blue with red trim, in a room decorated with cowboy-themed wallpaper—images of Pony Express riders and roping rodeo horsemen—hung maybe half a century ago. You take comfort from the comfort this place gives her. So much of her life has been spent in foster care and group homes that this house that grounds her with a vicarious family history partly grounds you.

The warmth of the kiss she places on your right shoulder when she stops drawing spreads up to your neck, and down past your chest.

"It should go here," she says, resting her cheek where she'd just placed her lips.

"I don't know if I want … to … something I can't be rid of."

"It should go here. If you want it. Reminder of when you were on the beach, with her."

You're unsure you've told her about the time Kristen fell asleep resting her head on your right shoulder at her parents' beach house. But you look at the Between pooling her eyes that are at times blue and at times gray, for they hold the Night bridging the two worlds on which she was born.

It doesn't matter if you've told her or not.

Later, while she sleeps, you pad downstairs in sweatpants bearing your high school's logo. You pass more cowboy wallpaper, and photos of awkward-looking, red-haired, freckled boys who had to be brothers, shot against generic Sears portrait backdrops. You pass the TV with a wooden cabinet and rabbit ears beside a light switch haloed with grime by decades of reaching fingertips and the his-and-her recliners upholstered in something like tweed: artifacts she insisted the probate lawyer leave behind when she rented this house for the cost of a studio apartment in Cambridge. You open your laptop, telling yourself you're treating your insomnia by looking at videos of cats and puppies, but knowing you're checking which of your instruments and what of your studio gear Lauren is selling online this week.

You make herbal tea, look at the webpages of tattoo artists nearby, decide against taking the fleur-de-lis and the droplets of blood that would mark your worry for Kristen this night. In bed, you curl around her, tasting the inhaler on her breath, under the sketch of the fleur-de-lis design she has tacked on her cork bulletin board. You touch it in the light filtering from the snow-haloed streetlamps outside, again think of the design on your right shoulder, then sleep.

Though her art now grounds you, as does this house full of purloined family memories, you walk through the hinted sounds of the sketch while you dream as if through a stranger's home.

You arrive and find her in her living room, her toes gripping the thick and stained carpet, the red and oranges of her locs standing out against the tweed of the chair. She's recently shaved the sides of her head, and her left-handed stroking of the stubble growing in calms her. Atop her clothing, her right hand traces the crescent of her caesarean scar, fingertips moving the way you're sure she'd have moved them to stroke the hair of her forfeited son. The antique 1940s-cop-movie black telephone rests on the floor beside her at the very place at least one loyal dog must have slept, and by her lap is the shoebox of letters and postcards that has been sitting on the end table beside her for most of the last century. She and you have yet to read through the entire shoebox. The oldest item you have so far found in the shoebox is a honeymoon postcard from Niagara Falls, dated 1936.

"Worst fifty bucks I ever spent," she said.

"What'd she want?"

"Investors."

When her mother had last spoken to her, it'd been to ask for money for a computer. Before that, a car. Before that, renovations for a place she only rented.

"Who'd she have in mind?"

"My boss. His wife. My foster mom. My foster mom's new husband." She looks away, then back at you and says, "Lauren," as if the transgression were her own.

Though your hands are still cold from the December air, you sit on the floor, take her feet in your lap, and rub them. When her mother—who came into her life the same day you did, on her birthday—crosses or disappoints her, she refers to her mother in terms of "fifty bucks," the amount she'd paid a private investigator to find the woman once the relevant court records were unsealed. Lately … maybe for more than a year … it is the only way she refers to the woman who'd lost custody of her by staggering damp and reeking with vodka before the family court judge.

"To invest in what?"

"Couldn't hear what she said, after a while."

Her eyes change.

Blue to gray.

As she looks at you.

The same shift that had happened when she'd told you, on the second time you'd been out with her, that she "saw" the music on your most recent demo as images she could draw.

The change in her eyes tilts the light of the room. Over the winter scents still on your clothes and coat you taste the autumn, the frost, the October cold, the leaves, she carries with her. You taste the scent of her skin that infuses her sheets, so that when you sleep beside her you dream of turning trees, passing seasons, the scent of air unique to apple orchards.

Beside her are her pills and inhalers; on the white lids of some stand out drifted hairs from her black cat. She has her meds out and visible. To declare she wishes to stay in *this* world, of the two into which she'd been born. Though *this* world has swallowed her child, taken from her by a scalpel and the immovability of an adoption agency she had to sue to cover the cost of the cesarean delivery.

She points to a new sketch in silence, for it's silence she needs now. She came into the dusk of her birth amid sirens and shouts and the scream of metal bent by hydraulic tools. Even her first breaths had been loud, coming from the clack of the oxygen tank of a fireman who'd expected nothing more serious that night than Halloween prank fires. Other times, she needs sound to anchor her in this world, be it on a dancefloor or the rush of a busy kitchen. The sketch by the chair, done in Rapidograph, is of a branching design at once like buck's antlers and a network of veins. From the size and shape of the design, you know she means for it to go on your right thigh.

You rub her feet until she sleeps. Then lift her smart phone from where it rests atop a doily cloth on the faux-mahogany dining room table and shut it off. You pull the old black telephone's four-pronged plug, of a kind you last saw while on tour, in a Kansas City motel that had Buddy Holly's signature on a page from a registry enshrined behind glass in the lobby.

You think of her hands as you walk frozen sidewalks, of their stillness as IVs are removed from and inserted into her wrist, of the wedding ring missing from her left hand.

You wonder if her husband took the ring, or had requested it be taken or cut from her finger, or if removing such jewelry is standard practice. Or if she'd taken it off before she'd been stricken. You don't dare ask the ICU nurses, who barely tolerate you as a non-family member, despite what is stipulated in her living will.

Her husband—whom she admitted she married for stability and the kind of household she'd never had, and that she'd *tried* to have, renting a house that could've belonged to the grandparents she'd wished for—had "overlooked" her living will. Amid all the forms and legalities and relics of "that old life of hers" that he'd isolated her from, her living will had stayed untouched, if unheeded.

Over the clatter of wheeled carts, and the TVs left on to stimulate the brains of comatose patients, the pale mark of where her ring had been makes a single chord in your mind that could not and should not exist within any audible realm, at once like a cello playing a D minor and the toll of a church bell.

You think of her hands—of the feel of both of them cupping your right as you placed it over her heart, when you made a soft quiet together in the storm of Industrial music sheeting down on the dancefloor you stood beside. You hold that lost moment as you grind down the winter night with your footsteps, until the time you can see her at the start of visiting hours. You have her fingerless gloves with you, to test if the feel of them against her palms will draw her back to this world, further from the other world that always claimed part of her. She'd left the gloves at your place, long ago. And arrangements had been made to get them back to her "When we next see each other!" that stretched until the medication expired in the spare inhaler she'd also left at your place, atop a folder holding all the art she has drawn for you.

You've not had the strength to look at that art since she has been hospitalized.

It will be hard to see her face today because it will hold the opposite of the flush that touches peoples' faces when they come in from the snow on a sunny day.

Your Guilt is kind as you walk the frozen waste of Kenmore Square, in the deep urban stillness before the first buses run. Your Guilt steps towards you, polite in answering your call, as it walks out of the very shadows in this Square from which you have seen bats and nighthawks and raccoons emerge, as if from woods in which children from folklore encounter witches.

Your Guilt is beautiful with the tattoos she designed to mark and heal your times of loss and grief. Your Guilt glitters with winter dew, hollow in its form that is, in truth, your form. The inverted fleur-de-lis defines its shoulder. The design like branching veins gland antlers on its right thigh shifts with the working of muscle that is not there as it walks, marking where it should be in memory of your brother John, in the place where he shot insulin to fight the diabetes that killed him.

Your Guilt stands, beckoning you to the shadows, the way you'd beckoned her into the past that'd once been yours when you'd lived in this Square, before it had been scrubbed and gentrified. Your Guilt bears the St. Xenia's cross she'd designed to honor the passing of your father and had intended for your chest, which hovers without the intermediacy of flesh before the reverse of the oak tree back piece she'd designed when your aunt passed into dementia. The cross and oak shift as your Guilt gestures for you to turn to the half-mirrored window of a high-end wine store, where your Guilt casts a reflection it never has before, becoming more a thing of this world, while the woman who drew the art that forms your Guilt slips into another.

The shadows in the window, in this improvised mirror.

Your Guilt would usher you into them.

Into the other world that marked her birth, and has partly reclaimed her.

Into the darker portion of the dusk that had midwifed her.

In the midst of a winter that could frost your eyes shut, the air takes the flavor of deep autumnk, and the shadows are tinted by the October blues and grays that shift in her eyes.

You grow colder beneath the layers of your leather and your hoodie, as the winter dew on your Guilt melts with the warmth your Guilt has just stolen from your blood and skin.

The shadows of this Square had been a comfort you'd shared with her. The Square is different now, but the shadows are not. Perhaps they've stayed unchanged from when there'd been a forest here, where River and marshland met, not yet cleared by charcoal burners and urban incursion. You'd told her of that lost forest late at night, standing here in the heart of the Square you'd known when you'd first come to Boston, playing at the many clubs that are now gone. You'd shared what those summer nights had been like amid these woodland shadows pooling in these urban alleys, where cigarette embers coaxed like will-o'-wisps. You walked with her along the streets where the moon once used to refract through the scores upon scores of empty beer bottles left on either side of club entrances for blocks in either direction. So much so, the moonlight danced upward through the glass, making an unreal glow against the bricks like what is supposed to come from a fairy underworld, while music seeped through nineteenth-century masonry abutting the back walls of basement club stages.

Someone long forgotten had looked upon the gently curving moonlight and dancing cigarette coals and called the bottles "glass pinecones." The Square and its light and its enduring forest shadows became known as the "Land of the Glass Pinecones," an ironic, ethereal enchantment of a name for a solid and enduring place ... that now no longer endures.

Your Guilt steals the comfort these shadows once gave you. The vine-wrapped lyre tattoo she'd designed to go over your heart after your grandfather—the first person to teach you how to play an instrument—had his crippling stroke stretches as your Guilt points to the darkness crowding the alley from which it came.

She is in those shadows, with the blue and the gray dusk

of her eyes, in the shade of a missing, darkened wood. She is in a cursed sleep between life and death brought on by the stress of a marriage she'd grasped at to have something *solid*, demonstrably *normal*, that she could call home, to have a tangible place in this world where she belonged yet only partly occupied. Much in the same way, she'd claimed a salvaged past when she'd rented a house full of artifacts of the previous occupants' parenting and grandparenting.

She'd grasped at her marriage to a husband who'd weaponized her asthma.

And you had done nothing.

Hoping she'd come out of the isolation her husband had imposed on her.

Yourself hollow.

Yourself paralyzed.

You had done nothing.

In the belief she'd ask for help when your help would matter. For you'd seen so many friends try to leave bad marriages before they were ready, only to return to them … the way you had twice returned to Lauren.

You had done nothing.

The Sin of Omission that made you hollow as wind in dry grass, that joined with the lesser omission of the tattoos you'd never taken.

You follow your Guilt into the shadows, hoping you can reclaim her for this world the way forced air from a fireman's oxygen tank once had.

Your hope is not consummated.

There are bottles here out for recycling; the moonlight refracting through them comes from a ribbon of sky. The window of time such light can strike this place can be counted in minutes. Here are echoes of what the ancient glass pinecones had once cast. In this otherworldly light, your otherworldly Guilt, sketched in increments by a woman trapped between worlds, now casts a shadow. Your Guilt becomes yet more solid as a small layer of you drifts from you like mist. You are lessened. Your Guilt and its newly stolen shadow fade, pulling the new scrap of materiality it has taken from you with it, as the moon's rim passes behind the building to your left.

You leave the alley.

Walk toward the River so you can follow its banks to the hospital, and once there, place earphones on her so you can play relics of your music that she had loved, that are all that's left of your non-commercial work, now that Lauren has finished punishing you for the apostasy of being a musician who had the arrogance of not dying young, denying her the widowhood she'd relied on having at this point in her life.

You have been served papers on behalf of her husband.

A kid came to your apartment door with a snow shovel in hand, asked if you were the building manager, and when you said no and identified yourself, threw the bulky packet at your chest.

You can no longer see her in the hospital.

You can no longer call to her with the touch of her gloves or with the music you'd composed for her on a child's desk painted forest green in a spare room of the house she rented, with her black cat on your lap whom her living will had entrusted to you should anything happen to her. There is no mention of the cat in the papers that you read while the cat twines around your legs.

Her mother can visit her … her mother, who could not keep sober in front of the judge while nominally fighting to keep custody of her.

Her husband can visit her … who turned on his heel and walked away when you met him, who forced her, out of jealousy hatched from his own failures, to break contact with all the artists she had known, all the friends of "that other life" that had been hers.

But you cannot see her.

You feed the old and thin cat who'd been a kitten when you'd first met her, and hate yourself for being too proud to call Lauren for money to fight this injunction, who never forgave you for the sin of being a working artist, and found it a personal project to escort you to the level of poverty she felt appropriate for you.

In your grief, you walk onto the ice.

Masked by driving snow.

Into the Between.

You walk through your own smoking breath into the deep

cold, onto the frozen River, knowing now why you had entrusted a friend to look after her cat. You walk amid the thick winter dawn that swirls with wind off the Harbor, into the Between of days, the Between of shores. You know from a call to the ICU that she is dying as you stand in deadly wind chill. And perhaps you are dying, too. Reaching to her. On neither land nor water. In neither day nor night. You can see the hospital from this part of the River. You try to recover her, as you think your Guilt had hinted for you to do. To reach her through the Between of her premature Halloween birth by standing in a place of Between, in the hinterland bordering the two worlds in which she'd drawn her first wounded breaths. To go into that deeper night realm and pull her back toward this world. Your lungs cry for the taste of autumn, your vision calls for the gray and the blue of the dusk she'd carried within her.

Through the wind …

Through cold that changes sound …

You hear your own tread coming toward you in the snow atop the River.

You turn as your Guilt approaches, now solid enough for snow to cling to the designs she'd made, but not solid enough for snow to cling to where bare skin would be if you'd taken her designs onto your flesh. Your Guilt is warm enough and solid enough to leave tracks of its bare feet.

There is urgency in your Guilt's movements.

The desperation of gait and posture a person takes leading another person from a burning room.

She is dying.

That is its urgency.

As it is yours.

But you do not know how to appease your Guilt, at this time of two lights beneath deep winter gales, at these last moments while the sun and moon share an invisible sky.

There is a new cracking in the ice, as the impressions of your Guilt's feet in the snow go deeper, as it steals more of you that exists in this world. It lifts its arm and you wonder if it will drown with you when your combined weight breaks the ice. At your Guilt's wrist, at the point on your body where the sleeve of ink she designed for you would end, a hand forms in outline, given shape by the blowing snow now clinging to it.

You are grabbed at your own wrist, cold fingers working where your glove and the cuff of your jacket meet.

Your Guilt steps into you, the way a man would step into a long coat held by a someone else. The cold of her designs slide under your skin as you realize how she had always intended those designs to be worn, as you realize this entity is not your Guilt but her wish for you. Her wish that has been given more weight not from what it has taken from you but from what of herself she has chosen to leave in this world ... entrusted sacred with you ... that you had first given her over the years she had been closer to you in friendship than any lover could be.

This is not your Guilt.

This is her Gift.

You hold her Gift beneath your skin as you feel her

leaving this world, as you feel the weight of what has been returned to you, as you feel the ice crack in a way that it did not beneath your feet when you'd walked away from shore.

You step carefully back to the riverbank, to live, to stay in this world and to remember the way she would wish you to.

AUTHOR'S NOTE: "Land of the Glass Pinecones" was what we punks and New Wave types in the '80s called the area around Kenmore Square in Boston, referring to the empty beer bottles that lined the streets and alleys by the clubs. They'd catch the light and the moon in a particular way. The phrase came from the song "Land of the Glass Pinecones" by the local band Human Sexual Response. The band themselves have since said the real inspiration came from a tree at a wedding they attended that'd been decorated with miniature beer bottles. But somehow, like in a game of telephone, the meaning got shifted to the light playing on bottles in Kenmore Square. And to a lot of us, that's what it will always mean.

'm not vengeful. I don't hold grudges. I mean, I work at a grocery store, uncrating produce and stacking heirloom tomatoes for display. I'm about freshness and vitamins and the power of sunshine. But I do balance the scales. When an accounting is called for, a reckoning, I see to it. What must be rectified, will be. And that's where we are now, at a reckoning with what has been lost and stolen.

With you.

I'm sitting in the kitchen staring at the phone. It rests neatly before me on the scratched butcher block table. Cardboard packing boxes are stacked around me. Fewer than I thought there would be after four years here. The small appliances went cheap at the garage sale, and the dishes. The table has a SOLD Post-it stuck to the corner. Ashen daylight seeps through the window. Outside, the Douglas firs shudder in the breezy drizzle. Daylight's all I've got. The electric company cut off the power last week. The water's off too, and the gas. By the sink there's a stack of FINAL NOTICE utility bills I never bothered opening.

But the phone bill, I paid.

The phone contains receipts.

The phone contains the entire text chain. It contains the history, this tale of Jamie Greenwood and Vicky Rich. I can't let the phone die, because it's the only thing that will allow me to even the score. And I *shall* see to it that the situation is rectified.

I must, before I'm out in the rain, under a tarp amid the firs down by the creek.

The cat slinks in and silks himself around my leg, purring. I pick him up and he settles on my lap, gray as the sky. Brady won't like the tarp life. Licking his paws is all the moisture he will tolerate. I bend my head to his, listening to him purr. (Yes, Brady is short for Number 12. *We get it, Jamie. Your cat is male.*) For a moment I hold still, prayer posture.

Namaste, Tom. An eviction notice will be coming in a few days. Unless.

It started with a *ting*, that sweet notification that a message had arrived. The number wasn't in Contacts. *Hey—Bandit got out!! Your back gate is open. I called him but he ran off.*

Thirty seconds later, from the same number: *He won't come when I call him. He took off into the woods toward the Interstate. I'm heading after him. Please get back to me*

A minute afterward, a photo arrived. It showed a Jack Russell terrier in prairie grass at the edge of a highway. The little dog sported a bull's-eye around his right eye and a cheeky blue bandanna around his neck. He was sniffing the grass while eighteen-wheelers roared past fifty feet away.

This is Vicky—your neighbor three doors down

Then, quickly: *Stephen, please please—I've been calling to him but your dog still won't come—too scared. Can you get here QUICK? I'm afraid if I get any closer he's gonna bolt onto the roadway. Treats? What? HELP*

Hindsight, perfect vision, all that. I don't need to rub myself raw seeing it again. Yet I do. And of course it's unbelievably clear now. It's been clear for weeks. I even reverse-image searched the Jack Russell photo and found it on Reddit. It had been posted on a dog lovers' subreddit—a scolding post from a traveler who watched a family of yahoos pop some Dews at a rest stop while they let their pup off the leash.

The post was six years old. Six. The danger to the dog was real. Online were more photos of that dog taken shortly afterward—a whole saga. Totally legit. Unlike the texts.

God. This is like those Stranger Danger lectures. *Never go anywhere with a grown-up you don't know. Not even if they ask you to help find a lost puppy.* This is Buffalo Bill luring the Size-14 girl into his panel van by wearing a fake cast. That obvious.

A fuckin' puppy. *Bandit.* How fitting. I grab the phone and scroll, like picking at a scab. *Jamie, why didn't you delete the messages? This is gonna kill you.*

Because the reply text is right there. *You have the wrong number.*

That one was intended to let Vicky know she was crying into the void. But Vicky's replies were instantaneous.

Isn't this Stephen?

Sorry

Crap

Now, I tell myself to stop. Put the phone away. I have this text thread memorized. But I don't stop. I stare at the screen, the thread with ME at the top. Five minutes after Vicky realized—supposedly—she was texting a wrong number, ME wrote: *Is the dog okay?*

After that came a painful wait. Vacuum. In space, no one can hear you scream for news about a fugitive terrier. Twenty minutes. Twenty-five. Finally, after half an hour, Vicky replied.

Got thru to my neighbor. Bandit is okay!

Masterful, really. Hitchcockian. Keeping everyone in suspense. In reply came thumbs-up emojis. Many. Profligate.

Then, from Vicky: *Thank you for your concern.*

And it went from there.

Look at you, I think to myself. *Jamie, searching for something.* There's no doubt about it, no point denying it. *All my life.*

Even when the chat with Vicky heated up, and after a few weeks veered, inevitably, toward the topic of money. My inner voice is excoriating. *That was when you started to bleed.* Openly, willfully, eagerly.

(Yes, I know I'm talking to myself here.) (I can't help it.)

You bled, not even feeling it. Vicky sent photos—not doggie photos anymore, but selfies. ("Selfies.") They were outdoorsy. Smiley. Goofy, even. The few backgrounds visible looked like Oregon. And you added *Haha* and thumbs up to her quippy messages.

I scroll. There's the heart she added to the selfie you sent her. Your photo shows a winsome smile, just a little desperate. Because this correspondence was never inappropriate. Always proper. Your texts were never over the line. You just felt inspired to be kind, supportive of your new friend; enthusiastic, really. Just telling her—how delicate she looked. How you couldn't resist.

Oh, Jamie.

I exhale. My eyes are red. *Don't go, Vicky. I need you. Just a while longer.*

Vicky had found a believer. No missing that.

(Stop it. *Stop.* This isn't helping.) (Shut up.)

You checked out all the advice Vicky gave you. Her uncle, she said, was a day trader, now into crypto. Can't miss. Don't be timid. *You're too smart to pass this up, Jamie. Don't let this chance go to waste.*

Vicky said she had nothing to hide. She sent screenshots of her crypto exchange statement. All those up-arrows and graph lines ascending like a moon shot. Fortune favors the scammers, but when Vicky's sending you photos and rubbing salt into wounds she has deduced you have (manhood, wealth, the job you lost, the look in your girlfriend's eyes, the guitar and amp you had to pawn to make rent) you lean into belief. Take the chance.

Back then, the olden days, last fall, the denial began.

Everything was fine with the crypto account. Look at the returns! On the exchange's site, it was cupcakes with sprinkles. Then, when it seemed like the right time to cash out, things changed. There were roadblocks with the account. Problems logging in. The statements showed all those huge gains Vicky and her uncle promised, but every time you tried to sell, the exchange slowed to molasses. *Processing.*

Abruptly, there was no way to access the funds. The sale was in vapor lock. Vicky expressed surprise. She said that she didn't have any difficulty moving her assets. What had you done wrong? Didn't you get the premium account? You should have. She told you to. (No, she didn't. There was no premium account available. All the money was gone.)

ME: *I need my money.*

Vicky: *Didn't you do your research?* Like a stiletto to the heart. *This is on you.*

The voice in my head won't quiet. *You never found anything you'd searched for.* That's what you thought. But with the money Vicky promised, you were getting close.

Before.

ME: *I gotta get the funds. If I don't, I'm screwed*

Even I can't bring myself to rehash the pleading that came after that, and the week-long silence from Vicky. Until—

ME: *I'm begging*

Vicky: *If you can't take the pressure, take the honorable way out. You're insured, right?*

At that point, Vicky the social engineering genius wanted to wrap things up. That was the end of the thread. February. It's now May.

The cat stretches, digs his claws into my jeans, and jumps. I pick up the phone. I type.

Hey girl. We cool? I know I got heated. Apologies.

I get it now. I need to access a premium account to get my funds disbursed from the exchange. You have one, you said?

How about we see if we can transfer my funds to your account, then you cash out and send me the $$

For a second I squeeze the phone, then drop it like it's a hot brick. My heart is racing. Outside, the wind blows rain against the windows.

I stare at the phone. Silently begging the universe to nudge Vicky into picking it up.

It stays dark. I shove back from the table and storm out to the patio, letting the rain hit me in the face. If this fails …

Faintly, inside: *ping*

When I run in and wipe my hands on my shirt, the message is on the screen. *So I guess we're not done,* she writes. *Good. I missed you, sweetie.*

My mouth is dry. I let out a breath, my vision pulsing. I text, *Thank you. You're my savior!*

Three dots. Please. My stomach feels full of moths.

OK, she texts. *Here's the thing. Your current funds are tied up in processing. They're stuck. To get them into my premium account you need to jar them loose.*

I reply, *How?*

More dots. *New deposit.*

Yes. There's the Vicky I was expecting.

I type, *So...I deposit more funds into my crypto account...*

She says, *Right. Then, basically, you'll set up a transfer to me for the* **whole** *amount you have invested. Everything will get pushed to my premium account, and I can cash it out to you.*

Vicky wants crypto. That won't work for me. I need to get her in meatspace. I have to get her physically in front of me.

I type, *Queen!!*

She hearts that. *Minimum transfer to a premium account is $2K. Let me know when you deposit the funds.*

I thumb the keypad. *One hitch. My bank account is overdrawn and credit cards have been cut off. I need to get the $$ to you another way.*

The pause lasts too long. Then, *Sorry, hun. You heard the rules.*

I clench my jaw. *This is my only chance to recoup the money I'm down. C'mon, Vic. I need this to get back on my feet.*

I send. I wait. Dangling the lure. But nothing.

I type, *But I can get cash. I have ways.*

Still no reply.

Cash money, I write. *I just need to get it to you.*

If she resists that, she's not the greed hound I know her to be.

The phone sits there like a block of lead. If this takes much longer I'll need to leave the house and find a Starbucks with an electrical outlet so I can charge it.

Then a ping. *No cash.*

The fuck?

She doesn't trust me, I realize. She's suspicious. I've

thrown her off her playbook. Maybe she thinks I'll put a dye pack in with a stack of twenties, or a glitter bomb, something to shock her and trace her.

I force myself to focus. She's open to the idea of getting more money. That's what I need to play into. What can I dangle?

I type. *I'll send you a money order.*

I know she may want a wire, or Western Union, but Western Union has cracked down on that since they got sued for letting so many grannies get taken by the Favorite Grandchild Scam.

Money orders are always paid for ahead of time, in full. They never bounce. Vicky should like that. And from what I've read, scammers have another reason to want them. With enough skill, they can change the dollar amount on the face of the order.

I play desperate. I feel desperate. *$2K money order. Made out to Victoria Rich.*

The phone is down to 2%. I rub my forehead with my knuckles.

You can mail it to me, Vicky writes.

I lean my head on the butcher block tabletop. Calming myself. *Cool. Address?*

She gives me a P.O. Box in Portland. Only a hundred-fifty miles away.

I'll get the money order and put it in the mail today, I write. As I stand up, my legs wobble. This has to work. When I grab my car keys and head for the door, Brady yowls at me.

"I hear ya. Eye of the tiger." I run out.

An hour later I snap a photo of the money order. A poor shot, only half of the order visible, so Vicky can't use it somehow for mobile deposit. I send the photo to her, then tuck the order in an envelope and write Vicky's address with a shaking hand. On the back, steadier, I write *Jamie Greenwood* and the return address in clean black ink. Just to make a point.

The local post office is my first stop. I hold onto the letter for a second, tell myself not to lose my grip. This is the way. I am the rectifier. I paper-airplane the envelope into the slot.

The next morning, I hit I-5 North and bomb to Portland. I drive in silence, no music, no podcasts. I drink coffee and focus.

The day is chill with rain, the traffic in Portland heavy. In the strip mall that hosts Vicky's post office, the parking lot reeks of moss and hot coffee. A supermarket dominates. Abandoned shopping carts dot the gleaming asphalt like bison.

At four p.m. I'm still sitting in the car. Rain sogs the view. The non-sun is giving up. Charcoal skies, headlights streaky through the windshield. Waiting. The post office is glass-fronted. It gives me a complete view of the P.O. boxes inside.

My hands aren't shaking. Not right now. I am cool, I am dressed up, nails painted a cyanotic blue, ready to make an impression.

I know that Vicky might not match the photos she has sent. If, that is, she is anything close to a she. Maybe Vicky Rich is actually an orc, outside as well as in.

Then a car pulls past, white Cadillac, and she jumps

out. Actual Vicky. Older by a dozen years, mouth pinched, moving quickly on kitten heels. Purse hanging from her forearm. Chunky frames, steampunk Gucci, reflecting the streetlights. Rain patters against her umbrella.

I get out of the car, moving as if in syrup. I watch her through the post office windows as she opens the P.O. box. I have pinned that box in my mind, have scoped it out ahead of time. She comes back out through the swinging door, bleary light flashing off the glass, and my head clears. Like a snap, a bark, a hammer hitting crystal.

She's alone. I can't wait any longer, and am not going to let her drive away. I won't follow her. Follow, and she might drive straight to somewhere I won't get satisfaction. This is it.

I text her a photo. As she walks past me to the Caddy I hear a *ping* from her purse. She pulls out her phone, stares, and slows. She frowns.

Then she looks up, and her head swivels.

I'm already approaching her. "I thought you'd appreciate a follow-up."

"Who are you?"

"I sent you the money."

She seems to harden, like cement curing. "Is this some kind of a joke?"

"You just picked up the letter I mailed. The envelope has the return address on it." I recite it.

"What game are you playing?"

Then, realizing she has made a mistake by talking to me, she moves toward the car.

"You want Jamie's money?" I said. "More of it?"

"Screw off. You're not Jamie."

"No. I'm not," I said. "I'm his widow."

For a moment Vicky's instincts fail her. She stutter-steps. Stops. She rips open the envelope. Her hopes run down the drain with the rain. The money order isn't for $2K. It's for $2.

She crumples the envelope and gives me a savage look. I'm not Jamie. But I'd found a believer. And moment by moment, she fell for it.

And yeah, that photo I just sent her—it's a follow-up on the little dog racing toward the Interstate. Scooter, his name was. Turn away if you don't want to know.

The mutt made it. He bolted into traffic between a beer truck and a bachelorette party heading to Nashville. The little freak shot straight across to another county.

Meemaw didn't. She was not half as fast as the dog. You can find the story online. Search "*Woman chasing dog hit by party bus.*"

Vicky hurls the envelope to the ground. She coils like a spring, ready to lunge, I think for my neck. Then she sees movement in the dusk, figures advancing, and reaches into her purse. Quick, no hesitation.

I charge her. I pin her to the Caddy as she squirms and claws and tries to bite me. *Get it, get it*—I reach into the purse, feel her hand scrabbling, and I claw her before she can draw it.

Her phone.

The phone that contains information on all her marks, those she had hurt, those she is targeting. She was half a second from hitting a code to lock it, wipe it, protect herself. I have her on mail fraud, but she wants to shield the list of men who are ready to empty their pockets and hearts into her maw. The phone's not a gun but is a weapon. I hold it up and catch her facial recognition, open it, then shove her back and retreat, clutching it to my chest.

Revenge. I thrill to it. The taste is poisonous.

Jamie rarely spoke of his yearnings, but I knew how he felt. That all his life, he was searching. For something, anything. He kept reaching for it, as if by extending his hands, grabbing at the air, it would come within his grasp. It never did. But his hopes—his blessed, ever-dashed hopes—always resurfaced, toxic, desperate, leading nowhere.

I loved that about him. I hated it. I hoped for him, which is why I stayed for too long, and why I never signed the divorce papers, even though I'd moved out and wasn't in the house when the lights were shut off.

Nothing satisfied him but he kept trying, scenting something ineffable, convincing himself he was getting close. But here's the thing.

I was the something. He could never see it. Right in front of him. Invisible.

And that doesn't matter now. None of it does. They found him at the bottom of a ravine on the McKenzie River, below the bridge he jumped from.

For a flicker I think I see you, your ghost, before the wind shreds it and I'm here on my own, wide open, ready to leap.

In my coat pocket, the blade lies cold in my palm, dark

but aching for the moment when I will sweep it out, when it will shine.

The FBI swarms from the shadows, blue jackets soaked, and cuffs Vicky.

I'm shocked at her mouth. Vicky's dressed like a top-performing realtor, like a megachurch pastor's wife ready for a Caribbean jaunt on the church Learjet. Chanel jacket and jeans, Louboutins. When the feds grab her the umbrella blows across the parking lot and her salon hair deflates like wet cotton candy. Her profanity is prolific and vivid. She's sticking to the canine theme that kicked off this whole nightmare, with me and my anatomy playing the role of female dog. She's spitting when they put her in the car, her face smeared against the window. Pouring it over me like hot coals, but she's helpless now. They drive her away.

For just long enough, the feds don't know that I have her phone. That's long enough for me to Air Drop Vicky's contacts and call records and text threads to my own phone, before I let hers slide to the ground beside the Cadillac. Long enough to import information that'll help me find the other scammers she works with.

The blue FBI jackets walk over, pull me aside, concerned and curious. We duck under the supermarket awning, out of the wet. Yes, I'll give a statement. I'll tell them everything.

I thought I'd feel lighter. The weight that's been chaining me down—it should be gone, yeah? Gone like you, Jamie. But the cleansing chill of the rain will have to do. At least the knife is light.

On to the next.

AUTHOR's NOTE: I have a playlist titled "Editing." I cue it up when I need to go hard. It features copious electric guitar and the occasional heart-shredding ballad. When I need to put the story into high gear, up the tension, and nail the emotional tone, I blast Foo Fighters. "DOA," "The Pretender," "Wheels," "My Hero," "Times Like These." And, when a deadline is biting at my ankles: "All My Life." I can count on the Foos to drive me across the finish line. I never considered using any other song for this story.

A long gravel driveway in the headlights, framed by thin branches from the trees all around. Gloomy, urgent synthpop from the state college radio station two valleys over, straining through static. Jared's hands, sweaty on the wheel. Ben checked the guns, one more time.

The driveway ended and the headlights glinted off four cars parked at angles off each other as if they had been thrown there. In front of them, a body, a piece of its skull missing.

"Is that the cop?" Jared said.

"Kill the lights," Ben said.

Jared stopped the car and they divided up the guns. The shotgun and two pistols for Jared. The hunting rifle and the big pistol for Ben, who was a better shot. The moon hid behind thin clouds, gave the whole sky a wan, gray light. They got out of the car, walked the rest of the way, letting their eyes get used to the dark. Soon, they could see, at the end of the driveway, the rickety house at the top of a small rise, light blazing from the first-floor windows. To their left, a dark barn, a cyclone-fence enclosure, and sleeping inside it, the shadow of the giant bird.

"What is that thing again?" Jared said.

"A cassowary," Ben said.

From inside the house, they heard shouting, a scream.

"That's my mom," Ben said.

"Let's go get her," Jared said.

Jared and Ben had met on the playground in first grade, under the jungle gym. They decided to look for treasure and dug with their little hands through the gravel, into the dirt below. They got in trouble for it, for having made a hole the janitor had to fix, for their dirty hands in class. It brought them together. After school they escaped into the woods behind the playground, found a clear stream that flowed into a drainage pipe. They wondered what was in there. By the end of fourth grade, they had picked thousands of spiders out of their hair, found three dead raccoons, and almost died twice—once when the pipe they were exploring almost got too narrow for them, once when a sudden rain caught them underground—but they knew how to get from one end of town to the other without ever touching a sidewalk.

They had other friends, but none so close. Jared took a bloody nose and some cuts on the face for Ben in sixth grade, when he jumped three boys who had jumped Ben after Ben looked at one of their girlfriends a little too long. The next year Ben held off a group of boys who had come to beat down Jared in the parking lot after school. He did it without throwing a punch. Ben wasn't big, or tall. But he looked hard. The kid who'd been hit a lot already, knew what it was and wasn't afraid of it anymore. The kid who would go for the eyes. In eighth grade Jared lied to the police who found them huddled in a bus stop at dusk, said Ben had been with him all day when it had only been an hour, without Ben having to ask. They were beyond owing each other by then. Beyond having each other's back.

"I know you and Ben are tight," Jared's dad said to Jared then, "but you have to watch it around that boy."

"Ben's not like that," Jared said.

"You're not hearing us," Jared's mom said. "It's not Ben. It's what's happening around him."

Jared knew what she meant. Ben had been to Jared's house dozens of times, eaten dinner at their table. They'd spent hours in the garage, making and breaking things out of scrap wood, daring each other to try to crack open the gun safe Jared's dad had. But Ben had never let Jared go to his house. It was always one line from him—*I gotta get home*—and then Ben would take off down the road, at a run, Jared waving goodbye to his back. Then how Jared would see Ben's parents around town, almost never together. His mom squinting at Jared, sizing him up. His dad staring through him without saying a word.

"I can take care of myself," Jared said.

"We know you can," Jared's dad said. "Just make sure you do."

Jared first thought he might be gay in the summer before ninth grade, watching porn from a grainy, dubbed VHS tape in the basement of a friend's house with nine other boys. He watched his friends get worked up at the straight sex, the lesbians, turning their lust into giggles and jokes. He felt nothing. But the gay characters drew him in. He didn't want to act like them, knew he wouldn't last long where he was if he did. But he did want to be around them. He also noticed they didn't get to fuck onscreen, not like everyone else. His friends wouldn't have liked that. He found books and movies of his own after that, knew he had to keep it secret. Being gay was something for somewhere else. A college, a big city. Not his town.

He couldn't leave yet. He could wait.

In the tenth grade Jared and Ben learned about the ruins of a small town in the woods a mile off the railroad tracks. They found it one summer day, a row of foundations like open graves for giants, a few houses half-standing up, a huge rotting barn leaning against a tree. They felt, for a moment, the sense of history, woods that were felled for farms and were now woods again, as if the trees allowed their devastation, knew they'd have their time again. They found one house that seemed more intact than the others. It wasn't. Jared fell through the floor, into the basement. He hadn't broken anything, but he was cut, bad, in seven different places.

Jared watched Ben pause as the blood ran. Felt the decision.

"My house isn't far from here," Ben said.

They walked each with an arm around the other's

shoulders. Ben's house, a squat place with a sagging porch in a stand of pines. Inside, a ragged couch, a folding table, rickety wooden chairs. Piles of things in the corners, clothes, a broken blender, unopened mail. Nothing on the walls. Ben settled Jared on the couch, came back with hydrogen peroxide, a ragged towel with the faded faces of the Superfriends on it, and bandages.

"Push up," Ben said, and Jared bared his leg. Felt Ben's fingers on him as he cleaned the wound, pressed down. Gentle and firm. Confident, Jared allowed himself to think. Caring.

"How does it feel?" Ben said.

"Better," Jared said.

"Hold this," Ben said. He moved on from Jared's leg to his arms, his cheek, his forehead. Jared looked around the room.

"I know what you're thinking," Ben said. "It looks like we just moved here."

"No," Jared said. "It looks like you're ready to move out."

Ben smiled. "That, too," he said. He finished and his fingers returned to the big bandage, kept the pressure on. They started to talk. About their friends at school. Who was fucking who, who would like to be. Who was in love. The rumors about their teachers that flew around town every six months or so that seventh graders were shocked to learn and eleventh graders couldn't remember ever not knowing. The things they wanted to do when they were done with high school. They hadn't talked about it since they were kids, when Ben wanted to be a long-haul truck driver and Jared wanted to work in a zoo. Now their dreams were hazier. They knew they didn't have the money for what they wanted and were trying to pull something else out of the world, something other than what they had.

"All I know," Ben said, "is that I need to get out of here."

"Out of this house or out of this town?" Jared said.

"You tell me," Ben said.

He blinked. A slow look of panic crawled across his face. They'd been talking all afternoon, and now it was dark in the house.

"You have to leave now," Ben said.

Jared swung his leg off the couch, trying to keep the wound safe. Ben grabbed his arm, started to pull him up.

"Hey, that hurts," Jared said.

"You don't get it," Ben said. His voice rose. "You have to leave now. My dad can't catch you here." Headlights passed on the road, swept through the house, and Ben wheeled in blind fear.

"Ben—" Jared said.

"What do I have to do to get you to go?" Ben said. Every word edged with broken glass. He ran to the back door and opened it.

"Stay off the road," he said. "At least for a mile."

When Jared got home he was bloody and dirty, too much for his parents not to ask. He told his parents the truth, about the dead town in the woods, going back to Ben's. About how he'd learned his lesson. His parents lingered. They weren't angry. But they weren't done.

Jared's mom told him everything. That Ben's mom was

quiet and kind, too kind, because Ben's dad was unstable, a loose temper. Violent. There were stories of fights late at night after the bars closed, Ben's dad ending up in jail for beating someone up, but the charges always got dropped. Stories, too, about some of the company his dad kept. People who ran over dogs. People who never came into town. Ben's dad wasn't just dangerous himself. He was involved in something even more dangerous, and not smart enough to see how dangerous it was.

"That's why we've opened our house to Ben," Jared's mom said. "Why we've fed him so often, let him stay here so much. His home isn't safe, not for him, and not for you."

That night, falling asleep, all Jared could think about was Ben's hands moving over his wounds. When he slept, he dreamed about it, except all the wounds were gone. He woke up with a thought so clarifying that it reordered his memories of the past.

I love him, Jared thought. It lit a fire in him, gentle and warm, made the colors all around him brighter, the late summer sun shimmering through the chattering leaves. *You look happy today,* his mom said. *I am,* Jared said. He didn't dare tell Ben. What would they do with it if Ben knew? Jared could wait, tend his secret flame.

Which made it hard a couple days later when Jared saw the car coming while he was walking home, a sedan losing its paint in blotches, rust spreading over the hood. It came at him too fast, swerved into the gravel on the shoulder to pull a U-turn that made the tires bark, made Jared stop walking.

Ben's dad rolled down the window, gave Jared a glimpse

inside the car. Ben's mom in the passenger seat, eyes down, unmoving. A pile of garbage bags in the back seat. Two rifles.

"Hey," Ben's dad said, his lips curling. "I see you."

Jared locked eyes with him, said nothing.

"I see you and your faggy little walk," Ben's dad said. "I see the way you look at my son with your faggoty eyes. I hear you've put a hand on my boy, I'll put a couple bullets in your face. Do you understand?"

Jared didn't move.

"Do you understand?"

Jared kept his face still, his voice even. "Yeah," he said. "I understand."

"Good," Ben's dad said. "Be seeing you."

He pulled another U-turn and drove off. Jared waited until the car was gone. He wasn't scared. He was angry.

A year went by, another fall, another winter, another summer, when Jared and Ben piled into a rusted Crown Victoria with three other friends and spent days escaping their town. They went to the raceway at Watkins Glen, dove into the gorges to swim in Ithaca, drank in the car watching *The Lost Boys* at the drive-in outside of Auburn, and Jared wished it was just him and Ben, alone.

That September, the start of their senior year, it seemed as though all at once their town was drowning in drugs. It must have happened slower than that, crept in, an invisible mist, in a leaning house, the apartment above the vacuum repair place, the riverbank by the dead mill. But then, from the end of one week to the next, it was in the news, three overdoses, three funerals. It was on the street just a few blocks from the police station, two people on the sidewalk curled against a building. Jared and Ben walked out of school and a man with greasy hair came up to Ben, asked him if he had anything, because Ben had that look.

"Sorry, man," Ben said. The man kept moving.

"What's happening?" Jared said.

"I don't know," Ben said.

That weekend they took the trail into the woods to the dead town. Everyone had found it by then, and someone had decided to throw a party while it was still warm out. They arrived to a crowd, a few small fires, flashlights on the ground pointing up into the branches above, making the smoke glow. A racket of voices, laughing, mocking. People gathered around a keg, cheering. A big boombox pounding out Slayer, blast beat drums, a thrashing electric guitar, people moshing in the leaves and shouting. Couples making out against trees, in the graves of the old foundations away from the light. Some of them just in the leaves, not caring who saw, who knew. It was a good time.

A skinny man too old to be there stepped into the light from somewhere in the woods and leaned against a tree. Soon he was handing out baggies of pills, taking money, rolling the bills and putting them in his pocket. Kids shrugged and popped the pills in their mouths, washed them down with mouthfuls of beer from thin plastic cups. The party changed.

More shouting, more laughing, more stumbling. A couple of fights that got broken up before they got bad. Moans from the shadows of the old foundations. Huge cheers from the keg, from the crowd dancing near the boombox, cups in the air.

Then a kid was down, another one, as though their strings had been cut. Both of them just lay there in the leaves. Cries of concern. *Oh shit, oh shit, oh fuck.* Someone said to kill the radio and the music snapped off. *Oh fuck.* One of those kids who, it turned out, didn't panic when things went south, started issuing orders. *We got to get them out of here. We got to get to the hospital.* It was what a half-dozen other people needed to hear. They lifted the fallen kids off the ground, disappeared down the trail back to the lines of cars by the road, making their plans. A hundred other kids still in the lit woods, reduced to murmurs. *Now what?*

"He's going," Jared said. Sure enough, the dealer shoved the rest of the baggies in his pocket, took a look around, pivoted, and headed into the woods, in the opposite direction of the road. Jared and Ben didn't have to say anything. They followed at a distance.

The dealer had a flashlight that bobbed among the trunks of the trees, a guiding star. They crossed a decayed set of railroad tracks. Broke out of the woods onto a dirt road, then plunged back in again. A sudden break that maybe was an old logging road, maybe was someone's driveway. A startled deer. Then, through the woods, yellow light from distant windows. They heard the dealer's footsteps crackle on gravel, the slam of a screen door. Reached the edge of the woods to see a house that could have been built from scrap, spare parts of other houses. The shadow of a barn, a fenced pen. Low voices from inside.

Ben pointed. There, in the moonlight, the outline of his dad's rusted car.

The screen door to the house screeched open, someone stepped out, and Jared and Ben heard a startled voice. They were just there, standing in the driveway. Nowhere to hide.

A voice from the house: "Someone's here, hit the lights." A set of floodlamps blared on, and now it was daylight in the woods. In the pen, the giant, colorful bird that had been resting there sprang to its feet and gave out a long, low, full-throated croak, a noise from before humans.

The man at the top of the stairs smiled. "Oh, Edna likes you," he said, in a high, pinched voice. A shotgun in his hands. "Please don't run, because I will shoot you."

Jared and Ben didn't move. The man with the shotgun called inside the house. "Anybody know who these two are?"

Ben's dad appeared in the doorway and glared. Ben withered.

"That's my kid and a friend of his."

"Should I feed them to the cassowary?" squeaked the man with the gun.

"Claude," Ben's dad said, "he's my boy." He was pleading.

"We don't just let them go, though, do we?" Claude said. "Boys need to be taught lessons." He leveled the gun at Ben. "Inside. Both of you."

The stench of mold, the tang of chemicals. A linoleum

floor streaked with dark stains, a buzzing fridge. Another refrigerator, unplugged, hanging open. A rusted electric stove. Plastic bags. Beakers. The ring of a naked fluorescent bulb stuck to the ceiling. Another man, the biggest of the three, waited inside.

"Who are these little fucks?" he said.

"One's Buck's boy," Claude sneered.

"The ugly one, I guess," the big man said. "Can I hurt them?"

"No," Claude said. "That's Buck's job."

"Claude," Ben's dad said.

Claude disappeared into another room, came back with a metal folding chair. "This'll *have* to *doooo*," he said, in a disappointed singsong. "Lie on the floor," he barked to Jared and Ben.

"Claude," Ben's dad said, almost in a whimper.

"If you didn't want to whip him," Claude said, "you should have raised him better."

Claude still had the gun. Jared and Ben got down on the floor, and Ben's dad raised the chair, brought it down. Jared heard Ben yelp, then his own voice cry out as the metal edge came down on his back, again, his waist, his legs. He understood it all then, the big man's stupidity, Claude's cruelty, Ben's dad's weakness. Then the edge of the chair came down on his head and he was out.

Jared came to again in the driveway, realized by the way he hurt that he had been dragged there. A bellow from the cassowary.

"He's awake," he heard Ben's dad say.

He was rolled over. Claude stood over him, pushed the end of his rifle barrel against his forehead.

"You tell the police or anyone about any of this," Claude said, "and I'll kill you and everyone in your families. Do you understand."

Under the pressure of the barrel, Jared nodded.

"I'm so glad we're clear," Claude said. "You should know you're only alive because of Buck. I would have killed you both."

Ben and Jared helped each other up and limped into the woods. They heard the bird in the pen bellow one more time, a rumble through the trees. Then followed the dim light through the branches and their memories back through the woods, across the road, and back to the dead town in the forest. The remnants of the party, a couple empty kegs, one half-full one. Plastic cups, a small slick of vomit. Three trampled sweatshirts. The trail back to town waited for them. But it was still dark, and they didn't know what time it was, and the adrenaline that had pushed them this far was wearing off. Ben swayed, then sat down, leaned against a tree trunk.

"What am I going to do, Jared? That was my dad."

"I know," Jared said.

"Now he knows that *I* know what he's mixed up in. Who he's mixed up with."

"I know."

"My dad will change his mind and kill us both."

"He won't," Jared said.

"How do you know?"

Jared sat down next to Ben, put his arms around him. Ben nestled in close and started crying. They warmed each other up against the night breeze, and soon they were both asleep.

They woke to the light sifting through the leaves and struggled to stand. They had bruises all over. Ben had a few on his face. Jared felt an angry lump on his head. It took them a long time to walk back. They stumbled into Jared's house, let the screen door bang behind them. Heard Jared's mom shriek, quick footsteps from the kitchen, and then both Jared's parents were there, their arms around Jared, both him and Ben. He'd been afraid they'd be angry with him, that he hadn't come home, and he was humbled by the release of their grief.

"What happened to you?" his mom asked.

Jared and Ben said nothing.

"Were you at that party last night?" his dad asked.

Ben didn't move. Jared nodded. Took a chance.

"Are those two kids okay?" he said.

"No," his dad said. "They died."

"Do you know anything about it?" Jared's mom said.

Jared shook his head. Ben still hadn't moved. He wouldn't, for hours.

The funerals for the kids were the next day. Jared and Ben stayed in the house, in Jared's room. They heard Jared's parents talking downstairs, couldn't make out the words. A knock on the bedroom door.

"Come on," Jared's dad said. "You got to talk to the police."

All Jared knew was that he wasn't going to give Ben up.

"Does anyone else know you're here?" the officer said.

"No," Jared said.

"Good," the officer said. "Start at the beginning." Jared and Ben gave each other a long look. *I'm not saying anything,* Jared thought. Then Ben started talking. He went back before the party, to his dad, all the years he was growing up. Told the police more than Jared had known.

The officer wrote it all down. Another officer standing near the door nodded. Watching them, saying nothing.

"We're going to find a way to get Ben's mom in a motel. Get her when she leaves the house without her husband," the first officer said. He handed Ben a card with an address and phone number on it. "We'll be taking her here."

They got a call at Jared's house an hour later, from Ben's mom. *Don't come here. You're safer where you are.*

"You can stay here as long as you need," Jared's mom said. "They're not going to do anything to us."

She was wrong.

For two nights, Ben slept on a mattress on the floor in Jared's room. They talked about the dumbest things they could think of. A kid's bad haircut. A crappy horror movie they saw five years ago. The spiders in their hair when they were kids. Ben fell asleep first, and Jared listened to his breathing, wished he was down there on the mattress with him, holding him close. He drifted off.

And woke. Still dark. A crash downstairs. Voices. His dad yelling down the stairs. *Who the fuck is that?*

Ben sat up. They looked at each other and didn't make a sound.

You motherfuckers, I'm gonna kill you, Jared's mom screamed. The blast from a shotgun. His mom screaming, his dad yelling. A crash, another crash. They ran out of Jared's room, onto the shadowed landing, lit only by the streetlamps outside. Someone was lying face down on the stairs, their head pointing toward the front door. One leg bent at a funny angle. Shouts and screams. *Run, get the cops,* Jared's dad said. The two boys vaulted down the stairs and saw the front door kicked in, splintered wood and bent hinges. In the dark living room, Jared's dad, covered in blood, his feet planted on the floor, a bear, roaring. He had something under his arm. No, someone's head. He punched it, punched it again, again, then dropped the body and kicked its face six times, the body jerking against the couch. Then it stopped moving.

Jared's dad stopped roaring, let out a long sigh, slumped on the couch in the dark over his unmoving attacker. His white T-shirt dark with spreading blood.

"You boys okay?" he said, his voice raspy and faint.

Jared ran for the phone.

"Your mom already called 911,'" Jared's dad said.

"Is she okay?" Jared said.

"She's the strongest, smartest person I know," his dad said.

"You're telling me not to call?" Jared said.

"I'm telling you that you have to get out of here, now."

"You're real hurt, Dad."

"I'll be fine. The police are coming. Now go."

Ben ran for the door and out. Jared turned to follow.

"You two be careful," Jared's dad said. "Look out for each other. I know you will, Jared. I know."

Jared nodded. He ran out of the house to the garage, unlocked the safe there, got the guns inside and boxes of ammunition. On the drive to the motel, they didn't say anything. Jared kept his hands on the wheel, listened to Ben load the guns.

They drove to the edge of town, saw the motel's flashing neon sign, and turned in. In the headlights, they knew already which unit it was. Two police cruisers in front of a busted-down door, three cops and a man in a striped, collared shirt, talking. No blood they could see. No ambulance. Ben rolled down his window.

"Keep moving," Ben said. They rolled by the scene, Jared trying to make it look like they were just looking for a spot. Ben listened.

"They didn't kill her," Ben said. "They took her. Her and the cop who was watching over her."

"Only one place where," Jared said. "Do we tell them?"

"I think they'll shoot my mom and dad as soon as they know the cops are coming," Ben said. He gave Jared a look. Didn't have to say anything.

"Okay," Jared said.

They took the state highway out of town. Ben turned on the radio, the state college station, crackling and fading. Driving drums, a high swooping voice. A burst of static garbling it all. Now lush synthesizers, a dance beat, a sense of symphony. The DJ, far away. *That was "Why Can't I Be You," from The Cure, then "True Faith" from New—*

Another volley of static. Jared turned onto a smaller road, less well paved, passed the road they'd crossed to get from woods to woods. Kept going.

"It's got to be here somewhere," he said. Ben pointed to a gravel driveway.

Thin branches. Four cars at angles. A body, a piece of its skull missing. The bird in the pen. Screams from inside the house.

"That's my mom," Ben said.

"Let's go get her," Jared said.

They made their way in the dark to the nearest window. There was Ben's mom on the floor, several men standing around her. One of them, Jared saw, was the second officer from the police station, the one who hadn't said anything.

Ben's dad, this time with a whip of a branch in his hand, whimpering. Claude squealing orders. *Hit her again.* The men laughed.

Ben's dad brought the whip down on Ben's mom.

"I can't watch this," Ben said, cocked his pistol, and fired through the window. The cassowary woke up fast, leapt to its feet, croaking and barking.

Jared followed Ben's lead, aiming at Claude.

But the gun was harder to handle than he thought it would be, louder, the kickback stronger. *You're aiming at a human being,* he thought. *You're aiming at a cop.* They both kept firing and missed everyone. But there was no whipping Ben's mom anymore. The men scattered. A few to the darkness of the rooms beyond the kitchen. Two hit the floor. Two of them headed for the door to the yard with guns of their own, and as the threat closed in on them, Jared thought of his mom and dad, protecting him and Ben. How they had worked together. How they had kept their heads. His nerves steadied and he trained his gun at the door, shot both men as they burst out, one in the side, one in the shoulder. They tumbled to the ground, shouting, in pain. The cop stumbled and rolled to his car, spun around in the gravel, and roared down the driveway. Jared and Ben backed away from the window, trying to find cover. The bird in the pen screeched and flapped, kicked at the fence, talons raking against the wire. Claude and Ben's dad came out of the house crouched, low. Jared shot and missed, shot and missed. He and Ben made a break for the nearest remaining car but weren't fast enough. Two bullets burned the air near Jared's head and then he was hit, in the arm. The pain of it knocked him down. Ben was down too, clutching his leg.

Claude laughed, a tinny cackle.

"Your boy's a worse shot than you are," he said to Ben's dad. He chuckled again and began to stride toward the boys, gun out.

Claude was going to finish them, Jared thought. Two bullets for each.

He saw a shadow flit across the yard. Ben's mom. She'd escaped the house. Now she was at the door to the cassowary's pen, and she opened it. Edna unleashed a string of metallic cries and seemed to float across the yard, then reared up on its legs. It was much taller than Jared would have imagined, and it was kicking at Claude, kicking at him with its talons. Claude screamed, a keening pitch like a teakettle. His shirt burst open, and some of Claude jumped out of the wound, spilled down his front and hung there for a split second until Claude did a half-spin and fell over.

Ben's dad fired at Edna and missed. The cassowary hissed and lunged toward him, traced two red lines across him. Ben's dad fired again, again, and buried bullets in the bird's body. It fell, squawking, and Ben's dad walked up to it and blew its skull open. Then he dropped down next to it and leaned into its fluffy black feathers. He gasped for air, as though drowning. A couple more men came out of the house.

"Claude's dead," Jared heard Ben's mom say.

The lights came on in the yard. She was there, a shotgun leveled at the men, something flush in her eyes Jared had never seen before. The men at the house flinched.

Ben's dad spat blood. "Oh, Penny," he said. "Our little operation here is just the beginning. What we're part of is bigger than the cops, bigger than this town. You're dead for what you've done, do you hear me? You and the whole family." He shot a glance at Jared and Ben. "Both families."

Ben's mom listened, and sadness crept into her face. She shook her head.

"Okay," she said. She planted the barrel in Ben's dad's chest.

"Wait—" he said.

She pulled the trigger.

The men at the house were gone, run off. Fleeing, Jared thought. Or getting more men, more guns. From the road, through the trees, they all heard distant sirens.

"Which cops are they?" Ben's mom said. She sounded tired. "The ones who tried to save me or the ones who tried to kill me?"

"You can't be here when they arrive," Ben said.

"Neither can you," his mom said. "Either of you."

"My dad," Jared said. "I don't know if he made it."

"I'll go find out," Ben's mom said. "But you have to get out of here, as far as you can."

"How will I know if my dad's okay?" Jared said.

"We'll find you when it's over," Ben's mom said. "Just don't come back." Her eyes welled with tears.

The lines of the state highway in the headlights, heading south, toward the city. Ben behind the wheel.

"Where are we going?" Ben said.

"I don't know," Jared said.

"What are we going to do?"

"I don't know."

They had to still be in shock, Jared thought, both of them. The things they'd seen, done, had done to them. It was all going to fall on them soon. But not yet. Now, his thoughts and feelings were as clear as they'd ever been.

"It's going to be okay," Jared said, "as long as I'm with you."

Ben kept his eyes on the road.

Now Jared was shaking. He was so afraid. But it was time. Long past time.

"Tell me you know how I feel about you," he said. "Tell me you've always known."

Ben's right hand left the steering wheel, floated downward and landed on Jared's thigh. Traveled upward until it found one of Jared's hands. Then Ben's fingers entwined with his, gave a little squeeze, and stayed there.

"I won't let go if you won't," Ben said.

They kept driving, toward the city.

AUTHOR'S NOTE: This story is a tough-love letter to the place where I grew up, decades ago now, and a real love letter to some of the people I knew then. The Depeche Mode song "Never Let Me Down Again" puts me right back there. I can remember where I was when I first heard it, as an early teen without the words or the smarts to come close to figuring out what he was. This song (and many others like it) felt like a portal opening, to knowing more about the world and who I was in it.

Ithaca, New York, was (and still is) a university town with a ton of hippies in it (then; now not as much), but underneath that was a gritty upstate New York town, much more connected to the much poorer rural towns in the surrounding hills than to the almost-literal ivory towers above them. There were (and still are) people who lived very precarious lives, just out of sight. But they were there, and too many of them slipped through the cracks. When they were kids, alternative music was part of their lifeline. I wanted to give people a chance to see them before they left.

SACRED MEATS

BY JEFFREY FORD

Two months prior Haffner Leeds began telling his wife, Ginny, about some streaming show he was watching. He spoke about it with the glee of a child on a carousel. She found the whole thing tedious beyond measure. Neither could she follow the plot as he told it. There were vampires and witches, and some kind of delivery service where sacred meats were ferried surreptitiously around a midwestern city by night in vans with the word OGOO in Day-Glo orange along the passenger side door.

She never got far listening to him before her attention drifted to what a loser he was, her wasted life, and then off into a daydream of a vacation in the Caribbean. Bits and pieces of his verbiage surfaced later in the day or days to come. They inadvertently bubbled up while she was at work, at the grocery, drinking devoutly every night out on the porch while he watched television. She recalled a woman crying into an empty baby carriage, an abandoned train station, a sacred meats barbecue attended by upper echelon religious figures, and something described as "dirty but sturdy."

Ginny sincerely thought Haffner was trying to give her brain damage or bore her to death. Leaving was no option because the house was in his name, and she didn't want to lose it in a divorce. At night, she was sleepless; during the day, she dreaded going home and sitting down to dinner only to listen to another summary of the show's latest installment. Ginny told her work friend Pam the entire sad saga of Haffner's metamorphosis from husband to nattering menace. "He was a fart-stopper long before this thing with the TV show, but now, Jesus, I just want to kick him."

Pam could only shrug and say, "What show is this? I never heard of it. And no show has new episodes every night of the week."

The light finally went on in Ginny's head. That night, in the kitchen, as she cut into her pork chop, Haffner said, "You'll never guess what happened in the show." Before he could launch into it, she said, "Wait." She held up her hand. "What's the name of this show? *Ogoo?*"

"No," he said. "That's the delivery service. The show is called *The Sadness of Sacred Meats.*" She wrote the title down on her phone as he, with jolly derangement, waylaid her with the latest. That night, after he finally went to sleep, she looked up the title he'd given her on the internet. Finding nothing after a half-hour on Google, she decided it was time to buy a gun.

The next morning, the light of day did nothing to dissuade her from her plan to arm herself. She bought a cheap .45 and kept it in the oven, where she knew he'd never find it. He didn't cook or clean or for that matter do anything else in the kitchen but drive her toward insanity.

Two nights after her purchase, when he said, "Wait till you hear this," she got up, walked to the stove, opened the oven, withdrew the gun from the top shelf, turned and squeezed off five shots in slow but steady succession. It was the first time she'd shot any kind of gun, and she was thrilled with how accurate her aim was. Every bullet that went through him was an angel getting its wings as far as she was concerned. The second one hit him right between the eyes, and she knew it was the kill shot, but given what he'd put her through, she calculated the damage and holistically came up with the fact that she needed to shoot him three more times.

His body jerked as the life fled him. He belched, he farted, then bled all over the place. She shook her head in disgust as gore pooled on the kitchen floor. The last she really looked at him, he was slumped over the table, his eyes wide open and crossed, his lips pursed in an O, like he was blowing her a kiss.

"Fuck you," she yelled at him. It didn't matter, though. He was the saddest sacred meat she'd ever seen, and she wouldn't be brought low by him. She rolled Haffner up in the braided rug from the living room. Grunting and cursing, she dragged him down the hall from the kitchen to the garage and stuffed him into the way-back part of his Honda CRV. "Get in there, you dumb fuck," was her parting salutation. Before she started the car and hit the garage door opener, she knew where she was going to dump him.

Out beyond Lake Road there was a defunct landfill. The place had been active for decades—ten acres of farm meadow, bounded by a tall hill, where local residents could leave non-organic waste: broken washing machines, cars, the contents of garages and attics and cellars. It had been bequeathed to the town of Threadwell by a local landowner, Trey Jake, and had been known as Jake's Dump forever. His plan was to give folks a place to dump their stuff and thus free the town from the eyesore of front lawn junk.

Some time back in the '90s, after Mr. Jake was long gone, dry cleaning companies, gas stations, manufacturing shops, and fast food places took to dumping their chemicals and oils and food trash overflow from their businesses. When the county government pulled the plug on the dump, it was a biohazard full of rats and who-knew-what. The grounds were poison, and there'd been a number of instances where local dogs had been found there eaten down to their skeletons.

Still, this didn't stop Ginny. She saw Jake's Dump as the perfect spot to unload Haffner. She drove to the south side of the place, killing her lights as she approached the old entrance and dirt road that led up and up to the peak of the enormous trash mound some locals called the Matterhorn. Once at the summit, the ground flattened out and she drove carefully to the edge of a precipice that overlooked the long drop from the heights of appliances, rusted busted station wagons, and construction debris down two hundred feet into the hills and fields of waste. The full moon complied and gave her a stunning view.

Ginny, a literature student in college, remembered Alexander Pope's dark side of the moon, where all lost things reside. "Fitting," she mumbled to herself, momentarily contemplating the years she lost to living with her idiot husband. Opening the back of the CRV, she hauled the corpse—rolled up in the rug like a giant death burrito—out onto the ground. It took all her remaining strength to get him to the edge of the cliff. She lined him up, and just before kicking him over the edge, she recalled the unkindest cut of all in their dreary marriage: Haffner's dick was perpetually bent at a right angle.

He careened down the slope, the rug unfurling and releasing his corpse to bang, slam, and dislodge wreckage in its descent. This action caused an avalanche of sorts, and his body was handily buried by it. After everything quieted back down, just beneath the night breeze, she heard the rats stirring and ran back to the CRV. For the rest of the night into daylight, she cleaned blood off the kitchen floor, smiling like a child on a carousel.

The rats started on Haffner before the sun came up. A threesome of rodents as big as chihuahuas tore through his belly fat, while a pair of smaller specimens tore off his eyelids to get the jelly of his green eyes. These two didn't stop there, though; they forged forward, squeezing through the orbital sockets and burrowing deep into the gray cake of the brain. At the crack of dawn, one of them reached the pineal gland and took a bite. It popped like a grape in the creature's jaws and flooded its senses with sweet nectar. The rats didn't notice, as their mission was sacred meat and nothing else, but when the pea-sized organ burst, it released a stream of mist which filtered up through the refuse covering Haffner like the trail of smoke from a cigarette, still lit, abandoned in an ashtray.

AUTHOR'S NOTE: I recently took a trip down memory lane and cued up the Black Flag video from 1981, "TV Party." If you're familiar with it, you'll recall Henry Rollins and the gang busting into a dark room holding only a couch, a TV, and a refrigerator with beer (or as the song tells it, "brews"). Chaos ensues, discordant metal, brews being spilled all over. While watching the video I had a thought of this taking place in our living room and my wife, Lynn, walking in and seeing the pandemonium. I knew right off the bat she wouldn't go for it and held onto the musically inflected daydream since for once it wasn't me fucking up. She stood there, hands on hips, acrimonious expression, and then I saw her leave. A couple of bars later into the song, she returned, holding a Sig Sauer P 226 X5 Legion. "Shut the fuck up," she yelled, and opened fire. She took no prisoners. That scenario was in my mind then. A married woman whose husband, a real schlub, can't think of anything to do but watch TV. From that image and scenario my mind took off in some decidedly strange directions and eventually gave birth to "Sacred Meats."

NEVER FORGET

BY ELENA MAULI SHAPIRO

The last thing Cornell remembers is counting down from ten.

Ten

His shaking from terror and pain botched the first attempt at putting the IV into the back of his hand. The veins collapsed, blue and bursting. There is still dried blood on the medical tape.

Nine

The new thing being pumped into his veins burns at first, but then it is cold like the first trickle of water from thawing pipes.

Eight

He is convinced he will not manage to go to sleep. He is an insomniac. They will cut him open, his eyes still staring and unblinking …

There is a roar—he never makes it to seven.

Under a radiant blue sky, human bodies hit the pavement, splashing into a gruesome red mist. Human bodies burn up inside, turning into a fine white ash. In the ash: pulverized metal, concrete, glass, file cabinets, computers, pictures of the family propped up on a desk. The clicking of keyboards, conversations by the water cooler, our illusion of safety—a fine white ash, carried by the wind. In the street, everyone is covered in that ash, breathing it in. Human bodies covered in human bodies. Human bodies breathing in human bodies.

The roar is back. He has a sense that he was gone for a while but he has no idea how long. The pain is what sears him into consciousness. He wants to call out but he can't move any part of his body. In the darkness he can only formulate one word—*Helen*. Inside he screams the name over and over, but his leaden body refuses him so much as a twitch. Goddamn, he must be dead, and this is Hell. Hell is this terrible pain, being trapped in an infinite loop of screaming his wife's name.

Finally, he gets the name out in a piteous little croak. *Helen*, he calls. Once. He waits. He still can't open his eyes. Twice. *Helen*.

You're in the ICU, a voice says. *You're doing well.*

He responds with a groan, and the nurse has the sense to blast a dose of morphine into his IV drip. He can still hear the roar. It sounds like rushing air, like falling from a great height at tremendous speed. He goes to sleep to that sound, and of course he has the dream again. He's had that dream every month for the past twenty years, and obviously his unconscious response to the wind tunnel roar in his ears is to put on that damn dream again, because that sound is what he imagines they must have heard during those final ten seconds.

He dreams about the jumpers. About their bodies tumbling down, so small against the enormity of what is behind them. Those towers were so huge. Those towers are no longer buildings; instead they are an image, forever inscribed into history as some kind of allegory. In the dream the jumpers fall forever. They never hit the ground.

Something was definitely happening, but he didn't know what. The floor was shaking as if there was an enormous engine rumbling immediately beneath it. Actually, the tremor was in the walls too, as if energy was radiating through the metal skeleton of the building. But the building was so massive, so strong, this didn't feel overly threatening. He was trading hot and he wasn't about to get up just for that. He only looked up when the guy at the terminal next to him said *what the fuck*.

What?

I'm pretty sure a piece of the building just whizzed by the window.

Come on, seriously?

Maybe we should get out?

If shit is really falling from the sky, I'm thinking we're safer in here than outside.

This was his eminently sage reasoning. Still, he was rattled enough that his eyes didn't lock back onto his terminal. He looked out of the window, an enormous pane of glass that went all the way up to the ceiling. Was there a weird smell in the air? A faint stench like hot metal, like when something is very wrong with your car?

There it was—holy shit—something falling outside. It flew by for just a split second, so that he was convinced he hadn't seen what he had seen. What he had seen simply wasn't possible.

Was that a fuckin' … person? The guy next to him said.

It was a woman. She had on a pantsuit, blue. With a white shirt. He'd seen her face. She wasn't screaming, didn't even look terrified exactly. Instead, she looked downright surprised, as if she too couldn't believe what was happening. It was her eyes, widened in shock, that convinced him that perhaps time was of the essence. Perhaps it wouldn't be such a bad idea to begin working his way out of the building.

He is so sick that when he turns his head the world spins, and he pukes on himself. He doesn't have the energy required to push the call button for the nurse. It's only then, lying there smelling the yellow smell of his thin vomit, that he remembers that Helen is no longer his wife, but his ex-wife. He'd forgotten, when he was in Hell. In Hell there is no time and every hurt ever done to you over your entire life is as fresh as the moment it happened. In Hell she is still leaving him.

When the nurse comes, she scolds him for his ruined hospital gown. While she's at it, she pushes the button to fold his bed upright—just slightly. Pain lacerates his guts. He gasps and tears fill his eyes.

"You have to try and sit up, sir, or fluid will gather into your lungs and you will get pneumonia. You have to try and move around as soon as possible," the nurse says.

Get pneumonia? Well shit, he should try not to do that now that the surgery was successful, now that the tumor is gone. It would be stupid to die of pneumonia after all that. The slight motion of his body makes him reel, and he spews again, but this time the nurse catches the dribble in a plastic receptacle shaped like a kidney bean.

You're a puker, the nurse observes. *Sometimes the general anesthesia does that to some people. Next time you should ask them to put nausea medication in the IV.*

Why don't they always put nausea medication in the IV? He would like to ask this question, but his throat burns awfully from the acid in his vomit. *Why does my throat hurt so much?* This question he manages to ask the nurse.

Probably from when they put the breathing tube down your trachea during surgery.

Jesus Christ. That woman has the bedside manner of rush hour traffic. He's not going to ask her why his asshole hurts too; he doesn't need to know. Knowing doesn't make it hurt any less, does it?

She left him because of money, of course. Because he didn't have any. He was a doctoral student and that's what student life was like. Student life was living in a shit neighborhood in a dump of an apartment where the pipes froze when the heat went out in winter. Then when the heat came back on, the pipes exploded. Frigid fucking water all over the floor. Their three-year-old daughter ran laughing and splashing around the place, impervious to the fact that she was wearing a parka and snow boots inside. Helen didn't find it nearly so amusing. He could see the tightness around her mouth, could see that she was two seconds away from asking why they had to raise their daughter in this shit. She didn't. She didn't say anything. She didn't leave then, though could he really blame her if after that she packed herself and the kid off to her parents' house, which was not flooded, nor was it sub-freezing.

He was in the doctoral program when she got pregnant. She knew what she was getting into, didn't she? Maybe she didn't realize it would take him years to finish. What was his attraction to physics anyway? Was he really a born scientist? He asked himself this. Maybe it was because it was hard enough to be interesting. It was difficult to stay interested when you were too intelligent, sometimes. His little daughter was adorable but she bored the shit out of him. Not that he would have ever said such a thing aloud. But sometimes he swore Helen could hear him thinking it.

He is only half-conscious when he pulls the tiny transparent tubes from his nostrils, the ones that are blowing oxygen-rich air into his lungs. The rushing sound of the air hisses unpleasantly through the vapor of his sedation, and he hates the feel of the tubes. His hand, operating of its own will, wrenches the tubes out of his face like delicate roots being yanked from the earth. The rushing air is blessedly gone. Everything is quiet and his breathing becomes smaller smaller smaller smaller …

Don't take these out! Don't ever take these out! the nurse scolds as she puts the tubes back into him. She speaks to him as if he is a small child or a senile old man—but he's in the prime of his life! Well, except for the cancer. Did he get the cancer from the fine white ash that covered everything on that day twenty years ago? Wouldn't that be poetic: he got the cancer because of the money. Because he had to go make some money.

The tubes are back in his nose, pulling him out of a choppy unconsciousness. He opens his eyes a little. If only he weren't here, maybe he could be happy.

Do you have a book I could borrow? he asks the nurse so quietly that she hardly hears him.

What's the matter, don't you watch television?

For fuck's sake. If he had the energy to feel disdain for her, he would revel in it. But instead, his dim awareness registers that his question is just as stupid as hers. What the fuck is he thinking, asking for a book to read? As if his blurry eyes could stay riveted to a page for as much as one sentence. His brain is roadkill like the rest of his body. As soon as he thinks the word *roadkill*, his brain, as if to protest that it is still functioning, pulls up an unbidden memory. His daughter, with him in the car, points at a smashed animal on the shoulder of the highway. *Daddy, what's that?*

Looks like a cat, he says, without thinking.

Fuck, why did he have to go and say that—he should have deflected the question, or thought up an animal that wasn't her favorite. Because now her eyes are filling with tears, and here he is thinking, like an asshole, that he should have pushed Helen harder to get that abortion. Because here is this little person, hurting, and it's his fault. Every hurt that will ever claw her heart is his fault: he brought her here.

In the end it wasn't the broken appliances or the ramen for dinner or the cockroaches that did it. It was the fucking dogs. Well, at first it was the tap in the kitchenette. It was belching brown water; it was disgusting. They weren't about to cook or clean anything with that, so he called the super. The guy was straight out of central casting, with his ass crack showing from the top of his jeans when he bent over to get into the cabinet under the sink. While he was on all fours rooting around under there, a heart-rending, high-pitched whine came from outside. They'd heard that sound nearly every day since they'd moved in. It sounded like dogs but they couldn't be sure what sort of animal it was. It sounded like suffering, that was for sure.

What is that? What the hell is that? Helen asked, exasperated.

That? The super's voice echoed from beneath the sink. *That there is the guy on the corner. He raises fighting dogs from puppies. He beats them so that they grow up mean.*

The guy had said it as if it was no big deal, it was just part of daily life in the neighborhood. The look on Helen's face was something else, something besides the usual stress. There was hurt in there for sure, but it also looked like a dawning realization. That look triggered enlightenment in Cornell. He knew right then their days together were numbered, it wouldn't be long before she would leave him. As a matter of fact, it didn't take two weeks.

The speed with which she hooked up with some trust fund asshole after she dumped him and took the kid with her was dizzying. She must have had the guy in the wings for a while, maybe they were even fucking while she was still married. Maybe it wasn't the dogs after all, maybe she just had to secure an escape hatch before she made her exit. In that guy she found what she wanted. Cornell had done her a favor, getting a graduate degree at an Ivy League university, because trust fund assholes were rather thick on the ground there. So, in a way he'd given her what she wanted after all, by putting her in the orbit of his replacement.

He could have moped around his dump of an apartment, spun his wheels frantically on his stalled thesis, but instead he said *fuck this place*, and went to Wall Street. They always wanted Ivy League science guys there, guys who knew how to think and were good with numbers. His first job was something called "quantitative analyst." People shortened that descriptor to *quant*, which always made him think of his professors saying *quantum*. Latin for *how much*.

It's a new day, and the nurse comes to yank the catheter out of his penis—she says, *this might hurt for a second.*

When a member of the medical profession says *hurt*, it's going to be terrible, he knows. Usually, they say *sting* or *pinch* or *you might feel a little bit of pressure.* If they actually say *hurt*, what new level of Hell is this? He barely has time to register this new development before everything is white with pain. Jesus Christ, aren't they supposed to count to three before they do something like that?

Heaven—heaven is the joy he feels once he realizes that the tube is gone from his poor brutalized dick. Heaven is short-lived, because the nurse immediately says, *you have to pee today or I will have to put the catheter back in.*

If he could, he would probably cry, but all he has left is the dull animal determination to piss—*piss, damn you!* The world has been reduced to the increasing, balloonish pressure in his bladder. The tiny plastic bedpan is unsteady beneath his tortured back. He heaves and squeezes for hours, but he is too swollen. For fuck's sake. The first time they put the catheter in, he was under general anesthesia. He really, really doesn't want to be awake to have that thing rammed up him again. He wishes he could rip all the tubes out of himself and run screaming through the hospital. But he'd probably puke and pass out if he even tried to sit up too fast.

Finally, his desperate efforts push a few yellow droplets out of him. Angels sing.

The few yellow droplets have sapped his strength utterly, even though the pressure in his bladder still throbs through his every sinew. How is he so full of piss his teeth hurt? He's only been allowed ice chips to drink, and his mouth is parched. He doesn't factor in all of the fluids from the IV as he fades out of consciousness, overcome by exhaustion and drugs and the relief of not having to get the tube clipped back into his genitals. The bedpan is still under him. It tips over as his body relaxes. When the nurse comes, he is passed out with his own piss all over himself. But it's all right: he is happy. He feels a real sense of accomplishment.

The news coverage of the cataclysm enervated him. On Fox News they were obsessed with this one woman who pulled down her skirt before she jumped. They harped on and on about how in her last dire moments, she still wanted to die with a little bit of decency. They loved this bit as if it was poetry to them—as if decency even existed when that lady would explode like a watermelon when she hit the pavement. As if it mattered whether the cameras caught a glimpse of her underpants when she would shortly be a shower of blood and guts. It was ghoulish, was what it was. Let those bastards die in peace—why do you have to take a picture, and make something of their every gesture, as if in that hour of utmost desperation any gesture could mean anything? For fuck's sake, there were restaurant workers jumping while gripping tablecloths in their hands thinking maybe they would act as parachutes and save them. As if the wind of the fall wouldn't rip those cloths right out of their hands. But no, they probably weren't thinking the tablecloths would save them. They weren't thinking at all, only feeling, like a tortured body in a hospital bed.

Those dipshits on TV also said that all the shoes on Washington Street had been abandoned there by running people. The high heels that women wore, possibly—but why were there so many men's shoes? The newscasters didn't know shit. What's the first thing you do when you relax into a long flight? You take your shoes off and you tuck them under the seat in front of you. Those shoes weren't left behind from the people in the building. He talked back at the TV: *these shoes came down from the planes, you assholes.*

The thing that really made him laugh was when those Ken Doll newscasters called the terrorists cowards for what they did. As if it didn't take huge clanging brass balls to fly a fucking airplane into a fucking building, ensuring they would be immediately incinerated. Come on. They lacked for morals, sure, but you couldn't very well pretend these fuckers lacked for courage. In the whole process, from learning to fly without learning to land, to boarding that plane, to staying on course straight into the tower—they didn't swerve once. You had to hand it to them. What they pulled off was fucking tremendous—it was more than the crime of the century: it was a crime that turned the clock from one century to another.

He should call somebody. He should call Helen. Everything moved so fast after the diagnosis that he didn't even have the time to compose how to tell her before they cut him open. What would he say now? He didn't have it in him to put a speech together. He'd have to tell her he was calling from a hospital, and then how he got to that hospital. The drugs would make him slur every word. She wouldn't understand and he would have to repeat himself. Plus, there is the possibility that the trust fund asshole she married would pick up the phone.

It's been enough years that he's learned to be civilized to Helen and her new family, but in the morass of his pain and vulnerability, he is suddenly as raw as he was when he first found out his little girl was calling the trust fund asshole *Daddy*. As if "father" was a title that could be shared. Fuck that guy, and fuck the money he dropped into straight from the womb. Fuck Helen, for calling Cornell a criminal because some of his market manipulation schemes weren't strictly completely legal. As if the trust fund, wife-stealing asshole was somehow morally superior for having the luck to have ancestors who were the ones to do heinous things for money. What was the saying? Behind every great fortune is a great crime? Nothing as spectacular as pulling a pin that would explode a civilization, but still. His blood is tainted, if not his soul.

The nurse comes in. She says: "I brought you something to read."

She puts an old copy of *Reader's Digest* on his bedstand.

Reader's Digest. For fuck's sake. A greater insult than all the tubes in the world shoved in all the holes in his body. And yet he wouldn't even be able to read *that* without falling asleep or puking from the letters dancing a whirligig on the page. Fuck. All he wants now is another ice chip a warm blanket more drugs a few more drops in the bedpan and *that is all.*

There was that crazy interval with one tower up, one tower down. He'd run from the first tower collapsing like he'd never run in his life. When he saw the enormous blast of black smoke coming at him, he was convinced that when it reached him he was going to die. By the time the second tower came down, he was in the sports bar where he sometimes had a cheeseburger on the way home from work, watching it all unfold on a big-screen television. You could tell among the huddled people riveted to the screen which ones had just escaped from there, covered as they were by fine white ash, still thrumming with adrenaline from their frantic run to safety.

For a bit, he had the crazy thought that somehow it would be okay, as long as that second tower stayed up. If the one tower stayed up then it would be alright, this wouldn't be the end of something. It was *something* to watch his last hope come down on a television screen while he was just a few blocks away. From the billowing blast, uncountable sheets of paper went flying—so many sheets of paper fluttering everywhere, and settling in the undistinguished rubble like fall leaves. He could see some of those papers wafting down the street through the window. How far would he have to get before the wreckage wouldn't follow him?

Cornell couldn't help but notice how neatly that tower telescoped while the news showed the footage over and over. There was no wrenching halfway up the metal skeleton, no toppling of a broken giant. Instead, the building almost dissolved into that uncanny white ash. He had to admit, it was beautiful engineering that allowed such a perfect collapse. The graceful destruction written into the act of construction, all those years ago.

The nurse gives him a translucent blue plastic device with a segmented white pipe connected to it. He is supposed to breathe from his mouth as hard as he can into this pipe, to make a white plastic marble rise inside the shaft of the device, all the way to the top. People in terrible pain who are stuck on their backs, people on heavy drugs—people who've just had extensive surgery, for instance—breathe shallowly. They risk accumulation of fluid in their lungs, and this weird toy is supposed to motivate them to breathe deeply.

He exhales as hard as he can into the pipe. It hurts. He gasps, sucks air weakly back into his lungs, though he has only made the marble rise halfway.

To piss, to breathe—to bother contracting his heart to push the blood along his circulatory system, his sluggish pipes—all of this is such fucking *effort*. Every process in his body down to his pulse is a desperate exertion. He feels his failures with searing awareness: he is a failure of musculature of organs of blood, indeed a failure on a molecular level. Atomic, even.

For some reason this strikes him as funny. Failure in all the systems that sustain his botched life is funny. He laughs softly into the blue plastic breathing device. The unsteady air from his quiet laughter makes the little white marble quiver. He pulls his parched mouth away from the hospital toy and lets the marble fall.

It was on his long walk home that he came upon it. It stopped him dead in his tracks, that hand. He stood there looking down at it for quite some time. How did it get all the way over here? How unfathomable the force that hurled this guy's severed hand all that distance. Nobody else stopped to look at it; it was a normal horror for that day. All those weary people wanted to get home already and didn't have time for this. But he did. The forearm past the wrist was a grisly hash of torn red meat, but the hand was whole. All five fingers were there. It rested on the pavement palm down. It looked oddly calm and expectant. It was still wearing a wedding ring. In a flash he saw himself pick up the hand, work the gold circlet off the dead finger. What was wrong with him? He would never do a thing like that.

For some reason it occurred to him that the hand couldn't be from a jumper. It wouldn't have made it so far from the site. The jumpers—not soon would he forget that sickening heavy thud their bodies made when they reached the ground.

He'd seen a couple of them hit. And yet even now he couldn't remember what that looked like. He could visualize the blood splatter and the pieces of flesh in the aftermath, but his mind refused to pull up the actual impact, the sliver of a moment when a person turned from a body into debris. He would never be able to remember what the moment looked like, though he would never forget how it sounded.

All the way across the bridge, he ruminated about what must have flashed through their heads when they flew off the building. Some of them jumped for sure, but some of them must have been pushed by the desperate throng behind them trying to get a gasp of air at the shattered windows. Ten seconds from the top of the tower to the pavement, that was how long the newscaster said it took to fall. Can you imagine? That's long enough to think, as the howling air rushes past your ears. That's long enough to count, like a hospital patient going under general anesthesia for surgery.

three

This is the last choice you will ever make: whether to burn or fly.

two

It is Tuesday and as long as I am alive you will keep falling forever.

one

AUTHOR'S NOTE: Soundgarden's "Fourth of July" starts with a low, ominous rumble like distant warfare. It gets darker from there, with Armageddon falling from the sky, its sound carried on the wind. It was the song that popped immediately to mind when I was asked to write a story for this anthology. The setting for the story grew organically from the lyrics: it's the apocalypse; it comes from the sky; it is deeply American. It has to be September 11th, 2001—the spectacular crime witnessed by an entire thunderstruck nation on television, the opening shot of the twenty-first century.

The chore wheel was a doomsday clock, ticking toward toilet week. Scorch had made it from a pizza box, with tasks Sharpied onto the cardboard square in back: dishes, dinner, trash, sweep 'n' mop, community outreach, and at the bottom, the dreaded toilets. They cut the box top into a circle, wrote our names around the perimeter, and nailed the thing to the kitchen wall, security deposit be damned.

I rented a three-bedroom house with a seven-person anarchist collective. Every room without a sink housed up to three people. If you shared a room, you shared a chore. Punks handed dishes through rising soap suds or swept up dust tornadoes while wearing bandito-style rags over their mouths and noses. I had my own room.

The collective held meetings in the kitchen. I'd be making lunch and rolling my eyes at their talk of armed uprisings and seizing the means of production, as if they were revolutionaries and not just a bunch of flakes in a depressed college town. But they were the flakes I rented from and, when everyone was home, I imagined us in one of those clear toy ant farms, bustling around or cozy in our little burrows. I was warm and, for once, I didn't think I was going to explode.

Our ant farm had some middle-aged construction workers on one side and the landlord's drug-front-ass pharmacy on the other. The pharmacy shared a parking lot with a church; park once, get saved twice.

I lived there for three months, or two full rotations of the chore wheel, before we got evicted. The working men next door set up a TV on a card table behind their house and would sit in plastic chairs pounding beers and watching racecars drive in a circle. One of the kind folks from the church complained, and we woke up to a six-foot-tall wooden fence blocking the backs of our houses. When I left for work the next morning, I clocked tall blue graffiti: SLUMLORD spray-painted across the fence. Imagine being told you're an eyesore. Imagine having rent due that week.

Wells, who got a kick out of sneering in the landlord's florid redneck face, came back from paying up with the news that we had a month to get out. "Of course, he told me *after* I forked over the cash," Wells said.

He shared a room with his partner Lorn, a knee-high pile of grease-caked bike parts, and a poster of The Clash standing on an empty highway and menacing the camera with a wooden baseball bat. He was a loudmouth who I'd heard shout, "This is *my* anarchist collective" during meetings, so of course he vowed revenge upon the landlord. The plan? Raise money to buy the house. Yeah, that'll show him.

You'd think that the rules would loosen up after that, but, as Tim put it: "We're self-governing, and some capitalist running dog landlord can't topple that." So, the chore wheel remained, even though cleaning the house felt like forcing veggies on a death-row inmate. I sorta did my chores. I couldn't focus. The ant farm had been shaken, and the ticking in my mind had emerged, louder and faster.

When I was nine, my mom took me to a Halloween fair in a church parking lot. I was on the carousel when I caught sight of the main attraction: a haunted house of mirrors anchoring the far side of the fair. Its facade was painted to be a dilapidated brick rowhouse, rectangular, with a leaning roof spilling tiles, light-up eyes blinking behind a top-floor window, and fangs hanging from the front doorframe. As the carousel spun past, I heard snatches of screaming keyboards and howling ghosts, maniacal laughs and creaking doors, echoing footsteps. I watched for as long as I could, craning my neck as my horse curved away, and by the time the carousel groaned to a halt, I knew I'd outgrown kiddie rides.

I hopped off my horse and bolted into the house of mirrors while the ticket-taker was flirting with some teen girls in hacked-up black Slipknot T-shirts. I bumped wall-to-wall, shoulder-checking my reflection, elbowing carnies in vampire and mummy costumes out of my way, until I got tired and hopelessly lost in a dead end the size of a toilet stall. As I whirled around, I saw endless reflections of myself, a kid with bedhead in the evening, and shorts I'd insisted on wearing despite the fall chill. My insides grew desolate. I crumpled against a mirror and slid to the floor, then my wails mixed with the creepy music, until a flashlight beam shot across every wall and a lady dressed as the Bride of Frankenstein took my hand and led me out to my mom, who was waiting in the house's shadow, face knit with terror, clutching the red snow cone she'd bought while I was on the carousel.

Mom pulled my head to her chest and squeezed my scalp with her fingertips. I should have been relieved, but I was embarrassed and as she led me away, I stared down the haunted house. The CD horror soundtrack skipped to a stop and in the new quiet, I heard a faint ticking, like a clock between my ears. Then I knew I had to go back, find my way through the house, and make it mine. But the church got a new pastor who called Halloween the devil's work, and the next year's fair just had apple-bobbing and a hay bale maze with stuff against premarital sex at the dead ends—a hairy-palmed devil statue wielding a box of condoms and a *Playboy*, a doctor gouging a bloody zombie girl's crotch with a wire hanger. I never went back to the festival and fought my mom until I didn't have to go to church either. The ticking stayed, and once I got used to it, I accepted it as a marker of my life easing by, moment by moment.

A decade later, I was mid-shift at the health food store, grazing the bulk bins and reading on my phone about the mysterious disappearance of a local indie musician/produce truck driver, when my uptight Deadhead manager walked by. While looking busy, I noticed a HOUSEMATE WANTED sign on the community bulletin board and wheeled my mop bucket closer to give it a read. The fine print just had a phone number and the slogan "Join us in fighting for the greater good." With a mouth full of date clusters, I grabbed the flyer and ducked into the break room to call.

I spoke to Scorch and asked to see the room, but they invited me for an interview instead. That should have been a red flag, but I was sleeping in a coworker's living room and he'd offered me shampoo because I was leaving a cloud of oil on his couch, so I knew my days there were numbered. When I asked who'd moved out and why, Scorch must have not heard because they were quiet for a second, then said they liked my vibrational energy and thought I could channel it into the collective. That was a little woo-woo for my taste, but I didn't ask any follow-up questions. The promise of having a door was just too alluring.

On the day of my interview, my bike lock clicked shut and the ticking got louder, distracting me for a moment before I registered what I was seeing: a leaning brick rowhouse, with dead black eyes for windows and an evil mouth front door. I couldn't look away.

After the eviction, the ticking sped up and made it impossible to focus on anything else. Sometimes a worry would creep in, about having to move back to my mom's or track down that old coworker and beg for their couch. But then another tick would come and my mind would go blank for a delicious half-second. I could still cook, especially my signature dish: Sloppy Joe mix with peppers, onions, and pinto beans poured over ziti. I'd chow down in my room, perched on the leaky beanbag chair I'd found outside the dorms, and play a punk record loud enough to drown out the ticking. I like the stuff you can shout along with: Limp Wrist, Swiz, a little Big Joanie when I'm sad. Tim was on toilets, which he cleaned with plastic grocery bags over his hands. I was considering dipping out before the end of the month and skipping my turn, but I wasn't sure where to run.

My chore that week was Community Outreach. I'd usually bike around for twenty minutes, nodding at people on their porches, before drinking a beer with the neighbors in the spirit of class solidarity. They'd ask me how those crazy, bomb-throwing roommates of mine were doing and I'd say I wished they were that cool.

I would have loved doing those things if the chore wheel didn't turn them into homework, so it was hard to get motivated. I'd get up, last bite of food still in my mouth, grab my bike from the pile of bikes by the front door, and pedal off, still chewing. Somehow, I'd always forget the plate.

Problem was, I'm an introvert, so Community Outreach would tire me out. I'd crash right away afterward, then rush to work, come home hungry, and bring a new plate up. Life kept passing by and, next I knew, there weren't any plates left in the cabinets. I had to improvise. Hot pan of food behind me, I scanned the dusty pantry staples and misshapen cookware that filled our kitchen shelves until my eyes landed on the chore wheel. It was a circle. With a hand planted on the wall, I yanked the nameplate free and splashed my food onto it.

Wells was on dishes that week. I was on my beanbag. *...And Out Come the Wolves* was on my turntable. People say that it's Rancid's sell-out album, but if writing a poetic rock record where every song hits like the first sip of beer on an abandoned rooftop is selling out then every single band should sell out as hard as they can.

Wells knocked on my door but Rancid and the ticking were loud enough for me to pretend not to hear. After the song died down, he swung the door open and peeked in. My mouth was stuffed with food, so I cocked an eyebrow at him like *What?* and he said, "Hey, we're outta dishes downstairs. Do you have any up here?"

I watched his eyes trace a path from the stack of mismatched thrift store plates next to me, to the soggy makeshift plate warming my lap, where tangy red sauce and parallelograms of bell pepper mingled with the permanent marker names. Then I swallowed, burped under my breath, smirked, and said, "Nah."

The next song kicked in and Wells stood there frozen for a second, muttered something about it being high time I pitched in, then gently closed my door and walked away, Doc Marten footsteps just off-rhythm from the music. The ticking got louder and I took a deep breath then tilted the plate to my mouth.

That night, I fell asleep on the beanbag, stereo on, needle skipping in the Rancid record's final, crackly groove. In the morning, the stack of plates was gone and in its place was a note that said "*For the greater good*" in familiar handwriting.

Lorn made coffee every morning and I knew that if I wanted a cup, I needed to hustle. I stumbled downstairs to the kitchen to find it wall-to-wall with roommates. Lorn knitting a black beanie or something. Wells in his day-laborer drag. Scorch in their overalls. Tim in his problematic honky pachuco get-up. Everyone was there. Even the one who secretly worked at Hot Topic; the reformed gutter punk who DJed anticolonial techno; and the one who'd sneak off to play video games, smoke weed, and listen to unfunky backpack rap with his bros from high school. The plates were gleaming in the dish rack.

I grabbed a mug. "Collective meeting?"

And Scorch said, "No. We're having a *house* meeting."

I sighed and looked for a seat. "Fine, but I gotta go to work."

"Damn right you have a job to do," Lorn said, needles clacking.

Between the usual clutter and the unusual cluster of people, it took me a second to notice the weapons. The AK-47s crossed on the table. The elaborate swap-meet dagger stuck to the magnetic knife strip on the wall. The blunt, cruel baseball bat leaning against the oven, in reach of Wells's soft hand.

The ticking got louder and faster and each one made my thoughts skip. Wells said something about how, even when I thought I was rebelling, I was still working with the collective. Scorch muttered " … martyr for the cause," and Tim said I knew too much to not be part of their plan.

I said, "I did Community Outreach," and turned to pour a coffee. The pot was empty and, when I turned back around to complain, they'd all stepped toward me. I felt an inch shorter with every tick. Then Wells swung his glare—and the baseball bat—in my direction. My nose exploded blood, and I landed on my back, looking up at the dead flies inside the light fixture, ticking pushing tears from my eyes. A couple collective members grabbed my ankles and pulled me across the floor, smearing my blood across the checkerboard tiles. For a second, I felt bad for whoever was mopping that week, but then blackness flooded in from the edges of my mind and it was just the ticking, echoing in the darkness and shivering through my veins.

I came to on the carpet in front of a bank vault. Footsteps ran around me. Someone screamed and Scorch told them to shut the fuck up or they'd blast them then and there. The ticking was faster, each one sending a quake through me and, before I could collect my thoughts, another would come. I tried to stand and felt that I was tied up, ropes around my ankles and thighs, binding my arms to my sides. I couldn't move.

I writhed and rolled onto my face. A boot hooked under my right arm and someone grunted and tripped over me, kneeing my kidney. I could think straight for the first time in weeks, and saw that life wasn't passing, it was counting down. The ticking had stopped. I jerked upward in the pregnant silence. Bike gears and chain links dug into my ribs and calves from under the ropes, and I saw my roommates in bandanas and ski masks, wearing normie thrift store business–casual khakis, pointing AKs at tellers, pulling open drawers, and corralling the poor souls who still refused to bank online. And Tim looked my way and mouthed, "Not yet" from behind a black ski mask. The last thing I needed was him telling me what to do, so I exhaled a lifetime of irritation and exploded.

The force of the blast tore open the huge circular vault door, and whirled fat stacks of cash into the air with a flapping like bat wings at night. The windows of the bank exploded, sending pixels of glass into the street. And my body was shredded into the tiniest bits, each one a second on a clock, a moment I could get back, a time when I was flying in my own direction.

As my pieces arced through the air—some smeared across bike parts, others stuck to hundred-dollar bills—I could see back in time, my trussed body rolling around the back of a box van with a produce company logo on the side, bumping my roommates as they whispered, "Your turn for toilets" and "For the greater good," and the ticking echoed off the van's metal ceiling. I saw a hoodie-cloaked Wells, spray-painting the fence before disappearing into the alley.

By the time the scraps of cash, flesh, and bike shrapnel rained to the ground, I'd seen the future too: Scorch dying from flying headfirst out of the bank and through the windshield of the produce truck. A bunch of normies who looked like older, softer Scorches at a funeral in a quaint town with a Waffle House and a different idea of the greater good. Tim getting a swastika tattoo in jail, wishing he hadn't used his last moments of freedom to scrub toilets. Lorn learning acupuncture after her parents' lawyer got her probation. Wells hightailing it out of town then using money from the bank haul to become a landlord himself.

The plates went back to the thrift store. The back of the chore wheel stayed on the wall until the house was demolished and replaced by an instantly dated condo with a rooftop pool. I want to live in the moment where the wall buckled and made a Salvador Dali clock of the cardboard, toilet week never coming.

With a metallic moan, the coin-shaped vault door rolled off its hinges. As the million little pieces of my body flew away, I heard the door gong against the ground, and from up high, I wished my roommates had all been in that house of mirrors with me when I was a kid. They were ticking, too, and we might have found our way out.

AUTHOR'S NOTE: Imagine a camera panning to a cocktail glass, a diamond ring-wearing lady hiding behind a plastic plant, then a character waking up, unable to remember a thing. That sounds like the start of a crime story, right? I really wanted to flip "Set Adrift on Memory Bliss" into an anti-femme fatale tale for this book, but music was segregated as fuck in the 1990s. PM Dawn, along with a slew of other left-of-center Black artists, were never considered "alternative" by the record labels or music programmers. It's easy to think of the Gen X alternative movement as a progressive paradise full of Fruitopia and nose rings, but not everyone was invited.

I internalized that exclusion. In junior high, I made mixtapes with rap on one side and punk on the other, never letting the Black bands meet the white ones. I was isolated in my own mixed-race Black identity crisis.

Rancid is a white punk band. One of the best to ever do it. Along with bellow-along choruses and poetic lyrics that hold their own against '70s Springsteen, a big part of the band's appeal is how they present as a tight-knit, interdependent group of friends, making their way together from the wrong side of the tracks. To my lonely self, that was aspirational.

When it dropped in 1995, "Time Bomb" was the song that punk ascetics would sing at parties to mock Rancid for selling out. I wondered: if the punks hated "Time Bomb" so much, how did they know all the words? The song's a gangsterish ska-punk cautionary tale, in the spirit of reggae classics like "Johnny Too Bad" and "Rudy a Message to You." I considered fleshing out the lyrics about the kid with the black coat, white shoes, black hat, Cadillac into a similar rise-and-fall tale but got stuck on ideas of loneliness and togetherness, and the punk rock tension between the desire for individuality and the need to be part of something bigger than yourself. Then I wondered what would happen if a boy was *literally* a time bomb, and I started writing a story with a title that will send chills down the spine of anyone who's had roommates. I got to have it both ways: doing my own thing and joining a bigger group. Thanks for including me in this book. Next time, maybe we can do Top 40 rap?

The strangest gig I ever had was fetish destruction. In July of 1995 I answered an ad in a newspaper asking for a reliable messenger and administrative assistant. My interview took place in a minuscule office above a deli, with the smell of burnt toast wafting through the window. Even though there was a fan spinning above our heads, it felt as hot as an oven in there.

The interviewer was a middle-aged man dressed in a black suit and tie who was sweating buckets and periodically dabbed a handkerchief across his forehead.

His name was Mr. Gaffey and the name of the business I'd walked into was the rather generic Useful Endings. Mr. Gaffey began by asking me the typical battery of questions: work experience, education, and the like, before moving into more esoteric territory.

"Are you superstitious?"

"I'm not particularly afraid of black cats," I said, wondering if this was part of a personality test. Or maybe it was one of those logic puzzles, like how'd you'd get a bag of corn, a chicken, and a fox across a river while paddling a canoe. I'd scored high on those, even if my résumé was a patchwork of unfulfilled potential and dashed expectations.

"Do you believe in magic?"

"Do I need to pull white rabbits out of hats or something?"

"You need to pull cursed objects out of boxes."

I stared at the man and laughed. Either this was the right reaction, or he was tired of talking to people. It was damn hot in the room. Maybe he wanted out of there quick. The man dabbed the handkerchief against his neck, then lit a cigarette. He waved the smoke away with a hand.

"Do you know what a fetish is? I don't mean an erotic predilection; I'm talking about magical fetishes." I stared at him, and he kept talking, looking pleased that he was schooling me. "A fetish is any object that is believed to possess magical powers. Rabbit's foot? A fetish. Lucky coin? A fetish. Spirit dolls, medicine bags, spirit boxes, talismans, and charms: fetishes. That's our business here: fetishes."

"You make magic charms?"

"We handle their safe, proper decommission. In the old days, people would make a charm, cast a spell, then dispose of its remnants by tossing it in a river, burying at a crossroads, or burning it in a pyre. There were also pieces that needed even more complex processes, like scooping dirt from under the hangman's noose and … Well, you get the point."

"Then it's like eco-friendly recycling?"

"Or toxic waste services."

"People pay for this?"

"Oh, yes. We have many individual clients, a few big companies. Have you heard of Madame Antoniette?"

"The lady with the psychic hotline," I said. I'd seen her ads half a dozen times while dozing off in front of the TV late at night.

"She has a standing contract with us. Now, the disposal of fetishes is easy enough. There's a color-coded manual you follow, it's all been standardized. But one crucial element is this: you must *not* believe in magic. That's the only way this works. For unbelievers, the fetishes are simply things. Musty old dolls, scraps of clothing, moth-eaten books. For believers, these are dangerous weapons. The best antidote against magic is indifference. You must be honest with me—do you believe in the supernatural? Are you superstitious? Any lucky numbers, or a passion for astrology?"

"Nah," I said. "My mom was a raging atheist and I take after her, so I don't have a religion and she didn't believe in lying to me, so there was never even any talk of Santa Claus or the tooth fairy."

"Then this kind of job, it wouldn't frighten you?"

"What's frightening is mold remediation," I said. I was overqualified and underqualified for nearly every job, with half a degree in cinema studies under my arm and a series of patchy temp jobs to show for all my efforts. "Quite honestly, if I don't get this job, I'm going to have to go into business with my cousin Alejandro spraying black mold with bleach, and let me tell you, that's a lot more of a drag than any crystal ball or voodoo doll."

We shook on it. I started the next day.

Useful Endings was an ordinary, dull business. Every morning, I walked to the basement and retrieved the items that arrived in the mail. I collated them by size, copied the information written in a form tucked inside the box or the envelope, then proceeded to browse through a three-ring binder labeled IDENTIFICATION GUIDE.

Aside from Mr. Gaffey, who tended to spend the day in his tiny office typing on the computer, the only other two people I ever saw regularly were Marsha, the secretary and receptionist who sat outside Mr. Gaffey's office going through invoices, and Dennis Duncan, the other Disposal Technician on staff. Dennis was about my age and smoked so much his teeth had passed stained-yellow and had arrived at a murky, algae green. Occasionally a Special Curator in expensive alligator shoes came in with a briefcase under his arm to discuss business with Mr. Gaffey, but the person I worked with every day was Dennis. I never interacted with any clients. The materials were mailed, and I carted them up to the room with a long green table where Dennis and I decommissioned fetishes.

When I was in high school, I'd worked at a fried chicken franchise. Useful Endings was just like the fast-food business. The manual told us everything we had to do. First, we weighed and measured the fetish, took a Polaroid of it, then looked up the type of fetish using the Identification Guide, and finally we followed the steps for the disposal of the object indicated at the back of the three-ring binder. We filled out more paperwork, stamped a pink sheet of paper with the word DECOMMISSIONED, and the accompanying carbon copy was stapled to a second Polaroid showing the object after its destruction. Then we moved on to the next fetish.

At the chicken joint it had been the same, a mindless loop of premeasured and prearranged steps.

The most interesting part of the job was leafing through the Identification Guide and determining the type of fetish I was dealing with. "Dolls" could mean a decapitated Barbie doll from the 1970s or a fourth century clay Louvre Doll impaled by thirteen bronze needles. Easy enough, right? Not so fast. Sometimes the doll might come with other items. The Louvre Doll was found with a *katadesmos*, which is a Greco-Roman curse tablet. So, should, that be filed under "Dolls", or did I place it under "Books and Writing"?

There were many tiny details to consider. *Voces magicae* referred to writing that had no translation. Gibberish, basically, or someone's special shorthand. But you couldn't assume that because you couldn't read something it was not a real language. You'd have to pull out one of the many dictionaries lining the shelves and check if it looked like this was actually Aramaic or gobbledygook.

Some of the items were brand new. Bottles of Pepsi wrapped with yellow string and filled with dead beetles. Others were antiques, like a bronze whistle with the words *Oh, Whistle, and I'll Come to You, My Lad* carved on its side.

There were erotic-binding spells on papyrus, bitter curses to shrivel a rival's testicles in clay, charms for wealth and health, bottles filled with the scent of faded perfume to obtain beauty. They were made of gold, of feathers, of shreds of newspaper. Some were expensive, others were silly. Some were true works of art, like an ivory idol the size of my pinkie, which despite its tiny size had been painted with the finest details.

Once the object was identified in its proper category and sub-category—brown for written materials, purple for dolls, blue for bottles and containers, and so on and so forth—I turned to the back of the binder for the instructions on how to disassemble and dispose of the spell. Eventually I got so good at identifying objects that I was able to tell from the moment I removed a fetish from its box whether I should soak it in brine and then burn it in the basement furnace that was especially conditioned for our use, or seal it with a layer of wax before smashing it with a hammer.

At times, I felt melancholic as I handled tiny cameos and bits of porcelain, thinking of how I'd imagined I'd work at a museum, restoring films from crumbling negatives. Live in Paris. Wear a beret. Eat baguettes. I don't know, something else.

I spent most of my shift listening to one of the CDs tucked in my Discman, and my lunch hour reading one or another beaten paperback I'd traded at the used bookstore around the corner. When I walked by Marsha's desk and she wasn't busy, I'd look over her shoulder and help with her newspaper crossword puzzle. She liked to crochet and gossip about the other tenants in the building. Mr. Gaffey did not gossip, and

Mr. Ridley, the curator, looked so posh every time he walked in with his briefcase that I thought if I got close to him he'd use his silver-tipped cane to shoo me away.

Dennis was the kind of guy who seemed ready and eager to make friends. I'd imagined him inviting me to weekend BBQs and bowling nights, but when I told him I didn't like comic books he grew a bit sullen. We chatted, but I hurt his feelings with my indifference to *X-Men*. No BBQs or bowling nights for us.

Still, we worked at the long green table and traded the occasional joke, made the trek downstairs to the deli or across the street to the Golden Dragon for lunch, and on one occasion when I was a few dollars short he lent me a bit of cash. He called me Nugget. I can't remember how the nickname got started, but it stuck.

Even though he'd been working there for three years, Dennis often relied on me for some of the more complex fetishes. When he was stumped, he'd say, "Nugget, please. You gotta!" and stare at me pleadingly.

A year passed. When July 1996 arrived, it was sweltering in the office. I played my music—Bikini Kill, Bratmobile, and Garbage humming in my ears—and sipped water from a thermos while I color-coded fetishes.

One afternoon, a lady walked into the office. She was dressed in black, her peroxide-blonde hair styled in the Rachel cut that every chick south of thirty seemed to have. I, not one for trends, had attempted Bettie Page rockabilly bangs that summer and concluded I looked like a clown, so I wore a rather stupid-looking, scalp-hugging toque with the Leafs logo for a week before I simply shaved the whole mess off.

Visitors were an oddity, so I could be forgiven for staring at the woman as she waltzed into the boss's office in her stiletto heels. Dennis, however, did not stare. He looked, shook and practically foamed at the mouth.

When the woman walked out of the office, slammed the door shut, and turned a furious glare in the direction of our table, I was smart enough to pretend I was checking a label. Dennis, poor idiot, grinned his crooked smile at the woman. She stormed off, her high heels clacking with telegraphed contempt. In a minute she was gone.

I slid by Marsha's desk. "Hey, do we have a new curator or something?" I asked, thinking of the guy in alligator shoes with the briefcase who was the only person in the building who looked like he earned real dough.

"God, no. That's Jennifer Powers," Marsha said, in a low voice that indicated someone of importance, but I shrugged.

"Don't know her. Is she on TV?"

She might be. She was pretty; her pale skin, slimness, and the dark circles under the eyes all combined to create the perfect heroin-chic look. I am not one for waifs or bony boys, but I saw similar, beautifully emaciated faces plastered on the covers of magazines and the sides of buses.

"Really, sometimes I wonder what you do in your spare time," Marsha said. I read James Bond novels and Doc Savage, caught black-and-white movies over at Kino Theater, collected travel brochures for places I'd never visit, but I let her talk. "She's a socialite. The daughter of Henry Powers. They make that jam. Tildbury Farms."

"Not Powers Farm?"

"No. Anyway, she's worth a fortune. Check the papers, she's always in the social pages. She was in a bad accident three years ago; her car went down a ravine. It was in the news, front page. You don't remember?"

Now that she mentioned it, I had a vague memory of the incident, of having seen that face before. Drunk driving, maybe? She'd recovered nicely enough by the looks of her.

"Okay, yeah. What's she doing here?"

"Well, I'm not quite sure. On Friday I got multiple phone calls for Gaffey from some woman. Mr. Gaffey wasn't too pleased and told me to say he was away if they called again. Then this morning Ridley phoned and said a young lady needed to see Mr. Gaffey, and couldn't she be squeezed into the boss's calendar? It was Ridley, so I had to do it. Ridley's the founder's brother, you know? Anyhow, he said 'Jenny' would be stopping around lunch time, and who walks into the office? Jennifer Powers."

"Hmm," I said, and slid my headphones over my ears again.

The next morning, I bought a newspaper. I didn't find Jennifer in the social pages; her picture was in the business section, with another one of a white-haired man and a fellow who looked like the youthful version of the white-haired gentleman. The headline was: FAMILY FEUD! Mr. Powers had recently experienced a heart attack and was recovering at the family estate. He'd been ill for a while, and the article wondered if Jennifer would gain control of the company, or if her stepbrother Jeremy would step in.

Lives of the rich and famous, I thought, and gave the paper to Marsha so she could solve the crossword.

On Wednesday, Jennifer came in again. This time she was the lady in red. Red dress, red shoes, red lips, and a ruby nestled against the hollow of her pale neck. Gold bangles adorned her arms. She walked into their boss's office and exited a few minutes later. This time, rather than slamming the door and looking aggrieved, she turned her blue, almost colorless eyes in our direction.

Marsha was out to lunch and Jennifer circled her desk and went toward the green table where we were working. I wiped the sweat beading on my forehead with the back of my hand while Dennis bobbed his head in greeting.

"Are you the Disposal Technicians?"

"Yeah, yeah, that we are," Dennis said with another ungraceful bob of the head.

"Only the two of you?"

"That's right."

"Do you ever do any freelance work?" she asked.

"We'd be fired if we did," I said, but the blonde kept staring at Dennis, as though she hadn't heard me. Finally, he cleared his throat.

"Yeah, we'd be fired."

"That's a pity," she declared, her gaze still fixed on Dennis. Her lips stretched into a smile. The contrast of her red lipstick and her pale face was startling, like when Rita Hayworth flipped her hair in *Gilda*, and I feared Dennis was going to swoon.

She turned around and walked out of the office with a strut that would have given Naomi Campbell a run for her money.

Something was brewing. Dennis was distracted and oddly quiet. On Friday, he invited me to lunch at the Golden Dragon. No sooner had our spring rolls been served, he leaned across the table.

"Jennifer Powers talked to me," he said.

"Lady Marmalade? She didn't talk to you, she stormed off."

"After that! She came back yesterday, waited outside, and tapped me on the shoulder before I got on my bike."

"What'd she want?"

"Her old man is sick. Apparently, there's a clause in a legal document that indicated if this happened, if he was terminally ill, they had to destroy a fetish. So, the fetish was mailed to the office a few days ago, but now she's placed an injunction. Her brother is countersuing her. It's a mess."

"Over a fetish?"

"That's what she says."

I dipped my spring roll in sweet and sour sauce. "Why's she telling you this?"

"Well, there's all this complicated legalese stuff and the company won't do anything until it's sorted out. She doesn't want it destroyed. Her brother is into some weird magic shit and she's afraid the destruction of the fetish would harm her dad. She'll pay me to take a picture of it and send her identifying information."

"You mean she doesn't know what fetish it is?"

"No idea, and she wants to know. Her dad told her it was custom-made by a warlock from Florence."

"Then the brother is not the only one into weird magic shit."

"She suspects it's something to keep a person in a state between life and death."

"That narrows it down. Necromancy." The foulest magic, that's what our manual said. It was color-coded black. We didn't get too many of those fetishes, but when we did inevitably the manual had a spooky story to reveal. Examples of bone magic used to create a revenant. Sticks tied in bundles to force the dead to speak. Corpses trailing black fluid and walking down a road, pestilent bodies that must be burnt after their heart was torn out. Or else, a *draugr* who looked like a dead loved one, and spoke with their voice, but their skin was terribly pale and cold as ice. They ate human carcasses. *Tales from the Crypt* tropes.

"No. It could be a protective charm. A health amulet. Even a *crepundium*."

I snorted. "No way."

The server came back with our order of Kung Pao Chicken. I spooned some onto my plate.

"We'd know if we looked at it."

"Dennis, this is none of our business."

"She's offering us thirty-thousand dollars. We can split it down the middle. The boss is keeping the fetish in limbo. You have the combination; just go into the morgue, get a picture, fill an identification sheet, and hand them to me. I'll slip the file to her tonight. No one will ever know it."

The morgue was a gigantic room of metal cabinets that housed the fetish paperwork. In some cases, even the remains of the fetishes were there, if the instructions in the binder indicated that the fetish needed to be "bagged and tagged" rather than completely obliterated. There was a small, adjoining room we called "limbo." That was where Ridley dropped off the top-notch fetishes that were not transported via mail or regular messenger. The Powers's fetish must be there, tucked in a safety box until the legalese around it was sorted.

"We'll be fired."

"Who's gonna tell? When you're signing off for the day, take a peek."

"And you'll get me a new job when they kick my ass out?"

"It's a dead-end job. Look, we both know it. It pays the bills, but that's about it. You want more of life. I've seen you eyeing the posters at the travel agency down the street, and there's that French dictionary that you sometimes pull off the shelf during our break. You're sitting there, practicing your vocabulary. This isn't what you imagined life would be."

No shit. A botched cinema degree and the weekly scraping-by weren't what I'd pictured as a youngster. I scrutinized the chicken on my plate, like a haruspex divining the future.

"Nugget, please. You gotta!" he said in that pleading tone that worked so well.

"Why don't you do it?"

Dennis seemed shocked at my response, but I've never been one to take a penny from the till or fuck around in the office. I'm all about clean references and steady paychecks. In the end, I'm also not much of a rule-breaker.

Dennis didn't explain, was sullen the rest of the evening. Could it be that he *believed* in the supernatural? What a joke! By the time we clocked out it had started to rain, but the rain was light, and the day was still warm. It felt like vapor. I hurried back to my apartment, opened a window, turned on a fan, and dozed off on the couch.

Around midnight I woke up, feeling like I was sticking to the fabric of the furniture, and poked my head out the window. I thought about giving Dennis a call. Telling him not to go through with it, because I knew he was going to get in touch with Miss Powers, and then I figured he knew thirty grand could get you places. I considered phoning our boss.

In the end, I may be a rule-follower, but I'm not a tattletale. I went back to sleep.

On Monday, the faces of Jennifer and Henry Powers stared at me from a newspaper stand. I palmed my jacket for change, bought the paper, headed to a coffee at a shop a few blocks from the office, and sat down to read. My hands were sweaty as I unfolded the broadsheet.

They were dead. Jennifer and Henry had perished in a fire the previous night. There was a statement from a Tildbury spokesperson and few details. I read the story twice. My coffee had grown cold. I drank it in quick gulps and proceeded to the office.

Marsha intercepted me as soon as I walked in. "Gaffey is in a foul mood," she told me. "Dennis opened the morgue and stole the Powers's fetish. They found it in a fireproof box at the Powers's house."

"Where's Dennis?"

"Nowhere. Ridley sent someone to his apartment, but he's not there. They're bringing in the fetish. Gaffey says you need to decommission it."

The fetish arrived that same afternoon and I stayed late working under the watchful eye of Ridley and Gaffey. It was a *Valdemar*: a small wooden coffin that had been stained black. A charm to control the dead. The lining of the coffin was stitched with the spell and the name carved on the back of it was Jennifer Millicent Powers. It had been made to keep her, not her father, in a state between life and death. It must have been commissioned after her accident.

The fetish, however, was not meant to outlast her dad. If something happened to Henry, it would be destroyed, and she would die. Why? Insurance, maybe. Or a rule of magic.

Since Jennifer survived the accident, she must have believed the fetish worked. When Henry fell ill, it triggered the destruction of the fetish, which she sought to prevent. That's why Jennifer bribed Dennis to retrieve the object.

According to the papers, Jennifer murdered her father and then set the house on fire. A twisted mercy killing since Henry was deadly ill. At the office, Marsha told me it must have been the other way around: Henry turned against Jennifer, set *her* on fire, then shot himself. Or maybe the stepbrother killed both of them. Or one of them? Marsha was full of ideas. After all, if you believe in magic, Jennifer was already dead, and the fetish was inside the fireproof box. That meant there might have been a charred corpse dragging itself through the hills that simply crumbled to dust the moment I decommissioned the Valdemar.

Anyway, that story concludes neatly enough with death.

Dennis's story doesn't have a clear ending. I'm unsure whether Jennifer asked him to steal the fetish from the start, or if the plan later changed, but he did take it from the office and deliver it to her. What happened next, who knows? Investigators did not find anything important missing from Dennis's apartment, although there was a bit of blood in the bathtub and the place was in disarray. But Dennis was not the most organized person at the best of times, so the chaos might have been him simply not bothering to tidy up.

Marsha and I traded theories. Had Dennis tried to ask Jennifer for more money, so she'd killed him and disposed of the body? Stepbrother Jeremy might have had a hand in the disappearance, killing Dennis in a fury because he believed his meddling had cost the lives of his father and his sister. Or else Dennis, fearing the repercussions of his actions, fled. This seemed the most likely outcome, as ten days later, a man resembling Dennis was spotted in New Orleans.

"At least he's alive," I told Marsha.

"Is he?" she replied.

"What do you mean?"

Marsha shrugged and returned to her crossword.

I left Useful Endings six months later. It felt too depressing, handling people's fears and dreams and desires.

Dennis has never resurfaced, and his face doesn't adorn any missing, or wanted, posters these days. He wasn't seen after that one glimpse in New Orleans.

You might think I have bad dreams, nightmares where a strange figure shuffles by my apartment complex, dripping a dark, viscous fluid. Or else that a perfectly preserved Dennis, looking like he's not aged a day since 1996, will knock at my door. You might imagine that I fear one day I'll receive a box that says "*Please disarm, Nugget. Please. You gotta.*" A fetish will be tucked inside, a black coffin with Dennis's name inscribed on the back.

But like Mr. Gaffey told me at that interview, the best antidote against magic is indifference. I do not carry amulets against the evil eye, or a red string tied around my wrist. I leave that to others, those with money, desperation, and faith enough for the services of Useful Endings.

AUTHOR'S NOTE: I told Nick Mamatas, when he asked if I'd be interested in contributing a story for this anthology, that I was going to turn in something inspired by Garbage's "I Think I'm Paranoid." Over a period of three months, I wrote and rewrote over 5,000 solid words of a story. Then I went into the hospital for major surgery.

My first night home, after taking a large dose of painkillers, I woke up from a dream where someone retrieved odd objects out of P.O. boxes. A doll, a bottle, a knife. I wondered why anyone would do that and wanted to write a story immediately.

Since I was trapped in bed, unable to shuffle close to the computer, I had to type most of it on my cellphone. I listened to Garbage while working, with no plot at first, only the image of strange objects lingering in my mind and the sound of "I Think I'm Paranoid" hurling me back to the rock of the 1990s.

I was groggy with the painkillers, and I thought at one point Shirley Manson belted the lyrics "*I'm superstitious.*" She doesn't, but I typed the word "superstition" at the top of the document and glanced at the amulet against the evil eye my mother had left on my night table.

The writing distracted me from the pain, and even though it was a completely unplanned story I think it made more sense, in the end, than the work I'd been carefully conceptualizing. Then again, improvisation is one of the crucial tools in a musician—and a writer's—toolkit.

TORNADO MOTHER

BY LIBBY CUDMORE

Kenneth used to dream of his mother as a tornado. She came in and destroyed everything but him, who was safe in the eye of the storm. All the women in his life were whirling dervishes; his mother Louise, his ex-wife Anastasia, his friend BT, his twin sister Dana before she vanished one night in the spring of 1996; she'd gone to the movies and never came home. They questioned her boyfriend, Billy, accused him of killing her, but no body was ever found. Billy's family had to movie to South Florida, and according to Facebook, Billy died a few years ago in a motorcycle crash. They never found Dana's body. For all he knew, she was still out there, spinning in circles through someone else's life. Kenneth just wished she could have left some way to chase her.

In Anastasia's eyes, Kenneth was the cyclone, an unpredictable storm of salt and fire and rum. He didn't blame her for leaving him. And BT? She always had been a storm, drifting in and out, stirring up dust, stirring up heat, stirring up trouble.

"You look just like my daughter," Mother said, patting BT's hand. "I was prom queen, you know. She gets her good looks from me."

"I've seen pictures," she said, unwrapping the blood pressure cuff. "You were very pretty."

BT was Kenneth's mother's new nurse. Mother had dismissed all the others ones; too pushy, too lazy, too dark. The racism was new, or maybe she'd just gotten tired of hiding it. But BT looked nothing like Dana. Dana had what the issues of *Cosmopolitan* he once hid under his bed called a *beach body*, model-thin blonde with breasts coming in and hips beginning to shape. She disappeared before she ever fully became a woman. He used to wonder if he saw her on the street, if he'd recognize her because she looked just like his mother did in the framed photos she kept on her white-and-gold vanity, next to a tiny bottle of Chanel No. 5 that had held the last few drops for the last twenty years, in reserve for another special evening that never came.

But BT was all grown up now, her red curls pulled back into a tight ponytail, curves hidden under her dark blue scrubs. He remembered her in tomboy overalls, his sister's best friend who'd become his best friend when Dana vanished. They used to play detective, try to figure out where Dana had gotten to—a tornado carried her off like Dorothy to Oz, or aliens beamed her up like on *The X-Files*. BT believed that Dana had run away and become a model like she always said she would. There was a girl in the Summer 1996 dELiA#s catalogue who looked just like her, preening in a blue-striped tank top and slim blue pants. She wrote to dELiA#s and asked. They didn't answer her question, but they sent her a silver star necklace that she wore until the chain broke. That was proof enough, she told him, but he didn't think she really believed that any more than he did.

"Ma, that's Bethany," he insisted. "Remember Bethany? Dana's best friend? You played bridge with her mother, Janice."

She ignored him. "My son isn't married," his mother said. "He's divorced, but that was her fault. She wasn't a good wife."

Anastasia was a good wife. A better wife than he deserved. He was the one who screwed it all up. But his mother believed a woman should stay with her man, even when that man turned into a mean and bitter drunk. And if his father hadn't died when he was sixteen, he'd be taking care of both of them. One parent was all he could handle right now. He'd only been back in Oklahoma City for a month, and his mother only for two weeks, but he already felt her wayward winds cracking his bones.

The neighbors had noticed it first; would find her wandering the backyard at odd hours, babbling about her prize-winning roses. Those roses, once the entire length of the fence line, were long neglected and dead, but she would cut and bundle up the sticks and present them like a bouquet, which the neighbors would accept with a stammered grace. It wasn't until she fell down her back steps that the cops got involved, found his number scribbled on the ASPCA notepad by the kitchen phone. He was on the next plane home. The waiting lists for memory-care facilities was long, so he needed to keep her in her house as long as he could.

But his mother's sickness had given him an excuse to come home, a place to land, somewhere to escape to that wasn't a studio apartment on the lonely side of town. Couldn't drink if he were taking care of her. Just had to just white-knuckle through.

"I'm sure he'll find a good woman someday," BT said. "How about some lunch?"

While his mom was napping, he found BT out on the back porch, drinking a Dr. Pepper. "Haven't had one of those in forever," he said.

"There's an extra in the fridge," she said. "My private stash. Help yourself."

He retrieved one of the cans and sat next to her. "Remember how Dana used to drink hers through a Red Vine straw?" he asked.

"And how she had to have four cavities filled before school started?" she replied.

He snorted. He stared at the wilted rose bushes, remembering the bouquets he would bring to BT on the anniversary of Dana's disappearance, casting the petals to the wind as though they might mark a pathway for her to return to them. BT could read tarot. BT could count crows. If BT's homemade sorcery couldn't bring her back, he decided one day, then Dana wasn't coming home. But he never let those words escape his lips. BT might never forgive him if he surrendered so easily.

"How are you doing?" she finally asked. "It must be hard for you to be back here."

"No harder than it was for you to stay."

She squirmed and slurped her Dr. Pepper. "Guess neither of us really had a choice," she said.

"I heard about your mom," he said. "I'm sorry."

"My biggest worry is that it's genetic," she said. "That one day my son Seth will have to spoon-feed me and wipe my ass."

"Didn't know you had a son."

"He's eight," she said. "His dad took off a couple of years ago. I'm starting to think it's me that makes people leave."

He couldn't tell if she was joking. "I'm not going anywhere," he said. "Not for a while."

She didn't respond right away. "The first thing I did when I got here was go into Dana's old room," she finally said. "I don't know what I expected; maybe that it would be preserved as a shrine, like with all those Lancôme lipstick ads taped on the wall and the zebra-striped Caboodle on her vanity, just absolutely stinking of Love's Baby Soft. But it was just ... a junk room. Where all the boxes of Christmas ornaments and old cards and mismatched pillowcases go. Like she'd never even been there. And with your mom's memory problems, it's like she doesn't even remember her either. Until you showed up, I was questioning my own sanity. Like maybe she was an imaginary friend or something."

"She was real," he said. "And I miss her every goddamn day."

"Me too," BT said.

The wind rustled what was left of the rose bushes. For a moment, he imagined he could smell them sweet on the summer air, mingling with BT's signature CK One and Banana Boat sunscreen to protect her fair freckled skin. He wanted to lean over and breathe her in. For a moment, he was thirteen again, his palm in hers as she read the fortune etched in his lines. *You'll have a long life and a pretty wife*, she said. *But there'll always be something missing*. The long life was still to be determined. The pretty wife was gone. And what was missing had been a hole in his soul for more than two decades.

"We should find a way to say goodbye," he murmured.

She shook her head. She picked up her empty soda can and stood. "I'm not ready for that yet," she said. "I might never be."

Kenneth woke to smoke. For a moment he was dreaming of the 54th Street bank fire, trapped in the vault with no way out. Seven people died, but not him.

Maybe that was the whole problem.

He'd been late to the call, trapped in the hellish void between hammered and hungover. He'd arrived at the scene of the inferno, got suited up and went in with the rest of his team. But he'd put his respirator on wrong. The room was spinning, the fire was screaming, it was too much for him to take. He stepped outside to vomit in the moments before it all collapsed. Seven people died, but they spun stories about how he tried to warn the others, tried to get him out, gave him a medal for bravery. After the ceremony he got so drunk that he crashed his car into a telephone pole, a suicide attempt that didn't work as planned. The cops just cleaned him up, told everyone he swerved to avoid a deer, told the hospital to leave off any evidence of blood alcohol content. *We protect our family*, they said. *It's tough to be the one who survives.* That medal was buried in a box in the garage. He never wanted to see it again. The ghosts of the men he didn't save would remind him, night after night.

But he wasn't at 54th Street. He wasn't even in his Hudson Street studio apartment. He was home, in his old bedroom, sleeping in his old twin bed laid with the green and purple geometric-print sheets. The smoke, however, was real.

In the kitchen he found his mother burning a pair of pajamas on the stove. Next to her was a cardboard box of his father's old things. He wanted to shout, scream, grab the fire extinguisher, and fill the room with foam. But the social worker had told him to react calmly, not to frighten her, as though she was a rabid coyote, a wounded tiger, a creature that might attack.

He choked on the smoke as he smothered the flames with a wool army blanket. He moved her to the bathroom and opened all the windows. He took the knobs off the stove and made a note to ask BT to up his mother's dose of Xanax so she would sleep through the night. He'd put her back to bed and clean up the evidence. That much he excelled at.

His mother stood exactly where he'd left her. There was a puddle of piss on the blue tile floor, a shit-filled diaper around her ankles. "I'm making pancakes," she said. "Dana asked for them."

"We can make pancakes in the morning," he said.

"Dana won't be here in the morning."

"Then we'll meet her at Jimmy's Egg. C'mon, let's get you cleaned up."

"Dad hates Jimmy's Egg," she said. "Says it gives him gas."

"Good thing he isn't here to complain."

"He wasn't a good husband."

"He wasn't a great dad either."

"Do you want chocolate chips in your pancakes?"

"Sure," he said. "I'll go to the store and get some first thing in the morning."

She patted his hand and smiled. "Anastasia was wrong about you," she said. "You're a very good boy."

Kenneth made coffee and got donuts from the Cambodian donut shop that took up residence where the old Winchell's used to be. He waited for BT on the porch and when she pulled up, he held out a cup of coffee. "She's still asleep," he said. "She was up late trying to burn the house down."

She took the coffee and sat. "My mom did the same thing," she said. "My son Seth was a newborn. She claimed she was heating up a bottle, but I found her sitting at the dining room table, completely oblivious to the smoke. I had to just go ahead and unplug the oven. You might want to do the same."

He nodded. "Put that on my list of chores," he said. "She was burning one of my dad's shirts. All his shit is still piled in the garage, and probably in Dana's old room too. I figure I might as well get a head start on getting this place cleaned out ready to sell. We'll need the money when we finally find a nursing home."

"Don't put it all out in the Dumpster," she joked. "Some of that stuff might be worth some money on the nostalgia market."

"Think your kid would want any of my old toys?" he asked.

"Maybe," she said. "He does love *Star Wars*. The new shitty ones, though. Not the good ones we used to watch. Which reminds me—I need to call my backup babysitter to watch him the rest of the week. The girl who usually sits for me had a family emergency and is going out of town."

"How about this," he said. "If he wants, he can come help me, and I'll let him take home whatever he wants. You save on the babysitter and I get some free child labor."

"Deal," she said. She stood. "Let me see about getting Louise up and ready. I thought I'd give her a manicure today. Make her feel pretty."

"She'd like that."

He put Seth to work moving boxes in his room. He made it into a game, a treasure hunt, gave him an empty box and told him he could fill it with whatever he wanted—action figures, comic books, clothes or games or music. Had to be careful, though, had to be strategic, couldn't make a mess. One box.

Each day they filled up the trunk and rode together to get rid of what they didn't want. Unloaded boxes at Half Price Books, the comic shop, Salvation Army. Seth said he'd grow into the flame-patterned bowling shirt; took Shredder and Leonardo, a Game Boy case with *Super Mario World* and *Link's Awakening* and *Kirby's Dreamland*. They got bags of tacos and brought them back to the house, Dr. Pepper Slurpees from the 7-Eleven. "We called these Icys when I was a kid," "he told him as the thick frost slithered into their cups. "Your mom and I used ride our bikes here; she always got banana and topped it with cherry."

"He really enjoys hanging out with you," BT said, later. "Every day he asks if he can go see 'my friend Kenneth.'"

He'd never thought about having kids of his own. Anastasia brought it up once, and he shook so hard and felt so sick at the thought that she never brought it up again. She knew about Dana, but there was no possible way she could ever know what it felt like to lose a sister, and he could never know what his parents felt like losing their child. He didn't want to know, couldn't even stomach the thought. *You don't want kids with me*, he'd told her. *My family is cursed.*

His mother had lost her own twin sister—his Aunt Lucille, who drowned in the swimming hole—when she was fourteen, pulled under by a current Louise couldn't save her from. Then Dana went missing, and his dad drank himself to death five years later. No wonder she lost her memory. There wasn't a whole lot worth remembering.

But Seth didn't feel like Kenneth's kid. His responsibility. He was just a little buddy, a ray of joy that lit up his day the same way BT did. Maybe this was what it felt like to have a family. Maybe it wasn't so bad after all.

"Bring him by any time," he said, smiling. "Plenty of boxes still to move."

A different nurse came by on the weekends. His mother mostly ignored her, pretended to sleep, demanded red wine and spaghetti from the Italian joint that closed down years ago. He promised her spaghetti when BT came back on Monday. "We'll all go out for a nice dinner," he said. "I got us a reservation and everything."

That seemed to satisfy her. She chewed with her mouth open like a child. When the nurse tried to give her the paper cup full of pills, she vomited up everything she had eaten and smiled. "I told you I wanted spaghetti," she said.

"I'm canceling our dinner reservations."

While the nurse cleaned up his mother, Kenneth went into Dana's room. He cleared a space on the bed and sat, staring at all the boxes piled up on her dresser. If she were here with him, she wouldn't put up with this. He imagined her coming back, taking one look at his sorry situation, and leaving again. He wouldn't blame her. He just wished he knew where she was so he could join her. Let the state take his mother. Let her spit up her spite someplace else.

He waited until his mother was in bed and the nurse was gone to start cleaning. He didn't want to have to explain what he was doing, didn't want to risk her seeing what all he was getting rid of. It was one thing to dispose of the boxes he'd left behind, it was something else entirely to clean out the tomb of a lost daughter and husband. He wondered if he might find his old notes from her case, composition books filled with scribbles detailing whatever sounded like a clue, a cigarette pack in the gutter in front of their house, a shifty-looking neighbor or a new postman, Billy's sudden disappearance. He wondered if any of them might now hold a clue that made sense. More than likely, it would just remind him that he was as helpless to save her then as he was now.

He opened a box of his father's clothes from the top of the stack. Kenneth only had the one suitcase and he sure as hell wasn't going to fit in anything he'd worn as a teenager. His dad's weekend jeans might fit him now, at least until he could get away to buy a few new things.

He took out a few polo shirts and a flannel for fall. A pair of brown loafers still in the box, a three-pack of white T-shirts with two still unworn. But at the bottom of the box was something that should not have been there.

Dana's diary.

He didn't remember how he got to BT's house. But the snapping glare of the motion sensor lights started him enough that he dropped the bottle of rum he didn't remember buying, splashing what was left on his shoes. "I solved the case!" he blurted. "Kenneth McCallister, brilliant detective!"

BT opened the door. "What the fuck is your problem?" she demanded. "You're gonna wake up the whole damn neighborhood."

"My dad raped her," he said. "He raped her and then my mom killed her."

"How do you know this?" she asked.

"I found her diary," he said. "She wrote it down. Said when she told Mother that Mother called her a slut. Said she looked just like her Aunt Lucille, that she'd been a slut too."

"She could have still run away ..."

"She didn't run away, BT!" he shouted. "My mother killed her own sister and she killed Dana too. Anyone who was a threat. She killed her and she buried her in the backyard underneath the rose bushes. That's why they grew so big. Like the Audrey II, right? Remember watching that movie? That's what happened to my sister."

"You're drunk," she said. "You're not making any sense."

"Of course I'm drunk," he said. "Shit, BT, I just found out my whole family's completely fucked up. My dad fucked my sister while my mom was in your house playing bridge with your mom. While I was at Boy Scout camp. While you were doing your nails and watching *Saved by the Bell*. And when she told Mother …" He flopped down on the cement steps, the rum absorbing the blow to his tailbone. "Mother killed her."

She sat down next to him. "Even if you could make her talk," she said, "she's got dementia. The cops wouldn't do anything."

"I don't care what the cops do to her," he said. "I just want to put my sister in a real grave. She deserves that much."

Seth came out in his pajamas. "Hi, Kenneth," he said. "Want to play *Super Smash Bros*? You can be MetaKnight?"

He laughed. "It's way past my bedtime," he said. "C'mon, sit out here with me and your mom. We're telling stories."

"Go back to bed," BT said.

"But I want to tell stories with Kenneth," he whined.

"Maybe another time," she said, glaring. "Kenneth has to go home now."

Seth sulked back inside. Kenneth waved to him, laughed a little, and then started to sob. "Why didn't she tell me?" he blubbered. "I would have protected her."

He didn't care if Seth heard him. Hell, he'd tell the kid the whole story. No more kindness to Ms. Louise. Let him know there are monsters in the world, and that sometimes they wear a kindly face, sometimes they give you cookies and pretend that everything's fine.

BT put her arm around him, holding him close. He sucked in the scent of her honey night cream and her almond lotion. "I'm sorry," he said. "I'm sorry I dumped all this on you. I'm sorry that I'm drunk. I'm just … sorry."

She kissed him on the forehead. "I'll drive you home," she said.

"I don't want to go home," he said. "I want to stay here. With you. I can't go back there. I'm scared of what I might do."

She stood up. She offered her hand. "I'll make you something to eat," she said. "And I'll make up the couch."

Kenneth slipped out before the sun came up, stole a pair of BT's sunglasses and left a note apologizing for the intrusion. He went right back to bed when he got home. Let his mother lie in her own piss for another few hours. He couldn't bear to face her, not with his hangover, not with what he'd learned. He got up a few hours later to use the bathroom and heard BT talking to her as though nothing ever happened. Seth sat quietly at the table, playing his Game Boy.

While his mother took her post-lunch nap, he quietly got a shovel out of the garage. "Can I help?" Seth asked as he passed through the dining room.

"Not today," he grunted. "Lots of thorns still on those rose bushes. I don't want you to get hurt."

"I'll be careful," he said.

"Another time, buddy," he said. "I promise."

"Don't go outside," Mother warned. "There's a storm coming."

There was a storm brewing, all right. The storm of his anger. Of the blue lights flashing when the cops came to retrieve her. Let them put her in a home, declare her unfit for trial, let her rot there until her own guilt consumed her.

The dry red clay came up easy. He dug until he was sweating, dug until he was parched, dug until his palms were blistered and his arms ached. Six feet down he hit carpet. Six feet down he saw duct tape.

"I'm sorry," he said aloud. "I wish you had told me instead."

BT glanced up at him when he came back inside. He nodded. She held everything they both wanted to say inside her mouth, chewed it around until she could figure out what to say. "Seth, baby, can you go into the garage and put Ms. Louise's laundry in the dryer?"

He paused his game and set it down. He went into the garage and she closed the door just enough so that he couldn't hear them.

Kenneth sat down next to his mother on the couch. She wouldn't look at him. "You killed her, didn't you?" he asked.

"There's a tornado coming," she repeated.

"You killed her because of what Dad did," he said.

"Dana was such a pretty girl," she said.

"You saw her as competition," he said. "Your own daughter."

"What will the neighbors think?" she asked. "No mother wants her daughter to be a whore."

"She wasn't a whore," BT said. "She was a victim."

"Did you kill Aunt Lucille?"

"Lucille stole Marvin from me," she said. "Marvin Rockefeller. He was such a handsome boy. A lifeguard."

"So you let her drown," he said. "You eliminated the competition."

Seth came running back inside the house. For a moment, he panicked that the kid had heard everything. But before anyone could say another word, the tornado siren blasted. "We need to get in the shelter," he said, taking his mother's hand. "We'll talk more about this after the storm."

She wouldn't move.

"Mother, now!" he said.

Her eyes were clear. He could carry her, fireman-style, sling her over his shoulder and risk breaking her fragile bird-bones to save her life. But what life was there to save? The life of a killer. The life of a liar.

The life of his mother.

Louise patted BT's hand. "You remind me of my daughter," she said. "I wasn't a good mother to her."

"You weren't," BT said.

"Leave her," he said. "We have to go."

"We can't leave Ms. Louise!" Seth insisted.

"Sometimes people make bad choices, baby," BT said. "And Ms. Louise doesn't want to come down into the shelter. But we have to. Come on."

Maybe his mother would land in Oz. Maybe she would see his sister's face in the eye of the storm, repent for the harm she inflicted, the blood she spilled. He'd never know, and she'd never tell. He took one last look at her before he closed the basement door. She was staring straight ahead. She was waiting. She knew what was coming.

BT hugged Seth close as the winds roared overhead. He sobbed against her. Kenneth found his dad's old radio and turned it on. Nothing but static until the radio announcer broke through to tell them it was safe to come out again.

Author's Note: As a third-generation Oklahoma woman, storms—winds, rain, human or otherwise—have always held a certain fear and fascination for me. Tori Amos's "Talula," specifically "BT's Tornado Mix" from the *Twister* soundtrack, captures the feeling of being at the center of a storm—and of being one yourself. We bury what we are afraid of, but the winds of time always find us in the end.

The first time I remember dying was in 1989, but I've been doing it a long time. You've heard of me. If you haven't, you've been living under a rock for the last however many fucking years. I have a bunch of names; I heard somewhere names give you power. There's a True Name somewhere around here, if there's any such thing as truth. But what's so special about me? I know *what* it is, I just don't know *why*. I read somewhere "why?" is not a spiritual question. Probably the Buddhists said it. Try to kill me, I just come back. How many times, I don't know. Fuck, I can barely remember what I had for breakfast yesterday. Just kidding, it was a speedball and a pack of Marlboros.

1988

I scream at my lingering bandmates and the overly enthusiastic groupies to get the fuck out so I can have some goddamn peace and quiet. I cover myself in frankincense oil. Draw the circle on the floor around the synths and over the cables in chalk and then salt. Lie down on the wood floor that's growing hotter by the moment. The smell of heating wood around me reeks like a sauna. Hot and wet and wood, but not burning. Only my skin is burning. My eyes are burning. I drank a fifth of gin before I started—all the greatest magicians were drunks, probably for some good reason. I don't know why the fuck, I'll just reverse-engineer this shit. Follow their lead. My True Will emerges. What I want, what I've *always* wanted.

I start playing and the incantation enters my body like a body and flows through me, like a song I've sung a million times before, speaking itself. The music rages louder, vibrations summoning leviathans. The tones change the air, twisting future. Time becomes a helix, the textures of the synth creating new futures. The vibrations which formed the world swirl around me.

I will be famous. I will be forever famous. Music is my Great Work. They will speak my names long after I'm gone. They will remember me and everyone I was after my body has turned to dust. They will graffiti my song lyrics on the walls of dying cities, decaying buildings, torn-apart streets.

I jerk off in the center of the circle, laughing like a maniac as I come, like a good magician. I'm a fucking genius, and I've always been a fucking genius.

<u>1989</u>

Me and Gabe are shooting speedballs, my favorite mix, my favorite bride. Nothing else feels like it. My body warms in the embrace of H, she cradles me in her arms, an affectionate love soothing every worry, every memory. She kisses my face and pain is an unimaginable myth. Pain becomes something mothers tell their children to keep them from behaving badly, from wandering in forests of reality, meeting monsters made of suffering. The terrors of real life retreat into their chilly, dark caves, and sleep.

The cocaine makes it so I don't sleep thru the magic of this experience. The taste of cocaine enters my mouth, but I don't experience it as revolting anymore. It's a signifier of where I'm at. Every moment becomes precious, even when I puke from the rush of uppers and downers colliding. The collision isn't a fight, it's a wedding of opposites, they can't help but love each other and elicit the best of both.

As invincible as I feel, my fucking heart still stops.

I descend into a hall of darkness. Towering fibrous walls surround me, changing colors from red to blue to green to black to gray.

The chasm stretches on, just restoring itself over and over. The space folds in and out, becoming bigger and smaller at the same time.

There's hundreds, thousands of me. Milling around, looking lost. They have different hair, different clothes. I catch a glimpse of one dressed in a mechanic jumpsuit, the name tag reads AL. They are all me. Some gather around a dark pool, lapping at it with their tongues. Some are dancing in the corner together. They whisper and shriek. They speak to themselves, to each other, in English, Danish, and

Spanish. I understand some of the words— "never", "wait", "tremble", "stuck."

I hover above them, bodiless. What the fuck am I supposed to do? Descending into the mass of Mes, I reach out to one. I can't help it, something wants to connect, wants to touch them. My hand settles on the shoulder of one, and he turns to face me. And then, I don't know, I absorb him, my teeth settle into his teeth, fitting perfectly. My face is already his but takes on his textures. New pores, new lines. Mine, and also not mine. Slightly altered. I slide into his body like a glove. My mind tastes his.

I'm shat back into reality. Or birthed, I don't know. Who fucking cares. Reality flashes me back into existence and somehow, I'm back, back *here.*

I'm awake in a Chicago hospital, or some facsimile of awake. I'm alive again, or some facsimile. I'm me, or some facsimile.

It smells like sterilizing fluids.

Get these fucking tubes out of my arms, these diodes off my body, give me my fucking works or replace the IV drip with another speedball for the *love of fuck*! I scream as much to the nurses. The one with the high and tight haircut, probably a white supremacist piece of shit, tells me, "Your heart stopped, you were dead for three minutes, and you're still asking for the same thing that put you here." I call him a stream of names. He tells me it's normal to be afraid after an experience like that. I tell him if he's not holding to get the fuck out or better yet get me the fuck out.

<u>1990</u>

It's one of the Wet Impressionz parties and I'm doing lines with Finn. Dave and Joe are taking turns blowing one of the cute young fags from the Art Institute. This one is wearing tiny hot pink shorts with a one-inch inseam, who is touching his own nipples thru a white mesh shirt. Probably ecstasy. Whatever. I only have eyes for the small mountain of blow in front of me right now.

Some smart asshole wants to talk to us. It's fine; he brought enough coke to share with the whole class. He's showing off about his mathematical prowess, like that means something, coked up and wanting to put his dick on the table, apparently.

"There's a beautiful simplicity of formulas," he's said for the eightieth time. I've had enough.

"Until you get to a higher level of math, then all that simplicity goes out the window," I say. Except, I didn't say it. Something else inside me said it. I don't know fuck all about math. How do I know this?

"A system of linear formulas only has one answer, until it has no solution or sometimes infinite solutions," I go on. What the fuck. The smarthead's gritting his teeth and getting more annoyed by the second. Good. Who cares where this knowledge is coming from, I like pissing him off.

"If solving the system leads to a false statement, then it has no solution. But with infinite solutions, we aren't talking about a limiting function, we are talking about expansive functions. Sometimes solving for x leads to an infinite number of positive and negative outputs. You fucking prick."

Smarthead gets up and leaves us with the now cocaine hill.

"What the really fuck was that?" Finn says, a ring of powder dusting his nostril.

"You're a mess, you know that? Line up the rest, I wanna do it all."

Who the fuck wouldn't be a heroin addict if they could live forever? Who the fuck wouldn't want to see what they could get away with?

I speed down Chicago's Western Avenue in my Supra. Max speed of 155 miles per hour, but maybe I can make it go faster if I push my foot down fucking harder. I'll break this gas pedal if I have to.

I speed through stoplights, four lanes of traffic, I wanna cross them all. I wanna destroy all the limits. I want to die in this. The faster I go, the harder it becomes to control the car. One wrong move, and hopefully it'll all be over. At least I'll have answers.

Won't I?

I don't know what happened. Between pulls from the Bushmills bottle and orange construction lights, the car careens and I hit something hard, harder than a human body. Time slows down. The car flips and I sigh in relief. Here it comes.

Back in the cathedral hall with a thousand copies of myself. Descending again, I can't help but touch one. I can't stop myself.

Wake again in the fucking hospital. The same nurse who talked shit last time. This time, he wants to know all about me. Asks me a bunch of fucking questions to "confirm" where I live, who's in the band, my fucking social security number. He's writing everything down. I'm so doped on the morphine they've given me, I tell him everything he wants to know. Then he asks if I know how I'm back here, how could I survive such a crash, why I'm not in heaven. My real self wakes up through the drip.

I laugh in his face. Heaven, of all places to go. I tell him to go fuck himself, that as soon as I'm out of here, I'm really out of *here.* I'll leave Chicago, the fucking city is finished with me anyway. I've made too many enemies, owe too many people money. My marriage is falling apart, Lisa is threatening to leave and take Holly. Fuck it, I'll go to Texas. I'll figure that out after tour.

Nurse Dickhead is on the phone. I can't hear what he's saying, but he keeps looking at me and raising his eyebrows. I catch: "you'll want to learn more."

1992

The fences are up, but the crowd is just too nuts. I don't know when or why it happened, but at some point, the audience for our shows decided they'd join us on stage. All of them. Breaking bottles, jumping off the stage, sometimes fighting. The security meatheads couldn't stop them. So, fences.

We're backstage, I'm doing rails of cocaine in the

greenroom off the glass table with the funny metal hoof feet. Just the campiest shit, probably Italian. I'll take my sweet time, these fuckers can wait all night. I can hear the crowd screaming, chanting.

"Are you finished? Can we start now? By the way, Bill showed up tonight." Roman is staring at me from the doorway. He's already got his shirt off, he's so arrogant.

"Why don't you back the fuck off? What do you care when we go on?"

"We have a lineup, man. We were supposed to be on a half-hour ago." God, I hate his nasally, soft voice, he sounds like a faggy librarian.

"So what if we fucked up the rotation?"

Roman turns, and I hear him say in a low, angry tone, "*You* fucked up the rotation." I see a feminine face as I lean over the mirror—the ghost of the last Me I brought back. I took her because, well, I'll try anything once. I'm haunted by myself.

We stand in the hallway, almost showtime. Almost time for worship. And as we enter the stage, that's when I realize the crowd is chanting my name. Not the band's name, *my* name. I'm here. I'm fucking famous. I'll live forever.

The sea of people surges. It's like watching a real-life painting of a Bosch hellscape. One of me saw it at the Prado in '70s Madrid. I remember, but the other Mes' memories are always more like dreams. I can watch myself through my own eyes walking through the dark halls of the Prado. The museum was way run-down and Franco's fascist idiots were all running around with machine guns, spouting about the dangers of the Leftist, Communist, and Masonic threat to Spain. Students were rioting at the University of Madrid. Not a lot of tourists, which made it great. I kept going back to Bosch and Goya. There was one panel, *Noli me Tangere* by Correggio, that I went back to daily. A taste of Catholicism, the shit I grew up swallowing. I wish it didn't comfort me, but the familiar is always comforting. That counterbalance to the pure hell of Goya's dark paintings, which kept drawing me in like some dark juju **WE ARE FUCKED HUMANS** altar. An altar to our dark and destructive-beyond-cruelty collective. The first time I walked into the room of his Black Paintings, I fell to my knees and wept for forty-five minutes. Some kind of Stendhal Syndrome overcame me, or maybe that Me was more sensitive than I am. Or maybe I would've cried like a bitch too.

But the Bosch. Black buildings with lights pouring out. Throngs of tortured people screaming and pushing each other. People vomiting over the edges of balconies. I worshiped there. I stood in front of it as a late teenager and knew that's the future I'd be destined for. I don't know if the other Me thought that, but I do.

We open the show with a long squeal of feedback, which pisses off the audience. Good. We go into the percussion, and everyone knows it's the opening track of our big hit fucking album. The track with the Vietnam film sample.

I am the Colonel, driven mad by power. I'll torture who I need to to win this war.

We play a throbbing set. We play some old stuff, even though I'm not that person anymore. After so much coke, I love screaming into the boneclad microphone. The audience is tearing themselves to shreds. A Bosch come true. After the show, William Burroughs meets us backstage. He told me ages before the show he'd bring someone he wanted me to meet. I asked if it was a hot chick. He laughed his tight-teethed sneer-laugh. "Better," he said.

It was Timothy Leary. I want to know everything about him. Shit, I wanna *be* him. He was once called the most dangerous man in America. He gives me his number and tells me he wants to try H sometime, says I can come by anytime to his place in California, for as long as I'd like to stay. "I have lots of space, especially for someone like you," he said, and he touched my ear.

I shiver. I can still feel it if I concentrate.

Me and Gabe are shooting up in the back of the tour bus. Roman is annoyed with us, but what else is new.

It wasn't the ritual. It's something else. Something inside me. My mother told me I was born months early, I shouldn't have lived. Did I die then? How many times have I died?

I don't want to think about it anymore. I don't want to think at all. How can I live when I might not be able to die? What could kill me? How destructive do I have to be? Or is it that time simply takes me? I don't want to think about decaying. My hair falling out, my teeth withering. My body becoming thin and fine and frail, with bones like a bird. Hollow and weak. I will *never* be weak.

Fame is here for me, but how long will it stay? Will my vision come true? Will fame fade, despite how undying I appear to be?

At least I can control the body, whichever body I am now. Control my own blood flow, which direction it goes in, whether it stays in my body or leaves. I could bleed myself out if I wanted to. Wouldn't matter. I'll dive headlong into oblivion again and again, how intense can the oblivion get, how far can I sink. Not thinking isn't enough, I just don't want to *be* anymore.

Roman is screaming in my face but seems very far away. Later, I smash a bottle of wine against Gabe's head.

<u>1995</u>

Chicago is done, been done. In Texas since the end of the big LaLa Land tour. I just bought a fucking compound in Marble Falls. Five acres, a former retreat center for twelve Texas Oil Big Fucks. Probably used it for their psychotic vacations from reality fueled by cocaine, sex workers, and whatever bizarro shit rich white dudes with broken moral compasses get up and off to. At least I'm just a garden-variety junkie who can't die. I'm nothing special.

It was about nine in the morning when the cops showed up. Jesus, how many cops do you fucking need to turn this junkie's ranch house upside down? The answer is thirty-two.

FBI, ATF, DEA, plus local, state, and county authorities. Overkill, if you ask Me. Any Mes.

I was sleeping. Sleeping, passed out, same thing essentially. I wake up to my door being broken down, and a swarm of black-clad SWAT cops screaming and shining shit in my face like God's flashlight aka the fucking sun isn't bad enough. I don't think, I just rise like I'm running in reverse and launch myself out of the window.

I smash against the giant oak on the way down. I can feel my head bounce off the trunk and my neck snaps in a few places with a wet crunching series of pops. Whatever. Here comes the InBetween Cathedral.

Floating down, this time I've got an idea. Landing on the cathedral floor, which changes texture and firmness even as my feet touch. Feeling like soft clay, then concrete, to almost a furry texture. I move my legs as though I could walk like in the Real World, but my feet sink into the ground. Then they don't.

The light in the cathedral has no source, the illumination total from top to bottom, though I can't see how high it goes. It's a building, but not. It's a cavern, but not. It's a palace with no ceiling, no end to the depth of it, endless night that must be illuminated by ... something. Something internal, intrinsic to the place itself. Whatever the fuck this place is.

I approach a group of Mes, directing my True Will, like Crowley would demand. They gibber to one another, it's language insomuch as all language is a series of sounds with meaning. Artaud said all true language is incomprehensible, and I don't know which Me knows so. Fuck it.

I rush the group, crashing into them, trying to touch as many as possible. I'm taking as many of these fucks with me as I can. Maybe I can empty the Hall of Me, like the Buddhist emptying of Hells. Let's all wake the fuck up.

The same sliding into a new body, I can feel my neck rebuild again. My spine stacks up correctly. My skull splintering repaired. I fit Myself into Myself, but who the fuck am I anyway? I live. Again. And now I'm dopesick in prison. I'll be here for at least a month. Shitting and puking. I love puke, it's so animalistic. There's no private shitter in prison, so I dopeshit in front of everyone. People leave me alone, and I'm too sick to think anymore. Good.

"Don't be primitive, son."

Merlot, apparently a very good year, is passed around again and again. Paul Getty Jr. is gesturing with his wine glass. We're on our seventh bottle, but Getty probably drank two himself. I wonder how this dude lives with himself, but he probably wonders the same about Me. Pretty funny for two old heroin addicts; the only difference is he has a trust fund and I don't.

"You'll never understand, Tim, you don't come from the same stock I do. Your father was a *dentist*." I'm tuning him out—lots of people would love to have your problems, asshole. I start making eyes at Laura. I don't give a fuck if she's eighty-four. I'll show her the time of her long-ass life.

Long life. Fuck. Will I be that old, older? Will I make it past one hundred years and just keep going?

I down my glass of wine, lick my lips at Laura, and prepare to ask her if she's ever seen anyone suck their own dick before and would she like to but then Getty is gesturing at me.

"And how's the experiment going, Tim?"

Tim looks stricken. I've never seen Tim speechless. Getty doesn't notice and keeps going.

"It's amazing you can just adopt a low-life musician and get paid by the feds to shoot him up. What does the government want with a degenerate like that, anyhow?"

My whole world freezes, chill as Chicago winter wind. "What the fuck are you talking about, you British-wannabe piece of shit?" I leap across the table, the H overtaken by adrenaline. My hands are on Paul Getty Jr.'s throat, I'm shaking him and screaming. Tim and Michael and Ronald Reagan Jr. are on Me, prying Me off. Getty's coughing and red-faced.

"You're not even a pet, you're just an animal," he manages to spit out.

"At least I didn't let Italians take my kid and leave him there for months. Now he's a vegetable, isn't he? There's a special place in Hell for people like you, Getty."

"I think this dinner has reached an organic conclusion." Tim smiles his cat smile. The world is crumbling around me.

"What did you expect? That this was all some transactionless encounter? You're novel, to be sure. I wanted to take the job, I wanted to know too. The key to all knowledge is somewhere inside you, I'm sure of it," Tim said.

"The state, though? The fucking state. You knew I'd never agree."

"But you did agree. *You* asked if you could come after the incident."

My blood freezes inside my veins with understanding. "The raid … that was orchestrated. It was never about finding shit. It was to get me here."

"You would've come eventually. Destiny is real. They just sped up the timeline." Tim shrugs. "You should be grateful they only wanted me to study you. You'd be a terrible soldier." Tim laughs.

My body as research for warfare. A tool for the fucking Man. Fucking never.

"I have to leave."

"Let's shoot one last time, my boy. Do it for your old man."

I let him. Holes in the sky open. It's Goya's *Saturn*, except Saturn's body has eight spindly legs and eight eyes on Tim's face. He's lifting my body to his dripping and bloodied mouth. I am devoured.

I can never tell anyone. Not even after he dies, which will certainly be before Me.

This is the most humiliating betrayal of my whole life. It feels like a play. I'll never let anyone suspect. Tim can stay my hero, everyone's hero, can't he?

"It's chaos that makes you what you are—don't know what that is, only what it's not," Tim says as I leave.

Whatever the fuck that means. I don't know where I'll

go, but there's a Me around here somewhere who does. If they're not in Me already, I know how to find them.

AUTHOR'S NOTE: Al Jourgensen once said Ministry's *Filth Pig* album was "music to kill yourself to." Every addict engages in a kind of death wish performance, whether that death is spiritual, physical, emotional, or all three. What if death is impossible? Worse, what if you return again and again with *more* self? Special thanks to Ministry, Revolting Cocks, Lard, 1000 Homo DJs, Pigface, Pailhead, and every other band that made our parents change the car radio station.

It's early March 1993 and Generation X sorely needs an antihero. Not a folk hero, you fucking hippies. Not a sponsored, manufactured musician in Chuck Taylors and unwashed hair, not even if he's a morosely self-aware and self-flagellating genius (sorry, Kurt). Certainly not one of those pre-packaged, obnoxiously beautiful sellouts from The Real World. We need one of us. We need someone who is living this shit for real and not someone washing themselves in a corporate spotlight. We need someone like Kelly G.

End of fifth period lunch and Kelly G. was in the courtyard, orange Walkman headphones around her neck instead of over her ears, music from a mixtape spilling out. She was sitting on top of her black Dickies sweatshirt under the lone spindly tree in the space. It had taken her more than a full academic year to claim that spot as hers. She didn't have many, or any, friends in Stoughton and she liked it that way. Kelly wasn't ugly. She wasn't pretty. She liked that her arms and hands and legs and feet were too long for her torso. She wore glasses with photochromic lenses that stayed shaded under the decrepit school's florescent lights. Her hair was dark, long, and curly, which, apparently, made her ethnically indeterminate based on the number of times white kids and teachers asked *Where is your family from?* She was mostly Portuguese with a name that ended in a "z" if you must know. But she knew who she was and she didn't care what anyone thought of her, which made her an intimidating one-of-one in that school. With five minutes left in the lunch period, a nineteen-year-old senior named Jared wandered over to her tree. He had been on the wrestling team until last year when the school shit-canned the program due to budget cuts. Jared wasn't ugly. Jared wasn't pretty. He didn't have any close friends, but he moved through the social strata of school freely and without consequence. The hallways and locker rooms whispered that he was tapped in the head, not someone to fuck with, not someone to be hanging out with— not after the cops had broken up the party in the woods near Ames Pond. The stupid freshmen believed he'd stayed back twice and had no mom. The annoying sophomores swore he'd stabbed a kid behind the football bleachers and he had no dad. Rumor and myth aside, he was the kid who crossed out the "S" on three NOW ENTERING STOUGHTON street signs as though he'd invented, or claimed, the *Toughtown* nickname.

Like the name and the whole fucking town, Kelly figured Jared was all bluff, all bluster. Jared stood with his scruffy Jordan Nikes inches from Kelly's boots. He rubbed a hand through his bangs and then the stubble undercut, waiting for her to say something first. She didn't. He turned his back to her and mumbled, "You work takeout at the Star?" She said, "Yeah, but I don't have your order." He said, "You work there on Fridays," like it was a pronouncement, a portent, and not a question. She said, "Sometimes." He said, "Maybe I'll see you there some Friday." Sometime between her standing and tying her sweatshirt around her waist and him leaving, the bell rang.

> *We need someone who was weaned on* Judy Blume, Kindred, *Stephen King,* Maus, The Handmaid's Tale, *stacks of Choose Your Own Adventures, but definitely not any of the Beats or any of the other books from the '50s and '60s that her high school teachers constantly push (okay, fine, in middle school I was totally into* The Outsiders). *We need someone who was weaned on shitty cable TV movies and* Barney Miller *and* Family Ties *and* The Facts of Life, *and yeah, fine, MTV, too. We need someone like Kelly G.*

That next Friday Kelly G. worked the takeout counter with two soccer players who only talked to her when they had to.

Not that there was time for chat because it was fucking Lent and every quasi-Catholic asshole in on the no-meat-Friday charade was getting pizza. Lenten Fridays got so busy the restaurant paid a dumbass cop to direct traffic in the lot and prevent fistfights over parking spots and near fender-benders. Town Star Pizza was hailed as the South Shore's best pizza, despite Stoughton being no-fucking-where near any shore. It couldn't have been more overrated as far as Kelly was concerned. Cracker-thin crust and personal-sized bar-style pizza. A wall with a single connecting door separated the takeout area—a square room that included soda fridges and a brand-new, standalone ATM next to a Keno screen—from the sprawling, always-packed restaurant and bar. Takeout even had its own parking lot, in theory. But on a Friday during Lent, all parking bets were off. At thirty minutes to closing, the ATM was out of cash and the line for takeout was a formless mob that spilled out the door. The whole night had been a blur of Kelly calling out first names with last initials and telling the occasional yuppie from Canton that the Star was cash-only and pointing out the ATM. Kelly allowed herself to look at the clock again and it was still, somehow, thirty minutes till closing. Thirty minutes to decide if she was going to beg a coworker for a ride or walk the two miles home in the dark. Someone in the kitchen slid a single pizza through the mail-slot-type hole in the wall between the kitchen and takeout and onto the counter behind the registers. She loudly read the name on the order slip: "Jared F!" Jared broke from the mob and stepped up to her register. He wore a Red Sox hat, pulled low, and a smile that was lower. Kelly told him the price. He passed her a ten. Kelly pressed buttons and opened the register, stuck the ten in its bulging slot, gathered the change, and closed the drawer. Jared said, "A lot of cash in there." Kelly said, "Fucking Lent." He nodded, sprinkled a single and change into a tip jar, and said in a voice that was lower than his hat and smile, "We'll talk."

> *Let's talk about the name Generation X. It kind of sounds cool, mostly. The "X" because you can't define us, right? It's already being overused and corporate-opted. And it's not like we're all cool. Some of us are the worst people we know, and they will only get worse as they get older. And hey, is it weird that Generation X came from some Canadian novel? Not that there's anything wrong with Canadians. And sure, fine, he got the term from somewhere else, but it's that novel people will remember and credit, and it wasn't even that good to be honest. Let's be honest because I will always be honest. People will remember Kelly G.*

Kelly G. was back at her tree during Monday's lunch. She was the only one outside because of a hard drizzle, the sharp and pointy kind. It was glorious and she didn't want to waste a day like this in school when she could be in her room with her window open and listening to music, so after lunch she went to the nurse and said she was coming down with something. The nurse didn't argue. Tuesday was different. The sun was out and it was warm, too warm for March, and half the school was outside. The underclassmen chased and wrestled and giggled, and the juniors roamed and mingled, and the seniors, who were tired, huddled in packs. Kelly hated it all and sulked under her craggy tree. At least her lenses were full dark. Nearing the end of the period, a tumbleweed of freshman boys rolled by and when their noxious cloud of acne and body odor cleared, Jared was there. His back was turned. Though she couldn't see his face, she knew he was smiling. He said, "Can we talk?" She said, "About what?" He said, "How much money are in those registers?" She said, "Depends on the day." He said, "I bet there's always a lot." She said, "Then why'd you ask?" He said, "Wanted to hear your answer." She said, "If you're gonna ask me to skim for you, you won't want to hear my answer." A teacher popped out of a door and yelled at some sophomore girls who were passing notes through an open cafeteria window. The girls ignored him. The teacher looked like a moray eel as he sank back inside his hidey-hole. Jared said, "I'm not asking you to skim." She said, "Are you asking me something?" He said, "More like telling you." She said, "You haven't told me anything." He said, "I'll be back to see you one of these days." She said, "Another Lent Friday?" He said, "A day when there's no cops outside." Kelly laughed. She didn't believe him, just like she didn't believe anybody, including herself. But she did believe he was being serious in the moment. She said,

"I'm not helping." He said, "I'm not asking you for help. You don't have to do anything. In fact, I'm here telling you to do nothing. No calls to no one—that part is important. And if anyone asks you anything, you say nothing. Can you do that? Can you do nothing?" Kelly said, "I do that all the time." He said, "I bet." She said, "Do I get anything for doing nothing?" He said, "Yeah. After I see how well you do nothing." The bell rang. Kids mock-screamed and scream-screamed. Their sneakers squished in mud. They funneled through the double-wide cafeteria doors. Kelly said, "Sounds like a threat." He said, "No, a threat would sound like '*I know you live in Wood End with your mom and your little brother and you don't lock your front door.*'"

The Lost Generation has a cool ring, but it tries too hard. O, woe is us. Like, how bad do we have it? They tell us we don't have it that bad. They always tell us that. The MTV Generation can go fuck itself. Latchkey Generation is okay and maybe the most accurate. But some of us can't be trusted with keys or the lock might even be busted. Are all our parents divorced? Do they all work late hours or just not come home sometimes? Whatever you want to call us, we don't care. We just need someone for whom heartbreak, loneliness, and alienation isn't a convenient pose and is instead their resting state. We need Kelly G.

Eighteen months ago, in the middle of her sophomore year, Lobsterman Dad—she sometimes imagined him with pincers for hands and beady black eyes, and sometimes what his subverbal grunts and huffs would sound like if he were plopped into a pot of boiling water—fled Gloucester for Maine. He called once every two months like clockwork. Mom, in an act of revenge and self-sabotage, moved Kelly, her younger brother Tommy, and their dog Peru south and inland, into a two-bed one-bath rowhouse here between big bad Brockton and affluent Sharon and Canton. Mom answered phones at the Department of Public Works by day and two, or three, or four, or five nights a week she either tended bar or just hung out at Doyle's. Mom said, "You're not funny," whenever Kelly creatively pointed out the bar's proximity to the Foxy Lady. Mom slept on a pullout couch in the living area so Kelly and Tommy could have their own bedrooms. Poor Peru was relegated to a too small penned-off area near the front door because of some skin disease that made her back and haunch fur fall out in clumps. Mom never tired of the observation that Peru's ass looked just like her ex-husband's balding head. That afternoon, Kelly got home a little after 3:30 p.m. The front door was locked but it didn't stay locked if you pulled and pushed up on the handle. She swung the door open slowly, careful to not ram it into Peru. A toxic fog of stench greeted her instead of the dog. There was an elephant-was-here pile of shit on the floor, just beyond the reach of the swinging door. She said, "Jesus, fuck—Tommy?" No answer. The middle school got out earlier than the high school and most days she came home to find Tommy playing Nintendo. He must've come home, saw the mess, and let Peru out—Peru spent more than half of her days roaming free in the complex; that she always came back made Kelly feel less guilty about her not being allowed in the rest of the apartment. Thomas probably went on his own roam of the complex or to the McD's in Cobb's Corner because he didn't want to deal with an oil spill of dogshit. It had a weird, gross film of mucus on top, too. Kelly was pissed at Tommy and a little worried about the insides of Peru's gut. Then she flashed to Jared saying that he knew where she lived. Maybe Jared had already come by and fed Peru chocolate or rat poison, or rat poison with chocolate. That dog would go to anyone and eat anything. She worried about Jared finding Tommy walking down Central Street or in line at McD's, and like the dog, Thomas would go to anyone and eat anything. The worries were vague enough in their threat to become even more worrisome. Kelly stepped over the adjustable fence, went to her bedroom, snagged Dad's old Polaroid, and paused in the doorway. Now, Kelly didn't believe in signs from the universe. She didn't believe the universe was a sentient, give-a-crap entity. That didn't mean this epic shit pile didn't have meaning. What it was, was a metaphor. Kelly believed you could find or make metaphors if you stayed open to them. Kelly went back into her room, opened the top underwear drawer, and plucked out a red-handled pocketknife with a single, squat three-inch blade. She had a plan. She had a plan for the shit, and a plan for Jared, for everything. Kelly pocketed the knife and returned to the scene of Peru's crime. With the toe of her boot, she slid the water dish next to the shit. She needed the dish for scale. She snapped a picture. The Polaroid whined. She stepped over the fence and put the photo and camera down on the coffee table. She gathered up paper towels, a quarter-full bottle of Pine Sol, and a garbage bag. As she cleaned, dry-heaving from the foulness of it all, and the shit pile, still, somehow, radiating heat through the wad of towels protecting her hand, she considered the metaphor more deeply. Maybe it represented what she'd been dealt in the short term. Maybe it represented what she would continue to be dealt if she followed Jared's "Do nothing" demand and threat. The shit cleaned up, chemical cleaner tanging the air, garbage cinched and tossed out front, Kelly patted the knife in her pocket and then hung the Polaroid photo of the dish and the shit onto the fridge with a Town Star Pizza magnet. She wrote a message on the photo's wide border at the bottom. The message was and would be for everyone: Look what Kelly G. had to fucking clean up!

> *We're the Loser Generation, and that's okay. There's dignity in losing. There's dignity in longing and needing. We need someone who's used to losing and used to being ignored, dismissed, or not even considered. We need someone who is invisible. We need someone who will make us feel her dotted outline. We need someone to make us feel something, anything. We need someone who might*

go away but won't ever die. The past isn't ours. We don't want it. We should've been dead already, incinerated in a thousand nuclear flashes. We have no future. For many of us, it has already been determined. We need someone who knows we're dead already. When we hear my story, some of us will pause and think and laugh and cry and raise a fist and curl a lip and sigh and shake our heads, and someday we will remember me not because I sang a song or wore cool boots or pouted for a camera, but because I showed us the consolation of losing is the same as the consolation of caring. It's May 1993 and Generation X still sorely needs an antihero. We need Kelly G. We need me.

Fucking Lent ends and more days and weeks pass whether or not anyone wants them to. Jared doesn't talk to Kelly G. again at school, doesn't even come outside during lunch anymore. He doesn't show up at the Star, either. No matter, because all the waiting makes what he has planned and what she has planned more real. Kelly runs through every possible scenario in her head, and daydreams about what everyone in school and in the town and in the country will think and say about her. She can't help but imagine angsty, noisy songs written about her; preferably at least one by Buzzcocks. The songs are popular but not too popular, and they piss off the right people. She can't help but imagine a movie, something dopey but still kind of awesome like *The Legend of Billie Jean*, being made about her. She hates herself for thinking that her antihero status requires pop culture approval but would welcome such approval with open arms and rolled eyes. Then, finally, on a sleepy Friday in mid-May, Kelly works the register alone because it's only 4:30 p.m. More register jockeys won't be coming in until after five. But Kelly isn't alone, the knife in her pocket keeps her company. Besides, the takeout area isn't empty; it's never empty. Someone's mom who smells like cigarettes and regret works the Keno window and register, and she half-assedly flirts with two grimy dudes who only have eyes for the animated Keno numbers appearing on the screen. There's a high school couple from Easton dressed in their obnoxious Oliver Ames High School gear waiting for their order. Behind them is Jack P., a reedy, melting candle of a mechanic from the body shop across the street. He always orders two pizzas pre-Friday rush: one with cheese and one with linguica. Kelly has her back turned, watching the counter between her and the kitchen, when the front door bursts open, accompanied by a heavy shuffle of feet and gasps and a scream or two and then above it all, a shout: "Everyone against that wall! Now!" Kelly turns and she has a smile on her face. She can't help it. The smile is nervous and hungry. Jared waves the handgun like it's a flashlight in a dark room. She imagined a beat-up shotgun, maybe sawed-off like in the movies. He quickly herds the customers up against the wall between takeout and the restaurant. Jared is dressed all in black, including a ski mask, and—good for him!—his sneakers. Kelly had imagined him wearing his stupid Nike

Jordans. The handgun and black sneakers are a sign that he put some real thought into this. Though not as much as she has. As ready as Kelly is, she doesn't know how this will turn out, and that only widens her smile. Jared orders the customers to lie on the floor and the two grimy dudes block the door to the restaurant with their whimpering bodies. Kelly wonders if a second person is waiting in an idling car in the mostly-empty parking lot. Either way, she knows Jared isn't planning on giving her a cut. The Keno mom on the other end of the counter has her hands up. Did Jared ask her to do that? Kelly has her right hand in her front pocket. Jared's view is blocked by the register. That hand pulls out the knife. She opens it, then curls her left hand around the knife's small handle. Jared throws a cloth bag to her and says, "Fill it." He turns and pivots, a weathervane in a storm, trying to keep an eye on everyone and everything at once, when he should be keeping an eye on Kelly because her plan isn't *do nothing.* She says, "I know who you are." Jared turns to stone, briefly. Then he approaches the counter, gun arm extended, no bend in the elbow. He says, "No you don't." She says, *"I'm pretty sure I do."* Keno Mom whispers something at Kelly, but Kelly doesn't hear it. She refuses to be distracted now that she's finally here, at the moment she's imagined nearly every waking minute of the past two months. This is her moment of chaos within chaos. Jared must sense this in some dumb animal way. His eyelids flutter and he bares his feckless teeth. "You don't know me," and he says it as bratty as a kid who doesn't want to share his toy. He licks his lips, and adds,

"But you're a problem, now. I have the solution right here." He stops walking, with the gun hovering halfway across the counter. His hand trembles. Kelly presses a button on the register. The drawer clangs open and Jared jumps. She laughs and says, "Nervous Nellie." He doesn't say anything. He continues blinking and continues not seeing her left hand, which is hiding under the bag he threw to her. Jared isn't all talk, but she's going to find out how much talk he is. Kelly says, "Do it." He says, "What?" She says, "Do it." He looks to his right, at the Keno mom and the customers on the floor, like maybe they'll help him. Kelly grabs Jared's wrist and pulls his hand and the gun toward her, pressing the muzzle against her own forehead. Momentum stumbles him forward until the tops of his thighs are pressed against the counter. He asks, "What are you doing?" Her eyes are on his eyes and she easily wins that wrestling match. She raises the knife, slow and smooth, and presses blade tip under his jawline, dimpling the skin. In one of her endless imaginings of this moment, she told him that she was a lefty the second before she bullied the knife under his skin. There were endless times she imagined a blood cloud billowing from the back of her head and her falling to the floor, a fall into grace. Now that the moment she imagined, that she crafted, a moment with only two possible future outcomes, is here, she wants it to last longer. She wants it to last forever. The best part is, is that it will last forever for us. After. After she says, "Do it," one more time.

AUTHOR'S NOTE: Buzzcocks don't get enough credit (or blame?) as antecedents and influencers of '90s alternative music. In a fair universe, their 1979 opus *Singles Going Steady* would be as famous as Nirvana's *Nevermind* or Green Day's *Dookie*, or at the very least, more well-known and better appreciated than, ugh, *Oasis*. Let's never speak of that band again. Buzzcocks did have a second act, of sorts, in the '90s, with the minor hit "Do It." The song's video—with the band looking vaguely mod—made a few appearances on American cable TV. It's a good song, one with Pete Shelley's typically playful, melancholic lyrics and melodic hooks. However, Kelly G. spends way more time listening to *Singles Going Steady*.

Jill paused at the bridge. It'd been a while since she'd been to Robbie Rubin's house, but she was pretty sure she would have remembered an entire bridge. She would never have forgotten something so spooky. It was covered—unusual in the South—and its dry rot and aged wood made it look ancient. She walked onto the bridge and relished in the shivers produced by her echoing bootsteps. Once she reached the middle of it, Jill leaned over the rail and smiled at herself in the flowing river below.

For someone who loved the idea of Halloween as much as Jill, October was always a month of possibilities that ended in discomfort and disappointment. The holiday in North Florida was always kind of lame. Nine times out of ten, it was swampy and your costume made you sweat terribly. Or the season would have flashed through fall and gone straight to a dry, bitter cold that made you hide your costume under coats and hats, making it pointless and joyless. But tonight,

Jill was getting nothing but *Sleepy Hollow* vibes, and it was a Samhain miracle.

Frogs groaned, cicadas warned, and the occasional laugh or squeal wafted down from the house with refrains of Oingo Boingo. Looking over the bridge and watching the lights from the house twinkle along with the reflected stars and waning moon, Jill felt elated.

All she ever wanted was a romantic Halloween.

"Something cozy and creepy, you know?" she had told Brom, when he asked her what her deepest desires were. And here he had magically delivered. He had told her to imagine the couples costume she wanted most, get outfitted, and he would meet her at the bridge. It had all been a little unbelievable and confusing, but now she understood what he meant. He had crafted this whole perfect experience just for her.

That was sort of Brom's whole deal, him being a demon and all. Jill and her best friend Jackie found him floating down the river like a rag-doll Moses. Someone or something had nestled it in a wren's nest before offering it up to the current, and it had washed up on the bank where Jackie and Jill always met when skipping class. Jackie fished it out and threw the doll at Jill's face. It landed in her lap, and Jill was repulsed by its absolute decrepitude and blankness. The doll had no clothes, no facial features, no hair. It was just a bland, stuffed pattern of a thing made out of potato sack and crude stitching.

Jackie immediately began yammering with her typical woo-woo biz of how it was some kind of demon-doll thing called a *Homhunkulous* and "blah-blah-blah grants unbidden desires." Jill gave it back to Jackie, told her she and it were full of shit, and Jackie gladly took it and stuffed it in her backpack while flicking Jill the finger goodbye.

That had been earlier this week, and since then Jackie had totally ghosted her until Jill decided to cold-call her at her house. That had been a horrible scene, and Jill was not proud of how she responded to it. But it did lead her to find Brom and the creation of this night, so whatever, who cares if Jackie's pissed. She'll live.

In the reflecting water, Jill watched a large shadow grow and loom over her. Brom! She resisted turning around to see his green, flaming eyes again, but she knew it would feel spookier to let the anticipation build. It grabbed her by the ribs, and she shrieked and struggled. When she was free and faced the shadow, her heart dropped. It was a girl like her in a hooded cape and dress. The girl dropped the hood back—it was Jackie in a Snow White costume.

"Hey, trick. Where's my treat?"

"Go away, Jackie. You're ruining it."

"Ruining what?"

"My cozy Halloween."

"That's what you are using him for?" Jackie rolled her eyes. "Of course you are." Jackie took a step back to take in Jill's costume. "Who are you supposed to be, anyway? Falco?"

Jill looked down at her mom's yoga pants tucked into some knee-high stockings.

"I'm Ichabod Crane, duh."

"You stole him from me so you could have a cute couples

costume?" Jackie cackled so hard it made her bend over the railing.

"It's better than what you were doing with him. Manifesting guy after guy just to vacate them and leave their empty husks on your floor."

"Oh, please. You thought I was full of shit when I told you what it was."

"Stop talking about Brom like that. He has feelings, you know."

"Ugh, I do know."

"You abused him!"

"Abused? He's a demon, a thing—you can't abuse a thing!"

"He's not a thing …"

"I swear to God, Jill—if you don't hand over that fucking doll, I will take it from you."

"Yeah, you and what army?"

Jackie wolf-whistled, and out of the bushes at the bridge entrance emerged seven vapid skaters dressed as Snow White's famous dwarves—sleeping caps and all.

Jill was overcome with dread. She had met these guys earlier that afternoon when she went to Jackie's house to confront her for ghosting. All the cars were gone, so Jill had snatched the spare key from under the welcome mat and let herself in. Babes in Toyland was blaring from Jackie's room and over the music she heard Jackie laugh in a fake and inane way she'd never heard her do before. The door was open a crack, and Jill pushed it further open and peeked in. Jackie was making out with some strange guy!

"You've been ditching me for a boy?" Jill yelled. The two pounced away from each other on the opposite sides of the bed. Once Jackie realized that Jill wasn't her mom, she scowled at her. But the guy looked at her pleadingly, almost thankfully, with wide green eyes with flaming pupils. Jill began to feel entranced by him, who seemed to speak in her head: *Save me!*

Jackie sighed and said, "Meh, I wasn't feeling it anyway." The guy's face, then body, began contorting. Jill tried to back out of the room, but he exploded into a blinding light that made her trip over herself instead. When her eyes recovered, she saw on the floor the empty husk of the boy, and on the pillows where he sat was the stupid *Homhunkulous* doll.

"Grab his ankles, would ya?" Jackie was bent over the boy, tugging at his arms.

"Is he dead?"

"No, he's a Hunk."

"What?"

"Just help me. They're fucking heavy." Jill grabbed his ankles and the two girls dragged him to Jackie's walk-in closet. Jill dropped the boy when Jackie kicked open the closet door and Jill saw arms and legs spilling out. It was brimming with a half-dozen other empty Hunk husks. Jackie busied herself with pulling the latest up and over the pile. Jill creeped over to the bed and stared at the doll in disbelief. *Save me! Save me now!*

Next thing Jill knew, she was running down the neighborhood street hand-in-hand with Brom, giggling and making plans for the perfect night. Somehow, she had managed to push the discomforting thought of the Hunks out of her mind until now.

Jackie caressed the nearest one.

"You know, it's funny. You wanted nothing to do with the doll until you saw that maybe I had something you didn't." She let her hand fall under his shirt and rummage around in his pants.

"Jackie, come on." Jill looked away, blushing.

"No, you come on." Jackie pulled from his pocket a switchblade. "Either you give him back to me, or I'll fucking take him from you."

Jill took a step back.

"Goddamn, Jackie—you're kind of taking this a bit far, don't you think?"

"Give. It. Back. Now!" Jackie stepped closer and put the blade up to Jill's face.

"He doesn't want you!" Jill shouted. "He wants me!"

Jill's response was drowned out by a flash of lightning striking a tree. Under its flaming limbs, a tall figure emerged—Brom as the Headless Horseman, replete with a flaming jack-o'-lantern head.

Jackie let go of Jill and shouted at the Hunks to go get him. The Hunks lumbered toward him, but when they reached the burning tree, he held his hands up, and they halted. They turned to face Jackie and Jill and as one began to convulse and contort. Their skin swelled and bruised with blood, and eventually each Hunk popped off like a gigantic zit. The released fluid boiled their skin and tissue off with acidic efficiency until all that was left was bone.

Brom stomped around the skelehunks, took off his

pumpkin head, and hurled it at them, bowling a perfect strike. Jackie and Jill ducked as ribs, limbs, jaws, and skulls went flying in all directions.

Jackie spun around to Jill and raised the blade up to her chin.

"Fucking give me the doll *now*, Jilly Bean."

"Fuck off, Jackie."

"We'll share him."

"I don't want to share."

Jackie started patting her down, Jill slapping her arms and hands away, and became more and more aggressive until Jill shoved her off so hard she slammed against the railing. Jackie crumpled over and howled in pain.

Overcome with remorse, Jill rushed over to help Jackie. Jackie raised the blade over her head and lunged at Jill. Jill caught her hand, but she lost her footing and the girls went down on top of each other. They wrestled on the ground until Jackie rolled Jill onto her stomach. She stabbed the small of Jill's back, and it hit the fanny pack Jill had tucked behind her coat. Here, the blade found the doll.

Jackie was thrown off Jill by a bright blue explosion that propelled her across the bridge and against the flaming tree. Jill herself was shot through the bridge and into the river, and she treaded water against the current until she found ground and stood up.

When she looked down at her clothes, she saw they were covered in blood.

"Oh, shit, Jackie!" She clambered out of the river and ran back up to the Jackie-side of the bridge—and was surprised to find the bridge was gone. Jackie was slumped against the now-smoldering tree. To Jill's horror, the doll was in Jackie's lap as whole as the day they found him. Jill slapped Jackie a few times and felt ill at the lack of response. She sat beside Jackie and retrieved the doll.

"Was this," Jackie coughed, "your idea of a cozy Halloween?" Her voice sounded like Brom. Jill jolted away from her friend, who stayed slumped against the tree, barely able to raise her head.

"No one was suppose to get hurt." Jill bowed her head and cried.

"Least of all you, right?"

Jill looked up and saw Jackie awake and smiling at her. "Jackie! Jackie, I'm so sorry!" Jill gave Jackie a hug and felt a searing in her heart. She looked down and saw the switchblade sticking out of her chest. Jackie was still motionless against the tree. Confused, Jill staggered back to the river, collapsed on the bank, and dropped the doll into the water. The last thing she saw was Brom being picked up by the current and carried away on a raft of pine needles and leaves.

AUTHOR'S NOTE: This story was inspired by Babes in Toyland's "He's My Thing," which appeared on their fourth album, *Painkillers*. The song is an interesting if not vituperative take on a love triangle that is masterfully illustrated by a creepy baby doll aesthetic unique to the band, and the accompanying video made by Phil Harder and Mike Etoll.

TRACK ONE – THIS NOT AN ALBUM (OR A PLAYLIST)

Leonard killed women. It was just a job.

Which didn't make him the devil, nor just a rat in a cage. On the rare occasions he allowed himself to give the matter undue thought, he maybe saw himself as a benevolent angel of death.

He killed the people other killers preferred to steer clear of. Someone had to do it.

He justified his job by always reminding myself that he carried out his work tasks with kindness. There was no unnecessary pain involved, no torture or lingering agony for the unfortunate victim to contend with. He took no joy in completing his assignments. He took no pleasure in the killing. It's what he was paid for and he was good at it. Precise, decisive, accurate, clean.

He killed women.

There was no element of hate or misogyny, just an acceptance that were he not do so, there were other operatives who would and they more likely than not would make a mess of it, falter in their aim, botch things up and leave the mark writhing in pain, bleeding away, her mind filled with despair, her body torn apart by terrible pain and abominable thoughts coursing through her brain as the light and consciousness ebbed away all too slowly.

He allowed his victims some dignity, even in death.

His weapon of choice was a Sig Sauer P229 Elite Compact, which he preferred to use at close range, when possible, and without a suppressor.

Some might say Leonard had a cold heart, but they would be wrong. He had an indifferent heart. He would never kill a child, he knew, though the possibility had fortunately never occurred. He loved music, and when alone in his SoHo apartment would have it playing all day long while he read his books. Only ever fiction.His musical tastes had initially been traditional: classical, the romantics, Berlioz, Grieg, Debussy, Satie. Then in his late teens he had experienced the flowering of folk music and only came to rock 'n' roll when Bob Dylan went electric and never looked back. Some songs and melodies were capable of moving him to the point of tears. Joy Division, R.E.M., The Incredible String Band, Bridget St. John, The Walkabouts, A Flock of Seagulls, The Flying Lizards; his tastes were suitably eclectic and admirable.

In outward appearance, he tried to blend in, his mode of dress balanced between ordinariness and the minor reaches of whatever fashion was trending, but never far enough to be noticed. Your everyday, reliable killer-for-hire. Word on the street had been positive since he had gone into the business. He would never ask why a particular person was a chosen target. It had no bearing on things. He had killed men too, of course. Leonard was an equal opportunity executioner but had somehow become known as the hitman who specialized in killing women. It was surprising how many of his colleagues drew a line at that. The go-to guy. Not that he readily accepted all the jobs that came his way. Certain cities he was unwilling to travel to and if an assignment coincided with the right concert at Webster Hall or an interesting gig downtown in the Village, he would invariably pass. Sometimes music was more of a priority for Leonard than death.

TRACK TWO – DANCE ME TO THE END OF LOVE

Anna had, like so many others before her, traveled to the city in search of an impossible dream. It hadn't worked out, but at least she hadn't chosen to go to Hollywood or, God forbid, Las Vegas. It could have been so much worse, she reckoned, a pragmatist at heart.

Manhattan was expensive. She briefly ventured out to Brooklyn and found to her disappointment it was no cheaper. She had lasted two years at a university in the Midwest but had never managed to generate enough interest in literature, or at any rate, the sort of literature taught in school. She had then supplemented her onerous student loan with some waitressing at a local dive near the campus, and thought that if nothing better came up, she could always do the same in New York, a city of bars, clubs, and busy nightlife. But even combining a daytime stint at an Italian diner on the corner of Broadway and Canal with a late-night shift at a bar south of the Bowery barely covered the rent in a shared apartment on Hester Street, where all the other women seemed to work as publishing interns with an ambition to succeed that Anna just couldn't summon up.

The burden of juggling two jobs took its toll on her energy and her mental health, so Anna took her pride in hand and found employment in a strip club a few blocks north of the Port Authority. If it had been the 1930s, she would have been merrily dancing for a dime a ticket or launching herself into a desperate all-hours dance marathon like the desperate heroine of a Horace McCoy novel.

She knew she had a decent body and was reasonably good-looking. The way men looked at her confirmed this. She was tall and rangy, and with the right clothes on could attract attention easily, mid-size natural tits holding high, thin in the waist but curvy enough below and with a dancer's legs. And Anna had always had a bit of an exhibitionist streak; always the first at summer camp to shed her clothes and lead the skinny-dipping rush into the still-cold lake. Maybe she thought she could dance for a couple of years, save some money, even study a little in her spare time, and learn things that would lead her by her mid-twenties to a more promising career stream.

And, oh how she liked dancing! She had taken ballet classes until high school. So what if she had to do it in the nude? It was only flesh, skin, and if men paid cash to watch, what was the harm?

She spent days preparing her mixtapes. Adding tracks, deleting others, reinstating some, and desperately trying to recall tunes she had heard just a year ago on the radio but the titles or performers of which she had failed to note. She was booked for two shifts, one in late afternoon and another at night when the tips were better. Rehearsed in front of the bathroom mirror. Agonized over whether she should just merely trim her pubic hair or dispense with it altogether. After much thought, she opted for the former, if only because she was aware her outer labia were slightly fleshy and she would feel overly self-conscious if she displayed them without a protective if ephemeral curtain of curls.

She could edit three songs into each set, each echoing the continuous shedding of her clothes until she was fully nude and lost in dance to the sounds, with the middle tune of necessity slower, to accompany her time wrapping her long white limbs around the pole. Anna was a tad nervous, as she had never done pole work before and had lied about in her interview. She'd wing it. And if her gyratory gymnastics around the cold metal pole might initially be lacking in poise and dynamics, she was confident the music she would be dancing to would soothe the thoughts and loins of the male audience. Velvet Underground, Chris Isaak, John Cale, Terry Reid, Lou Reed, and Television would underpin her set, she decided, and she would twirl under the naked glare of the pink and gold spotlights, her mind and limbs in thrall to the heartbeat of the bass, the wail of the electric guitars, and the *doo-doo-doo-doo-doo-doo*s of the colored girls harmonizing along.

TRACK THREE – THE NIGHT COMES ON

The city sleeps. Restless souls gather in its web. The lost and the found, the good and the bad, the gray and the black because only the sheets in which they are tangled are white, and then only occasionally.

Anna at 3 a.m. Wandering the streets in a daze. Emerging from University Place and making her way toward Washington Square and Sullivan Street. A night without stars of clouds, just a blanket with all the colors of darkness. The arch is illuminated and looks cinematically artificial. The fountain is empty. A flutter of breeze timidly slithers between the trees. The squirrels whose domain it is, and whom she often feeds at the weekend, are nowhere to be seen and she wonders where they all stay or hide at this time of night.

She feels dizzy. She has broken one of her initial vows. She'd insisted from the outset of her time in the clubs that she would never do lap dances. Nor would she sleep with customers.

The man was rougher than she expected and out of fear or resignation she hadn't had the energy to ask him to stop. She feels dirty.

Her only relief is that she didn't do it for money, although he had been showering her with small gifts in his steady rite of seduction. First flowers, then a cashmere wrap, and finally jewelery. She knows so little about the latter, whether it's cheap or valuable. Fake or real.

And she'd given in.

Yes, she had appetites and took some form of wicked pleasure knowing she could arouse men. Not that any woman standing naked and exposed on a stage with the glare of the spotlight highlighting the fragility of her flesh could easily turn on a guy.

She had agreed to have a drink with him. He was coarse, not the sort of man who would normally attract her. Shorter, over-cologned, articulate with his hands rather than his words. Someone she had little in common with. But her damn curiosity condemned her. From the moment she first wondered "What if?" when he had casually revealed he was familiar with the Lou Reed song she had stripped to and had once met the man himself.

"I love that song," he had said. "But you know it's all about trannies?" He did have a wicked smile. "But I know I'm safe with you, aren't I? You don't have a bad surprise down there … You're the real thing. You've shown me and a thousand others the goods."

"I know that Lou Reed had a trans girlfriend, Rachel Humphreys," she said. "She was the real thing, too,." Maybe the man liked a brat, and she liked carving out a bit of independence.

They'd been sitting in a sheltered alcove in a late-night speakeasy close to Alphabet City. Anna was in civilian garb, wearing a short denim skirt and a T-shirt with a Ramones logo. He wore a thin gold chain around his neck. Later, once he assumes ownership, he will buy her a gold ankle chain and insist she wear it at all times, even on stage. But now, his leer both attracted and repelled her. She had never known bad men and curiosity killed the cat. She agreed to go to his apartment, a plush open-plan loft overlooking the Hudson. The first time he fucked her, he took her from behind and crushed her against the plate glass window as she giddily watched the lights of New Jersey glimmer like distant stars.

"I love you, babe," he said as he came with a caveman's grunt. "You're mine now …"

He had offered to call her an Uber, but Anna wanted to walk back, collect her thoughts, resigned but anxious in the knowledge she had made a bad mistake. She hadn't showered, his seed was still inside her, and when she reached Bleecker Street she began to cry and now felt terribly alone.

TRACK FOUR – CLOSER

Leonard was between jobs and restless.

At his third-floor window, looking out over Wooster Street. 3 a.m. He should be sleeping, reading, watching something on TV, anything, but was unable to get his mind to focus on anything. Thoughts crowded each other out. The faces of men and women past. Like ghosts. Haunting him, reproaching him. Those he has killed. His roll call of death.

A movement in the shadows on the cobbled street. Almost in slow motion, a young woman in a tight-fitting black T-shirt and denim skirt. Long legs. Ballet shoes. Leonard squints: braless. Her blonde hair a mass of untamed curls. From his vantage point at the window, he is unable to make out the color of her eyes. Blue, he guesses. She walks slowly, her face a study in concentration, visibly in distress, crying maybe? She seems in no hurry to reach a destination, her feet delicately skimming the pavement as she makes her way down Spring, oblivious to her surroundings. Like an Eadweard Muybridge model whose movements have been deconstructed.

Leonard's heart skips a beat. The lingering phantoms of his past victims crowding the room instantly evaporate.

He wants to call out to her, somehow catch her attention. The window doesn't open. He brushes his finger against the glass. Peered into the growing darkness as the young woman moves out of the impoverished circle of clarity she had briefly inhabited as she passed the streetlight. He raps on the window harder, trying to catch her attention. A yellow cab rushes down the street. She turns her head slightly. Toward him? Toward the speeding car? Looks up at his window. He is overcome with shame: will she think he is just a creep, some Hitchcock voyeur out of a noir movie? Can she even see him properly? The light is on in the apartment's front room that looks out onto Wooster and he must just be a dark shadow to her. She looks away. But he will never forget her. His night vision. His Edward Hopper, the very picture of loneliness and beauty. His very own Sweet Jane.

She has walked on, out of sight.

Leonard hurriedly slips on a jacket and steps into his shoes, opens his door and rushes down the stairs, in too much of a rush for the elevator.

He almost stumbles as he emerges onto Wooster Street. Runs down toward the corner with Spring, hoping to catch another look at her. Glances left, right, and center but there is no sign of the young, distressed woman. How come? She wasn't even walking very fast. Could she live nearby, have disappeared through her own front door? The streets are empty in all directions.

Leonard takes a deep breath.

Leonard is in love.

And it hurts. Badly. It makes no sense, but there you are.

TRACK FIVE – UNKNOWN PLEASURES

Could the man at the window have any idea that two hours ago she was being unceremoniously fucked overlooking the Hudson River, and that she still carried the evidence in her cunt? Of course not. But the shame was overwhelming. She had whored herself out. And cheaply at that. What had come over her? She didn't even remember the damn guy's name!

Her next set at the club was not until the following

Tuesday. She was booked in for six days in a row, afternoon and evening sessions.

She jumped into the shower and cleansed herself of him, banishing his tobacco and booze breath from her skin, rubbing herself pink. She took a morning-after pill; he had not used a condom. "I like my women raw," he had insisted. "I'm a no-nonsense man."

He was back Tuesday, propping up the bar, clapping over-enthusiastically as she stripped, making it clear she was now his. He'd brought a bottle of champagne along, thinking it made him classy. And was waiting for her at the door after she had changed into civilian garb.

"You're coming with me."

She tried to make excuses, but he would have nothing of it. On her final night of the week at the club, he brought her the thin gold anklet and told her to wear it on a permanent basis.

A few weeks later, he demanded she move in with him, and she did not have the courage to resist but also kept the payments up on her shared rental downtown, leaving some of her personal belongings there. He still tolerated her working at the club, which allowed her a modicum of financial independence as he insisted on paying for everything: food, new clothes, expensive restaurants, accessories.

Anna began saving for a rainy day, as she knew deep inside either he would tire of her fast enough or she would strain too far at all the restrictions he was imposing on her, his possessiveness, his crudeness.

Once, she had found pleasure in her dancing, the shameless flaunting of her body, the way her limbs embraced the music as she moved to its languorous beat, every movement and moment resonating deep inside her, oblivious to her audience, ignoring their collective lust. It was a celebration of her beauty, her power of seduction. Now the joy had gone and her performances were mechanical, just muscle memory.

She felt like a captive in an old black-and-white movie full of clichés, the gangster's moll. He was a bad man. She was there, sitting politely on the sofa when he had meetings, unavoidably listening in to his phone calls, his plans. She found out he had a sizeable investment and control of the club where she danced, which explained some of the shady goings-on in the backroom, the small envelopes changing hands, the drugs being sold. Anna found out she was not the first dancer he had been involved with. There were dark whispers about her predecessor, a Ukrainian beauty with thoroughbred looks that had far outshone her artistic talents. Something had caused her departure. Some said she had been moved to another city and was now being pimped out, even.

Out of the blue, she was approached in front of the Angelika, on the corner of Houston and Mercer. A law officer who was aware of her relationship with the bad man, asking for her cooperation. She agreed to provide information.

Anna knew the risk she was taking.

She began listening to his calls, taking notes thereafter. Agreed to accompany him to meetings, stored compromising information she had picked up on. Maybe it was a way out, a chance to rid herself of him before it got worse.

He asked her to sleep with another man. Just the once, he said. A friend who was on the run and needed a woman, and hiring an escort was too much of a risk. She reluctantly agreed and leaked the fugitive's location to her contact. By the time they pounced, though, he had moved on, so it was all for nothing. Encouraged by her docility, her bad man lover arranged a threesome with another of his male friends. Anna had never been with two men before. He was aggressively vocal as he watched, and filmed, her being mounted by the stranger. "Get her!" he shouted. "Teach her what she is!"

Later, as they drank, she had to tiptoe her way to the bathroom and was sick. The two men never even noticed her discomfort and kept bantering about her and her performance in bed as if she was not even present. They insisted she watch the short clip of her being pounded, and Anna was sick again. They laughed. After they left the room to visit the hotel's bar downstairs, Anna rapidly inserted a memory stick into the second man's phone and, the following day, handed it to her police contact.

TRACK SIX – EVERYBODY HURTS

"We are fully aware you prefer not to take on assignments in the city proper."

Leonard nodded. "It's where I happen to live. Involves more risks. 'Never shit where you eat,' as they say."

"We know the saying. We say it too."

It was a voice on the telephone. They'd never actually met. This was how business was conducted. Never in person. Information conveyed through dead letter boxes. Payments made to offshore accounts.

"The matter has a degree of urgency."

"I'm not sure," Leonard said.

"We can make it worth your while to make this one exception to your rules."

"Why me?"

"Because you complete jobs other operatives are reluctant to take on."

"Ah, a woman."

"And the man she consorts with. She betrayed him, but he was the one who made the mistake of trusting her."

"You know I have no interest in the reasons for the hit," Leonard reminded them.

"So? We'll double your fee if you can resolve the problem within the week."

It had been several months since Leonard's last job and he was restless. Ever since he had caught a fleeting glimpse of the young woman, his ghost of Wooster Street, he had made attempts to find her. To no avail. How many tall blondes with curly hair and a ballet dancer's walk could there be in the city? And maybe she didn't even live here, had been just a tourist finding her way through the SoHo night?

He had tried. A few false leads. Once catching sight of someone with similar characteristics waiting to board a train to Connecticut at Grand Central, only to find when he caught up with her that she was nothing like his all-too-brief apparition.

And what was it that made her so special, tugged on his heartstrings and loins in the few seconds she had walked unsteadily into and as quickly out of his life? Made him feel like a fool for lust?

Damned if he knew …

It made no sense, this obsession.

Organizing a new hit would clear his mind, banish her maybe forever, Leonard thought.

So, he accepted the job.

"He's connected, but doesn't normally carry," Leonard was told. He wrote down the name and the address. Peered closely at the photo that had been messaged through to him, then deleted it. "He owns a stake in a strip club and is shacked up with one of the dancers. She's your main target. Her next shift is Saturday night. We don't have a pic of her, but she's a leggy blonde, but with natural tits. That should narrow it down for you. The two of them normally leave the club together. Hit them then. No need for discretion."

"Half now, half on completion," he said.

"As usual."

"Done deed." The line went dead and he put the phone down. He'd been standing by his window, looking out on Wooster Street. It had become a bad habit.

TRACK SEVEN – THIS IS NOT A LOVE SONG

The week before Christmas, winter arrived in Manhattan with a vengeance.

Leonard stood in the shadows across the street from the strip club, observing the comings and goings under the awning of a Korean deli, filtering the sounds of music leaking out, at one stage recognizing the chorus of Lou Reed's "Walk on the Wild Side" and humming along.

He drew his coat's collar tight around his neck; he should have brought a scarf to protect him from the growing cold.

Finally, the bouncers waved the die-hard customers away, and the club's neon sign was switched off. Half an hour later, he recognized the mobster as he left the joint. He was followed, as if reluctantly, by a thin woman wrapped in an army trench coat, trailing behind him. She must be the dancer.

The couple made their way down the block and turned into an unattended parking lot.

As they approached a metal gray BMW, Leonard quickly crossed the street and, as an electronic ping sounded and the car's parking lights flashed, drew his gun. He shot the man first in the back of the head and adjusted his arm to bring the woman into focus. The guy crumpled to the ground and in the same moment the dancer turned toward Leonard. Her face was a dagger to Leonard's heart. But his finger was already squeezing the trigger and the bullet punctured her heart before she could say a single word, eyes wide open, terror spreading through her consciousness until the curtain fell. She slowly stumbled against the side of the car before sliding down slowly to the parking lot ground like a marionette being reeled down by its strings.

Leonard lingered a moment, his whole world in disarray, even as his nervous system screamed to flee before the gunshots attracted any witnesses.

Leonard hadn't cried since childhood. But he did now as he looked one final time at her face, now in repose and strangely peaceful.

Finally, he forced himself to face away, and, just as he did, snow began to fall on Manhattan.

A few days later, on Christmas Eve, Leonard brought home a string of lights, put on a CD, strung the lights over a high pipe running across the ceiling, and before Iggy Pop had finished singing about sister midnight, hanged himself.

AUTHOR'S NOTE: In the mid-1980s I worked for the Virgin Group, running their publishing operations. Which made quite a change from traditional book publishing offices, what with musicians roaming the corridors, visiting the record company on the floor below, peeking into my office with often preposterous impromptu book proposals. As a die-hard rock music fan, it was a curious experience. Getting daily advance copies of tapes, albums, and free tickets for all London gigs by groups and singers signed to Virgin, and having a hi-fi system in my office was a welcome bonus.

Sadly, none of the music involved was ever much to my personal liking, as in no way did the Sex Pistols, then Public Image Ltd, Magazine, XTC, Killing Joke, Orchestral Manoeuvres in the Dark, Human League, assorted reggae bands, and Phil Collins cater to my idiosyncratic melodic tastes! At any rate, I managed to commission a children's book from Sting based on his song "'Message in a Bottle," and corralled my old friend Michael Moorcock into writing a novelization of the (distinctively unlikeable and unmarketable) Sex Pistols movie *The Great Rock 'n' Roll Swindle*, which we had in part financed. Possibly not the greatest accomplishments of my book publishing career …

Across from my own office was the company art studio run by designer Peter Saville, who also freelanced as Art Director for Manchester-based Factory Records and is now best-known for designing all that label's covers, including those for Joy Division and New Order. Thus, the sublime and poignant strains of "Love Will Tear Us Apart" spreading across the floor became the sonic wallpaper of my daily life for day after day—a wonderful distraction and a song now deeply embedded in my soul.

A few weeks ago, my friends Adam and Melissa and I cruised down to see Munly and the Lupercalians at a gritty but iconic Denver institution on South Broadway called the Hi-Dive. It was a good show, and we were wired afterwards, so instead of heading home we popped in for a drink and a bite to eat at Sputnik, the restaurant right next door.

Since *hipster* is one of those words that has lost all meaning through linguistic drift, let me explain that when *I* say hipster, I mean the alternative subculture aesthetic that began, kind of, in the 1990s, but really had its heyday in the first decade of the twenty-first century. I'm talking about indie sleaze: skinny jeans-wearing fixed-gear bicycle enthusiasts who fetishized lo-fi, dying media like the 'zine and the mixtape, and felt nostalgia for their youth while still, technically, being pretty young.

Hipster establishments used to be gloriously grimy dives with shitty vinyl seats held together with duct tape. Their menus included clearly labeled vegan items before that was typical. Then as now "hipster" was a kind of pejorative (no hipster would ever call themselves a hipster), but a hipster joint these days means a restaurant, perhaps a "provisioner" with bare Edison bulbs as lighting, charcuterie boards, and twenty-one dollar cocktails featuring house-smoked salt and a Fernet rinse.

Sputnik is the first kind. It has a drink on the menu called "The Professional," which is a shot of espresso dropped into a Pabst Blue Ribbon.

The service at Sputnik is legendary for its shittiness. Nobody writes anything down and it's always slow, no matter if there's four people in there or forty. But we didn't mind, especially when the opening chords of Weezer's "My Name Is Jonas" came on the sound system to palpable general approval.

"Hell yeah," said Adam.

I nodded my agreement, and the conversation moved on—until the second song on the *Blue Album*, "No One Else," came on.

"Are they playing the whole thing, I guess?" asked Adam.

"This is the crowd for it," said Melissa, teasing us a bit. She's younger than us, a *SpongeBob Squarepants* Millennial, not a *Ren and Stimpy* Millennial.

"Awesome," said Adam.

Weezer's first, self-titled album, often called the *Blue Album*, is, indeed, awesome. It was one of my favorites in high school, but I had not listened to it all the way through for over twenty years.

As the final track approached, our food arrived. Melissa had ordered her ramen mild, but it came out so spicy I could almost taste it from across the table. The overpowering chili and the sight of the bright red oil just intensified my discomfort. Spicy food, Weezer ... Individually they're bad enough, but together, they evoke a memory of a night I'd rather forget—the bad decisions I made; a childish prank war gone terribly, fatally wrong.

"Holiday" wound down, and I steeled myself, waiting for the iconic opening bass line of "Only in Dreams," the eight-minute-long work of genius that ends the *Blue Album*. But some other song came on instead.

"*Awwww*," protested the entire restaurant, like an elementary school class being told recess was canceled.

In the face of such unanimous disappointment, someone quickly switched the music over to "Only in Dreams." This was greeted with applause and scattered cheers.

"If you're gonna play the whole album, you have to play *the whole album*," said Adam.

"Yeah," I agreed weakly.

Melissa made a squeaking sound and began to cough. She was bravely soldiering through her meal even though she was already sweating and red-faced.

"Do you want to trade?" Adam asked once she'd recovered. He'd gotten a bahn mi and fries.

Melissa shook her head no.

"Come on, switch with me!"

"My lips are *numb*," she mumbled.

This exchange gave me time to get a hold of myself. I was also struggling, but for very different reasons.

My friend and lover Tyler Matthews had likely died while "Only in Dreams" was playing. And I don't mean, like, *playing anywhere in the world*. That's true of every song; a very emo thought. I mean he probably died while *I* was playing "Only in Dreams," during my radio show on my college's station, WPRK, 91.5 FM, "The Best in Basement Radio." Not only that, he died of an allergic reaction to chili—and where I was during those eight minutes became part of the police investigation into his death.

As I did my best to push away the thoughts and memories that, for me, weave their way alongside the artfully lazy high hat cymbal in "Only In Dreams," it occurred to me that my friend Nick Mamatas had recently solicited me for a story for a noir anthology he was editing called *120 Murders: Dark Fiction Inspired by the Alternative Era.*

I'd told him I'd be happy to … *if* I could come up with an appropriate idea. That was, I admit, a *very* big if. I write science fiction and fantasy, not crime fiction—or any sort of fiction set in the real world.

But that night, as I listened to the peerless crescendo toward the end of "Only in Dreams," I realized I didn't need an idea. After all, I'd once been a character in a real-life crime story—and, unfortunately for everyone involved, that incident requires no embellishment whatsoever.

During the spring of 2002 I was a sophomore at Rollins College, a small private university located in Winter Park, Florida. You likely won't have heard of it unless you're in the business world. For twenty-five years or so Rollins has been ranked by *U.S. News and World Report* as the best regional university in the South, yet it remains relatively obscure.

This is likely because, while the college takes warranted pride in the excellence of its professors, small class size, and the beauty of its Spanish Mediterranean buildings shaded by ancient, mossy live oaks, it is—or at least was, while I was there—also a starter country club for the children of the wealthy. When I was attending Rollins, most of the cars you'd see parked on campus were BMWs or Lexuses. *Playboy* ranked the college as the number-three party school in the country. That caused a bit of a kerfuffle with the trustees, as you can imagine—the official story from Rollins was that a fraternity had done a write-in campaign and the ranking "did not accurately reflect the school's culture." I disagree; Rollins was very much a party school. If the ranking didn't accurately reflect the school's culture, then why during my tenure did the extraordinarily preppy fraternity Phi Delta Theta hang an enormous, hand-painted sign reading COLLARS UP, PANTIES DOWN! over their house's front door during Parents' Weekend? And there were plenty of other incidents like that.

I'd come to Rollins on an art history scholarship thinking it would be like Hampden College in *The Secret History*. Instead, it was more like Camden in *The Rules of Attraction*.

Ah, but that's not quite fair. I was serious, studious, and

artsy, and quickly found a vibrant community of like-minded friends and colleagues, and my classes were fascinating and diverse. That spring, I was taking History of Renaissance Art, Medieval Art and Architecture, Creative Writing: Short Stories, and Gender in Science Fiction, a class which introduced me to Ursula K. Le Guin, Connie Willis, C.L. Moore, and the anthology *Dangerous Visions*, all of which would influence me greatly. I was volunteering at the radio station, as I mentioned, and I was also sleeping with Tyler, my close friend Holly Haldeman's boyfriend.

Here I should remind you that this is all true. Yes, my name is Molly, and I really did have a friend by the name of Holly. We lived in the same dorm, and we both volunteered at the radio station. We even looked similar, enough that we were often mistaken for one another in passing. She was slimmer, but we were about the same height. My hair was darker and wavier while hers was paler and straighter, but we had cuts of similar length, and we both wore straight-leg jeans, white T-shirts, and Chuck Taylor high-tops. We smoked the same cigarettes, too: Marlboro Ultra Lights 100s.

That said, in terms of our taste in men we couldn't have been more different. I had sexually imprinted on Jeff Goldblum as Ian Malcolm in *Jurassic Park*, so I tended to go for guys with leather jackets, black jeans, and horn-rimmed glasses—sadly thin on the ground in hot and muggy Central Florida. Holly, on the other hand, liked the most basic men imaginable: tanned surfer dudes with hemp anklets who wore board shorts to class and had nary a thought in their head.

This type of man was common at Rollins, even though the campus is right smack in the middle of the state, about two hours from any beach. Tyler, her boyfriend, was perpetually sunburned and rarely without his acoustic guitar. When he wore shoes at all, it was a pair of beat-up Birkenstocks, of course. He was the opposite of dark and brooding, but he could *really* fuck—which is why what should have been a one-time drunken mistake became a months-long affair.

It all began on the night of the Tau Kappa Epsilon mixer. I didn't go to frat parties—in fact, I'd never been to one before that night; never even considered going. I don't enjoy drinking out of Solo cups, and believed on the evidence of every movie ever that I'd find the people who attended such functions to be unspeakably tedious. Additionally, my dorm, Pinehurst Cottage, had a cultural bias against frats that I had embraced.

Pinehurst was—and still is—an old wooden house that stands out from the Spanish brick-and-tile of the rest of the campus. We'd now call it the "woke" dorm, but that wasn't a term back then. Members enjoyed single rooms, for which we paid dues, and were required to put on one campus-wide program of a "socially conscious" nature per semester. For example, my friend Brad invited a bunch of professors to participate in a panel called "How Artists and Scientists Think." Another friend, Daniel, hosted an event where we made a square for the AIDS Quilt. I once brought in the Guerrilla Girls to speak about inequality in the art world.

My only real interaction with "Greek life" was in my Art History classes. For some reason, Art History was *the* sorority girl major at Rollins in the early 2000s, specifically for the sisters of Kappa Kappa Gamma.

I got along well enough with them, and in particular with a stunning blonde named Reese. She was always perfectly coiffed and wore those matching velour tracksuits with JUICY spelled out in rhinestones across the rear end. We were fascinated by each other, I think; I didn't know anybody like her, nor she like me.

Reese told me about the frat party. She said I should come. I said thanks, and that I might check it out. I'd said the same thing the other times she'd invited me, but this time, I found myself considering it.

As I mentioned, I was taking a writing class that semester, and my professor, Dr. Dalton, had recently declared that we all needed to seek out as many "experiences" as possible. Only through these experiences would we come to know ourselves and the world enough to make our writing feel "real."

I enjoyed Art History, but I had always wanted to be a writer, in that way of lifelong readers. I'd taken my professor's advice to heart. I reasoned I could go to the party as an anthropologist and still retain my identity as "someone who didn't go to frat parties." Maybe, I thought, I might even come away with my mind changed.

I did not. It was exactly as I'd expected. The music was generic—Sugar Ray, Jack Johnson, and too loud. I didn't have much in common with anyone, and worst of all I was dressed incorrectly. I had donned my usual white T-shirt and jeans, thinking I'd blend in. Instead, I was shocked to find the guys were in blazers and pressed khakis and the girls were wearing extremely short cocktail dresses with expensive flip-flops. This was the era of body lotion containing lots of glitter, so between that and the sandals when they stood together they looked like a cluster of goddesses in one of the Botticelli paintings I'd been studying that semester.

I was over the party after about an hour. All I'd done was stand near my KKΓ acquaintances while they swapped stories about the various male attendees they'd slept with, none of whom I knew. But when I started to say goodnight, Reese took me by the hand.

"The party hasn't even gotten started," she said. "Come get a drink."

"I think I've had enough …" I said.

"Then you *definitely* need a drink," said Reese. I was charmed by her pleading with me, and decided one more couldn't hurt.

The booze was limited to an unappealing mix of cans of inexpensive light beer and a cooler full of a heady concoction of frozen limeade, Kool-Aid powder, and grain alcohol that everyone was calling "Magic Jesus." I knew this because one of the longer conversations I'd had that night had been with some random frat guy as I got my first cup.

"We usually call this Purple Jesus, you know. But tonight it's called *Magic* Jesus," he'd said, clearly expecting me to be impressed.

"What makes it magic?" I'd replied, wondering momentarily if I'd been roofied.

"We made it with Magic Twist Kool-Aid," he said grandly. "It changes color when you mix it. It started out green and it turned blue."

"Wow, amazing," I'd said, at which point he'd slunk away from me, clearly aware just how badly he'd failed to impress me.

Reese escorted me back to the Magic Jesus. As we lined up for the plastic ladle, one of the guys sidled up to her and whispered something in her ear. She nodded.

"Hold on," she said to him, and turned to me, her expression suddenly very serious. "Do you want some coke?"

I thought about what my professor had said about experiences … but that was a little too much for me. I shook my head. "No thanks."

"Are you sure? It's good coke," she said, with more sincerity than I expected.

"I'm okay. I think I'll stick with Jesus," I said, waggling my cup at her, with a wink that I hoped would seem conspiratorial and lighthearted. She nodded and waved at me as she giggled her way elsewhere.

"It *is* good coke, you know."

I managed not to jump even though I hadn't realized anyone was behind me. When I turned, I recognized the speaker, though we'd never met. I knew him by the moniker "Pink Pants Guy" as—you guessed it—he wore pink Dockers before that was more of a thing. He also wore a navy blazer with white piping that would have made him look like a cruise ship captain even if he hadn't frequently worn a white skipper's hat with it—though not at that moment, to my relief. He was in Phi Delta, one of the "Collars Up, Panties Down" crew. The collar of his robin's egg blue Lacoste shirt was indeed popped.

"No doubt," I said. "I just have zero desire to inhale deeply in the bathroom of this place."

"Fair enough," he said, and extended his hand. "I'm Kevin."

"Molly," I said, shaking his hand firmly, as if we were about to conduct a business transaction.

"I don't think I've seen you before," he said. "Are you ..."

"I'm not in a sorority," I said. "I came here with some friends."

"Interesting," he said. "Well, what do you think so far?"

"Honestly? I think this drink is disgusting, and that whoever is DJing has terrible taste in music," I said, pitching my voice over the Creed currently assaulting my ears.

"Well, you're not wrong about that," said Kevin. "So, if you're not in a sorority, do you live on campus?"

"Yeah, in Pinehurst," I said.

"Oh!" he said, with genuine surprise.

"*Oh?*"

"I just ..." He really did not know what to say. My dorm's reputation was clearly on his mind. I smiled and said nothing. I had wrong-footed him. I found I liked the feeling; another new experience.

"You just what?" I asked.

"I guess I didn't realize anyone cool lived there."

"Am I cool?"

"You know you're cool," he said, and it finally dawned on me that he was trying to pick me up.

The worm had turned. I was now wrong-footed.

I wasn't a virgin, but 1990s public school sex education had terrified me into avoiding casual sex. I've always been a bit of a hypochondriac, so the full-color slides of genital warts and, of course, the AIDS crisis, had been an extremely effective deterrent.

But going back to a stranger's dorm room would be a new experience for me … Maybe Professor Dalton, on whom I had a bit of a crush, would perceive the increased verisimilitude in the sex scenes in my stories. Even then I knew that was a nutty reason to sleep with a stranger, but I let Kevin talk me into it anyway. I figured at worst whatever happened would be forgettable.

I was wrong about that. Kevin was *really* drunk, drunker than I was, drunker than I realized. He couldn't perform despite my best efforts to rally him with my hands and my mouth. Eventually he pushed me away.

"Stop," he said. "Sorry."

"Don't be, it's fine," I said, as I pulled away from him. "We can totally stop, but if there's anything else I can do to help, I'm open to it."

"Yeah?"

"Why not?" I said.

"Okay. Hand me that." He indicated a dark blue towel hanging over the back of the desk chair.

I was confused but retrieved it anyway.

"Hold it over my face," he said.

This was new for me. I hesitated, but he looked up at me so eagerly that I figured I'd give it a whirl.

"Wait," he said. "First put your glasses back on."

He then proceeded to jerk off as I held the towel down over his face, gently at first, then more firmly at his urging. It was all a little unusual, sure, but it turned me on to watch him pinching his balls with one hand as he mauled his dick with the other. He moaned pretty loud when he came all over his hands and chest.

"That was hot," I said, when he'd finished. But when I tried to take the towel off his face, he grabbed it back with his cummy hands.

"Get out," he said.

I pulled away in surprise. "Really?" I asked. His voice was a little muffled, and I was still tipsy, so I wasn't quite sure I'd heard right.

"Just get the fuck out," he said, "and if you tell anyone about this, I'll tell them your pussy is loose."

This pissed me off. I felt I'd been more than generous with this guy, and it annoyed me to receive threats and abuse in return.

"Whatever, *loser*. You couldn't even get it in my pussy," I said, as I put my clothes on as quick as I could. When I got the fuck out, as requested, I closed the door to his room behind me with more force than necessary.

It was very late when I emerged into the balmy Florida night. Even so, I didn't feel like heading back to my dorm room. I knew no way could I sleep after the party and the weird sex, so I headed down past Pinehurst to sit by Lake Virginia and smoke a cigarette.

Lake Virginia has always been an integral part of Rollins life, appearing in school songs and, of course, sales brochures. It was starting to show stresses from fertilizer runoff, but it was still gorgeous, especially at night. A fingernail moon hung above the placid waters as I settled in on a bench just beyond the treeline. A slight breeze ruffled my hair as I tried to light my cigarette behind my cupped hand.

I was working on my second, musing on whether Professor Dalton's advice was really all that great, when I heard a twig snap behind me. Before I could turn around, hands covered my eyes.

"Surprise," said a male voice I recognized as belonging to Tyler, Holly's boyfriend. I pulled away from him. Tyler's smile turned into an expression of horror when he realized I was me, and not Holly.

"Oh my god I'm so sorry," he said in a rush. "I thought …"

"Don't worry about it," I said.

He was carrying his acoustic guitar with him, of course. He'd clearly come down to do some late night al fresco jamming. I wondered where Holly was.

"Would you like this bench?" I offered, feeling stupid the moment the words left my mouth.

"Oh, there are others," said Tyler, just as awkwardly.

"Nah, it's cool. I was just about done with my cig … and anyway it's been a long night."

Tyler set his guitar against the bench and sat down next to me.

"Actually … can I bum one?"

"Sure," I said. Mine was almost done, so I put it out in the soft wet earth by the lakeside. I lit two more in my mouth, handing him one. Everyone knows that smoking is actually cool, in spite of what anti-smoking propaganda says, and I felt *especially* cool with that move.

"So, what happened?" asked Tyler. "Holly said you went to a frat party."

"Oh gawd," I said, and told him the whole story.

"Holy shit," said Tyler. "That's wild. I can't imagine asking for that on a first date."

"Oh? What's the right number of dates before asking a girl to hold a towel over your face while you jack off?"

We both froze. Something changed between us in that moment; or rather, I had changed something, however unintentionally.

"Fuck," said Tyler, and leaned in to kiss me. Or maybe we both went for it. I can't really remember. I guess it doesn't matter, because before long he had his hand on my breast, first over my shirt, then under it. I slalomed my hand down his chest, hesitating before going further. He moved my hand to his cock. It was stiff, and even through his pants I could tell it was big.

"So," I said, somewhat breathless between kisses, but also definitely playing it up a bit, "if a towel isn't involved …"

"You're going to do a lot more than jack me off," he said. I liked that.

"Let's go back to your room," I said. Tyler lived in Lyman Hall. He also had a single; he was a member of the Rollins Outdoors Club, or R.O.C., the other organization, like Pinehurst, that was given "non-Greek special-interest housing."

"No, let's go to yours. Holly has a key to mine." Tyler was the R.A., which I assumed was how he'd managed to pull off such a feat.

I wish I could say that Tyler speaking Holly's name made me come to my senses. I wish I'd been a better person in that moment, for a lot of reasons. But I wasn't, and this is a true story. I led the way back up to Pinehurst. I let us in through the back door, which was closer to my room, and well away from hers. And I said yes when he pulled down my panties so we could fuck in my university-issued extra-long twin bed.

It has been my experience that boring people are bad in bed. Tyler was an exception to that rule. He could really lay it down. We both lay there for a while afterward just saying "wow" and "seriously" before discussing how this had to be a one-time thing. It had been very wrong, and while we couldn't undo what we'd done, we could make sure it never happened again.

It happened again. Many times, always in my room, since we agreed that it was less risky for him to sneak out the back exit of Pinehurst than me to go to his room. We both felt awful about it, but not awful enough to stop. Not when the sex was that good—because it was *that good*. And we both got a little illicit frisson out of sneaking around, it's true.

It was never serious between us. We were never in love, but we came to like one another quite a bit as our affair continued. I started looking forward to seeing him, not just when I knew he'd be stretching out my pussy before grunting his fascinatingly intense orgasm into me. We never talked about it, but it seemed to me that he felt the same. His smile, when he saw me, was genuine, and he began to come around Pinehurst more—to hang out, not just to canoodle with Holly. He'd show up to play Fluxx or Settlers of Catan when we'd all head down to Dave's Down Under, the campus hangout with late-night food service. Sometimes he'd even show up to Pinehurst programs.

It was a Pinehust program that marked the beginning of the end for us. Smita Sanghrajka, Pinehurst's R.A., ran a program that semester where she took us to a local Indian restaurant to eat and talk about Indian food and its relationship to Indian culture. The evening of the event we were all hanging out in the common room, discussing who would drive, when Smita mentioned she'd made a reservation for more people than had signed up, so there were still a few spaces available.

"You could totally come if you wanted, Tyler," she said.

Tyler and Holly were snuggling on the couch. I was kind of studying some flashcards for my upcoming Medieval Art midterm, but I couldn't help looking up.

"Nah, I don't think so," said Tyler. "Thanks, though."

"Aw, are you sure?" I said, before I realized I probably shouldn't seem interested at all.

"Yeah," he said, as I avoided Holly's gaze by turning back to my flashcards. "I'm busy. Plus, I probably shouldn't be seen *fraternizing with the enemy*, you know?"

We all chuckled at that. Tyler was referring to the annual "R.O.C.-Pinehurst War," which was basically a week of the organizations playing pranks on one another. I don't know when the tradition began, but by the time I arrived at Rollins, in 2000, it was an established part of the spring semester. It had no official start date; at some point, someone would initiate it, and then it would escalate until one of the dorms surrendered, or we all got bored.

"Hold up," said Dojo Martinez. Dojo was Pinehurst's biggest R.O.C. War fan. He'd initiated it this year, by ambushing R.O.C. members with water pistols as they'd come back from a kayaking expedition to Wekiwa Springs. "How's that gonna work with you two dating?"

"We're staying neutral," said Holly. "I hate R.O.C. Wars anyway."

"Me too," I said, not looking up from my flashcards. I always thought it was all rather juvenile at best and disruptive at worst. Plus, R.O.C. always—*always*—kicked our asses.

"You guys are such haters," said Dojo.

"Guilty as charged," I said.

"*Personally*, I think it's inappropriate," said another Pinehurst habituée, Caitlin Fenton, who could always be counted on to be a pious killjoy about everything. "After all, in the wake of the horrors of 9/11, I don't know if *war* is something that belongs on this campus."

Dojo looked like he was gearing up for an argument, but Smita put a stop to it by announcing it was time to go. Tyler kissed Holly goodbye.

"See you later?" he said.

"Yeah," she said, but I thought she seemed a little less enthusiastic than usual.

That night, it seemed to me like Holly wouldn't meet my eye. She rode to the restaurant in a different car. I acted like nothing was off, which was easy enough after all my recent outright lying. And anyway, we were in a large group and I was occupied by the panoply of new-to-me dishes Smita ordered for us: chana masala, butter chicken, saag paneer, papadum, and more.

Soon enough, Holly seemed more like her usual self. The good food and good company had cheered her—as had watching Dojo and the other guys compete to see how much spicy chutney they could put on their food and still eat it.

After the meal, we visited the Indian market next to the restaurant. I remember being amazed by the selection of foreign beverages, British items like digestive biscuits and HP Sauce, massive bags of lentils and rice, and colorful spices. I saw a few of the guys congregating in that aisle as I headed out with a Dairy Milk bar in my bag; I'd remembered reading about them in Roald Dahl's *Boy* as a kid.

Holly was standing there, smoking a cigarette. I sidled up alongside her and lit one of my own.

"You doing okay?" I asked, feeling like a shit for asking, but also, she was my friend.

"I guess."

"What's up?"

"I dunno."

"C'mon."

She shrugged. "Things have seemed weird between me and Tyler."

"Oh, really?" I said, wondering if she could hear my heart beating. "You guys seemed good earlier …"

"He's been kind of, I dunno. Distant?"

"Maybe it's midterms," I said, as if I didn't know Tyler wasn't particularly studious.

Holly laughed. "Yeah, right!"

Our dormmates were pouring out of the shop, their plastic bags bulging with purchases.

"Are you guys meeting later?"

She nodded.

"Good," I said, putting my cigarette out in one of those trash can ashtrays you never see anymore.

"Yeah," she said. "What'll you do tonight?"

"I have to finish *The Left Hand of Darkness*," I said. "Maybe I'll go down to the radio station and listen to whatever new CDs have come in while I read."

"We got an advance copy of the new Polyphonic Spree."

"What about the new Wilco?"

Holly shook her head. "Next week."

I never made it to the station that night. We came home from our jaunt to the Indian restaurant to find Pinehurst in an uproar. During our absence, members of R.O.C. had broken in and stolen all our shower heads. We'd started the war, but they were already winning it.

I know the portrait I've painted of myself in this story makes me seem like a terrible person. That's because I was a terrible person. In fact, I still am. Professor Dalton was right—experiences change us. They help us understand ourselves. What he didn't tell us was that sometimes that understanding doesn't improve us.

I'd like to tell you I've learned my lesson about cheating after everything with Tyler, but the truth is, all I learned is that I like to sneak around. That said, I've never again snuck around with a friend's boyfriend. And for what it's worth, after seeing Holly so unhappy, I did vow to end things with Tyler. I went through with it, too—the following day, during Holly's radio show. For obvious reasons that had become a favored hook-up time for me and Tyler.

I waited until after he'd fucked me stupid. I'm only human.

Tyler didn't fuss. He agreed our affair had been a mistake, if a happy one, and we needed to be better to Holly than we had been.

"How was it after she got back last night?" I asked, as we were putting our clothes back on.

"Totally fine," he said. "Sorry I couldn't come to dinner, that probably would have helped the situation. But I can't eat spicy food."

"Yeah," I said. "There were definitely some dishes that were too hot for me."

"No, I mean, like … I can't eat spice. It fucks me up. I've had some weird reactions to chilis in the past, I think I might be allergic. Just don't tell anyone, okay? It's so embarrassing."

"Why is it embarrassing?"

"It sounds like some kind of white person disease, being allergic to spice, you know?"

I chuckled. "Okay. I can see that. Your secret's safe with me."

It was an amicable parting of the ways, but I ended up feeling sadder than I anticipated. I was able to hide it well. There was a lot going on, between my reading, my writing, studying for my upcoming midterms, and the trials of the R.O.C.-Pinehurst war.

Not long after that, I was walking home from my writing class, feeling grouchy, and dirty—we still hadn't gotten our showerheads back. I spied Holly sitting on the porch swing, her cigarette dangling elegantly between her middle and ring fingers. I waved as I walked up.

"Don't go in there," she said, offering me a smoke. I took it as I sat down beside her.

"What's going on?"

"I dunno, but it smells horrible."

"Another R.O.C. prank?"

"No. Some of the guys are planning something. I don't know what."

Then Holly turned to me. She looked like she was about to say something, but I never found out what, because that was when Dojo stumbled out the front door, coughing and waving his hand in front of his face.

This wasn't unusual for Dojo; nor was it unusual that his eyes were totally red. Dojo was our resident pothead. I should probably explain that his name wasn't really Dojo, he was Dominic Joaquin, but he was very into anime. Indeed, he was wearing the pants to the ninja costumes he and his friend Andrew had bought at MegaCon, and a *Neon Genesis Evangelion* T-shirt with some weird reddish stains on it.

"Oh man," said Dojo. "Oh man."

"What's going on in there?" said Holly.

"We are going to get R.O.C. so good, *so* fucking good."

"How?" asked Holly.

Dojo's smile was wicked. "I shouldn't tell you … I'm not supposed to tell anyone who's not involved …"

"Come on," I said.

"We're making homemade pepper spray," said Dojo, giddy with excitement. "We bought some peppers at the Indian market and Chris found a recipe on the web. We're gonna spray down all the door handles, and if we can get inside we'll hose down the sinks and faucets and toilet seats too."

"That's fucked up," said Holly. "You could really hurt someone."

"Oh, come *on*," said Dojo.

"Seriously!" I said. "I mean, what if someone is, like, allergic to spice?"

Too late I remembered that Tyler had said his spice allergy was something he kept secret. Out of the corner of my eye I saw Holly stiffen up and felt her staring at me.

"An allergy to spice?" Dojo said. "What is that, some kind of white person disease?"

"Look, I dunno," I said. "It's still a bad idea, all right?"

"We have to fight back!"

"Or what?" I asked.

This baffled Dojo, but he was saved from needing to reply by Chris Harris and Andrew Garcia joining us on the porch. Andrew was an all right guy, he once helped me get a big lizard out of my room—big for Florida, so you can imagine. Chris, however, was a constant thorn in my side. I could not stand this man. "Toxic masculinity" was not a term we used back then, but it described him perfectly. He was one of those little guys with something to prove. This was before the days of "short kings" and all that, so looking back on it I have more sympathy for him; at the time, I found his macho schtick obnoxious in the extreme.

"Victory is ours," bellowed Chris, as Andrew brandished a spray bottle with an evil-looking red liquid inside. "Behold!"

"Put that away." Dojo gave us a sour look. "We've got some goody two-shoes out here. And a possible traitor."

"I am not a traitor," said Holly. "I'm neutral. I'm Switzerland."

"What's the problem?" asked Andrew.

"They think our plan is *dangerous*," said Dojo, rolling his eyes.

"It could be," I insisted. "What if someone gets it in their eye? Or like, I dunno—I mean do you always wash your hands *before* going to the bathroom? What if some guy comes home to take a piss and gets it all over his dick?"

That just made the prank sound even better. Andrew, Chris, and Dojo all cracked up at the idea.

"Don't worry, Molly. It's only, like, half-strength," said Andrew. "We diluted it. It wouldn't be that bad."

"Oh yeah?" I looked at the three of them, a challenge in my gaze. "Well, if you're so sure about that, why don't one of you spray it on *your* balls?"

They exchanged uneasy looks. Then they turned to Holly.

"Don't look at me," she said, holding her hands up.

"If it's really and truly not that bad, I won't say another word about it," I said, making eye contact with Chris specifically. "You afraid?"

None of the three guys moved. After a long moment, I snorted derisively.

"Thought so," I said.

"Fine," said Chris. "Give it to me."

"Dude," said Andrew.

"What? It's not gonna be a big deal," said Chris, grabbing the bottle from Andrew. "Watch."

Indeed we did watch as Chris pulled out the waist on his jeans and boxers and sprayed it on himself. He immediately collapsed onto the porch, frothing at the mouth. The spray bottle went rolling off the edge into the bushes as he clutched at his junk and tried to swallow a scream.

"Oh my god," said Holly, as Andrew and Dojo watched on in horror.

I chose to say nothing.

"Dude, are you okay?" said Andrew, as Chris squirmed.

"I'm fine," he managed to gasp. "It's … it's not that bad."

"Clearly," I said, in my best *Daria* deadpan.

"Get up, dude, get up," said Dojo. "Smita's coming."

Usually, Smita was one of the cheeriest people on campus, she always had a big smile on her face and a kind word to say. But today, she looked mad. Her cheeks were red, her brow was furrowed. Something was clearly very wrong.

"What is going on here," she snapped, as she stomped up the wooden steps, "and what is that *smell?*"

"Uh," said Andrew.

"This better not be some kind of R.O.C. Wars thing," said Smita.

"Oh, it is," I said helpfully. "It's pepper spray, they made it in the kitchenette, from stuff they bought at the Indian market."

Dojo shot me a dirty look. Smita looked incandescent with fury.

"I just came from the Dean of Students' office," she said. "Tyler was there, too. The war is off—do you hear me? It's done, it's over. It seems that *someone* was running around campus today with a paintball gun, shooting at R.O.C. members, and accidentally hit a professor." Smita turned to Dojo. "Witnesses said the individual was dressed up like a ninja."

"Why are you looking at me?" said Dojo—bold, as he was still in his ninja pants, and even the ninja shoes with the toe thing.

"Go take those off right now," said Smita. "I told the dean

I had no idea who would do such a thing—and as far as I'm concerned, I still don't. But I'm serious. No more R.O.C. War. I will personally see to it that any Pinehurstian who pulls another prank will be out of the dorm. Forever."

"That's bullshit!" said Dojo. "They still have our showerheads!"

"They gave them back. I have them in my bag," said Smita, patting her sling bag. "Now go back inside and clean up whatever is making Chris cry, and we'll forget any of this ever happened."

"I'm not crying," said Chris, who was definitely crying. He got shakily to his feet. Smita didn't even seem to hear him as she herded them all inside, leaving me and Holly on the porch swing.

I couldn't decide if the silence was awkward or not. Holly had been about to say something when Dojo had joined us, and I'd made that gaffe during the pepper spray incident … In order to circumvent her going back to either topic, I sucked my teeth and shook my head.

"I can't stand those guys," I said, as I lit another cigarette, one of my own this time. "I mean, Andrew's all right. But Chris and Dojo, they're beyond obnoxious. I don't even know why they're in Pinehurst. Chris is the poster boy for traditional masculinity, Andrew is so baked all the time he barely knows he lives here, and Dojo's programs are terrible." That was no exaggeration; Dojo had screened some bootlegged episodes of *Record of Lodoss War* as his program the previous semester. When asked how that could possibly be viewed as socially conscious, he'd said he was *exposing a majority-white campus to Japanese culture*, which I admit was a good answer even if it hadn't been a good program.

"So let's get them kicked out."

I choked on my smoke, which I hadn't done in years. "What?"

"Let's get them kicked out."

"How?"

Holly got up and walked around the side of the porch. When she came back, she had the bottle of pepper spray in her hands.

"Think about it," she said. "What if we went through with their prank? Smita knows they wanted to do it. They'll take the blame, and you heard what she said the consequence would be."

"That's kinda messed up," I said. I've always had a gift for understatement, it's true.

"It's not like we're getting them kicked out of *school*," said Holly, as in the tone of one explaining something simple to an especially dim child. She handed the bottle to me so she could light up a cigarette. "They just won't be in Pinehurst anymore."

I was not cool with this plan, not at all. But before I could say anything, Holly fixed me with a stare that made me shiver in the warm morning air.

"Come on," she said. "Why not?"

I realized she was testing me, seeing if I'd bring up Tyler's spice allergy again. I tried to think of other reasons this was a bad idea. "For one thing, they're likely pouring all the spray down the drain," I said. "We have the bottle. They don't."

"Andrew always leaves his door unlocked. We can split it in half and put the other bottle in his room."

I couldn't decide which was more shocking—the deviousness of her plan, or the casual way she proposed it. It seemed so out of character for Holly … But then again, could anything be out of character for either of us? We were nineteen years old. Our characters were still forming.

Holly cocked her head. "So, are you in, or are you out? I mean, you said yourself that they didn't deserve to be in Pinehurst. Or is there some other reason you don't want to do it?"

I could have said yes. I could have said it was a cruel and stupid idea, which it was. Or, I could have said I knew about Tyler's allergy—and if Holly had asked why I knew, how I'd found out, I could have told her the truth.

But I didn't. Instead, I shrugged.

"Why not," I said. "I'm in."

This was the plan we came up with:

I had class that afternoon, so Holly ran out for a second spray bottle. She would divide the pepper spray, putting one bottle in my room and the other in Andrew's. Thursdays were when Dojo's anime club met. Andrew was Vice President. He'd be sure to be gone.

We would pull the prank in the middle of the night;

or, rather, during the wee hours of the morning, after most people, even college students, were in bed, and before most people, especially college students, got up.

Tyler would be Holly's alibi. Mine would be my radio show, which was on Friday mornings, four-to-six a.m. I'd leave as usual, clock in at the station, and then at some point I'd put on a long song—I'd chosen "Only in Dreams" by Weezer—so I could sneak out to apply the pepper spray to the door handles and be back before it was over. Plenty of DJs put on long songs to nip out for a smoke, so it wouldn't look unusual at all. Just "my usual movements." (Holly and I watched a lot of *Law & Order* together, between classes.)

We argued a bit about whether I should try to sneak inside R.O.C., as Chris, Andrew, and Dojo had hoped to do. I was unwilling, even when Holly offered me her key; she didn't need it, as she'd be with Tyler. I pointed out that entering that way would give me away. Rollins had converted to key card access before I arrived, but certain doors on some of the older dorms, like Pinehurst and Lyman Hall, still could be opened with a room key. Students were supposed to use the card swipe, though. The keys caused the fire alarms to chirp.

I said sneaking inside seemed like a great way to get caught. Holly said if I snuck out of my show early, like right around 4 a.m., everyone would assume someone was just coming back late and drunk. Furthermore, dousing the bathrooms was way worse than just the door handles. She claimed it was the only way to be certain we'd get Chris, Andrew, and Dojo in trouble. I stood my ground, but even so, when I got back to my dorm that night, I found the spray bottle and Holly's key on my desk.

I didn't take the key with me. When my alarm went off, I pulled on my jeans and grabbed my bag. The spray bottle was nestled in there with my *Blue Album* CD, my cigarettes, a tin of Altoids, my flip phone, and whatever else I deemed crucial in 2002.

I hadn't slept well the night before; I never do when something's weighing on me. I was crabby and jumpy. As I walked down to the basement of the Mills Memorial Center, where WPRK broadcasted from, I squealed when a baby black snake slithered across my path even though every Floridian is fairly casual about snakes, spiders, even alligators.

When I got in, I waved at the DJ who had the two-to-four a.m. slot and headed into the library to select the music for my show. In 2002, WPRK hadn't even begun to convert to digital. These days I don't even know anyone with a CD player, including myself. It makes me sad. Maybe it's just hipster nostalgia, but I've never felt as personal a connection to music as I did back then, handling physical media, pulling unusual-sounding bands or albums off the shelf to check them out, reading liner notes.

WPRK played indie rock. And I mean *indie*—Ani DiFranco was too mainstream for us, and anything that might have gotten airtime on an "alternative" station was right out. Even so, we all cheated a bit at times, bringing in our own CDs, which is why I had to bring the Weezer with me. Holly had disapproved of my choice—of course, with so many albums at our fingertips there were plenty of even longer songs, but I reasoned that I had a better sense of how long "eight minutes" was because I knew the song so well.

The DJ left, some song still playing. When it ended, I did my station identification, welcoming my listeners to my show, *One Fish, Two Fish*, where they could expect "two hours of great indie rock here on WPRK, 91.5 FM ... the best in basement radio." I had Phantom Planet's "Always on My Mind" queued up and planned to play "Labour of Love" by Frente! and "I Don't Want to Get Over You" by The Magnetic Fields before putting on the Weezer and sneaking out. My reward for a job well done would be Neutral Milk Hotel's "In the Aeroplane Over the Sea," even though our general manager had recently begged us all to stop playing so much Neutral Milk Hotel all the time.

I remember fidgeting, wondering if I was really going to go through with it—if I was really going to frame three students because I found them annoying. Because I was afraid to tell my friend I knew of her boyfriend's allergy. Looking back on it, it was a perfect example of Sayre's Law: "In any dispute, the intensity of feeling is inversely proportional to the value of the issues at stake." But I was young, and I had never heard of Sayre's Law. Instead what pushed me out the door, as I hit PLAY on "Only in Dreams," was once again recalling Professor Dalton's admonishment that writers should be hungry for new experiences. This was all certainly very new for me.

The sky above the live oaks was just beginning to brighten

as I stole out into the quiet early morning. Rollins isn't a large campus; you can see Pinehurst Cottage from the entrance to WPRK, which meant I didn't have far to go to reach Lyman Hall. I didn't take the straightest route, along Mills Lawn and down Rollins's Walk of Fame, featuring stones honoring figures from Aristotle to actual Rollins alumnus Mr. Rogers. No, I selected a more discreet path, though it would take more time—which is why it took me longer to realize that Lyman Hall was not dark and quiet like every other dorm. It was ablaze with light, and I could see people moving around inside. There were students outside as well, gesturing animatedly at one another, kayaks and other equipment strewn all over the ground around them.

I withdrew behind some azalea bushes. Not being particularly "outdoorsy" myself, I had forgotten that R.O.C. excursions often required an early start. Holly hadn't told me about anything like that going on, and for the first time I wondered if she'd been setting me up.

The thought unnerved me, and I hightailed it back to the radio station, making a quick detour to pitch the spray bottle into the dumpster behind the cafeteria. I felt dizzy and sick to my stomach, but also enormously relieved that I'd had a good reason not to go through with the plan. Chris, Andrew, and Dojo were all annoying, but trying to get rid of them wasn't my style; I've always preferred to complain about things rather than take action about them.

I got back as the "Only in Dreams" bass line was fading out, and queued up my beloved Neutral Milk Hotel, hoping the familiar singing saw and Jeff Mangum's nasal warbling would restore me, as they have ever done. The rest of my show passed without incident, but my relief was short-lived. The DJ after me burst into the studio as I was winding down the second hour with a little Magic Dirt and Orange Juice, and before even really checking to see if I was on the air, started to breathlessly tell me her news.

"Omigod there's an ambulance outside of R.O.C.," she said.

"Oh shit," I said, trying to act concerned-but-normal as every muscle in my body tensed. "Is everyone okay?"

She shrugged. "I saw a stretcher ..."

I had a bad feeling about this news, but I told myself it was a college campus. People were always injuring themselves.

It could have been anybody on that stretcher.

I didn't hurry out of the studio. I put all my CDs away, I signed the logbook. I only began to hurry once I emerged into the dawn, where this time I took the direct path to Lyman Hall. The ambulance had left, but the cops were still there, along with a big crowd of students and administrators and Campus Safety officers. Holly was in the crowd, and when I saw her face was red and swollen and tear-streaked, my heart sank.

She saw me as I approached. I put my hand up in a half-wave. She did not return it. Instead she pointed at me.

"*You*," she said, and everyone in the crowd turned to look at me. "*You* did this!"

Tyler had died from anaphylactic shock brought on by his spice allergy, and after her public accusation, it was my word against Holly's as to how it had happened. She said I'd been the one who came up with the idea to douse R.O.C. in pepper spray, to get Chris, Alex, and Dojo kicked out of Pinehurst, and that I'd pressured her into giving me her key so I could get inside to coat the faucets, toilet seats, and doorknobs. She pointed to the spray bottle she'd planted in Andrew's dorm room as part of my master plan, saying I'd done it.

It was a compelling story, but I had the truth on my side. I pointed them to the spray bottle I'd ditched in the dumpster. The barrel was empty; I'd never used it. Plus, the faucets and toilet seats had been sprayed before I even left the radio station; the CCTV and key card access log confirmed it. The early-morning hullabaloo I'd witnessed was all the students who had risen early to go kayaking dealing with tingling hands and other parts, pretty much proving it couldn't have been me.

Then Tyler was autopsied. His allergy wasn't severe enough to have been triggered by touching a faucet. He would have needed to consume the pepper spray, so once again I became a "person of interest," especially after Holly told the cops that Tyler had broken things off with me. In her story, I'd been angry and looking for revenge. The problem was, when the cops looked for any evidence that I'd ever been inside R.O.C., there was none—not even a hair or a fingerprint. I'd told them to go look, all those hours of *Law & Order* working in my favor this time. Holly had assumed there would be forensic evidence, given that we were sleeping with each other. She didn't know I'd never been in his room, not even once.

After this, she finally broke down and admitted she'd done it—or, at least, that she'd been the one to bring the pepper spray inside of Lyman Hall. Holly's plan all along had been to get *me* kicked out of Pinehurst as revenge, framing me for trying to frame Chris, Andrew, and Dojo. She'd also hoped Tyler would get some on his hands and eyes—a little payback for his dalliance with me. And, not knowing we'd ended things, she'd hoped it would sour him on me. Surely, I would look like the world's biggest bitch, pulling such a prank while knowing about his allergy.

She'd put the pepper spray in her Nalgene water bottle. She'd rinsed it out afterward but hadn't done a good enough job. There had been some residue in there, and when Tyler, bleary-eyed from the early-morning wakeup, had tried to drink from hers, a few drops had gotten into his mouth. Even watered-down, the dose was fatal.

What happened to Holly is Holly's story to tell if she ever decides to do so. All I can speak to with any authority is what happened to me.

So, did this experience change me, as my creative writing professor had prophesied? Yes, and also no. Grief changes us, and I grieved—for a lover, for a friendship, for a life, and for my life, which did change after the dust had settled. I felt a lot of anger, another form of grief. I felt a lot of guilt; I still do.

On the other hand, I had a more-or-less regular experience at Rollins for the rest of my time there. Yes, I stayed. I wished I'd had some kind of literary novel-type experience of "seeing Tyler everywhere I went," but I really didn't. I never forgot him, but the human mind is amazing in its ability to compartmentalize. For better or for worse I was able to carry on fairly easily once I moved off campus. Having no social life to speak of, I graduated in the top five GPAs in my class, and completed two internships, one at the Enzian, a little independent movie theatre in Winter Park, and another at a school for girls who weren't thriving in the public school system. I met the man I would one day marry, and one day divorce.

I suppose the biggest change for me was allowing myself to be distracted from my goal of becoming a writer. A bit sick of seeking out those pesky experiences, I detoured first through social work and then graduate school.

But one cannot avoid experiences—and, for those of us who feel the compulsion to write, one cannot avoid writing. After all, here I am, finally telling this story, after a decade and a half of publishing more fantastical fare. I have at times wondered if I write stories about sentient spaceships, aliens, and androids to avoid writing stories like this one. Yet even in my science fiction the characters and plots are based on those real-life experiences Professor Dalton told me to seek out, the ones I tried to have, the ones I couldn't avoid having. A reversal of fortune affects everyone, real or imagined. A profound betrayal is a profound betrayal, whether the betrayer is me, or at least someone very like me, or a devious and dastardly alchemist. Setting and characters aside, joy appears in my stories, and sorrow, and regret, and, for that matter, weird sex stuff. I do my best to depict the real, but in the end it's up to the reader whether or not it feels true.

AUTHOR'S NOTE: While not everything in this story is true (thank goodness!), the Molly Tanzer of "The Best in Basement Radio" and I are in agreement on the perfection of Weezer's debut album and, in particular, "Only in Dreams." Many thanks to Rivers Cuomo, Patrick Wilson, Matt Sharp, Jason Cropper, and of course the amazing Brian Bell, who recorded all the guitar parts on the *Blue Album* in one take. Many thanks as well to Rollins College—I know I go a little hard on my alma mater in this, but the education and experiences Rollins gave me made me the writer, and the person I am today. Fiat lux!

ACKNOWLEDGMENTS

Who does one acknowledge for a lifetime of music? My uncle Peter, who brought in LPs and weird little zines and comix from the wilds of the East Village to my family's *Saturday Night Fever*-era Bensonhurst apartment, to start. Donna Donna, my favorite DJ on WLIR. My high school pal Don Zaros, who tried to teach me guitar. My friend Sara Grosky who made me a zillion mix tapes and brought me along to shows all over Manhattan in the early 1990s. Ted Leibowitz of BAGeL Radio, a stranger whose *480 Minutes* stream kept me going for years. My faves from the podcast *Communion After Dark*.

And for two decades of short fiction: all my co-editors of anthologies and magazine projects past. Joe Clifford, who started the craze for music-themed crime fiction anthologies. My agent Michael Curry who can never have too many doors slammed in his face on my behalf, and to R. B. Wood, who is ready to make a short fiction in publishing (by starting with a large one).

CONTRIBUTORS

WILLIAM BOYLE is the author of eight books set in and around the southern Brooklyn neighborhood of Gravesend, where he was born and raised. His most recent novel is *Saint of the Narrows Street*, available from Soho Crime. His books have been nominated for the Hammett Prize, the John Creasey (New Blood) Dagger Award in the UK, and the Grand Prix de Littérature Policière in France, and they have been included on best-of lists in *The Washington Post*, *CrimeReads*, and more. He currently lives in Oxford, Mississippi.

SELENA CHAMBERS is the author of *Babes in Toyland's Fontanelle* for Bloomsbury Academic's 33 1/3 series and the Weird short story collection *Calls for Submission* (Pelekinesis). Her writing has been translated in five countries, as well as published in the U.K. and Australia. Nominations include: the Pushcart, the Colorado Book Award, the Best of the Net, as well as the Hugo Award and World Fantasy Award (twice). For more info, check out: www.SelenaChambers.com.

JEFF CHON is the author of *Hashtag Good Guy with a Gun* and *This Is the Afterlife.* As a much younger man, he used to sit in front of his computer on Sunday nights and write sad stories about people who mostly asked for it, while music videos played softly in the background.

LIBBY CUDMORE is the author of *Negative Girl* (Datura, 2024), *The Big Rewind* (William Morrow, 2016), and the Wade & Jacks series in *Ellery Queen Mystery Magazine, Alfred Hitchcock Mystery Magazine,* and *Tough.* A Shamus and Black Orchid Novella Prize winner, her work has appeared in *Dark Matter, The Dark, Shotgun Honey, Stone's Throw, Monkeybicycle,* and *Smokelong Quarterly,* as well as in the anthologies *Burning Down the House; Lawyers, Guns and Money; A Beast Without a Name;* and *At the Edge of Darkness.*

JEFFREY FORD is the author of the novels *The Physiognomy, Memoranda, The Beyond, The Portrait of Mrs. Charbuque, The Girl in the Glass, The Cosmology of the Wider World, The Shadow Year, The Twilight Pariah, Ahab's Return,* and *Out of Body.* His short story collections are *The Fantasy Writer's Assistant, The Empire of Ice Cream, The Drowned Life, Crackpot Palace, A Natural History of Hell, The Best of Jeffrey Ford,* and *Big Dark Hole.* Ford's fiction has appeared in numerous magazines and anthologies from Tor.com to *The*

Magazine of Fantasy & Science Fiction to *McSweeney's* to *The Oxford Book of American Short Stories*, and has been widely translated. It has garnered World Fantasy, Edgar Allan Poe, Shirley Jackson, and Nebula awards, as well as a *New York Times* Notable Book of the Year.

MEG GARDINER is the #1 *New York Times*-bestselling author of seventeen novels. Her thrillers have won the Edgar Award and been summer reading picks by *The Today Show* and *O, The Oprah Magazine*. In August 2022, *Heat 2* (co-authored with Michael Mann), debuted at #1 on *The New York Times* bestseller list. A former lawyer, two-time president of Mystery Writers of America, and three-time *Jeopardy!* champion, Gardiner lives in Austin.

TODD GRIMSON is the author of the novels *Stainless* and *Brand New Cherry Flavor*, and short fiction which appeared in *BOMB, Juked, The Quarterly, Bikini Girl*, and the *Voice Literary Supplement*. He now lives in Oregon somewhere.

CARA HOFFMAN is the author of *Running*, a *New York Times* Editor's Choice, *Esquire Magazine* Best Book of the Year, and *Autostraddle* Best Queer and Feminist Book of the Year. A crime reporter and an environmental journalist, she first received national attention in 2011 with the publication of the feminist classic *So Much Pretty*, which sparked a national dialogue on violence and retribution and was named a Best Novel of the Year by *The New York Times Book Review*. Her second novel, *Be Safe I Love You,* was nominated for a Folio Prize and named one of the Five Best Modern War Novels by *The Telegraph* UK. A MacDowell Fellow and an Edward Albee Fellow, she has written for *The New York Times, The Paris Review, Bookforum, Bennington Review, The Daily Beast, Rolling Stone, Teen Vogue,* and *NPR.* She has been a visiting lecturer at Oxford University, and is a founding editor of *The Anarchist Review of Books.* Hoffman lives in Exarchia and New York City and teaches in the Krieger School of Arts and Sciences' Advanced Academic Programs at Johns Hopkins University.

Maxim Jakubowski is a British writer and editor who worked in publishing and the music industry for many years. He has edited over 100 anthologies and issued four short story collections (*Death Has a Thousand Faces,* 2023, being the latest) and twenty-one novels. Ten of those were written under a pseudonym and repeatedly reached the British Top 10, and were published in thirty languages. His latest are *The Piper's Dance* (2021), *Just a Girl with a Gun* (2023), and *The Exopotamia Manuscript* (2024). He lives in London surrounded by too many books.

Alex Jennings is a comedian, educator, and award-winning author whose writing has appeared in *Current Affairs Magazine, Pseudopod,* and *New Suns (Volumes 1* and *2).* He is an instructor of Popular Fiction at the Stonecoast MFA program as well as a columnist for *The Magazine of Fantasy & Science Fiction.* His debut novel, *The Ballad of Perilous Graves,* was released by Orbit/Redhook in 2022. His fiction and poetry have been short-listed for numerous awards, including the Ernest J. Gaines Award, the Ray Bradbury Prize for Speculative Fiction, the Locus Award for Best Debut Novel, and the World Fantasy Award. He is the winner of the 2023 Compton Crook Prize from the Baltimore Science Fiction Society. He lives and works in Baton Rouge, Louisiana. As of this publication, he has lost 135 lbs and counting. Find out more at www.alexjennings.net.

CYAN KATZ is a criminal QTPOC elder living in Berlin, Germany. Born and raised in Alaska, they've been advocating for *your* right to party since 1979. They love being Arab Jewish, medically trans, and a collection of paradoxes. By day, a gothic Borg Queen; by night, an extremely sleepy kitten. In 2010, they discovered butoh, a contemporary Japanese dance, and have since collaborated globally on performances, workshops, residencies, and films. A longtime Buddhist practitioner, their meditation/ dharma study group, Weirdos Only Meditation, recently turned ten. This anthology is their debut publication! Their stories are bodycentric, often dealing with themes of otherness, neurosis/ trauma, and familial structures. They're preoccupied with transformation, ontological and epistemological questioning, and the care and feeding of monsters in our personal oceans.

JOSH MALERMAN is the *New York Times*-bestselling author of *Bird Box* and *Incidents Around the House*. He's also one of two singer/ songwriters for the Michigan band The High Strung, whose song "The Luck You Got" can be heard as the theme song to the Showtime show *Shameless*. He lives in Michigan with his fiancée, the artist/ musician Allison Laakko.

MICHAEL MARANO was a bouncer for a whole weekend in 1987, and was a roadie for the (blessedly) short-lived Boston-area band The Bed Spins for their first (and final) tour—an experience that left Marano, after earned wages, $20.00 in the hole. Marano dropped out of grad school, and produced the novel *Dawn Song*, which garnered The Bram Stoker and International Horror Guild Award. His novella *Displacement* was nominated for the Shirley Jackson Award, and his collection *Stories from the Plague Years* was named one of the top ten horror publications of the year by *Booklist*. Building upon his experience hosting *Mad Prof. Mike's Cool Punk Rock Show* on WBNY in Buffalo, Marano became a nationally syndicated commentator on genre films for the Public Radio Satellite System program *Movie Magazine International* from 1990 to 2022. Marano's written genre commentary has appeared in venues such as *The Arts Fuse*, *Paste Magazine*, *The Boston Phoenix*, *The Weekly Dig*, and many others. "MediaDrome," Marano's regular column in *Cemetery Dance*, has been one of the more popular features of the magazine for 25 years. Since 2008, Marano's been teaching genre fiction writing in the Boston area, in addition to remote classes, book-doctoring, and editing (www.BluePencilMike.com). As a hobbyist circus performer, Marano has choreographed, and performed narrative aerial pieces for lyra based on the works of J.G. Ballard and Philip K. Dick and on Yiddish theater and folklore.

Silvia Moreno-Garcia is the author of *The Seventh Veil of Salome*, *The Daughter of Doctor Moreau*, *Mexican Gothic*, and many other books. She has won the Locus, British Fantasy, and World Fantasy awards.

Zandra Renwick has written copious short stories under variations on her birth name, including Camille Alexa and Alex C. Renwick. Her award-nominated fiction has been adapted to podcast, performed on stage, and optioned for television. She currently lives in Montreal.

Jason Ridler is a historian at Johns Hopkins University and creative writing teacher for the Google Arts and Culture program. He's the author of ten novels, including *Dead in the Ring* (forthcoming), *Harvest of Blood and Iron*, and the Brimstone Files series. He's published seventy-plus stories at such venues as *Berkeley Noir*, *Beneath Ceaseless Skies*, and *The Territories* anthology series. A former punk rock musician and cemetery groundskeeper, he lives in Parts Unknown, California. www.jasonridler.com.

Veronica Schanoes is an American author of fantasy stories and an associate professor in the Department of English at Queens College, CUNY. Her novella *Burning Girls* was nominated for the Nebula Award and the World Fantasy Award and won the Shirley Jackson Award for Best Novella in 2013. She lives in New York City. *Burning Girls and Other Stories*, her first collection, came out from Tordotcom in 2021.

ELENA MAULI SHAPIRO was born in Paris, France, and moved to the United States at the age of thirteen. She's amassed several degrees in literature and writing around the San Francisco Bay Area (Stanford University, Mills College, UC Davis), where she still lives with a scientist husband and a sassy little black dog. She is the author of two novels, *13 Rue Thérèse* and *In the Red*.

BRIAN FRANCIS SLATTERY (www.bfslattery.com) is the author of four novels—*Spaceman Blues*, *Liberation*, *Lost Everything* (which won the Philip K. Dick Award), and *The Family Hightower*—and numerous short stories. He's also a journalist and musician and lives outside of New Haven, CT.

MOLLY TANZER is the author of five novels, two collections, and two novellas. Her work has been nominated for the Locus Award, the British Fantasy Award, and the Wonderland Book Award. Her novel *Creatures of Charm and Hunger* won the Colorado Book Award in 2021, and her work adapting manga for English-speaking audiences has been nominated for the American Manga Awards. Her critically acclaimed short fiction can be found in *The Big Book of Cyberpunk, The*

Magazine of Fantasy & Science Fiction, and *The Year's Best Dark Fantasy & Horror*. Follow her on Instagram @molly_tanzer. Molly lives outside of Boulder, CO, with her many houseplants.

CHRIS L. TERRY is author of the novels *Black Card* and *Zero Fade*, and co-editor with James Spooner of the *Black Punk Now* literary anthology. Terry was born in Boston to a Black father and Irish-American mother, and spent his teens and early twenties touring in different Richmond, Virginia-based punk bands. He lives with his family in Southern California, and teaches creative writing.

PAUL TREMBLAY has won the Bram Stoker, British Fantasy, and Massachusetts Book awards and is the *New York Times*-bestselling author of *Horror Movie*, *The Beast You Are*, *The Pallbearers Club*, *Survivor Song*, *Growing Things and Other Stories*, *Disappearance at Devil's Rock*, *A Head Full of Ghosts*, and the crime novels *The Little Sleep* and *No Sleep Till Wonderland*. His novel *The Cabin at the End of the World* was adapted into the Universal Pictures film *Knock at the Cabin*. He has a master's degree in mathematics and lives outside Boston with his family.

NICK MAMATAS is the author of several novels, including the instant cult classic *Move Under Ground*, the speculative thriller *The Second Shooter*, and the posthuman riff on Shakespeare: *Kalivas! Or, Another Tempest*. His short fiction has appeared in *McSweeney's*, *Best American Mystery Stories*, Tor.com, and many other venues. Nick is also an anthologist; with Ellen Datlow he co-edited the award winning *Haunted Legends* and with Masumi Washington the acclaimed *The Future is Japanese*. He also produced an anthology of progressive weird fiction *Wonder and Glory Forever*. Nick's fiction and editorial work has been nominated for the Hugo, World Fantasy, Locus, and Bram Stoker Awards. He is also a member of the editorial collective of *The Anarchist Review of Books*.

OTHER WORKS BY NICK MAMATAS

<u>NOVELS</u>

Kalivas! Or, Another Tempest
The Second Shooter
Sabbath
I Am Providence
The Last Weekend
Love is the Law
The Damned Highway (with Brian Keene)
Bullettime
Sensation
Under My Roof
Move Under Ground

<u>COLLECTIONS</u>

The Planetbreaker's Son
The People's Republic of Everything
The Nickronomicon
You Might Sleep …
3000 MPH an Hour in Every Direction at Once

<u>ANTHOLOGIES</u>

Wonder and Glory Forever: Awe-Inspiring Lovecraftian Fiction
*Mixed Up: Cocktail Recipes (And Flash Fiction) for the Discerning
Drinker (and Reader)* (with Molly Tanzer)
Saiensu Fikushon (with Masumi Washington)
Hanzai Japan (with Masumi Washington)
Phantasm Japan (with Masumi Washington)
*The Battle Royale Slam Book: Essays on the Cult Classic by Koushun
Takami* (with Masumi Washington)
The Future is Japanese (with Masumi Washington)
Haunted Legends (with Ellen Datlow)
Realms and *Realms 2* (with Sean Wallace)
Spicy Slipstream Stories (with Jay Lake)
The Urban Bizarre

Clever and curious reads for
lovers of the strange and mysterious.

Current and Upcoming Releases

Available Now

Winter in the City - Anthology
120 Murders - Anthology

Coming Soon

The Black Fire Concerto by Mike Allen
Spring in the City - Anthology
Born of Malice by Xan van Rooyen
Five Funerals by Jeff Somers

RUADÁN
BOOKS

Coming April 22nd

Now Available for Pre-Order